MARGARET BROWNLEY is the author of several highly acclaimed historical romances, including her recent bestseller *Pistols and Petticoats*.

RAINE CANTRELL is the author of many historical romances, including the acclaimed *Darling Annie,* and the winner of ten writing awards.

NADINE CRENSHAW, whose latest romance is *Viking Gold,* was a nominee for the Romance Writers of America RITA Award, and winner of their Golden Heart Award.

SANDRA KITT, a leading romance writer, is the author of *The Color of Love.*

For The Love of Chocolate

Margaret Brownley

Raine Cantrell

Nadine Crenshaw

Sandra Kitt

St. Martin's Paperbacks

FOR THE LOVE OF CHOCOLATE

"Sometimes You Feel Like a Nut" copyright © 1996 by Margaret Brownley.
"The Chocolate Shoppe" copyright © 1996 by Nadine Crenshaw.
"Sweet Dreams" copyright © 1996 by Sandra Kitt.
"The Secret Ingredient" copyright © 1996 by Theresa Di Benedetto.

ISBN: 0-312-95791-2

Printed in the United States of America

St. Martin's Paperbacks edition / May 1996

10 9 8 7 6

CONTENTS

SOMETIMES YOU FEEL LIKE A NUT

Margaret Brownley

❋ Chapter 1 ❋

The door of the Certified Nuts And Chocolate Factory swung open and any hope Holly Brubaker had of closing up shop early and starting on the stack of special orders faded away with the sound of jingling bells.

She peered between the gold-foiled ears of a chocolate bunny and caught sight of a tall, broad-shouldered man dressed in a gray suit. Dark windblown hair fell across his furrowed brow. He had a square, rugged face—the kind of face that was all angles and planes and might have been too harsh had it not been for the sensitive curve of his lips and the intriguing indentation centered on his chin. He pulled off his sunglasses and gazed about the shop. In the late afternoon his eyes looked almost golden in color. He spotted her and the lines of concentration deepened.

He stood at the door looking like a man allergic to his surroundings. Obviously, he didn't want to be there.

Probably forgot his wife's birthday, she decided. Or an anniversary. In either case, she was willing to bet he'd buy a box of assorted milk chocolates. That's what most men bought. Women were far more adventuresome, preferring to pick out each chocolate piece by piece.

Something about this particular man didn't seem to fit. Curious, Holly moved to the right to get a better look. The nondescript gray suit was an unfortunate choice—and as out of place in the beach community of Santa Monica, California, as a polar bear in the desert. Though, given the width of his shoulders and the length of his hard, lean body, the suit was less of a liability than one would expect.

He was not one of her regular customers, nor was he a tourist. He was definitely not a chocolate lover. Chocolate lovers were more freewheeling and fun loving. This man looked too serious. He also seemed immune to the heavenly smell of chocolate that floated on the air like a warm friendly smile. Almost everyone who walked into her shop stopped and took a deep breath, eyes closed for a moment, to absorb the warm, rich, tantalizing odors. Even the two holdup men who had robbed her last year had shown honest appreciation of the rich chocolately smells before demanding her money—and a sample of every chocolate candy she sold.

Obviously, this man had a wooden nose or a head cold. Maybe both.

She had no idea why he was in her shop, but her instincts told her he hadn't come to buy chocolate.

"What did the chocolate say to the caramel?" she asked, hoping to solicit a smile. He looked startled at first, then interested, or at least the corners of his mouth turned slightly upward and the frown softened.

He slid his sunglasses into a black eyeglass case. "I give up."

"I've got you covered."

He chuckled and she smiled back. She liked men who laughed at silly jokes. This particular man looked as if he hadn't had a good laugh in ages. All too soon he grew serious again, and she fought the urge to tell another ridiculous joke. "You aren't a spy, are you?"

"A spy?"

"Come to steal my secret chocolate recipe?"

This time when he smiled, she noticed a dimple. "Ah, not exactly." He gazed at her for a moment, then suddenly, as if to catch himself doing something illicit or out of character, cleared his throat, managing somehow to distance himself in the process. He's definitely married, she decided. Not that he was her type or anything.

"I'm looking for the owner," he said gruffly, as if to discourage any further attempts on her part to cheer him up.

If he was, indeed, married, he must really be in the dog house, she thought. This called for a twenty-five-pounder. "I'm the owner. My name's Holly Brubaker and the dog-house specials are on that table over there."

He glanced at the table she indicated, then averted his gaze back to her, amusement dancing in his eyes. "If I ever find myself in the dog house, I'll know where to come." He moved toward her and slid a white business card across the counter. "Mark Spencer from Woodson-Meyers Insurance Company."

"Oh, dear. Don't tell me I forgot to pay my premiums."

"No, nothing like that."

"Oh, I thought . . . Woodson-Meyers insures some of my personal belongings. They came highly recommended."

"This has nothing to do with your policy. I'm investigating a series of burglaries in the area. I'd like to ask you a few questions."

"Burglaries?" Openly curious, she nonetheless hesitated. "Would you mind if we go out back? I can work as we talk."

"Not at all." He accidentally knocked against a large stuffed gorilla, catching it before it hit the floor. No sooner had he righted the gorilla than he backed into a blow-up dinosaur.

She quickly hid a smile. The investigator with his broad movements definitely needed a lot of space. The poor man would probably feel crowded in the great outdoors. "We just poured a mold," she explained. "It's too big for the fridge and my air conditioner's acting up. It's cooler outside than it is in here."

He lifted his shoulders in a careless shrug, but there was nothing careless about the way he assessed her. Nor was there anything relaxed about the energy that seemed to coil within him. "No problem." He walked into a dangling mobile, ducked beneath an overstuffed lion that hung from the ceiling fan, and seemingly dodged from one near disaster to the next while she closed up. Amused and more than a little curious, Holly kept him in her ken as she followed her usual end-of-the day routine, knowing full well she was being watched with equal fervor. What could an insurance investigator possibly want with her?

It was Mark Spencer's opinion that the Certified Nuts And Chocolate Factory was a bloody booby trap. He steadied a tottering display of stuffed animals, and backed into a barrel filled with chocolate samples wrapped in cellophane and tied with bright ribbons. The woman didn't waste a bit of space. Even the space out of reach between ceiling and floor was filled with large pink balloons floating atop colorful strings. The balloons bobbed and shifted with the ever-changing air currents, creating more movement and more reasons to duck. Antique display cases were crammed with molded chocolate carousel horses. Unicorns with gold-foiled horns, chocolate roses, and silver-foiled engagement rings vied for space.

He wasn't particularly fond of chocolate, but the tantalizing smells in the shop tempted him.

Gazing at the pretty store owner, he decided she looked even more intriguing now that she had emerged from behind the counter and he could see her more fully. From the moment he first glanced over the shiny glass counter and into eyes as clear and blue as twin mountain lakes, he was intrigued—in a strictly professional way, of course.

Surprised to catch himself staring, he purposely turned his attention to the luscious chocolates on display behind the glass counter. Sizing up the suspect, he told himself. What else would explain his keen interest? He certainly had no personal interest in her. She was definitely not his type. For one thing she was too restless or flighty, or something. Everything on her, from her shiny blond ponytail to her silver candy-kiss earrings and arm full of bangles, shimmered, jingled, or otherwise moved. Even her slim body seemed to be in constant motion. She was all over the store, straightening a display here, a sign there like a bee visiting all the flowers in a garden. Following her progress around the store was definitely a challenge. Though admittedly, the payoff was worth the effort.

Chocolate brown stretch pants molded around her shapely legs. A pink oversized T-shirt with the logo *Give me your chocolate and no one will get hurt* fell to midthigh. Clearly this was a woman who put heart and soul into her business. Watching her cute derriere wiggle as she moved a lace curtain and reached into the front window to flip the sign from open to closed, he decided that wasn't all she put into her work.

"This way," she said at last. She led the way through a door to a spotless kitchen. A slightly built Hispanic man dressed in a brown and pink uniform looked up as they entered and grinned, a decorating tube in his hand. Trays of chocolate molds filled with tantalizing mounds of marshmallow cream were spread on the counter in front of him. He was surrounded by a group of freckle-faced cub scouts.

"I'll take care of Marilyn," she called. Using both hands, she picked up a huge metal mold shaped in the form of a voluptuous girl in a bikini. Holly turned toward the investigator. "Meet Marilyn. She has a date with a bachelor party." Holding the mold in both hands, she headed for the door leading to the parking lot in back.

"Let me help you with that," he said, chasing after her.

"It's all right. I'm used to these things," she called over her shoulder. She pushed open the screen door with a swing of a shapely hip and disappeared outside.

He followed her to the alley that ran behind the building. She seemed oblivious to the cold wind that had been blowing all day long. She was too busy waving the darned full-figured mold through the air like some tribesman performing a ritualistic fertility dance.

The mold was at least three feet long and appeared heavy. "There's nearly twenty pounds of chocolate in this thing," she said, as if to guess his thoughts. "It's great for keeping in shape."

"So I, eh"—his gaze slid down the length of her—"can imagine."

She lifted her lashes to glance at him. "Now what did you want to talk to me about?"

He noticed the color of her lipstick matched the pink of her T-shirt. Normally his powers of observation were confined to crime scenes or suspects. This woman wasn't a suspect—not yet, at least. He decided she was older than he'd first supposed, probably in her late twenties. "Is that Miss or Mrs. Brubaker?" It was hard to tell. She wore a ring on every cotton-picking finger.

"I'm not married," she replied. Her gaze dropped to his hand as if to do some ring checking of her own. He wore no rings, and only wore a watch during working hours. He lived a streamlined life and that's the way he liked it. He hated clutter, unnecessary conversation, and anything else that served no purpose other than to take up space or fill in time.

"You said you were investigating some burglaries?"

He nodded and reached into his suit coat pocket. The woman sure could move that body of hers. She was graceful as a dancer and every bit as agile. Hips and torso were in perfect harmony with her arms and legs, as if they moved to some inner music. Surprised to find his thoughts straying away from the purpose of his visit, he gave himself a mental nudge and pulled out a candy nougat wrapped in gold foil. "Do you sell these?"

"Not only do I sell them, I make them."

"Does anyone else sell this particular candy?"

"No one. If you peel back the foil, you'll see the raised chocolate initials HB. That's my trademark."

It was the trademark that had led him to Holly Brubaker in the first place. Why none of the police detectives who had worked on the case from the start hadn't bothered to check out the trademark indicated how low art theft was on the priority list. Though art theft was a big problem, causing over two billion dollars in annual losses worldwide, most police departments were forced out of necessity to allot their dwindling resources to crimes of a more violent nature. No where was that more true than in Southern California. That's why the Woodson-Meyers Insurance Company maintained its own highly trained investigators.

He slid the candy back into his pocket. Suddenly Miss Brubaker was embroiled in a daredevil juggling act. Quickly assessing that her fancy two-step was not part of the cooling process, he hurried to help her, catching hold of a pointed metal breast and doing some two-stepping of his own.

"Grab the legs!" she cried.

"I'm trying." It took some doing but he finally had a firm hold of Marilyn's ankles. "There."

No sooner had he spoken than one of the leg clips sprang open and a stream of warm liquid chocolate gushed out.

"Yeow!" He jumped back and slid in the creamy slick chocolate spreading on the asphalt. Arms windmilling, he fought to regain his balance. Finally, his feet flew out from beneath him and he hit the ground, hard.

✦ Chapter 2 ✦

*M*iss Brubaker cried out in alarm. "Mr. Spencer! Are you all right?" Her eyes and mouth were rounded in horror as she gaped down at him, hand on her chest.

He scowled through the curtain of chocolate that dripped down his eyebrows and lashes. All he could see was a damned metal breast. He gave Marilyn a shove, sending the mold flying. He moved his arm and groaned. He ached all over, but because Miss Brubaker looked so worried, he tried to make light of his injuries. "I always wanted to be a chocolate Easter bunny."

"Don't move," she said. "Jose! Hurry!" No sooner had she called his name when Jose came running out the door. He was followed by the group of cub scouts who stared at Mark as if he'd just landed from outer space. Upon seeing him sprawled spread-eagle on his back, Jose froze.

Miss Brubaker waved her arms. "Get the hose. Hurry!" Jose took off running, and disappeared around the side of the building. She turned to Mark. "Stay here while I call 911."

He struggled to sit up. "No need. I'm okay. I think."

She squinted as if trying to see through the thick coating of chocolate that covered him. "I don't think you should move. You look rather pale."

He groaned. "How can I look pale? I'm covered in chocolate."

"I'm talking about your aura."

"My what?" Before she could reply, he was hit with a blast of icy cold water. "Yeow! Get that damned thing away from me!"

"Turn it off!" Miss Brubaker screamed.

"I'm trying," Jose yelled back. Miss Brubaker hurried to Jose's side and together they finally got the hose turned off, but not before Mark was thoroughly drenched to the bone.

His teeth chattering, Mark sat hugging himself, trying to coax some warmth into his frozen body. Miss Brubaker appeared at his side with a handful of clean terry towels. "I'm so sorry, Mr. Spencer. I don't know what to say. Nothing like this has ever happened before. . . ." On and on she went, apologizing profusely and fluttering around him like a nervous hen.

Somehow she'd managed to escape the torrential downpour of chocolate with little more than a nickel's worth on her pink T-shirt and a tiny dab on the tip of her nose. He pulled a soaking wet handkerchief from his pocket. "Your nose," he said.

"Oh!" She blushed prettily, but held still while he gently rubbed the spot away, though she chatted constantly. "Of course, we'll replace the suit, and pay for any injury. . . ."

"Forget it," he grumbled. He was too damned cold to know if he was seriously injured and he didn't give a hill of beans about the suit. He was going to catch pneumonia, he was sure of it. Hell, he was so cold, he was probably going to die of hypothermia.

"You're shivering." A worried frown creased her smooth forehead. She tugged at his arm. "Come inside where it's warmer and I'll find you something to wear."

A blast of cold air hit him as he stood. He was dripping wet. Even his shoes were filled with water. Holding his arms and legs as stiff as a mechanical man, he followed her inside, dripping a trail of water across the kitchen floor. He ignored the group of wide-eyed cub scouts, who watched his every move.

"Make room for the nice man," Miss Brubaker said. The

boys cleared a path, gaping up at him as he dripped past them. Only one boy had the ill grace to snicker.

He followed her into a small pantry with no windows.

"My office," she explained. "Take your clothes off and I'll find you something to wear."

Before he could respond, she left him, closing the door behind her. As quickly as his frozen fingers allowed, he stripped off his wet clothes and tossed them into a pile by the door.

A knock sounded and Miss Brubaker's musical voice called out. "Are you decent?"

He glanced around for something to cover himself and grabbed a five pound bag of chopped English walnuts. His dignity protected by the nuts, he called out, "Under the circumstances, Miss Brubaker, I'm uh . . . very decent."

The door opened slowly and she peered inside. She took one look at the bag of walnuts and quickly averted her eyes. Her cheeks turned a most becoming red as she held out her hand. "This is the only thing I could find. I really am sorry. If you like we can . . ."

His heart sank. Whatever it was she held in her hand was bubble-gum pink in color, and trimmed with brown piping. He took the garments from her and prayed it wasn't a dress. "Don't worry about it."

She fell silent. Finally, she peered at him through lowered lashes. "I'll let you get dressed. I'll be outside if you need me." She scuttled out the door quicker than a rabbit down a hole and he couldn't keep from laughing. Miss Brubaker obviously wasn't used to having naked men in her pantry.

He walked out of the pantry a short time later wearing the chocolate factory uniform. Although the garment was clearly marked extra large, the pink trousers rose to flood-water heights above his ankles. His broad shoulders stretched the fabric to the fullest and try as he might, he hadn't been able to button the shirt. He wore his gun strapped beneath his arm.

Looking red faced, though ultimately composed, Miss

Brubaker handed him a check. "I do apologize." The check was made out for a thousand dollars. "I hope that covers the cost of replacing your suit. And of course, I'll pay for any medical expenses."

"My company will take care of any expenses." He looked at the check and chuckled. "I doubt that my entire wardrobe cost that much." He handed the check back. "Don't worry about the suit."

"I insist." She tried slipping the check into his shirt pocket, but he stopped her with his hand.

"I can't accept your money," he said. "It might look like a bribe."

"A bribe?" She thought for a moment. "Shall I send it to the insurance company direct?"

That's all he needed; the guys at the company would razz him no end. "Forget it!" He glanced around. The cub scouts were still gaping at him. Obviously, they'd never seen a man dressed like an ice cream cone, wearing a gun.

He debated whether to leave and return the following day, or to stick it out to the end. "Is there somewhere private we can talk?"

She nodded and led the way back into the shop. He followed, his wet shoes making strange little sucking sounds with each step he took. She sat down at a glass ice cream table in front of the window. The wrought-iron chair didn't look strong enough to accommodate his six-foot-three body, but he sat down akin to a man who was being strapped into an electric chair, and folded his arms across his chest.

"Are you sure you weren't injured? You fell pretty hard."

At the moment he wasn't sure of anything. "I'm fine." When she continued to look worried, he sat forward. "Listen, it's no big deal. I was covered in chocolate—"

"Enrobed," she interjected.

"What?"

"In the business it's called enrobed. You were enrobed in chocolate."

"Uh . . . yes, well, no harm was done."

"Would you like something. Hot chocolate?"

He groaned inwardly. After that little episode out back, he never wanted to see anything remotely resembling chocolate for as long as he lived. He held up his hand, trying to ward off her concerns. "Nothing, thank you."

"You were asking about my chocolate nougats?"

He brushed his finger through his damp hair and almost knocked over the display of nuts stacked pyramid-style behind him. He was tempted to leave and come back the following day, dressed in a suit of armor. The woman and her shop were a menace. "The thief leaves one of your nougats at the scene of each crime."

Miss Brubaker sat back in her chair and stared at him in disbelief. "Really? I read in the papers that the thief left chocolate nougats, but I never dreamed they were mine. What do you suppose it means?"

"That's what I want to know. It would help if you would give me the names of the customers who buy your nougats on a regular basis."

She pursed her full pink lips together. "I think that comes under privileged information."

"Privileged?" He sat back and grimaced. His shoulder ached like the devil. "You sell candy. What's privileged about that?"

"Most of my customers come in here because they're lonely or depressed. Chocolate makes them feel good, but so does a friendly ear. I know more about my customers than most doctors know about their patients."

"I'm not asking for personal information. All I want are names."

"Names?" She looked as if he were asking for the moon. "Let's see, there's Sally and Evan. They're a husband-and-wife writing team. Then of course, Boo-Boo. He was in earlier. Oh, yes, there's Superman and Charley. Oops! Forget Charley. He's more of a gentle soul. He prefers soft centers. Let's see. Dr. Mandel. He used to like soft centers until his wife left him—then he switched to nougats. I think that's a good sign, don't you?"

"I'm not sure what you mean. Why would that be a good sign?"

"It means he's taking charge of his life. He's not sitting back, feeling sorry for himself. You tell me the chocolate they prefer and I'll give you a psychological profile. It's much more accurate than a Rorschach test."

"So what kind of person is the Nougat Thief?" he asked, curious if her profile matched the profile worked up by the police psychologist.

She thought for a moment, but everything continued to jingle and jangle. Her earrings, her bracelets, the layers of gold chains around her neck. "The thief is a man. No question."

"Why do you say that?" he asked.

"Men prefer milk chocolate. Women prefer dark. Since nougats are made from milk chocolate, chances are the nougat thief is a man."

"Are you saying women don't buy nougats?"

"I would say about seventy percent of my nougat customers are men."

"Interesting. Why do you suppose women prefer dark chocolate?"

She shrugged. "I'm not sure. Maybe dark chocolate brings back childhood memories of baking brownies and chocolate chip cookies. It's my guess that boys spend less time in the kitchen than girls. Maybe they grow up with less appreciation for baker-type chocolate."

He shook his head and chuckled. "So you think the thief never baked chocolate chip cookies." That wasn't in the psychological profile. "Why do you suppose the thief goes to the bother of leaving chocolate nougats?"

The question brought an odd look to her face. Something akin to pain touched her eyes, veiling the intriguing blue depths with dark shadows. As quickly as the look came, it was gone, but he sensed that she had retreated somehow, pulled back, as if he'd touched a nerve or had lost her trust. Normally, he would make it his business to dig deeper, to find out what she was hiding. Today, he felt a sudden urge to reach out and protect her, protect whatever secret had put that haunted look in her eyes, protect the rapport that had sprung up between them, however tenuous.

Feeling uncomfortably hot, he glanced at the ceiling. The moving balloons told him there was nothing wrong with the air vents. Maybe he was running a fever. In any case, he felt silly dressed in that ridiculous getup. It had been a mistake to stay. He should have taken his leave and returned the following day.

"Maybe he feels bad about stealing," she offered. "Maybe he's a kleptomaniac and can't help himself. The chocolate nougat is his way of apologizing."

So far the thief had stolen somewhere in the ballpark of two million dollars worth of paintings. Chances were the thief used the nougats to draw attention to himself. There was no end to what some sickos would do for publicity. Mark was convinced it was only a matter of time before the Nougat Thief would pop up on *Geraldo* boasting about his exploits.

"So what else can you tell me about this man?" he asked. The fact he was asking these questions surprised him. He wasn't normally into this psychological stuff, and he certainly didn't make a practice of asking opinions from someone outside the police department. But he was intrigued by Miss Brubaker. Or maybe he was simply hypnotized by the constant movement of the shapely leg that swung beneath the glass-top table, mere inches from his.

"He's a man of discriminating tastes. My guess is that he breaks into expensive neighborhoods and takes only the most valuable art."

She could have read as much in the paper. "Go on," he said, keeping his voice even.

"He's flamboyant. Methodical. Thinks things through very carefully. Never leaves anything to chance."

"Does this bring any of your customers to mind?" he asked.

"Only about a fourth of my customers," she replied.

He reached for his pocket before recalling he didn't have his notebook. "Do you have something I can write on?"

She jumped up and dashed behind the counter, reappearing a moment later with a notebook and pencil.

"Thanks," he said, flipping the notebook to the first page. "Start at the beginning. And I need first and last names and addresses."

"I don't have first and last names." She took her seat opposite him. "My customers pay by cash and we don't have any reason to take addresses unless we're shipping something."

"So you don't maintain a mailing list?"

"Not yet," she said. "I'm thought about getting a computer, but . . ." She shrugged. "We take pride in hand-dipping our chocolates and doing things the traditional way. A computer seems so high-tech, don't you think?"

"I guess so," he said. He wasn't much for technology, himself. In the last few years, forensics had grown increasingly sophisticated, but nothing could replace an experienced investigator's gut feeling. He liked to think that's why his record for solving cases was higher than any police detective's. "How many customers do you have who buy nougats on a regular basis?"

"I don't know. Maybe a hundred or so."

"Do you mind if I hang around for a few days? See if I can come up with some leads?"

"Well . . ." She frowned.

"Your customers won't even know I'm here."

She glanced at his gun. "I didn't think insurance investigators were armed."

"I got my license last year after an attempt on my life. Some people don't take kindly to having their insurance scams go up in smoke. In any case, I assure you the next time you see me, my pink pants and my gun will be out of sight."

Smiling, she unfolded her long legs and rose to her feet. "Would you like some samples to take home with you?"

He shrugged and followed her to the counter. "Why not?"

She walked behind the counter and studied him for a moment. "I would say you're a chocolate/chocolate kind of guy." She slid open a door and reached inside the counter.

"What?"

"Chocolate inside and out," she said. "No nuts. Just plain. What you see is what you get."

He watched her carefully place the chocolate swirls into a pink paper bag, and he felt a sense of uneasiness that had nothing to do with the outlandish outfit he wore. Not willing to concede she was right on target—or that he really was as boring as she obviously believed—he pointed to the triangular-shaped chocolates. "May I have one of those?"

She lifted her gaze to him and their eyes locked. "Are you sure you want a bubble gum delight?" she asked.

Bubble gum! What was the world coming to? "Positive," he lied.

Pulling her eyes away, she placed a chocolate triangle in the bag. "Anything else?"

"That'll do me for awhile," he said, taking the bag from her. "What do I owe you?"

"It's on the house."

"Appreciate that."

She watched him with cool assessment. "Unless of course, you think it'll look like a bribe."

"It'll be our secret," he said, winking. He stood gazing at her for a minute. "What do you like?" She looked confused and he clarified himself. "Chocolate. What kind of chocolate?"

She dimpled. "I like rocky road. It's hard and crusty on the outside with a soft marshmallow center. Some people are like that, you know. If I ever get married, it'll probably be to a rocky road type of guy." She walked him to the door, her bangles making a soft, tinkly sound. "I really do apologize for your suit."

"I needed a new suit, anyway," he said.

"I hope you find your man, Mr. Spencer."

"Don't worry, Miss Brubaker," he said with grim determination. "I always find my man. I hope you find yours."

⚹ Chapter 3 ⚹

After leaving Holly Brubaker, Spencer sat behind the wheel of his car, tapping his fingers on the steering wheel. Today was the day he was due to stop by his elderly aunt's house to curb her trash, but because she was at present without a handyman, he'd also promised to cut her lawn. If he drove home and changed out of the ridiculous pink uniform, it would be dark by the time he reached his aunt's house.

He didn't dare not show up. Aunt Beatrice was his mother's oldest sister. An active woman in her late seventies, she refused to give in to old age. Last week, he had found her painting the kitchen. The week before, she had bowled a two hundred game. If he failed to make an appearance, she'd curb her own trash and cut her own grass. The last time she'd messed with the mower, she'd required eleven stitches in her hand. That's why he'd asked to be assigned to the Nougat Thief case, so he could keep an eye on his aunt until she found another handyman to replace the one who'd recently quit.

He really didn't have any choice but to stop by, pink pants and all. Sighing, he started the engine, turned the heater on full blast, and pulled away from the chocolate factory, vowing to seek revenge on the first person caught laughing at him.

Some twenty minutes later, he pulled into the driveway

of his aunt's one-story bungalow and felt his heart lurch. A ladder stood perched next to the house. Leaving the door of the car open, he dashed across the lawn to the ladder. "What's the matter with you, Aunt Rice? Are you trying to kill yourself? Are you . . ." He stopped when he found himself gazing up at Ricky Sloan, the eighteen-year-old youth who lived three houses away. Ricky had been in trouble with the law on two occasions, once for tagging, another time for petty theft. The boy came from a broken family. His mother tended bar in some sleazy nightclub and his brother had served time in the state penitentiary. In Mark's estimation, the boy was trouble. Big trouble.

"Neat duds."

Mark didn't want to discuss his attire. "What are you doing up there, Ricky?"

"Mrs. Albright said I could earn some extra money by cleaning out the rain gutters."

Mark grimaced. On her fixed income, Aunt Rice couldn't afford to tip a fly. He walked up the steps to the porch just as the screen door flew open.

"I thought I heard your voice," she said in her usual scolding voice. Upon seeing him, her mouth dropped open. "Mercy sakes, what happened to you?"

"It's a long story," he said, then told her about the mishap at the chocolate factory.

Amusement danced in her eyes. "You were covered in chocolate?"

"Actually, it's called enrobed."

She gave him a strange look and shrugged. "Did anyone ever tell you that pink suits you?"

"Thanks a lot."

"Now tell, what were you doing shouting at Ricky?"

"I was shouting at you." He followed her through her cluttered sitting room to the kitchen in back. She was dressed in tight red pants and an oversized T-shirt. "I thought you were on the roof."

"I don't have time for that nonsense. I've got more important things to do. My guitar teacher is due in less than a half hour and after that, it's my monthly board meeting." She was the chairperson for the Golden State Art Association Ways and Means Committee and was always making him purchase tickets to afternoon teas and dull dinners.

"Are you still taking guitar lessons?"

"I most certainly am," she said proudly. "I'm learning to play "Hound Dog." I'm telling you, Elvis had nothing on me."

He grinned. "Good for you, Aunt Rice. But getting back to Rick, I don't want him hanging around the house. His whole family has been in trouble with the law."

"Nonsense. The only thing wrong with the boy is he can't read."

"If he can write, he can read."

"What makes you think he can write?"

"I saw what he wrote along the Santa Monica pier."

"Oh, phooey. Just because he spray-painted a few words onto a pier doesn't mean he can read." She pointed to a stack of books on the dining room table that had been left over from her days as a grammar school teacher. Aunt Rice had been retired from the Los Angeles School District for over fifteen years, but she'd never stopped teaching. The age of her students had changed, of course, since she'd left the formal classroom; the students she taught now were considerably older, but that didn't stop her from ordering them about. When Aunt Rice decided to take on a student, she took total command. "When I get finished with him, he'll be writing poetry."

"If he writes it along the pier, it'll still be illegal."

Aunt Rice frowned. "That's not funny."

"It wasn't meant to be. What happened to Mr. Chin?" Mr. Chin had been his aunt's handyman.

"He landed a good job at the Beverly Hills Hotel."

Mark sighed. Mr. Chin was another one of Aunt Rice's students. When Mark had first hired him, he spoke maybe three words of English. He could hardly deny the man an opportunity to move on to bigger and better things, but it was damned annoying to have to keep replacing handymen.

"What do you think about chocolate nougats?" he asked, suddenly changing topics.

His aunt studied him through her tri-focal glasses. "I love them. Why?"

"You love them?" Why didn't he know this? "You *love* them?"

"Especially the ones over at that wonderful chocolate factory on Santa Monica Boulevard."

He stared at her aghast. "You don't mean the Certified Nuts and Chocolate Factory?"

"That's the one," she said with a naughty laugh. "Now don't you go telling old Dr. Stoneface that. The man has some fool notion that chocolate causes cholesterol."

Old Dr. Stoneface was Aunt Rice's name for Dr. Myers and he was probably in his mid to late thirties. "You buy nougats at the Certified Nuts and Chocolate Factory?" he asked in disbelief.

"For goodness sakes, Mark. There're a lot worse things I could be doing."

Wonderful, he thought. His very own aunt was now a suspect. He walked out the back door to the side of the house and, thinking he heard Christmas bells, stopped dead in his tracks. The soft sound of musical bells reminded him of the owner of the chocolate factory and he searched the yard, half expecting to see her there. The sound was coming from the wind chimes that hung from the redwood trellis shading the patio. Funny. He hadn't noticed them before. They had to be new. He only hoped his aunt hadn't hung them up herself.

He hauled the two plastic trash cans out to the curb, checked the tire pressure and oil in his aunt's car, and carried the bottle of spring water from her front porch to the kitchen. He then fired up the gas lawn mower and cut the grass in the backyard. There was no way in hell he was going to cut the front lawn dressed in pink pants.

"I'll cut the front lawn this weekend," he called through the screen door, raising his voice to be heard over the strident sounds of a guitar. If that was "Hound Dog," it was a good thing Elvis wasn't around to hear it.

The guitar stopped and Aunt Rice came to the door, followed by a bearded man wearing faded blue jeans consisting of more holes than denim. His hairy chest was bare beneath his leather vest, his meaty arms covered in tattoos. A tattoo snake coiled up his neck, disappearing behind a dangling earring.

"Did you ever meet Peter, my guitar teacher?"

"Can't say I have."

"Hi, man. The old lady here, told me all about ya. Said you were a P.I. or somethin'." His eyes traveled the length of Mark. "You must be working undercover."

Mark swallowed back his irritation. *Chrissakes, where did she find these characters?* "No, actually I like to wear pink in my free time."

"That's weird, man." Peter rolled his eyes, then sauntered back to the living room.

Mark shook his head. "He calls *me* weird?"

Aunt Rice followed Mark to his car. "Don't mind Peter. He's really very intelligent. He just hasn't had a proper upbringing. But when I get finished with him, you won't recognize him."

"I thought he was your guitar teacher."

"We made a deal. He teaches me to play guitar and I teach him how to read."

He gave her parched cheek a kiss. His aunt sounded so determined, he suddenly felt sorry for the man. He wouldn't wish Aunt Rice on his worst enemy. "Where'd you find him, anyway?"

"I didn't find him. He found me. My reputation as a teacher is well known. He might look like riff raff, but he's eager to learn, though he is a bit set in his ways. It's taken me all of nine months, but he's finally agreed to get a haircut."

"Is that part of the deal?"

"Not exactly," she said, looking mischievous. "But how can a person's brain function with all that hair?" She gave him a playful tap, but her face was serious. "Stop looking so downright serious. Mercy me, Mark. Since your divorce, you've become so . . . I don't know . . ."

"Boring?" he asked.

She thought for a moment. "You were always boring." She glanced down at his ridiculous pink pants. "At least you were before today."

"What?"

"All right. Predictable. But you've gotten more so since the divorce. You're so careful. As if you never intend to make another mistake as long as you live."

In other words, boring. He opened the door to his car and slipped behind the steering wheel. The little pink bag of chocolates was on the seat next to him. On impulse, he reached for the bag and pulled out the chocolate triangle. A vision of blue eyes and pink lips came to mind. He handed the chocolate to his aunt and watched her face light up in delight.

"Bubble gum," she said, looking surprised. "I do declare. How did you know that was my second favorite?"

He started up the engine. "Next time, I'll bring nougats," he called through the open window.

He left her grinning like a schoolgirl.

Yawning, Holly pushed herself away from her work counter and stretched. It had been a long day. She had worked on orders for nearly four hours, ever since that nice insurance investigator had left.

Just thinking about Mark Spencer brought a smile to her lips and a hot flush to her cheeks. Lord, if he didn't look a sight enrobed in chocolate. But it was the memory of him standing stark naked in her "office" that commanded her thoughts. Who would have guessed that beneath that dull gray suit dwelled such a splendid—and ultimately manly—physique? Imagine him thinking he could hide that body behind a mere package of English walnuts. The thought made her giggle.

Cindi, her assistant looked up. A tall slender woman in

her mid-thirties, she had short brown hair and soft doe-brown eyes. "Don't tell me you're thinking about that man, again." Holly had regaled Cindi with all the delicious details almost as soon as she'd walked in the door. Today had been Cindi's day off, but she had agreed to come in after hours to help Holly catch up on the back orders.

"I can't help myself," Holly said, trying to keep her giggles under control. "You should have seen him." More laughter bubbled out of her, making it difficult to talk. "Stark naked . . ." This was the third or maybe even the fourth time Holly had recounted the strange encounter with the investigator. What she hadn't told Cindi was how the man had affected her on some primitive, though ultimately feminine, level. Though the way Cindi was smiling at her, she'd probably already figured that out for herself.

Holly cleared away the empty bowls of frosting while Cindi piped eyes on the last of the five hundred chocolate robots that had been ordered for the wrap party of a high-tech thriller filmed at Paramount Studios. Cindi yawned.

Holly gave her a sympathetic look. Cindi hadn't been herself lately. She seemed tired, distracted, and forgetful. Last week, she'd forgotten to order chocolate. Fortunately, the distributor caught the error and no real damage was done. Still, it wasn't like Cindi to make mistakes. Any attempts on Holly's part to find out what was bothering Cindi had been unsuccessful.

"What do you say we call it a night?" Holly said. They still had a lot of orders to fill, but she planned to get an early start in the morning.

Cindi ran a sponge over the marble counter. Behind her, Jose was stacking dishes into the dishwasher. "You won't get an argument from me." Cindi was a single mother with two school-aged boys. Only on rare occasions did Holly ask her to work nights. "What do we have tomorrow?"

Holly glanced at her schedule. They had a wedding and a baby shower. "Two hundred roses in white chocolate, five hundred mints, and twenty-five baby cradles. The mother-to-be called and said it was a boy." She also had to repour the Marilyn mold for that bachelor party.

"I'll be in after I get the boys off to school."

"Oh, by the way. The insurance investigator will be back. He's looking for a thief."

Cindi's eyes widened. "You mean he was working on a case? What makes him think he's going to find a thief in our store?"

Holly quickly explained about the nougats. "It's hard to believe, but the insurance investigator thinks one of our customers is the Nougat Thief."

Cindi frowned. "Did he say if this thief is dangerous?"

Holly shook her head. "I'm sure Mr. Spencer would have told me if he was. Besides, how dangerous can a man be who leaves chocolate nougats as his calling card?"

"I hope you're right," Cindi said, looking unconvinced. She pulled her tote bag from a cupboard. "See you first thing in the morning, Jose."

Jose looked up from the dishwasher and grinned. "Not if I see you first."

After Cindi had left, Holly noticed the light was still on in the pantry. Stepping inside and reaching for the light chain, she spotted a package of English walnuts on the floor.

Releasing the chain, she stooped to retrieve the package and was startled by the racy thoughts that flashed through her mind. He wasn't even her type. She liked her men adventurous and unpredictable, traits not likely to be packaged in a gray suit and gray tie. The fact that he had affected her in such a way proved how much she'd been neglecting her social life. She'd worked night and day for the last two years trying to establish her business. She couldn't even remember the last time she'd stepped out on an honest-to-goodness date.

No wonder the investigator made her pulses fly. Come to think of it, he was probably the closest thing to what you might call a normal, single male who'd stepped into her shop for quite some time. At least he didn't sport nose rings, mohawks, tattoos, body paint, or wet suits as did ninety percent of the other males who walked through her doors. No indeed.

Only a package of English walnuts.

Laughing softly to herself, she turned off the light. Before leaving for the night, she checked the shop. Mr. Spencer's business card was still on the counter where he'd left it. It was a plain white card that further confirmed he wasn't her type. Sighing with regret, she slipped the card into her shoulder bag and hurried outside to the parking lot.

Chapter 4

*B*y midmorning on the following day Holly decided she'd had enough. When she'd agreed to allow Mr. Spencer to stake out her shop, she'd expected him to keep a low profile. Fat chance.

Dressed in a gray suit that was an exact clone of the one he'd worn on the previous day, he stood out among the skimpily dressed beach crowd like a cherry on white chocolate. More than once, she glanced over the counter and realized he was the only one in the shop whose hair was not shaved, spiked, or dyed purple.

Still, he managed to fill the shop with his commanding presence and virility. His height didn't help, of course. So far he'd towered over everyone who'd walked through the door. Maybe he'd be less noticeable if he wasn't wearing that plain gray suit of his. Or that spicy aftershave that managed, somehow, to assert itself over the smell of chocolate. Or if he didn't have such a charming way of engaging even the most reticent customer into a discussion as to which box of chocolates he should purchase.

He told everyone he wanted something special for his favorite aunt. Naturally, this set every female heart aflutter. Women old enough to know better were falling all over themselves to give him their name and even their telephone numbers, just in case he needed advice in the future.

Oh, he was charming and smooth and clever, all right,

with just enough male vulnerability to melt the heart of every woman who walked in the door, no matter what her age or circumstance.

Well, Holly didn't like it. She resented him tricking *her* customers. She resented him watching them as if it were a crime to buy Holly Brubaker Chocolates. She resented him watching her employees, watching *her*.

More than anything, she hated the way her customers were fawning all over him like he was Mel Gibson and Brad Pitt all rolled into one.

"How are you today, Miss Holly?"

Holly had been watching the investigator with such intense purpose, she failed to notice the homeless woman standing in front of the counter. "I'm fine, Myrtle," she replied. "And you?"

The thin, haggard woman peered at Holly with tired, faded eyes. Myrtle pushed a grocery cart filled with her belongings up and down Santa Monica Boulevard, day in and day out. She refused to stay in shelters or otherwise accept help and had told Holly on numerous occasions that she was an "independent woman who don't cotton to charity."

Today, she looked more needy than independent. "You wouldn't happen to have any samples, now would you?"

"It just so happens I do," Holly said. This was a familiar routine that occurred daily. She reached on the shelf for a bag she'd set aside earlier that was filled with a generous sampling of chocolates, oranges, and assorted granola bars, purchased from a local health store.

"There you are," she said, passing a bag over the counter.

The woman gave Holly a toothless smile. "I just can't seem to make up my mind which candy I like best. As soon as I do, I'm going to buy a truckload."

"You let me know in advance so I'll be ready," Holly said. She watched the woman shuffle out the door, her thin shoulders bent over as if burdened by the weight of the thin shawl. After the woman left, Holly directed her gaze to Mr. Spencer. He stood talking to one of her customers who always came into her shop dressed in a bear costume. She knew him only as Boo-Boo.

Under normal circumstances, she might have found humor in the sight of a gray-suited investigator somberly questioning a man dressed in a bear costume. Today, she was incensed.

She turned to Cindi who was refilling the display counter with a fresh supply of chocolate bonbons. "Cover for me."

Boo-Boo greeted her with a formal bow as she approached. He wore a little blue vest over his bear costume. "Howdy, Miss Holly. You got a problem here at the shop?"

"None that I can't handle." Holly glared at Spencer. "Do you mind if I have a word with you in back?" Without waiting for him to respond, she spun on her heel and headed for the door leading to the factory area.

It was impossible to have a private conversation in the factory at this time of day. The telephone was ringing, delivery men were hauling bricks of chocolate and other supplies through the service door, her driver, Harry, was preparing to make a delivery, and a group of noisy first-graders watched in rapt attention as Jose creamed the fudge across a marble counter.

She had no choice but to take the detective into what she had jokingly called "the office" the day before. In reality it was a small storage room, with barely enough space for two people to stand. If she could ever find a way around the city's strict building codes, she would add a business office and small conference room. For now, the storage room would have to do.

Big mistake.

If the detective filled the shop and factory, he positively absorbed the tiny space. Worse. Since she entered first, he blocked her only means of escape. Though it was *her* property and *her* conference, he clearly had control.

He folded his arms across his chest, crossed one foot over the other, and leaned against a stack of boxes containing English walnuts. Strangely enough, the harsh light of the naked bulb softened his sharp, rugged features. He looked as debonair as Cary Grant in the late-night movie she'd watched the night before and that alone was playing havoc with her senses.

"Is there a problem, Miss Brubaker?"

"Yes, there's a problem. I don't like you questioning my customers."

"I'm only doing my job."

"And I would like to do mine."

"If I'm in any way interfering with your work, all you have to do is say so."

"You told me you would only question the ones you thought fit the profile of your thief."

"The thief is a nutcase. He steals thousands of dollars worth of paintings, then leaves a Holly Brubaker nougat on the victim's pillow."

"So what's that got to do with Boo-Boo?"

He looked surprised. "Boo-Boo is a grown man who walks around in a bear costume and seems to have nothing better to do than buy chocolate nougats. In my book, that makes him a suspect."

Her eyes flashed with azure blue sparks. "Maybe you better get a new book, Mr. Spencer. Boo-Boo almost lost his life in a fire when he was a child. Despite over a hundred operations, he literally has no face—or at least not one that anyone wants to look at. That's why he walks around in a bear costume. It's the only way he knows to make people smile at him rather than turn away in disgust. Does that sound like a nutcase to you?"

He rubbed his chin and looked genuinely apologetic. "I'm sorry. I didn't know. But you have to understand, in my business, everyone's a suspect until proven otherwise."

"Even me?"

They stood staring at each other for an electric moment and might have continued staring at each other longer had Jose not knocked at the door to tell her she had a phone call.

Since the detective made no move to leave, she had no

choice but to suck in her breath and thread her way past him. She brushed against him lightly, but otherwise had managed to maneuver the slender opening without bodily contact. For all the good it did. For just as she reached for the doorknob, he wrapped his fingers around her arm.

Caught off guard, she glanced up at him. "I'm sorry," he said. "About Boo-Boo. Can I make it up over lunch?"

"I'm sure Boo-Boo would be happy to have lunch with you."

"What about you?"

Suddenly, she couldn't breathe. "That depends. Am I a suspect, too?"

"I can't dismiss any possibility in this stage of my investigation."

"Then I don't think we'll be having lunch together, Mr. Spencer. I wouldn't want to compromise your case."

She tore open the door and hurried to the wall phone. She grabbed the handset and pressed the lighted button. "Holly Brubaker." It was one of her distributors returning an earlier call. She reached for a file folder, surprised to discover that her hand was shaking. Upon flipping open the folder, she dropped the papers on the floor. "May I call you back, Mr. Collins?" She hung up and stooped down to pick up the papers, painfully aware that the investigator was watching her every move. This made picking up the scattered sheets of paper that much harder.

What in the world was the matter with her? She was acting all jumpy and nervous and for no apparent reason. She had nothing to hide. Absolutely nothing.

When she finally got the file together, she inadvertently set it on the fudge that was cooling on the counter. Realizing what she had done, she quickly grabbed the file and sent the papers flying for a second time. Spencer shook his head and disappeared through the door of the shop.

No doubt she had gone up another notch on his suspect list.

* * *

Holly rose earlier than usual the following morning. Mozart, her orange marmalade cat, scooted out the open door as Holly reached for the newspaper on the porch.

Her apartment was on the top floor of a two-story building. It was all glass and wood and provided an unimpeded view of the Pacific. At night, she could hear the ocean waves crash on the rugged cliffs below. Now she walked through her living room, ducked beneath her collection of wind chimes, and stepped out to the balcony that ran the entire length of her living quarters. Embracing the spectacular view, she sat in one of the white wicker chairs facing the ocean, and spread her paper on the table next to her coffee and the leftover pizza she'd heated in the microwave.

The Nougat Thief had made the front page. Neither her name or the name of her company was mentioned in the article, and for that she was grateful. Mark Spencer, acting as the spokesman for the insurance company had been quoted as saying there were no suspects, but he was working closely with the police department, and together they were following every possible lead. It was a standard statement made by a pretty standard guy. So why did just seeing his name in print start her pulses racing?

It was much the same question she asked herself later that morning when she arrived at work and found him casually drinking coffee in the kitchen and kibitzing with Jose and Cindi.

He leveled his brown eyes on her. "Good morning, Miss Brubaker. Jose, here, was explaining your production procedures. You have a pretty impressive company."

"Thank you." She helped herself to coffee. "The paper said the Nougat Thief struck again."

He pulled a gold-foiled nougat out of his pocket and placed it on the counter. "I don't suppose you can tell when that particular piece of candy was made or sold?"

"'Fraid not."

"Then it could have been sold yesterday or a week ago, maybe even a month ago."

"I'm afraid that's true."

"It would help if we had a way of knowing the approximate time a nougat might have been purchased. Is there a way you could adjust the recipe slightly each day?"

"I couldn't do that. My regulars would know. I once changed the chocolate suppliers, and got complaints from customers."

"Maybe we could change the foil," Cindi suggested. "You know, color-code it in some way. Use red foil one day. Blue the next."

Holly pursed her lips. "But these are gold nougats," she said. "Don't you think the thief might get suspicious if I try to sell him something other than what he's used to?"

"I agree," Spencer said.

Cindi set her coffee cup down. "Maybe we could make it look like an experiment. You know, have the customers fill out a card giving their opinion. Ask them how they feel about red- or blue-foiled nougats. Leave a place for them to fill in names and addresses. Tell them it's for a drawing. We could promise a box of chocolates to the winner."

"I suppose we could try it," Holly said. Though it was for a good cause, she hated doing anything underhanded. Her customers trusted her and that was important.

Spencer shook his head. "Actually, I'm not sure that's such a good idea. This thief is no dummy. He's likely to grow suspicious should the nougats appear different in any way. There's no telling what he might do if he feels we're trying to trap him."

Cindi's eyes widened. "Are you saying he might be dangerous? That he might try to harm one of us?"

"We have to consider every possibility. Actually, I don't think he's dangerous, but if he thinks we're on to him, he could change his MO or lay low for awhile, making it that much harder to track down."

"Isn't it difficult to get rid of stolen art?" Cindi asked.

"Not as difficult as you might think," he replied. "A painting could be stolen from Bel-Air and be sold to an art dealer in Belgium. You'd be amazed how many stolen artworks show up in the catalogs of legitimate museums or auction houses. The problem is by the time the piece reemerges, there's no way to trace it back to the thief."

"It must be frustrating," Holly said.

His gaze met hers. "It can be." He glanced at his watch and stood. "I want to check with the police department. See if they found any prints at the latest crime scene." He shrugged. "You never know. Even the best of thieves can grow careless."

Mark Spencer returned to the shop later that afternoon looking grim. He paced an impatient path in front of the counter, dodging balloons and stuffed animals while Holly tried to ignore him and concentrate on her little six-year-old customer. Kevin lived in the apartments two streets over from the factory and couldn't seem to make up his mind what he wanted to buy. "So what's it going to be, Kevin?" she asked. "What do you think your mother would like for her birthday?"

"Do you think I have enough money for that one?" He pointed to the five-pound deluxe assortment costing nearly forty dollars plus tax.

"I don't know, let me see." She peered over the counter. He opened up his palm. "I have a whole dollar," he said proudly.

"A whole dollar, eh? I guess that should be enough." She took the dollar from him and slipped the five-pound box into a paper bag. "There you are, Kevin. Wish your mother a happy birthday from me."

"I sure will, Miss Boo-Baker. Thanks a lot."

She watched the jubilant boy leave the shop. Next to her Cindi shook her head. "I swear one day, you'll give away the shop."

"May I have a word with you, Miss Brubaker?" The insurance investigator glanced at Cindi. "In private?"

"Of course, Mr. Spencer," she said, noting his grim look. *Now what*?

He turned on his heel and headed for the factory door. Leaving Cindi in charge, Holly followed him. He was already standing in the pantry when she joined him. It irked her that he thought he could walk into her storage closet any time he damned well pleased.

Feet apart, eyes ablaze, he barely gave her time to close the door behind her when he began his tirade. "I have spent the better part of the morning questioning some of the people Jose told me had access to your factory. I questioned your driver, the laundry man, and the rep from your main distributor and everyone of them knew all about me and my investigation. They said you told them."

"Of course I told them. I thought they had the right to know what's going on around here."

"Any one of those people could be the thief! Your driver, for example."

The thought of Harry being the Nougat Thief was too preposterous for words. "He has twelve grandchildren, for goodness sakes," she said, as if this was proof enough of his innocence.

"He also lost his last job under suspicious circumstances."

"He lost his last job because one of the partners was embezzling money and Harry threatened to turn him in."

"And you believed him?"

"I wouldn't have hired him if I didn't."

"Who else have you told?"

"No one. Except Hank, our paper distributor and Judy Daggs over at—"

"Dammit! Do you think this is some sort of game? This man could be dangerous. No one's been hurt—yet—but we've been lucky. We have no way of knowing what might happen if this man is surprised during a robbery, or feels cornered."

Resenting his condescending tone, she turned to leave, but he held the door closed with the palm of his hand, preventing her escape. "If you would be so kind as to remove your hand," she said coolly.

"Miss Brubaker, I mean it. There's a connection somewhere between the Nougat Thief and this shop. I don't know
what it is or how it all comes together, but with or without
your help I intend to find out."

⚹ Chapter 5 ⚹

The following Wednesday, Holly left the shop just after the noon hour and strolled down Santa Monica Boulevard to the beach. Now that the wind had stopped, it was a beautiful warm day. The sky was cloudless and the calm blue Pacific sparkled beneath the sun. She followed the path along the beach to the canopied wagon that sold sandwiches and cold drinks. She was greeted by the man known as Cory, a big jovial black man who always had a smile for everyone. "Well, if it isn't the candy lady," he said, his teeth flashing white against his dark gleaming skin. "What it'll be today?"

"I'll take a turkey sandwich and a diet," she said.

"Make that two turkey sandwiches and add an ice tea."

Recognizing the deep, husky male voice, she spun around. "What are you doing here, Mr. Spencer?"

Dressed in his usual gray suit, he looked every bit as out of place on the beach as he had in her shop. What she couldn't understand was how he managed to make ordinary looked so damned sexy. "Just enjoying the view, like everyone else." He paid Cory for both their lunches, handed her the wrapped sandwiches, and picked up the drinks. They strolled over to the beach and sat on the concrete curb. Music from the carousel rose from the crowded pier. Further out, seagulls circled a lone fishing boat.

"I'm sorry I yelled at you the other day."

The apology surprised her. "I'm sorry, too."

He set the drinks on the curb between them. "How does one get into the chocolate business?" he asked at length.

It was a strange story; one she seldom talked about, even to her best friends. She didn't generally talk about her past, at least not in a serious vein. To combat the pain—or at least short-circuit it—she'd developed a humorous, almost flippant approach to any awkward questions regarding her background. Today her stock answer rolled off her tongue like a ball rolling down hill.

"Hey, I was born under a Hershey bar. End of story." She shrugged carelessly and reached for her drink, only to find her hand stayed by his. She looked up and almost panicked when she realized her old tricks weren't going to work on him.

"Want to try again?" he asked gently.

She snatched her hand away. How dare him! What gave him the right to intrude on her privacy? Make her think things she didn't want to think, feel things she didn't want to feel? "All right," she snapped, sensing he was not going to back down. "I was left on the steps of the old San Fernando Mission as an infant. A nun found me in a bassinet with a change of clothes and a Hershey's candy bar."

"Are you serious?" He looked so shocked, she didn't have the heart to stay angry at him. "You were abandoned?"

"Like an old mine."

A shadow crossed his forehead as if it pained him to hear her make light of it. "I can't imagine how it must have been for you."

She let her gaze drift across the ocean. An oil tanker broke the otherwise straight line between the sky and the sea. "For years, I tried to figure out why anyone would leave a chocolate bar in a baby basket. As a child I thought I was related to the Hershey family. I daydreamed about being a heiress or something. I guess in a way the chocolate factory gives me a feeling of having roots. That's why I resent . . ." Embarrassed at revealing so much to a relative stranger, she bit down on her sandwich.

"What do you resent?" he probed. "My suggesting your employees or business associates might be suspects?"

"Something like that. I know it sounds silly, but the people I work with are like family to me." It was crazy, really, the way she never stopped trying to create a family for herself, going so far as to collect old photographs from antique shops. "What about you?" *That's it, Holly, change the topic. It works every time.* "What made you become an insurance investigator?"

"I started out as a cop just like my father and, before him, my grandfather."

"What happened?"

He hesitated as if to weigh the wisdom of revealing too much. "I still think of myself as a cop. The only difference is I no longer have to deal with politics."

"Did you always live in Santa Monica?" she asked.

"Actually, I'm only living here temporarily. I've spent most of my life in San Bernardino," he said. "I had two hard-working parents. I was born and raised in the same house and never missed a day of school. After college, I entered the police academy. I married my high school sweetheart and bought a house with a picket fence. I guess that makes me a pretty ordinary guy. What you call a chocolate/chocolate kind of guy."

"You make it sound like ordinary is something to be ashamed of. When I pegged you as a chocolate/chocolate kind of person, I meant it as a compliment. See that guy over there?"

Mark followed her gaze. "The one with the purple hair and tattooed body?"

She nodded. "I happen to know him. He comes into my shop regularly to buy candy for the homeless shelters. He says it's the luxuries that make people feel good about themselves. Do you know how long it took me to find out what a great person, he is? Whereas with you, one look and . . ." She paused, trying to find the right word.

"One look at me and you know I'm great."

"Absolutely." Feeling suddenly self-conscious, she

flashed him a smile. After they finished their sandwiches and drinks, she shoved their wrappings into an empty paper cup.

"Miss Brubaker . . ."

She glanced up at him. "I'd like for you to call me Holly."

"Holly," he said softly. He touched the candy-kiss earring at her ear, sending it spinning. "About Boo-Boo . . . I really am sorry."

It wasn't until she tried to speak that she realized she'd been holding her breath. "I know." Her heart was beating fast, her cheeks burned. Flustered, she rose to her feet and shakily walked to the waste receptacle. After tossing their refuse, she turned. Several feet stretched between them and still she was having a hard time breathing. "I have to go back to the shop and relieve Cindi."

He nodded. "I have a meeting. It's one of those boring annual events that everyone is expected to attend."

"Oh." She felt strangely disappointed, like a child whose birthday was about over. There really was nothing more to say, no reason to stay, but she stood looking at him, just the same, and he stood looking at her.

"I hope you catch him soon," she said finally, but only because it seemed necessary to say something, even something inane.

"I will," he said with quiet resolve. "Make no mistake."

His confidence filled her with envy. Her life had taken so many unpredictable turns, she was never certain anything would work out as she'd hoped.

Suddenly he stooped over and retrieved a paperback romance that had fallen out of her shoulderbag. "I think this is yours." His eyebrows raised when he studied the numerous bookmarks sticking out of its pages.

She took the book from him. "I like to mark the passages that talk to me. That way I can read them again." She saw the look of interest in his eyes, could guess what he was thinking. He probably wouldn't believe her if she told him the truth; that the passages marked were about acceptance and love and had nothing to do with sex. "Thank you for lunch, Mr. Spencer."

"My name's Mark," he said.

"Mark." It didn't seem right to refer to an insurance investigator by his first name. It didn't even seem right to stand with him in public and recall how he looked standing tall and naked in her makeshift office, hiding behind a package of walnuts.

Feeling her emotions doing strange flip-flops, she took two steps backward. "Well, I guess I better go. Cindi can't have nuts—uh—lunch until I get back." Good grief, nuts! What a thing to say? "See you later," she stammered.

It didn't take much to figure out he knew exactly what carnal thoughts had caused her slip of tongue. Amusement danced in his eyes. "Are you going to be turning another mold?"

Oh, yes, he knew exactly what she was thinking, all right. "Yes. This afternoon," she said forcing her voice to remain calm. "Feel free to drop by and watch."

Without waiting for his response, she turned and quickly followed the footpath back toward Santa Monica Boulevard, crossed the street on the green light and joined the noon-hour thong on the sidewalk heading toward the Third Street Promenade. She glanced back at one point, craning her neck to see around the midday crowd. Her heart skipped a beat to discover him standing exactly where she'd left him, watching her. Even from that distance, the heat of his gaze affected her, touching her on such a deep level as to frighten her. She picked up her pace in a futile attempt to outrun the deep-rooted feelings he'd unwittingly uncovered.

The next morning, Holly found one of her favorite customers waiting outside the door when she arrived to open up shop. Holly greeted her with a smile. "My, my aren't you the early bird?"

"I'm trying to get my errands done before it gets hot." Mrs. Albright immediately grabbed a basket and started browsing.

Mrs. Albright was in her late seventies. She always wore red; Cinnamon red nail polish matched her red plastic high-heeled shoes. The doctor had ordered Mrs. Albright to give up smoking and high-heeled shoes. "The damned fool doctor won't be happy till he sees me wearing old lady shoes," she'd complained on more than one occasion.

Although most people her age generally avoided nuts, Mrs. Albright's order always included a half pound each of nougats and peanut brittle. On occasion, she even purchased a handful of chocolate with bubble gum centers. Although Holly felt obliged to point out that her doctor was acting in Mrs. Albright's best interests, she secretly admired the woman's tenacity.

Cindi arrived, apologizing for being late and looking as if she'd been up all night. "Are you all right?" Holly whispered behind the counter.

"Of course I'm all right. Why wouldn't I be?" Cindi looked so distressed, Holly decided not to press. Instead she turned her attention to Mrs. Albright, who had finished browsing and was now peering at the chocolates displayed behind the glass counter.

"The usual?" Holly asked.

Mrs. Albright gave a mischievous nod. "Today I'll take three-quarters of a pound instead of the usual half. I have a doctor's appointment this afternoon. Just a checkup, mind you. Try as he might, the fool doctor can't find a thing wrong with me." She winked and lowered her voice. "It makes him feel useful to scold me about my eating habits. Today, I intend to munch on nougats while he's examining me."

Mrs. Albright paid for her purchases and was just about to leave when Mark Spencer walked into the shop.

"What in dang blazes are you doing here?" Mrs. Albright demanded. "It's getting so a woman can't do anything without being spied on."

Startled by the woman's outburst, Holly stared over the counter at the investigator. Oh, no! Had he been checking up on Mrs. Albright, too? How dare he harass her customers!

Mark smiled and surprised Holly by kissing Mrs. Albright on the cheek.

"Would anyone like to tell me what's going on?" Holly asked.

Mark put his arm around Mrs. Albright's slight rounded shoulders. Even with her heels, Mrs. Albright barely reached his shoulder. "Holly Brubaker, I want you to meet my favorite aunt."

"Your aunt?"

"It's hard to believe, isn't it?" Mrs. Albright said, her gaze swinging back and forth between her nephew and Holly. She moved away from her nephew and lowered her voice. "He's not really such a bad guy. Once you get to know him, that is. He'd make good husband material."

Mark, who was busily setting up a sign he'd knocked over, turned. "What are you whispering about, Aunt Rice?"

"Oh, nothing," she said, looking innocent. With another wink at Holly, Mrs. Albright picked up her bag of candy and walked to the door, her high heels clicking across the brown and pink linoleum floor.

Mark opened the door for her. "I'll stop by later."

"What a woman," Holly said. "I hope I can have as much tenacity at that age."

"I have a feeling you and Aunt Rice are cut from the same mold," he said. "But don't worry. I won't hold it against you."

"Gee, thanks."

He leaned over the counter. "We need to talk." Without saying as much, he managed to convey the message that another trip to the pantry was in order. She wondered if it was her imagination or if they were already talking in some sort of secret code like an old married couple.

"I'll be in back," she called to Cindi, who was helping a customer pick out a box of chocolates for his secretary.

Less than a moment or two later, she stood in the small space of the closet facing the detective and trying with all her heart to keep her senses calm.

"I had the police department run a check on your employees."

She stared at him in disbelief. "You what?"

"It's routine," he explained.

"You could have told me."

"Why? So you could warn them?"

Holly couldn't believe her ears. "Warn them. You make it sound as if my employees have something to hide." Something in his face filled her with alarm. "Is that what you're saying?"

He rubbed his chin. "Jose has a record."

'That was years ago, when he was in high school."

"He served time for car theft."

"That was years ago," she repeated stubbornly.

He glanced at his notes. "Then there's Cindi."

"Cindi?"

"There's a pending shoplifting charge against her. She goes in front of the judge the middle of the month."

"Shoplifting?" She couldn't believe it. No wonder Cindi had been acting so strange. She hated this, hated sneaking behind people's back. Maybe snooping was his job, but it wasn't hers. "Is there anything else?" she asked, coolly.

As if he guessed her thoughts, he rubbed his forehead with his fingers. "This is all public record."

The need to protect the people she thought of as family was so great, she could hardly see straight. "You put this on your public record, Mark Spencer. I stand behind my employees one hundred percent. Not one of them is the Nougat Thief. I'd bet my life on it."

At the end of that same day, Holly closed the shop at five, grabbed a cup of yogurt from the refrigerator and joined Cindi and Jose. The three of them sat around a marble counter.

"Jose, is there a way we can mark the nougats so we can keep track of them without anyone knowing?"

Jose thought for a moment. "The only way I can think to do that is to find a way to number the foil pieces."

"See what you can come up with, will you? Make sure no one can spot the numbers." Mark had been against her marking the nougats, but she hated not knowing who she could or could not trust. The sooner the Nougat Thief was caught, the better for her peace of mind.

Holly finished her yogurt, donned an apron and carried a bowl of green frosting to the work table. A hundred little white chocolate baskets waited to be decorated with pink icing. This was the third night in a row she and Cindi had worked late. If business continued to flourish as it had in recent weeks, she would have to hire a full-time candy decorator.

Holly set to work piping tiny green leaves and vines around Cindi's artful pink rose buds. "How are the kids?"

"Fine," Cindi said. "Stevie's on the honor roll and Brian made the all-star softball team."

"That's great." Cindi had been divorced for only about a year, and the children were still trying to adjust. She glanced across the work table at Cindi. "Is everything okay with you?"

Cindi glanced up. "Of course. Why do you ask?"

"Lately, you seem . . . distracted."

"Are you saying there's something wrong with my work?"

"Your work is fine. I couldn't wish for a more conscientious employee. It's just . . ."

"I'm fine," Cindi said, in a tone that clearly forbade any more questions.

Holly debated whether to force the issue or let it rest. She hated this, hated knowing something that Cindi would probably hate for her to know. Hated the seed of distrust that had been planted in her mind ever since Mark Spencer had told her about Cindi's shoplifting charges.

One had nothing to do with the other. She was positive of it. She clamped down hard on the cone in her hand and a green line of frosting shot across the table. It was going to be a long night.

It was almost ten by the time Holly drove into her carport and took the stairway to her apartment. Ocean waves from a tropical storm hundreds of miles off the coast crashed on the nearby rugged cliffs as she let herself into her apartment. She froze in front of the open door, her hand stopping short of the light switch. Something was wrong. She felt it in her bones, in the prickly chill that crept along her scalp, in the cold metallic taste of fear lining her mouth.

Something was very wrong.

✦ Chapter 6 ✦

*A*ndy Warhol was missing.

Rather the painting of the Hershey Bar she had bought on a whim at a charity art auction was missing. How she ever worked up the nerve to turn on the entry way light, she would never know. She half expected to find a dead body or a gun pointing at her. Instead she found a blank wall and an empty frame.

The painting had cost her an arm and a leg and had it not been for the small inheritance she'd received from her parents, she could never have afforded it. Jim and Sharon Ferguson had convinced her it was a good investment. The Fergusons lived downstairs and owned both the complex she lived in and one of the largest art galleries in the area.

The painting made a great conversation piece. No one entered her apartment without commenting on it. Still, she was surprised by the depth of emotion as she stared at the wall. She felt devastated, violated. More than anything she felt angry.

Suddenly, it occurred to her that perhaps the thief was still in her apartment, lurking in one of the dark rooms, ready to attack her.

Horrified at the thought, she backed her way out of the still open door and raced downstairs to her landlord's apartment. It wasn't until she reached their front porch that she remembered the Fergusons were still in Europe on an art purchasing expedition. They weren't due back for another couple of days.

She ran to the carport and locked herself inside her car. Hands shaking she fumbled in her purse for the business card Mark had given her and picked up the handset of her cellular phone. Holding the card up so she could read it in the dim glow of the streetlight, she punched in Mark's number. *Please, please be there.*

Counting the rings, she held her breath as she glanced around her. The ocean breeze made the night seem alive with moving shadows.

The phone picked up on the third ring. "Spencer."

She let out her breath. Thank God. "Mark."

A moment's silence stretched between them. "Holly? Is that you? Where are you?"

"I'm home. The Nougat Thief—he was here."

"All right. Give me your address."

"Two thirty-two Gulls Crossing Lane."

"Is the thief still on the premises?"

"I don't know. I don't think so. I'm calling from the car phone."

"Did you call the police?"

"I'm going to call them as soon as I hang up."

"I'm on my way." The line went dead.

She dialed 911 and made her report. Why she called Mark before calling the police, she couldn't say. All she knew is that she wouldn't feel safe until he arrived.

She replaced the phone and slid the key into the ignition. At the least sight of anyone lurking around, she intended to be out of that driveway in a flash.

Though it seemed to take forever, little more than six minutes passed according to her watch before she spotted the flashing red lights in the distance.

Mark arrived on the tail of two black and whites, his wheels screeching to a stop. She was never so glad to see anyone in her life. She jumped out of her car and rushed into his arms.

"Holly!" He slipped his arms around her waist. "Are you all right?"

She nodded. "I think so."

He glanced at the two-story building. "Is this where you live?"

She nodded. "Upstairs."

He called over to one of the uniformed policemen. "Upstairs." His arms still around her, he studied her face in the glow of the security light. She was shaking and couldn't seem to stop. "If you want, you can sit in the car and wait."

"I want to go with you." She pulled away from him. His presence had both a calming and a spine-tingling effect on her. "I'm all right, really I am. Now that you're here."

"Are you sure?"

She managed a smile. "Positive." They walked up the stairs together as she filled him in on how she discovered the theft. "When I saw the painting was missing, I was too afraid to go inside."

They were greeted by Officer Green, a blond-haired, blue-eyed man in his mid-twenties. He talked in a slight southern drawl. "Same MO as the Nougat Thief," he told Mark.

"He took my Warhol," she said, pointing to the bare spot next to the hat rack. The empty frame leaned against the wall.

Mark studied the frame. "Campbell soup?"

"Hershey bars," she replied.

He locked gazes with her, surprising her with the look he gave her, a look that conveyed sympathy. But there was more, much more. She also saw understanding and she felt an inner tug as if someone had literally pulled her heart-strings. He understood something about her that not even she had understood until that moment. The horrible feeling of devastation and violation had less to do with the painting and more to do with what the painting represented. The thief had stolen a part of her legacy, dammit. As irrational as this was—as illogical—Mark understood her feelings without question, accepted them, and by George, so would she.

Something happened at that moment between them; something changed, but she was too distraught to analyze what it meant, other than to know that for the first time in her life, someone understood her. Really, really understood her.

"Was this insured by Woodson-Meyers?" Officer Green asked, obviously wondering why Mark was on site.

She nodded and reached in the glove drawer of the antique hat rack for a snapshot. "For fifty thousand dollars. This is a photo of the painting."

Officer Green took the photo and whistled. "This is worth fifty grand? I wouldn't give you two cents for it."

"I don't think Miss Brubaker is interested in your opinion!" Mark said sharply.

Officer Green turned red. "I'll check the rest of the house." Like a dog with his tail between his legs, he hastened away.

"Damned kid better learn to keep his opinions to himself," Mark said.

"Don't be so tough on him," she said softly, tugging on his arm. "A lot of people feel that way about Warhol."

"Officer Green is here to investigate a crime, not to give his opinion on art."

Mark was right, of course. Some people might have been offended by the rookie's thoughtless comments. Perhaps under other circumstances, she might have been too. But tonight it was enough that Mark understood the painting's true value had nothing to do with monetary worth. There was nothing more she could want.

She followed Mark into the living room and watched him duck beneath her collection of wind chimes that hung in front of the sliding glass doors. He pulled out his handkerchief and, careful not to leave prints, slid the door open. The wind chimes moved in the wind, filling the room with something akin to metal laughter. Under other circumstances, the wind chimes might have lifted her spirits, but tonight they sounded hollow and reminded her of the many days and nights they had been her only company.

Mark stepped onto the balcony, looked around, then studied the edge of the door. "It looks like he jimmied the lock."

He lifted his voice to be heard over the wind and the sound of crashing waves. "You'll have to call the locksmith."

He stepped inside, closed the door, and ducked back beneath the wind chimes. In so doing, he almost toppled a three-tiered table holding her china angel collection. He quickly righted the table before any damage was done and practically turned over the little tea cart that displayed her African violets.

"How the thief managed to maneuver without knocking anything over is amazing," he said.

Holly resisted the urge to point out that not everyone required as much space as he did. Besides, she was too busy holding her breath and waiting for the next mishap.

She was almost relieved when he started down the hall toward the bedroom.

The bedroom! She tore after Mark and found him standing next to the queen-size bed, staring down at her pillow. It wasn't until she moved closer that she could see the gold-foiled nougat on her Willie Wonka pillowcase.

Mark lifted the pillow. "Willie Wonka?" he mouthed, so that the two policemen who were checking out her walk-in closet couldn't overhear.

She blushed. The pillow slips were a gift from the Ferguson's five-year-old grandson.

She watched one of the policemen pull out a ballpoint pen and use it to ease the nougat into a plastic bag.

She took a deep breath. How dare the thief break into her home, take her things and flaunt what he did by leaving one of her custom-made candies on her pillow! A candy that she herself might have sold him. She felt violated and used. More than anything, she felt enraged, as if by choosing her candy as his calling card, he had made her an accomplice to his dastardly deeds.

"Holly."

She looked up, surprised to find Mark's face blurred by her tears. Suddenly, she was in his arms, her head against his broad shoulder. "He had no right to do this," she sobbed.

"He had no right to come into my house, into anyone's home and . . ."

Mark sucked in his breath. "I know. We'll find him. I promise you." He pulled her so close, their hearts seemed to beat as one. He pressed his lips against her smooth forehead. Hands in her silky smooth hair, he felt her press against him as if to seek comfort and shelter. At that moment, he would have done anything for her, given her his last breath had she wanted or needed him to.

A movement caught his eye and he turned his head. He saw the two cops exchange a glance. He realized how his hand in her hair and his lips on her forehead must look. Embarrassed to be caught acting unprofessional, he quickly pulled away. She gazed up at him, questioning, no doubt, his sudden withdrawal.

"I don't think you should stay here tonight. Is there somewhere else you can go?"

"I'm not leaving," she said stubbornly. "But I was just thinking, maybe we should check the apartment downstairs. The Fergusons are away. They're art dealers and own a lot of valuable works. I have the key to their place."

She started past him and he caught her by the wrist. "Are you sure you're up to this?"

"I'm taking care of their place while they're gone. It's my responsibility."

He nodded and released her hand. She waited while he asked Officer Green to accompany them, then led the way outside and down the stairs.

Her brave front deserted her as soon as she reached the Fergusons's front porch. She hesitated, keys in hand. He took the keys from her, unlocked the door, and flipped on the entry light. Although there was nothing in the entry way that would indicate a robbery had occurred, Holly felt a cold chill travel through her body.

After a whispered exchange, Green pulled his gun out of his holster and Spencer followed him into the living room. Only a moment passed before he called to her. "Could you come here, Miss Brubaker?"

Miss Brubaker. She wondered if the sudden formality was for the policeman's benefit. She hoped so.

She walked into the living room and stopped. "Oh, no!" she cried. The Ferguson's entire collection of original oils was missing, along with a signed Beatrice Wood sculpture.

It was midnight by the time the place had been dusted for prints, a full report had been taken from her, and everything checked out. Mark was the last to leave. He lingered in the entry way of her apartment and looked for all the world like he didn't want to go. "Keep everything locked up tight," he cautioned her. He glanced at the sliding glass door. Earlier he had battled the wind chimes to wedge a broomstick into the sill. "Be sure to call a locksmith first thing in the morning."

"I will," she said. "I'll be all right, really."

He gazed at her pale face and felt something stir deep within. She looked like she didn't want him to go. Well, that made two of them. He didn't really have any choice in the matter. He was investigating a crime. It would be unprofessional of him to stay. Unprofessional to give into the feelings that were clamoring for release. The best thing for both of them was for him to get the hell out of there, fast!

He hurried, almost ran, down the stairs, through the gate, and down the driveway to his car. The wind blew sand and salt into his face, but did nothing to cool his fevered body. High waves crashed against the nearby rocks with thunderous force filling the air with mist, but even this failed to cool the heat generated by desire and want and, more than anything, need. God almighty, what was he thinking? Even if he wasn't working on a case, Holly was off-limits. She would drive him crazy with her bangles and wind chimes and constant clamor. Why, there wasn't room to breathe in her place, let alone her shop. She was, to put it kindly, a nut. A lovable, charming, but very much off-limits nut.

There was no room in his strange though infinitely ordered life for someone like her.

Traffic was light. It took him less than ten minutes to

drive back to his own place, this time following all the speed limits. While working on the case, he'd rented a temporary room on the edge of the city on the second floor of an old but graceful Victorian house. He owned a small house in San Bernadino, but hated the commute. The room probably saved him four hours driving time a day.

His monthly rent included kitchen and sitting room privileges. He never used either room, preferring to keep himself confined to his own cheerful quarters, which included a sunny, glassed-in porch.

Tonight, no room pleased him. Not the sparse and orderly bedroom. Not the living room with its perfectly ordered bookcases. Not even the techno-thriller bestseller with its single bookmark could hold his attention. He kept thinking of Holly and those blue tear-filled eyes of hers.

He sat in a large overstuffed chair and flipped on the TV. Holding the remote control toward the screen, he surfed the channels in the futile hope that something would catch his attention. Nothing did. He was too busy thinking or, rather, trying not to think about Holly. What was she doing at that very moment? What was she thinking? Suddenly, he realized he was actually watching a commercial for chocolate frosting.

Disgusted with himself, he flipped off the TV and began pacing the floor. This was wrong. He was an investigator. His job was to solve the case, not get involved on a personal level. But he *was* involved. He'd felt her pain as he looked into her face that night, felt her loss as if it were his own, and his sense of professionalism was compromised by a sense of outrage. Heaven only knows what he would have done had he met up with the thief in person.

This was no good. No investigator worth his salt would allow himself to get personally involved. Either he was going to have to get his emotions under control or he was going to have to remove himself from the case.

That's what he'd done when he was a cop and his wife's brother had been arrested for pushing drugs: He'd had himself removed from the case. Lynn had been furious. She'd begged him to step in and do something. When he'd refused to do as much as testify on her brother's behalf, the marriage fell apart.

He didn't blame Lynn, of course. It was a well-known fact that before the police department had been overhauled, things happened: Evidence disappeared, reports were lost, and light sentences were imposed on the family members of certain privileged officials. A judge's son had practically walked away free from a drunk-driving charge. Charges for pandering were dropped against a councilwoman's daughter for no good reason.

He could have gotten Lynn's brother off had he wanted to, or persuaded the judge, a friend, to consider a lighter sentence. But that wouldn't have served the public interest. As much as it hurt to admit it, Lynn's brother was bad news. He deserved to be behind bars.

Mark was a firm believer that if you do something wrong, you pay the consequences. Besides, he had no sympathy for anyone who messed with drugs. Drugs were the root of too many broken lives. Seventy-five percent of all homicides were the result of drugs.

Lynn accused him of being hard-nosed and uncompromising. The day her brother was sentenced, she filed for divorce.

Mark had always played by the rules, even as a kid, no matter what it cost him. He once passed up on a chance to play on his high school all-star team rather than cheat on an exam.

Play by the rules, Mark, that was him and no matter how many times he'd been tempted in the past by someone he'd met during an investigation, he'd always managed to keep a professional distance. Until now. Now he was simply Mark Spencer, a lonely bachelor who had the sudden urge to do something wacky and completely out-of-character.

He wanted to eat a piece of chocolate-covered bubblegum, for God's sakes. To wear something that wasn't gray, to laugh like he hadn't laughed in years. To do something really off-the-wall crazy with a certain blue-eyed nut.

❧ Chapter 7 ❦

The knock at the door sent Holly's adrenaline skyrocketing. It was after 1 a.m. Far too late for visitors, salesmen, or sugar-borrowing neighbors. She considered the possibility that it was someone returning her cat, Mozart, missing since the burglary.

She flipped off the TV and listened. Another knock sounded, this one louder. Her heart beating fast, she walked to the door, her oversized slippers flip-flopping against her heel. Telling herself that a burglar wasn't likely to knock, she held her hand to her fast-beating heart and called out. "Who . . . who is it?"

"It's me, Mark."

With a sigh of relief she undid the bolt and chain as quickly as her quivering fingers would allow, and threw open the door. Dressed in blue jeans, white sneakers, and a gray jacket, he stood lean and tall, conveying a feeling of permanence and security. Never was she so glad to see anyone in her life. "What are you doing here?"

"I was just passing by. . . ." Obviously realizing how ridiculous that sounded he laughed. "I was worried about you. So I drove over here to make certain everything was all right. When I saw your light, I thought maybe you could use some company."

She leaned her head against the edge of the door. "That depends. Is this a formal visit?"

"Does it look like a formal visit?"

She gave him a soft smile. "In that case . . ." She backed away to let him in. "Want some hot chocolate?"

He grinned. He hadn't had hot chocolate since he was a kid. "Hot chocolate would be great." He followed her toward the kitchen and slid onto one of the high stools at the counter separating the kitchen from the dining room. She was dressed in a short terry robe that stopped midthigh. She had abandoned her usual ponytail, and her slightly damp hair fell around her shoulders. Moving with a grace and energy that belied the lateness of the hour and the harrowing events of the night, she poured milk into a pan and put it on the stove to heat.

"Are you hungry?" she asked. "I could cook up some corn."

He wasn't sure he'd heard right. "Corn?"

"Bought it fresh today. White corn on the cob—" She broke off, looking embarrassed. "It's my favorite midnight snack, but I could make you a sandwich if you prefer. . . ."

"I don't generally eat after nine," he replied.

"Don't tell me you get nightmares."

"Not nightmares. Insomnia. Especially if I'm working on a case."

"I get my best ideas at night," she said.

"Really? Well, I don't want it said that I stopped the creative process. Corn on the cob and hot chocolate sounds . . . different."

She grinned and reached for a large pot. "I think chocolate goes with everything." She filled the pot with water and placed it on the stove to boil.

He watched as she made hot chocolate the old-fashioned way, with milk, cinnamon, and real whipped cream, using none of the lowfat, low-calorie substitutes that were so popular.

She carried two mugs of the steaming beverage to the counter and slid on a bar stool opposite him. There was something intimately satisfying in sitting in a warm, cozy kitchen in the wee hours of the morning drinking hot chocolate with Holly Brubaker.

"How do you think the thief knew he would find valuable artwork at my place?" she asked.

It was a good question. He'd checked art museums and associations and supply houses in the area trying to find a link. The thief always knew which houses to break into and he was getting that information from somewhere. "I have no idea," he said. He didn't want to talk about the robberies; actually, he didn't want to be reminded that he had no business being here, in Holly Brubaker's apartment, sipping hot chocolate and wondering what she wore beneath that skimpy robe of hers. Furthermore, he had no business toying with the idea of lifting her into his arms and carrying her into that feminine pink bedroom he'd seen earlier and laying her onto that queen-sized bed with its ridiculous Willie Wonka pillowcases.

"Very few people knew I owned a valuable painting," she said. "I'm hardly a collector."

"No, but the Fergusons are. My suspicion is that they were the targets. When the thief realized there was an upstairs apartment, he decided to take a look and got lucky."

"I hate this," she said. "I hate the idea of working in the shop tomorrow and wondering if every customer walking through the door is the thief."

"It could be an employee," he said gently, knowing how much she resisted the idea.

She shook her head stubbornly. "I don't believe that for a moment."

"You don't want to believe it." He hadn't wanted to believe Lynn's brother was a drug dealer. After Lynn's mother had died, he and Lynn had taken the boy into their home; Mark had taken him fishing. He had practically treated him like a son or, at the very least, a younger brother. It had hurt, dammit, to find out that the boy had betrayed his trust. Lynn thought she was the only one in pain. She was wrong. She was wrong about a lot of things.

He took Holly's small hand in both of his, seeking to comfort, but strangely enough receiving far more comfort than he could give. It was as if she were responding in some mysterious way to his private pain. "It'll soon be over," he promised. "We'll find the thief and put him where he belongs."

She nodded. "The problem is, he can only be punished for stealing artwork, not trust."

"That's true of any criminal," he said. His brother-in-law had been sentenced to fifteen years for selling drugs. He'd received no additional time for breaking up a marriage.

"The water's boiling," she said and after a while added, "I better put the corn in."

Startled to find himself still holding her hand, he released her. "Oh, I'm sorry . . . I . . ."

"It's all right . . . I . . ."

He watched her glide from the refrigerator to the stove, wondering why suddenly they were talking in breathless half sentences. It must be the air. Maybe the storm was forcing a low-pressure system onto the coast, taking the oxygen out of the air. He stared at the glob of whipped cream floating on his hot chocolate and wondered why he was suddenly thinking like one of those TV weathermen.

She sat down again. "The corn won't take long." While they waited for the corn to cook, he talked about his divorce and the reasons he left the police department. Later, they slathered real butter across the steaming hot corn. He ate his corn in tidy rows; she ate hers with wild abandon, taking a nibble here, a nibble there. Watching her, he shook his head. Watching him, she shook hers.

"I better let you get some sleep," he said after awhile. The clock on the wall told him it was after two. He wiped the last of the melted butter from his mouth and stood. She followed him into the living room.

"I appreciate your coming over," she said. A gust of wind rattled the windows and she jumped slightly, then shivered. "It's really windy out there."

"Yeah." He glanced at the sliding glass door. "Be sure to get that lock fixed tomorrow."

"I will," she said. "I . . . my cat's missing. I'm afraid he must have escaped. The thief probably left the door open. I thought Mozart would be back by now. He doesn't usually stay away this long."

"I'm sure he'll be back by morning."

"I hope so. It's amazing how much company a cat is. Even one as independent as Mozart."

Their gazes locked and held like sunlight on glass. "Would you like me to stay?"

Her eyes widened in surprise. "What?"

He swallowed hard. Now he'd done it; offered to stay when he knew damned well there was no logical reason for him to do so. She was perfectly capable of taking care of herself. And there wasn't a reason in the world to think the thief would come back. "I . . . I could stay the night," he offered. "Sleep out here on the couch." He added the last so there'd be no mistaking his intentions.

"That's not necessary," she said slowly.

His heart missed a beat. *It's not*? Well, if it wasn't necessary for him to sleep on the couch, then she was suggesting . . . "Holly, I'm sorry . . . I don't think we should, you know?" He groaned inwardly; he sounded as virtuous as a choir director. "Under the circumstances . . . it wouldn't be right."

Her face flared red. "I didn't mean . . ." She looked flustered and bewildered. "I meant to say . . . it's not necessary for you to stay. . . . I mean . . ."

She was talking in those run-on sentences again like she did when he was covered—uh, enrobed in chocolate. Like she did when he stood naked as a jaybird. He rubbed his chin and wished the floor would open up. "It was my mistake. I . . . I want you to know it's not that I don't want to sleep with you and . . ." Now he was the one talking in run-on sentences. "It just wouldn't be right," he finished lamely.

Somehow she managed to recover first. "You don't have

to explain yourself. I know you would never do anything you considered improper."

He frowned. What was she saying? That he was a prude? What? Somehow this didn't sit right with him. Nor did the idea of leaving her. She wanted him to stay. He could see it in her eyes, her face, hear it in her voice. What kind of man would he be if he walked out, knowing how she felt? "Oh, hell, give me a blanket and a pillow."

She bit her lower lip. "Are you sure?"

"Positive."

"All right, then. I'll"—she waved her hand in the general direction of the bedroom—"be right back." She disappeared down the hall, returning moments later with an arm full of bedding. He hurried to take the blankets and pillow from her, brushing her hand with his own. Jumping back as if he'd been touched by a flame, he bashed his elbow against the china cabinet. Dishes rattled, but fortunately nothing broke. He smiled sheepishly and moved carefully toward the couch, ducking to avoid the grabby tendrils of a flirty Boston fern.

"It's kind of you to stay," she said. Watching the hem of her robe inch up the back of her shapely legs as she bent to make his bed, he felt like a fraud.

She moved the toss pillows and stuffed animals from the sofa and stacked them in wild abandon next to the overflowing bookshelves. "The bathroom's down the hall to the right," she said. "Is there anything else you need?"

Oh, yes, he thought, there was plenty he needed, starting with the need to see if her lips tasted as good as they looked. "Nothing."

"Good night," she murmured softly.

"Night."

She turned to leave, stopping just before she started down the hallway. She glanced back over her shoulder. "Mark—thank you. I'll sleep a lot better knowing you're here." With that she was gone and after a moment, he heard her bedroom door close.

He pulled off his shoes and stretched his body the length

of the oversized couch. The wind howled and the waves crashed against the rocks, but the storm outside seemed mild compared to the feelings that churned inside him. He rolled over on his side and felt her nearness. *Sleep tight, Holly, because I sure in hell won't.*

✵ *Chapter 8* ✵

$\mathcal{M}$ark woke with a start and, forgetting how narrow the couch was, landed on the floor with a thud. Stunned for a moment, he lay between the couch and the coffee table and tried to make sense of his surroundings. It was still dark, which made the infernal racket that much more incredulous. Who in hell was playing the piano at this hour?

Mark fought with the blanket that was twisted around his body and stood. He reached for the lamp and turned it on just as Holly hurried into the living room, dressed in an oversized T-shirt that stopped midthigh. Her soft, rounded breasts with their pointed tips were outlined beneath the fabric. Sleep-tousled hair fell around her shoulders in a golden halo. She looked all at once angelic, earthy, and sexy.

"I'm sorry," she said breathlessly. "I honestly thought Mozart had escaped."

Mozart? He turned to face the piano. A large orange cat strutted up and down the keyboard, its marmalade tail flitting through the air like the baton of a tipsy conductor.

"He's hungry," Holly explained. "He only plays the piano when he's hungry or feeling neglected. That's why I named him Mozart. I didn't leave his food out because I thought he was gone."

She lifted the cat off the piano and stroked him lovingly. "Poor baby. Where have you been? I've been looking all over for you." Holly and the cat disappeared into the kitchen.

Mark sat on the edge of the couch and ran his fingers through his hair.

"Do you want some pasta salad?" Holly called.

Good God. Pasta salad? At this time of the morning? He glanced at the clock. It was just after four-thirty. He seldom rose before seven. Unless, of course, he was on a red-eye flight for his company. "No thanks."

She walked into the living room, looking bright and perky, and sat down on the couch next to him. "Are you all right?"

"Yes." No. He wasn't all right. For one thing, he was having an adolescent hormone attack or something. For what else could explain the desperate urge to take her in his arms and kiss her. He covered his face with his hands so as not to look at her, but that didn't seem to help much. She was wearing some sort of delicate fragrance. No one should smell that good at four in the morning. Or look that good.

She stood. "I'll let you go back to sleep."

There was no way he was going to get any more sleep. "Don't go," he said softly. He reached for her hand and stood. "Don't go."

Her lips parted as she looked up at him, her eyes soft and inviting. He slipped his free hand around her waist and pulled her to him until they were standing mere inches apart.

He whispered her name and brushed his lips against hers. Her mouth was soft and yielding, warm and sweet. Overcome by the urge to possess her, he crushed her to him. Covering her mouth hungrily with his, he pushed his tongue through her lips. She ran her fingers through his hair and he deepened the kiss. He held her so tight it was as if they breathed and moved as one.

His lips left hers momentarily to nibble at her earlobe and to sear a path of warm kisses along the length of her smooth, warm neck. She arched back, and moaned softly, her lovely firm breasts pressing against his chest.

Capturing her lips more urgently than before, he reached for her breast. The lovely firm mound filled his hand as tenderness filled his heart. He felt her shiver at his gentle touch and the tiny rosebud peak grow taut against his palm.

Her hand dropped down to his zipper and a thrill of excitement shot through him like an electrical charge. Grimacing in pain that was both sweet and agonizing, he wrapped his hands around her waist and pressed his forehead against hers. "I didn't come prepared." He gazed into her eyes. There hadn't been anyone for him since the divorce, and that was God's honest truth, but he couldn't ask her to take him at his word.

"Oh," she whispered, in what he hoped was disappointment. "I don't think I have . . ." She brightened. "Maybe I do." She took him by the hand and led him down the hall and into her bedroom. In a whirlwind of energy, she pulled out a drawer and dumped the contents onto the bed. He blinked in disbelief. Never had he seen so many earrings in his life.

"Holly, what in the world?" His zipper was about to burst and she was playing dress-up.

"It's here somewhere," she muttered, sending earrings flying in every direction. Finally, she held up a silver earring shaped like a bullet. "Here it is!"

He stared at the earring. "Here what is?"

"One of those . . . what we need. One of my customers gave these to me for my birthday."

He took the earring from her. "Are you serious? There's actually one . . . those things we need . . . in here?" He held the earring up to the light and managed to knock a half dozen framed photographs off the nightstand. "How do you open this thing?"

"Try twisting it."

He tried but the capsule didn't budge. "Do you have pliers?"

She left the room and returned moments later carrying a toolbox. Soon tools were scattered on the bed with the earrings. "See if this pair will work."

He took the pliers and gripped the end. It took a bit of doing, but he finally worked the top off the silver capsule. He closed an eye and looked inside. "Do you have a pair of tweezers?"

She nodded and reached for the pair on the dresser. Like a surgeon performing delicate brain surgery, he worked the little foil packet free. Lord, this was crazy. He was crazy. Still, he couldn't help but feel a sense of triumph when he'd accomplished his mission.

She smiled up at him. "I knew you could do it."

He ran his fingers through his hair. "I don't think this is a good idea."

She studied his face. "I know. You're working on a case and you're concerned about professional ethics."

He *was* concerned about professional ethics. But what he was feeling at the moment went far deeper. "It's more than that," he said, reluctant to get into a complicated discussion. "It's the relationship thing. There's no room in my life right now." It was the truth, but that didn't mean he liked it. Especially now, when she looked so beautiful and soft and, more than anything, desirable. "If I'm in town for more than a month at a time, that's a lot. I'm afraid that's the nature of my job."

He set the foiled packet on the nightstand, knocking over another picture frame. "The truth is I don't think there's room in your life for me."

He could tell by her face he'd hit a nerve. "How can you say that?"

"Look around you, Holly." He indicated the amazing collection of photos around the room. "Your life is so full and rich. How could I possibly give you more than you already have? Especially with my job."

"Do you want to know who all these people are?" With a sweep of her arm, she sent the frames flying. "They're strangers. All of them! I found these photos in antique shops." She stood looking around her, looking lost and confused, as if suddenly seeing her surroundings for the first time.

"Holly, I'm sorry." And because he felt guilty for having stripped her of her protective armor, he pulled her in his arms and held her close.

She fit so naturally into the curve of his body it was as

if she was meant to be there. Her warm breath mingled with his as he offered her comfort. Soon, his heated lips found hers.

This time there was no stopping the all-consuming passion that flared between them. He picked her up in his arms and carried her to the bed, knocking over a stack of books in his haste. Easing his body next to hers, he gently worked the hem of her T-shirt upward, skimming the velvet softness of her thighs and hips with the sensitive tips of his fingers until he'd exposed the full beauty of her breasts.

He gazed at her lovingly. He feathered his tongue across one rosy peak before taking the tiny bud in his mouth.

"Oh, Mark." His name came out in a breathless whisper. Her flesh tingled with fire; her breasts seemed to melt at his touch. She tugged on his shirt, desperate to feel him, desperate to explore every part of her body as he was now exploring hers.

Smiling at her impatience, he pulled his shirt over his head and discarded it. Then his hands dropped to his belt buckle. In no time at all he was naked, his heated body hard as steel and flushed with burning desire. She skimmed her hands over his chest, down his hips, then wrapped a hand around his heated shaft. He shuddered at her touch and moaned softly.

He slid her lacy panties away and touched the nest of tidy curls between her thighs. She was ready for him; more than ready. Taking but a moment to protect her, he slid on top of her and plunged deep into her feminine depths.

Thrilling to the touch, the feel, and sheer manly power of him, she surrendered to the heated swirl of sensations. He filled her to the brim. He filled her heart, her soul, her body.

Later, sighing with sweet exhaustion, they clung to each other, not wanting to let go. They might have remained in each others' arms forever had the deafening sound of bells and buzzers not filled the air.

She slid out from under him and already missing her, he sat up. Much to his amazement, he counted at least ten alarm clocks around the room, and everyone of them was yelling at the top of its mechanical lungs. It was like being in a hospital nursery at feeding time.

Holly raced around the room turning off the alarms. "Ow!" She bent over and retrieved an earring. It was the mate of the earring he'd pried open. Suddenly she began to giggle. "I just remembered who gave these earrings to me for my birthday. They were a gift from your aunt."

Moaning, Mark laid back and covered his head with a pillow. *What the hell was Aunt Rice doing giving out condoms?*

He waited for her on the balcony while she dressed for work. The sky was blue and the wind had died down, but the waves still pounded the rocks below. Overhead, the seagulls circled and cawed.

Presently she stuck her head outside. She was dressed in her chocolate factory getup. "Would you like some ice cream?"

He turned and hit his head on one of the blasted hanging pots that was swinging from the overhang. "Ice cream? In the morning? Don't you do anything like normal people?" His words held an edge that had more to do with his own confusion than anything else. He was working on a case that involved Holly Brubaker and he had no right to become personally involved. The insurance company frowned on that kind of thing; he frowned on it. And even if it weren't for the case, he was hardly in a position to offer a woman much more than an occasional night out on the town.

Still, seeing the hurt look on her face filled him with guilt. It wasn't her fault. The responsibility was his and his alone. He brushed his fingers through his hair. "I didn't mean that like it sounded."

"Yes, you did." When he made no reply, she sat quietly in a wicker chair, or at least as quietly as someone wearing a ton of bangles and jingling earrings could sit. "Listen, I know what you said about your job making it impossible for you to get close to anyone. . . ."

He sighed. "I never know from day to day where I'm going to be sent next. Art thieves consider the world their marketplace. I know this sounds jaded, but for me that means I've got to look at the world as one big crime scene."

She watched his face. "This isn't about your job."

"Of course it's about my job."

"It's about me and you and how unsuited we are for each other."

"I can't deny that we are different. I live a simple, regimented life. Yes, even when I'm on the road. I admit it; I'm boring. But that's how I like it. I eat proper food at proper times. A bowl of whole-grain cereal in the morning, a well-balanced dinner at day's end. I swear, I'd drive you crazy."

"I like that you're a bit eccentric."

"I'm not the one who's eccentric. You are. Not that I'm complaining, mind you." He leaned over to kiss her on the nose. "I like you just the way you are."

She looked up at him, her eyes questioning. "But you think I'm a nut."

He straightened and leaned against the railing. "I don't you think you're a nut. I think you're eccentric and that's an important difference."

It might be to him, but as far as she was concerned it was still a label, and that brought back too many memories of the past. During her growing-up years she'd been branded with all the fashionable labels of the day; they'd called her hyperactive, manic, gifted, lazy—you name it. No one knew for sure what made Holly zig when the rest of the world zagged, but an army of so-called experts had a name for it and it almost always preceded rejection.

"All right," he said, his eyes filled with warm lights. "Have it your way. I think you're a nut and you think I'm boring."

"I don't think you're boring." Never had she met a man who excited her more. "Conservative, maybe."

"Don't we make a fine couple? I think you're a nut and you think I'm boring. . . ."

"Conservative."

"Holly . . ." The teasing lights left his eyes. "Last night was very special. You'll never know how special."

She braced herself. *You're a special little girl, Holly, and that's why we're sending you to another school . . . another doctor . . . another home.* She stood abruptly. It was time to bring out all the survival techniques she'd perfected in the past. "Last night wouldn't have happened if I hadn't been robbed." She fought against the tears burning her eyes, prayed her voice wouldn't give her away.

He frowned. "What are you saying?"

"You were trying to comfort me and . . . things got out of hand. We took a roll in the hay." She managed a flippant tone. "It happens."

"Try again, Holly," he said softly.

Her temper flared. How dare he see through her? She glared at him. "Why are you making such a big deal of it?"

He looked at her long and hard. "This rolling in the hay business . . ." His voice sounded curt. "Does it happen often?"

"Mark . . ." For a moment, she almost gave herself away; she wanted so much to go to him and hold him. But that would be a mistake for it would only open her up for the rejection she knew awaited. No, in order to survive, she had to be the one who pushed away. She averted her eyes. "I guess it was the combination of having someone break into my home and Mozart disappearing." She chanced another look at him. "I'm really grateful to you for helping me through a difficult time."

"Grateful?" he said evenly, his face so bland she was positive she saw relief written all over it.

Feeling as if her resolve was about to shatter, she started for the door. "I better go or I'll be late." She ran through the living room, snatched up her shoulderbag, and raced out to her car.

She'd saved him the trouble of hiding behind his job or making up some other excuse as to why he wasn't ready for a relationship. Saved herself the pain of once again being rejected. She'd gotten good at this over the years, this walking away from a possible relationship before anyone got too emotionally involved. Damned good!

Sure it hurt. Sometimes. Timing was crucial. The break had to be made before she cared too much.

This time she'd waited too long.

❋ *Chapter 9* ❋

*H*olly arrived at the shop feeling shaken, confused, and angry and she had only herself to blame. She knew the requirements of his job from the start. She even recognized how different they were in personalities. Yet, she had jumped in with her heart and soul—her entire being—hoping against hope that this time would be different. That someone could love her, really love her, without reservations or censure or recommending a psychiatric evaluation.

When would she ever learn? It was not the first time she had opened herself up to rejection and failure. Not by any means. It was a lifelong habit. Well, no more. She had her full of people considering her odd, starting with her adopted parents. Bless their souls, she loved them dearly and was heartbroken when they died less than six months apart. That had been three years ago, but she still missed them and wished with all her heart that just once they had approved of something she'd done. It hurt to recall that the very last thing her mother had said to her on her death bed was, "Holly, must you wear those ridiculous earrings?"

They weren't entirely to blame. Lord knows they tried to be loving parents and maybe in their own way, they were. They'd adopted her late in life. Both were in their forties, but the other two couples who had considered adopting her had backed out. After spending her first ten years in various foster homes, she was considered a child with "special problems." It was thought at the time that an older couple would know how to handle her.

They didn't really, but they never gave up trying. They were constantly shaking their head and meeting with school teachers, principals, and psychologists. She remembered the countless times she'd overheard them discussing her latest antics in hushed worried voices.

She'd been analyzed to death. Well, no more!

If Mark couldn't accept her the way she was, tough tacos. She didn't need him in her life—no matter how much his kisses set her afire or how much it pained her to let him go.

Swallowing hard against the lump rising in her throat, she blinked back tears. It would be all right. She would land on her feet just as she had all those other times. Eventually, she'd forget Mark and the night they'd shared. Forget his kisses. She'd continue to fill her life as she always filled it, with work and clutter and do-good causes. So what if she didn't have a love life? She could make a whale or two happy. Raise money for the library, help clean up the Santa Monica Bay. Prowl antique shops for old photos. She wiped away a stubborn tear and threw back her shoulders in firm resolve. No, sirree, she didn't need Mark Spencer or anyone else in her life.

Hearing Jose in back, she walked through the open door to the factory area. "Any luck coming up with a way to trap the thief?"

Jose was hauling a brick of chocolate from the storage room. He slid the block on the counter. "I think so. See if you think this will work." He waited for Holly to sit on a stool then dangled a roll of tickets in front of her. "I purchased this at the party store. If I hide a ticket in between two pieces of foil, then wrap the nougat as usual, no one will suspect a thing."

She studied the nougat. "What if the two wrappers separate?"

"I doubt if anyone would think a thing about it. As for the thief, we don't know that he eats the nougats. He may simply use them for calling cards."

What Jose said was true. "How do we keep track of the numbers?"

"See this little sticker? The number corresponds with the one inside the foil. All you and Cindi have to do is jot down the name of the customer on the sticker."

It sounded easy enough and they would only have to do it for regular customers. They didn't have to keep track of nougats sold to tourists or schoolchildren. "We'll give it a try," she said. "But for now, I think it best if we keep this among ourselves."

Jose agreed.

"How long before the nougats are numbered?"

"This tray is already numbered," Jose said. "You can use these for the regulars and sell the ones on display to tourists and others you don't want to keep track of."

Holly nodded in approval. "Thanks, Jose. Let's hope we catch ourselves a thief."

For the rest of the morning, Holly went through the proper motions. She smiled at her customers and said all the right things. No one guessed how much she was hurting inside.

Only once did she let down her guard and that was during a lull between customers. As she was restocking the display counter with chocolate/chocolates, she broke down in tears.

Cindi rushed to her side with a box of tissue. Tissues had landed on the permanent reorder list when Cindi was going through her painful divorce. Now the tables were turned and it was Holly who needed comforting.

"Oh, you poor thing," Cindi cooed, throwing her arms around Holly. "I have a feeling Jose's number system is going to work. And as soon as the police catch the thief, I'm sure they'll find your painting and everything will be back to normal."

"Nothing's ever going to be the same again," Holly sobbed, the tears flowing harder than ever. "And it's all because I'm a nut."

Cindi drew back. "That's not true. You might be a bit eccentric. . . ."

"Oooo."

"Now calm down, Holly. Eccentric is good."

"Since when?"

"I don't know. Since . . . do you remember how you hired me for this job?"

"We met at Disneyland."

Cindi laughed. "On the Small World ride. My sons and their friends sat together and I just happened to be seated next to you. As our little boat was winding its way through the canal, you spotted those gigantic plastic lollipops and said you were looking for a candy maker."

"And you said you were one."

"And you interviewed me on the spot. If I recall, we had to shout to be heard above the 'It's a Small World' song. By the time the ride was over I had a job."

Holly wiped away her tears and blew her nose. "So what's your point?"

"The point is that most people would have told me to call for an interview."

"So what you're saying is I'm not just eccentric, I'm a nut."

"Let's just say, you march to a different drummer." Cindi gave her an affectionate hug. "Mark doesn't know you like I know you. But when he does . . ."

Holly frowned. "Mark has nothing to do with this. Even if it did, it would never work out between us. Mark's job requires him to travel all over the world."

"You always said you wanted to see the world."

"It's not just his job; we're so different."

"Opposites attract. Look at me and Tom."

"You and Tom are divorced."

"All right. So that's a bad example. But I know other couples who are opposites and who still manage to be happy."

"Mark and I aren't just opposites. We're from different galaxies and—" She quickly wiped her tears away when the sound of jingling bells announced the arrival of a busload of tourists.

They did a brisk business that day. A lot of the regulars

came by. Holly and Cindi took special care to mark each sticker with the name of the person buying the nougat, but in reality, Holly didn't consider any of them suspects. She would know, wouldn't she? If one of her regulars was the suspect? Wouldn't she feel bad vibes or something?

It was entirely possible that it could take weeks or even months before one of the marked nougats found its way to a crime scene. That meant she and Mark were going to have to pretend nothing out of the ordinary had happened between them. She'd have to pretend that his kisses hadn't set her afire and that his touch hadn't left an indelible mark on her. It would be hard; she knew it would be hard. She might be many things, but she was no actor.

Business slowed down just before closing. Holly decided to broach the subject she wished she could avoid. Cindi was wrapping a basket full of chocolates with clear cellophane. The basket was going to be given away as a door prize for an AIDS benefit. Holly donated at least a half dozen of these baskets a month to local charities. "Cindi, I know about your shoplifting charges."

Cindi's hand stilled. "Who told you? Mark?"

"It's not important how I know. Do you want to talk about it?"

Cindi dropped down in a chair behind the counter and held her head. "I'm so ashamed. I don't know what to say." She looked up, her eyes filled with tears. "Brian stole a baseball glove."

"What?"

"He slipped it into my shopping bag when I wasn't looking. I told him I couldn't afford it, and . . . I don't know what got into him."

"But Mark said *you* were arrested."

"I could hardly turn in my own son, could I?"

Holly stared at her in disbelief. "Are you saying you took the blame for something Brian did? How's he going to learn to accept responsibility for his actions if you protect him?"

"He's only ten. He made a mistake. He promised me he'd never do it again."

"Listen to me, Cindi. This is serious. You could go to jail."

Cindi looked close to tears. "My attorneys said since it's my first offense, the judge will probably be lenient."

"You can't take a chance like that. Judges are bowing to public pressure to get tougher with first timers. In any case, you've got to think what's best for your son. Tell your attorney the truth. Please, Cindi, promise me you will."

The bells on the front door chimed as a man with a sheepish, almost panicky look hurried into the shop, his credit card in hand. Cindi rose to her feet, took one look at the man, and whispered, "Want to bet he forgot his wife's birthday?"

The Nougat Thief had struck again. No sooner had Holly opened up the morning paper and read the headlines than the phone rang.

It was Mark.

"Did you see the paper?"

She leaned against the kitchen counter and tried to breathe normally. She hadn't heard from him in over a week. Not since the night he'd filled her apartment, her bed, and more than anything, her heart with his presence.

"Holly?"

"I've only glanced at the headlines," she said, her voice husky. "Any further clues?"

"None," he admitted. "But don't worry. Two million dollars worth of artwork isn't going to stay hidden forever. Sooner or later one of those hot properties is going to show up in a museum or auction catalog."

She hesitated. "Did he leave a nougat?"

"Yeah. Just like all the other times."

She chewed on her lower lip and wrapped the telephone cord around a ringed finger. "Was . . .?" She hesitated, not sure how he would react to her meddling. "Was the nougat double wrapped?"

A moment's silence stretched between them. "What do you mean double wrapped?"

"Jose figured out a way to mark the nougats."

"Dammit, Holly. I told you not to do anything that could put you or your employees in danger."

"We were careful," she said, wondering if it was her imagination or if he really was as concerned about them as he sounded. "But if it's numbered, I can tell you who purchased it."

"What? Are you serious? How soon can you meet me?"

"I can be at the shop in fifteen, twenty minutes."

"I have to stop at the police department first." The phone clicked in her ear. No good-bye, nothing. Just *click*.

She hung up the phone and wondered how long it would take for the pain to go away. How many days, months, or years would have to pass before she could forget the feel of his arms around her? Forget the one glorious night they had spent together?

However long it would take, today could be a step in the right direction. If the nougat was double wrapped, she and Mark might never have to see each other again. He would have his man. At least one of them would be happy.

Less than twenty minutes later, Holly let herself into her shop. It was still an hour before Cindi and Jose were due to arrive. Thinking to catch up on some light bookkeeping while waiting for Mark, she pulled out her ledger and stared unseeing at the column of figures. She finally pushed the ledger aside and began to pace.

She was nervous about seeing Mark again. She was also worried; what might this latest nougat reveal? She didn't want the thief to be one of her regular customers. She didn't want it to be someone she knew and cared about.

Mark walked in the door, his eyes shining with excitement. "We've got a number." He filled up her shop with his presence as he held up a piece of paper, and looked oblivious to how the mere sight of him affected her. She began to tremble so much, she could hardly breathe. Every bone in her body ached with sweet memories of being in his arms. Her lips burned as if his kiss still lingered there ready to ignite anew at the least provocation.

"Number ninety-one."

She moistened her dry lips and wiped her damp hands on her pants. "I'll check." Saying a silent prayer, she flipped through the pages that held the stickers in numerical order until she found the number she was looking for.

Her finger on ninety-one, she stared at the customer's name, not wanting to believe what she saw. Dear God, don't let it be true!

Chapter 10

"*H*olly?" He was by her side in a flash, his hand cupping her elbow.

She spun around to face him. *Don't touch me*, she wanted to cry out, though she longed for his touch. *Don't look at me*.

He searched her face, his brow creased in worry. "Are you all right?"

"Do you mind if we sit down?" Taking a deep, unsteady breath she moved away from him and lowered herself onto a chair next to the glass-top ice cream table.

Mark sat down opposite her. "Is it Boo-Boo?" he asked gently, and when she didn't immediately reply, he gave a sympathetic nod. "I'm sorry, Holly. Really I am."

She shook her head. "It's not Boo-Boo."

He sat back. "Who then?" He frowned as he gazed at her trembling lips, but his eyes were warm with concern.

She wet her lips and swallowed hard. This was the hardest thing she'd ever had to do. "Mark—it's your aunt."

His eyes widened in astonishment. For several moments he said nothing; he only stared at her. Finally, he leaned forward. "Aunt Rice?"

"I'm so sorry. I wish I didn't have to tell you this."

He jumped to his feet, practically knocking over his chair. He did knock over the blow-up dinosaur. "Aunt Rice! How can this be? It's a mistake. It's got to be."

As much as she wanted to believe he was right, she knew better. "We were so careful not to make mistakes. Cindi and I checked every number twice before we recorded it."

"Damn!" He spun around and headed for the door.

"Wait, Mark!" She ran after him, but by the time she reached the curb out front, his silver gray Olds had pulled away.

The television was so loud, Mark was required to bang on the screen door and shout her name before he could rouse Aunt Rice from her chair. He suspected she was asleep, but knowing her, she would deny it.

"Sakes alive! I'm coming and this better be important." She looked surprised to see her nephew. "Mercy me, is it Thursday already?" She unhooked the screen.

"No, it's not Thursday, Aunt Rice. I need to talk to you." He followed her inside. "Would you turn that thing off?" he shouted.

Aunt Rice picked up the remote control and pointed it to the TV. "Now what are you all riled up about? It's that woman, isn't it?"

He was taken aback. "What woman?"

"The candy store owner. Holly Brubaker and don't tell me it's not. I saw how you two looked at each other."

Just hearing Holly's name brought a stabbing pain to his heart. To think the night they'd spent together had meant nothing to her, that she could so easily dismiss it as a tumble in the hay both shocked and pained him. Upon realizing his aunt was watching him closely, he quickly turned his attention to the point of his visit. There would plenty of time later to ruminate. "Have you heard about the Nougat Thief?"

"Course I've heard of him. Everyone's heard of him. Mercy me, just because I'm seventy-something, don't go thinking I don't know what's going on in the world."

"We set a little trap to catch the thief."

"Now isn't that nice. Did it work?"

"I sure as hell hope not, because if it did, we're in trouble."

"We are?"

"Yes, Aunt Rice. We are. You and me. The nougat left behind during this last burglary was purchased by you."

Aunt Rice's eyes widened. "Me? Mercy me, are you accusing me of being the Nougat Thief?"

"Certainly not. You're seventy-seven years old, for chrissakes."

She looked insulted. "Are you saying I'm too old to be the Nougat Thief?"

"What I'm saying is that you purchased the incriminating nougat. I want to know how one of *your* nougats ended up at the scene of a crime."

Aunt Rice sniffed and stuck out her jaw. "How am I supposed to know?"

"All right, all right. Let's start from the beginning. How many nougats did you last buy?"

"I always buy a half pound or more," she said.

"The doctor said you're not supposed to eat nuts," he reminded her.

"Harumph!"

"Aunt Rice!"

"All right. I don't eat them. Not all of them. I give some to my students."

Mark stared at his aunt in astonishment. "You're teaching the Nougat Thief how to read?"

"Well . . . I . . ." For once in her life, Aunt Rice was speechless.

Mark paced around the floor. It was beginning to make sense. His aunt belonged to the Golden State Art Association. The thief was probably pumping Aunt Rice for information while she taught him phonics. Mark took his aunt's hands and sat her on the sofa. "Now think carefully. Do you have a student who's interested in art?"

"They're all interested in art," she said. "I'm very selective in who I take on as a student. They must be interested in art or music. That's my requirement." Suddenly she looked every bit her age as she slumped against an overstuffed pillow. "I can't believe what you're saying. I know my students."

Feeling sorry for her, he squeezed her hands. She'd devoted her life to helping people. Now it looked as if someone had used her kind and generous nature for his own gain. "You know I'm going to have to check them out. I need a list of your students' names."

"What will happen to him? The Nougat Thief?"

"He'll be arrested and stand trial."

Aunt Rice sighed and reached for her address book. He jotted down the names and addresses of her students as she read them aloud. There were ten in all.

"Thanks, Aunt Rice. Now do me a favor and cancel classes for the rest of the week. Tell them you're feeling tired or under the weather."

"I'll do no such thing."

"Do as I say, Aunt Rice," he said, and because he knew better than to try to dictate to her, he gave her one of the smiles she could never seem to resist. "Please, for me."

"Very well. But if you don't want me to make anyone suspicious, I better come up with a more believable excuse." She thought for a moment, then brightened. "I know. I'll tell them I'm flying to Vegas for a fling with a younger man."

He grinned. "That's my girl."

Mark left his aunt's house and called Detective Riley at the police station. He was convinced that one of the names his aunt had given him would turn out to be the suspect. He read the names and addresses to Riley then drove the half block to Rick's house. Rick hardly fit the profile of an art thief. For one thing, he was too young. For another, he lacked the sophisticated knowledge that was needed to successfully smuggle and market stolen art abroad. He doubted the kid knew Madrid from Bosnia. Still, he could be working with his brother, who had served time for robbery. It wouldn't be the first time a man sent up the river for one crime, came back an expert on another.

Rick greeted him warily. "What are you doing here?"

"Just want to ask you a few questions."

Rick stepped outside, closing the door behind him. "What sort of questions?"

"Ever hear of Warhol?"

"I think I saw that advertised on TV? It's insurance, right?"

"I think you're confused. Warhol is the name of an artist."

Rick shrugged. "Never heard of him. The old lady . . . uh . . . Mrs. Albright told me about some dude named Ren Brand."

"That's Rembrandt. What about your brother?"

"Kirk?" It was difficult to see that Rick thought the idea absurd. "He don't know nothin' about art, either. But if you want to ask him about sports, he's an expert."

"Maybe another time. Where's your brother living now?"

"Out in Covina."

"Got an address?"

Rick looked worried. "He hasn't done nothing."

"Then there's nothing to worry about."

Rick gave Mark the address, then turned and walked into the house, slamming the door behind him.

Mark hurried down the steps to his car. His gut feeling told him Rick wasn't involved. He glanced down at the list of his aunt's students. One down and nine to go.

Holly rubbed her stiff neck and turned her head from side to side. She'd been piping icing on chocolate baby booties for the better part of three hours. She glanced at the clock. It was after eight. She decided to work until nine and call it quits.

Jose checked the tempering machine to make sure the chocolate was flowing smoothly. "It seems to be working okay now," he said. Earlier the temperature had dropped, causing the chocolate to seize up for the third time that week.

It had been a month of mechanical problems. First the air conditioner, then the freezer, now the tempering machine. "What we really need around here is a full-time repair person."

Jose grabbed his Dodger baseball cap and grinned. "We

already have that, Miss Holly. There's no one who can wield a screwdriver better than you. Seriously, though, we do need more help."

"I'm running an ad in Sunday's paper."

"I'm glad to hear it." He put on his cap. "I'll see you in the morning. Make sure these doors stay locked. Adios." She heard the back door slam shut as he left.

Holly continued to pipe little pink flowers amid clusters of green leaves. She really was lucky to have found two such conscientious employees as Jose and Cindi. She wondered if she could be lucky a third time. Moments later, she heard the key in the lock.

"Did you forget something, Jose?" she called.

When no answer came, she looked up and gasped. The barrel of a gun pointed straight at her.

Chapter 11

She dropped the tube of frosting and froze. "What . . . what do you want?" she stammered.

"Just keep calm and you won't get hurt." The gunman was dressed from head to toe in black. He wore a black knitted cap over his head.

"There isn't much money. We made a deposit earlier and—"

He held out a gloved hand. "I don't want your money. I just want information."

"I-Information?" she stammered. "If you think I'm going to tell you my secret chocolate recipe, you're crazy!"

He surprised her by laughing. "I don't want your recipes." He reached into his pocket and pulled out a square of paper. He slapped it on the table in front of her. "What does that number mean?"

She recognized it as one of the numbered tickets Jose had hidden between the foil wrappers. "I . . . I have no idea."

"The numbers weren't in the wrappers before."

Holly thought fast. "I recently changed companies."

"Why would they put numbers in between two pieces of foil? That's an added expense. It makes no sense."

"If you like, I'll call the company in the morning and ask."

He stood staring at her as if he was trying to make up his mind whether or not she spoke the truth. Finally, he stepped back and looked as if he was about to leave. If only someone hadn't chosen that particular moment to start pounding on the back door.

Moving quickly to her side, the gunman pressed the gun to her temple. "Whoever that is, get rid of 'em. Any suspicious moves and you're dead." He held the gun with both hands, the barrel pointing upward, and flattened himself against the wall. "Do as I say."

The bitter taste of fear filled her mouth. She swallowed hard and walked to the door. Beads of perspiration rolled down her back. She glanced back at the gunman and took a deep breath. The banging started up again, this time with more urgency. The fire code required that the door, though locked on the outside, could be opened easily from inside.

Mark filled the doorway with his presence. He looked so tall and strong, almost invincible, it was all she could do to keep from throwing herself into his protective arms.

"We've got to talk," he said. "I've been acting like a jerk."

"I can't talk right now, Mark. I'm working."

He narrowed his eyes. "Now whose job is coming between us?"

"There isn't any *us*, Mark. Please go." She tried closing the door on him, but he stopped her with a well-placed foot.

"I must talk to you now. I'm leaving for Madrid tomorrow."

Crushed by the news, she momentarily let down her guard. That was a mistake, for it allowed him to push his way inside. He reached for her hand. "I can't believe what you said about us. You made it sound like the night we spent together meant nothing to you." When she refused to look at him, he put his hand beneath her chin and turned her face until she had no choice but to meet his probing gaze. "Holly—are you all right?"

He was looking at her so intently, he failed to notice the gunman behind him. If she could just get him to leave. "I'm fine, Mark." She pulled her hand away and stepped back. "You surprised me. I didn't think you'd be leaving so soon."

"It's another case," he said. "Actually, it's one I've been

working on for quite some time. I thought we had it solved, but it turns out we don't have the king pin. Holly . . . about you and me . . . you have to know how special I think you are."

There it was again, that dreaded word *special*. She didn't want to hear this. Not now, not ever. "I'm busy, Mark. Maybe you can call me when you get back from Madrid."

"We have to talk now."

She felt desperate. "We have nothing to talk about!" she snapped. "Just go!"

"Tell me it wasn't just a tumble in the hay," he said. "It wasn't for me and I can't believe that's all it was for you."

"You don't want to believe it!" she said, sounding almost hateful. At that moment, she would have done anything to protect him. "Your ego won't let you believe it!"

Disbelief and confusion clouded his face. He stepped back as if to leave, then suddenly stopped. "You're trembling," he whispered. "Are you all right? Holly? Talk to me. I'm not leaving until I know you're all right."

The gunman stepped forward, his gun pointed at Mark's temple. "Now, isn't that noble of you?"

Mark went white. He turned slowly to face the gunman. "Let me guess. Peter DeVeer, right? My aunt's guitar teacher."

The gunman reacted by pulling off his ski mask. Aunt Rice had kept her promise. Gone was the unkempt hair and scraggly beard. If it wasn't for the coiled snake tattoo on his neck, Mark wouldn't have recognized the man.

"Well, well, if it isn't Aunt Rice's nephew." He grinned. "I didn't recognize you without your pink pants. Perhaps you'd be kind enough to toss your gun on the floor. Or do you only carry a gun when you're dressed in pink?"

Mark glanced at Holly, then reached beneath his jacket for his Glock. The well-spoken, polite demeanor of the gunman was a long shot from the devil-may-care attitude he'd portrayed during their past encounter.

"That's good. Now toss it across the floor, nice and easy."

Mark did what he was told. The gunman grinned. "I believe you were saying something about going to Madrid."

Mark narrowed his eyes. "Why would you care where I'm going?"

"Let's just say I have a vested interest."

"I bet you do." It wasn't until Mark saw the background check on Peter DeVeer alias Peter Vandenbilt that he suspected there was a connection between Madrid and the Nougat Thief.

"I'm going to miss the old lady. I gave her guitar lessons and she kept me up-to-date on the members of the art association. The poor woman never guessed I could read and when she caught me with her address book, she believed me when I told her I was trying to sound out the word *address* on the cover." He laughed.

Mark's fury rose. He hated the idea of his aunt being used by some two-timing thief.

"How did you do it?" DeVeers inquired. "Was it the foil wrappers? Ah, yes. I was right to be concerned. Did you not think I wouldn't notice the numbers?"

"We didn't think the thief actually ate the nougats himself," Holly said.

"But how could I resist? They are delicious. Perhaps I *will* steal that recipe of yours, Miss Brubaker. Since I must now relocate, I'm going to miss your candy."

"Why'd you leave your victims a nougat?" Mark asked.

"Actually, that began quite by accident. During my first theft. I inadvertently left behind a nougat that Aunt Rice had given me earlier. I believe it fell out of my pocket when I climbed over a balcony. Well, I must say, I was quite taken aback to see myself described the next day as the Chocolate Nougat Thief. It's quite distinctive, don't you think? In any case, I decided to continue the practice. I thought putting the nougat on the pillow was a nice touch, don't you?"

"Very nice," Mark agreed. The nougats had fooled investigators into believing the series of local art thefts were not related to any of the known international crime rings. "We know you're fencing the stolen goods in Madrid. If you turn yourself in, perhaps we can get the authorities to work a deal. Your Madrid contact for leniency."

DeVeers laughed. "Surely you jest?"

"I think you should know the police are on their way to your place with a warrant for your arrest."

DeVeers shrugged. "They won't find me, now, will they?" He checked his watch. "Oh, dear. I have a plane to catch." He grinned. "Don't get your hopes up, Spencer. It's a private plane, leaving from a private airport." He wagged his gun. "Get over there, both of you. That's the way." He pulled a roll of silver duct tape from his pocket and tossed it at Holly's feet. "On the floor, Spencer. With your hands behind your back." Mark did as he was told. "That's the way. Now, Miss Brubaker, since you're so handy at wrapping things, perhaps you'd be kind enough to wrap your boyfriend. Move it!"

Holly picked up the roll and proceeded to truss Mark's wrists. After Mark's hands were securely taped behind his back, the gunman indicated she was to do the same to Mark's feet.

"That's the way, "he said when Holly had completed the task. "Now sit on the floor with your back against his. That's the way." In quick order he had taped her hands and feet. He then secured her and Mark to the leg of the counter, wrapping tape around their bodies until they were almost as tightly wrapped as mummies.

"That should hold you," he said straightening. "By the time anyone finds you, I'll be long gone."

"Don't count on it," Mark growled.

DeVeers grinned. He appeared to be enjoying himself. "Oh, but I do." He slipped his gun in his pocket and grabbed a handful of nougats. "It has been a pleasure. Tell your aunt to keep practicing her guitar. She might bring Elvis back from the dead, after all." With a wave of his hand, he slipped out the back door.

Mark cursed. He had left police headquarters that night with the intention of driving home to pack. Coming to the chocolate factory had been a last-minute decision. No one knew he was there. It looked like they were stuck until morning. Aware that Holly was unnaturally quiet, he glanced over his shoulder. "Holly, are you okay?"

"I'm okay," she said softly. "This is the first time I've ever been bound like this."

"It's my first time, too. What time does Jose come in?"

"He's coming in early, tomorrow. Around six."

He glanced up at the wall clock. It was only a little after nine. That left nine hours of sitting in this uncomfortable position. He stared at the telephone. It was probably not more than fifteen feet away. It might as well have been on the moon. "How'd DeVeers get in here?"

"I think he had keys. I thought it was Jose."

"Jose?" He frowned. Come to think of it, didn't he see Jose's car in the parking lot? Was it possible the two of them were working in cohorts. Knowing how Holly felt about Jose, he decided to keep his suspicions to himself. At least for the time being.

"This is all my fault," she said. "If I hadn't interfered . . ."

"Thanks to you, we tracked down the Nougat Thief. And I have a funny feeling he's going to lead us to the kingpin in Madrid."

"That would be wonderful," she said. "Maybe you won't have to go to Madrid, after all."

"I have to go."

She fell silent for awhile and then, "Mark?"

"Yeah?"

"What you said earlier about the night we spent together." She bit her lip, knowing full well that to admit the truth was to open herself up to the pain. "It was special for me too."

He took so long to answer that she began to think he never would. Finally, he said, "Then why did you tell me it was just a roll in the hay?"

She closed her eyes. It was enough that her hands and feet were bound; she could no longer hold back the truth. "I didn't want to admit how much that night meant to me; how much you mean to me."

He pressed his back against hers. It wasn't a hug, but it felt close to it and though she couldn't move, her heart took flight. "Maybe one day, you and I can work something out," he said.

Her spirits crash-landed. At least he knew how to reject someone with class and dignity. "Yeah. Maybe." And maybe one day the world would be a perfect place.

The hours crept slowly by. Holly's back ached, her shoulders ached, her legs and behind grew numbed. She'd never felt so miserable in her life. She was also hungry, but the trays of chocolates were out of reach. "You know what DeVeers said about the first chocolate nougat being left by accident?"

"Yeah."

"Do you suppose that's how the Hershey bar came to be left in my bassinet. By accident?"

"I suppose that's possible."

She thought for a moment. "All these years, I've been trying to figure out what the candy bar meant, and it turns out it meant nothing."

"I guess there's no way of really knowing, is there?"

"I guess not."

"It seems to me you're asking the wrong question. To my way of thinking, you should be asking why your mother abandoned you on the steps of a church. There were organizations even back then that handled adoptions. Why didn't she ask for help?"

"She was young. Terribly young. And desperate. Don't ask me how I know, I just do."

She sounded so positive, he didn't have the heart to tell her what he thought of her mother, of any mother who deserted her child. He pressed the back of his head against hers, wanting so much to take her in his arms and comfort her. "Maybe it's best to forget about the chocolate. There's no way you'll ever know."

"If only I had the answers, I wouldn't feel like a part of me was missing."

"Is that how you feel? Like part of you is missing?"

"Sometimes. I guess that's why I have this compulsion to fill up all the physical spaces around me."

"Does it work?" he asked. For if it did, he might give it a try. He might wear rows of chains around his neck, a ring on every finger, fill his living quarters with clutter.

"Not really. The only time the empty feeling went away was the night you and I were together."

He closed his eyes. That night had worked for him too. Suddenly, his life seemed to have purpose and direction. It wasn't until the next morning that the doubts began to plague him. "Maybe after this Madrid case is over, I'll have more time to devote to a personal life. Would . . . would you mind if I call you, sometime in the future?"

"Oh, no!"

"No?"

"The tempering machine."

"What about it?"

"It's stuck again. I thought I'd fixed it but . . ."

He tried moving, but couldn't. "So what's the problem?" Suddenly a blob of chocolate as thick as lava fell on his forehead and began inching its way down the ridge of his nose. He cursed beneath his breath and tugged at his hands. "How much chocolate is in that thing?"

"At least forty pounds," she said.

"You gotta be kidding. Forty pounds!"

Another glob of chocolate hit him, this time on the back of his neck. He pressed his head against hers and let out a moan.

Suddenly, she started to giggle. "What do you call a crusty investigator covered in chocolate?"

He couldn't help but chuckle. "I give up."

"A plainclothesman."

Her jokes got worse as the night wore on. But it didn't matter. He laughed at each and every one and it felt good. It felt very good.

❧ Chapter 12 ❧

It was Cindi who found them the next morning, not Jose. After her initial shock at seeing the two of them bound together and dripping in chocolate, she doubled over in hysterics. "Don't tell me. Kinky sex, right?

"Ambushed by a bad guy," Mark explained. "But I like your explanation better."

"If you're finished laughing," Holly said irritably, her face streaked with chocolate, "would you mind getting us out of this mess?"

Cindi shut off the tempering machine and reached for an unwieldly butcher knife.

"Be careful with that thing," Mark said.

"Hold still." Cindi reached for a roll of paper towels and set to work wiping the chocolate away from their hands. "What a mess," she complained, cutting through the layers of tape. She freed Mark first, then turned her attention to Holly.

Mark pulled off his shirt, washed up and grabbed the phone.

Cindy cut the last of the tape away from Holly's hand and tackled the tape at her feet. "How did you two get in this predicament, anyway?"

Holly worked the circulation back into her wrists. "The Nougat Thief spotted the marked foil and smelled a trap."

Cindi's eyes widened. "The Nougat Thief did this?"

Mark hung up the phone, grinning. "The Nougat Thief is locked behind bars."

"That's wonderful," Holly said. "But how . . .?"

"It seems that Aunt Rice remembered catching her guitar teacher with her address book. She then recalled how he quizzed her about her friends in the art association. She put two and two together and decided she didn't like the sum. She tried to reach me and couldn't. That's when she reported her suspicions to the police. They caught him at the Van Nuys airport." He glanced down at his chocolate-covered pants. "I have a meeting with my boss to give him a rundown on everything that's happened."

"Maybe Jose can find you something to wear. . . ." Holly headed for the sink. "Speaking of which. Where is Jose?"

Cindi glanced around. "I thought he was here. I saw his car outside."

"Wait a minute," Mark said. "His car was in the parking lot last night."

"Oh, no." Holly quickly turned off the faucet, grabbed a handful of paper towels, and started for the door.

They found Jose bound and gagged in the back seat of his Toyota. Mark undid the gag, cut the rope at his wrists and ankles, and helped him out of the car.

Holly checked him over. "Are you all right?"

Jose nodded. "It was you I was worried about. This man with a gun was waiting for me outside. He took my keys and—"

"That man was the Nougat Thief," Mark explained, "and thanks to your little number ploy and the help of my aunt, he's now out of business."

Jose's gaze traveled from Mark to Holly. "What happened to you two? You're covered in chocolate."

"The tempering machine seized up," Holly explained.

Jose shook his head. "Again? If you like, I can give you a uniform to wear."

"Thanks," Mark said. "But pink isn't my color. I think I'll head on home." His warm gaze settled on Holly. "Are you all right?"

She nodded. "I'm going home myself. I could use some sleep. If I don't see you again, good luck in Madrid." Exhaustion was a blessing; it helped to deplete her voice of emotion.

He looked hurt, or maybe just tired. It had been a long night. "I'll stop by and say good-bye."

"That won't be necessary," she said, her voice flat. He looked at her strangely, but she quickly walked away. She didn't want to say good-bye. Not now; not ever.

She didn't see him for two days. Not until he showed up on her doorstep with a package wrapped in brown paper. It was her Warhol painting.

"I got the police department to release it. Otherwise, it would have been tied up in evidence until well after the trial."

"Thank you," she said, trying to ignore the lump that had suddenly formed in her throat.

"I'm leaving first thing in the morning. I'll be in Madrid for a couple of days to wrap up some loose ends. After that, my company wants me to check out an art auction in Paris. It looks like a stolen painting that had been heavily insured by my company is going on the auction block."

"Good luck." She managed to sound reasonably cheerful and distant. Maybe she was a better actor than she thought.

He rubbed his chin. "Keep your eye on my aunt for me, will you?"

"I will. Take care of yourself."

"You too."

She laughed one of those forced laughs that sounded flat and hollow and strained. "Don't worry about me. I always hang in there."

She feared by the look on his face he was going to tell her to "try again" as he had so many times in the past when she had tried to her hide her true feelings by being flippant and funny.

To her relief, he didn't. Instead he turned and left, left so quickly he was out the door before she could stop him. She stared at the door hoping against hope he would come back to her. When he didn't, she ripped the paper off her Warhol and was struck by the irony of it all. First her mother, and now the man she loved more than life itself had walked out of her life, leaving behind little more than a chocolate bar. And it hurt. Dammit. It hurt a lot.

She carried the painting downstairs to the Fergusons and asked them to find a buyer. Later she stood in her living room staring at the windchimes, the angels, the stuffed animals and the rest of the unbelievable clutter. Every single item, no matter how artistically arranged, was a grim reminder that filling up space was the worst possible way to combat loneliness.

She drove to the market for empty cardboard boxes, then began packing up knickknacks until the tables and bookshelves were free of unnecessary clutter. Maybe Goodwill could make use of the stuff. Later, she glanced around the room. Mark had only spent one night in her place, but the memories of him seemed ingrained in the very walls.

She might have stood there forever, recalling that one magical night they'd spent together, had Mozart not announced dinner time by strutting across the piano keys.

She picked up the cat and headed for the kitchen. Getting rid of the unnecessary clutter in her life had been easier than she thought. Getting rid of the memories of Mark was going to be a whole lot harder.

Two weeks later, she stood behind the counter and flipped through the stack of resumes that had flooded her shop since the ad ran in the paper. She settled on a handful of qualified candidates, and set them aside. Cindi was so much better at scheduling appointments than she was.

Holly glanced at her watch. Today was the day Cindi was to appear before the judge. Holly had planned to accompany her, but Cindi's ex surprised them both by offering to go with her.

This last week had been hectic. The media had practically parked themselves in her shop following the story in all the papers about her connection with the Nougat Thief. Unfortunately, an overzealous reporter on the *Los Angeles*

Times dug up the story about her being abandoned on the steps of the mission some twenty-five years earlier and. before she knew it, her shop was filled with cameras and reporters.

Her life had definitely become more hectic since that story broke. Though her regulars didn't seem to mind the intrusion of reporters as much as she did. Boo-Boo was particularly supportive. "I thought I had it bad. But I was never left on a doorstep," Boo-Boo said, his voice muffled by his bear costume.

His out-pouring of love and concern filled Holly with guilt. He had so little, yet gave so much. The costume he wore to hide his disfigurement covered up something far deeper than outward appearances. He had his disguises; she had hers.

As if on cue, she went into her usual "hey-isn't-everyone-born-under-a-candy-bar" routine. Silently, she added, *I don't need Mark. I don't need anyone.*

When he didn't laugh, she picked up his furry paw. "You don't have to wear your costume for me, Boo-Boo."

The furry round bear head wagged from side to side. "And you don't have to wear yours for me."

A busload of senior citizens arrived before noon for a tour of the factory. They oohed and ahhed as Jose poured chocolate batter across a marble counter and spread it out with a wooden fudge spade. Following the tour, they streamed into the shop to purchase chocolates for their grandchildren.

Cindi called that afternoon with good news; her attorney had been able to get the department store to drop the charges, providing the family enter counseling. "Even Tom agreed to attend counseling with us."

Holly knew how hard Cindi had tried to get Tom to agree to marriage counseling before the divorce. "That's wonderful," Holly said. "I'm so happy for you. Take the rest of the day off." Hearing the bells jingle, Holly lowered her voice. "I've got to go. Someone's here." She hung up. "May I help you?" she called to the woman who was standing just inside the doorway as if she didn't want to be there. Holly was reminded of Mark and how he looked on the day he'd first walked into her shop.

The woman was dressed in an elegant black and white suit. Her smooth blond hair and carefully made-up face was half hidden behind a pair of over-sized sunglasses. She looked perfect enough to be on the front cover of *Vogue*.

There was something strangely familiar about the woman. Holly decided she was probably an actor or some well-known personality.

"I'm looking for Holly Brubaker." She spoke in a well-modulated voice.

"I'm Holly Brubaker."

The woman stared at her for what seemed like forever. "How can I help you?" Holly asked.

The woman slowly removed her sunglasses. "My name's Jennifer Mason. I'm your mother."

❧ Chapter 13 ❧

*H*olly had imagined this moment countless times in the past, had envisioned every possible scenario, but nothing had prepared her for the actual meeting. "My . . . mother?"

Jennifer Mason nodded. "I saw your photograph in the paper and I knew I had to see you in person." Her eyes filled with tears. "You're so beautiful. . . ."

"I . . . I can't believe this." Holly grabbed hold of the counter with one hand. "I never thought . . ."

"I'm sure it's quite a shock. It was quite a shock to me to read the story in the paper. I hope you can find it in your heart to . . ." She bit her lower lip and glanced away momentarily as if trying to compose herself. "I would really like for us to get to know one another."

The mother Holly had envisioned was nothing like the well-dressed, well-spoken woman who stood before her now. "Why?" she whispered. "Why did you abandon me?" The question slid out so quickly, as if it had been poised on her lips all these years, waiting for the first possible moment to be put into words.

The carefully made-up face seemed to crumble and Holly saw the mask for what it really was, a way to hide the pain, much like she had hid her pain behind knickknacks and bangles and flippant jokes, much like Boo-Boo had hid his behind a furry face that everyone just naturally loved.

"I was young and afraid of what my father would do if he knew about the baby. Please understand, it was different back then. My father was a prominent judge. I would have brought shame and dishonor to him. To the entire family. As soon as I knew I was pregnant, I ran away from home and stayed with a girlfriend. I wanted so much to keep you but, I was barely seventeen. I couldn't even support myself."

Holly wanted so much to understand, to embrace this woman as one would embrace a mother, but for once in her life, she was unable to pretend. She'd spent a life time pretending it hadn't mattered that she'd been abandoned on the steps of a church. Today she knew how much of a lie that was. "But to leave me . . ."

"I didn't just leave you. I hid behind a tree until you were found." She searched Holly's face beseechingly. "I know this is a terrible shock. Maybe it would be best if I leave and let you get used to the idea. I'm staying at the Hilton."

Holly nodded. She needed time to think. "I'll call you."

"Very well, then." Jennifer Mason slipped on her sunglasses.

"Wait." Holly hurried from around the counter. "The candy bar . . ."

Jennifer looked startled. "What?"

"The candy bar you left in my bassinet. Why did you leave it?"

"It was all that I had with me." There was no mask on her face this time to hide behind. No cool elegance to hide the grief. "I had nothing else to give you."

"Did you call her?" Cindi asked. It had been three days since Jennifer Mason had walked into the shop and made her startling announcement.

"Not yet." Holly reached for a wrench. She'd been working on the tempering machine for the last hour. She had taken the entire machine apart, cleaned and oiled the motor, and put it back together. It still kept seizing up. Clearly she was going to have to call in an expert or break down and buy a new one.

"What are you waiting for?" Cindi persisted. "This is your mother." Now that she and Tom had grown close again, Cindi seemed to think any relationship could be fixed.

"I don't know. I just can't seem to get over the anger and hurt."

"Is it the same anger and hurt that let Mark get away?"

The screwdriver slipped. "What?"

"You let him walk out of your life and didn't even try to stop him."

"How could I have stopped him? I know how important his job is to him."

"Would he think his job was that important if he knew how much you loved him?"

Holly slammed the screwdriver onto the counter. "Just once, I would like someone to think me important enough to fight for. My mother gave me up rather than embarrass her family. My adoptive parents allowed every Tom, Dick, and Harry psychiatrist to label me like I was package of meat being stuffed in a freezer. Never once did they tell those so-called experts with all their fancy terms where to go."

"This isn't about your parents, Holly. This is about Mark."

"Mark walked out on me because of his job and because I eat pizza for breakfast and display candy bars in my family album. The point is, I want someone who can *love* me despite all my craziness. Someone who thinks I'm important enough to fight for. Someone who's willing to give me some slack and make sacrifices. Who'll stick with me through thick and thin." She shoved her toolbox away. "Is that asking so much?"

She flipped on the switch of the tempering machine. Even now, she was reluctant to give up on it. Damn! It was only a machine. Why couldn't just buy a new one? She *knew* why.

The machine made a strange noise as the blade began to spin rapidly.

"Look out!" Holly ducked to avoid the splatters of chocolate that were flying everywhere.

"Holly."

Her heart leaped at the sound of his voice. She turned. "Mark . . ."

His gray suit was covered in chocolate, but to her wondrous eyes, he'd never looked more magnificent. She quickly turned off the machine and grabbed a hand full of towel. "What are you doing here?"

She reached up to wipe the chocolate from his face. He caught her wrist and gazed down at her. "God, I must be crazy to think I could walk away from all this . . . this nuttiness that is you." He cupped her face with his other hand.

"That's me, nutty as they come."

"Try again, Holly," he said softly.

Through thick and thin. She bit her lip, grateful that he could see through her ploy. "I missed you," she whispered, her eyes filled with tears. For once in her life the need to express her love was far greater than her fear of rejection.

"I missed you too."

"But your job . . ."

"What good is my job when I can't stop thinking about you? All the time I was in Madrid, I wanted to be here. Every lonely night I lay in bed and wanted to be with you. I'm through traipsing around the world. I'm going to talk to my boss and see what options are available. If worst comes to worst, I'll change jobs if I have to. I'll do anything as long as we can be together."

Sacrifice.

"But Mark . . ."

"You're all that's important to me."

"But you said we were too different to make a life together."

He shook his head as if he couldn't believe he'd said such a thing. "Before I left for Madrid, I stopped to say good-bye to Aunt Rice. She handed me a bag of chocolate/chocolate mixed with nougats. She said it was a perfect combination."

"And was it?" she asked.

"In every possible way." He kissed her tenderly on the lips. "Normally, I wouldn't think of asking a woman to marry me while I'm covered in chocolate, but somehow it seems like the right thing to do. So, Holly Brubaker, I want you to know I love you and I want you to be my wife."

Love! The word wrapped itself around her heart and filled her with the warmest possible glow.

Unable to believe how perfectly her life had suddenly turned out, she flung her arms around his neck and ran her chocolate covered hands through his hair. "I love you, too, Mark Spencer. And, yes, I'll marry you!"

His face beamed with happiness. "What do you say we have a quiet dinner for two and start making plans?"

"I'd love to." She gazed into his eyes and felt a sense of wonder at the love and devotion she saw mirrored in their depths.

He kissed a dab of chocolate from her nose. "Promise me you'll never change."

She felt a tugging inside. At last she had found someone who loved her and accepted her just the way she was. That's all she ever needed or wanted. Maybe now, she could do a bit of accepting of her own. "Before we have dinner, would you mind if we stop at the Hilton? There's someone I want you to meet."

He didn't mind, nor did he mind later when she came up with the idea of getting married on the carousel on the Santa Monica pier. Or when she suggested eating corn on the cob at three in the morning because they were too crazy in love to sleep. Nor did he mind being awakened at four by Mozart playing the piano—or a few hours later by those confounded alarm clocks.

He didn't mind because even conservative, chocolate/ chocolate kind of guys who wear boring gray suits and drive boring gray cars can sometimes feel like a nut.

THE CHOCOLATE SHOPPE

Nadine Crenshaw

❧ *Chapter 1* ❧

*L*ondon lay in the clutch of a bitter, cold day. The frost was old, and the Thames was frozen hard as always in January. Muffled in a cape, Judith Browne studied the new sign swinging above the street. Such signs hung everywhere in the city, with golden lambs, blue boars, ruby-red lions, the Stuart crest or the profile of dark, black-haired King Charles II, his father's crown restored to his head. The sign Judith studied read: DUGDALE & SON, CHOCOLATIERS. A colorful wooden Jamaican parrot sat with its feet perched on the words.

How Judith envied Evan the experience of sailing across the ocean to lands that few Englishmen, and fewer Englishwomen, had ever seen. He'd been part of the British expedition that had captured Jamaica almost by accident in 1655, seven years ago, an expedition unworthy of Cromwell's New Model Army, being poorly equipped, poorly supplied, and poorly led. Two thousand sailors died, but Evan Dugdale had survived, and on Jamaica he'd discovered chocolate.

And now his dream had come true. He'd opened the shop that would make his future secure. Judith studied the diamond-paned windows on either side of the door, feeling a completely unselfish pride for him. Chocolate and coffee-houses were more popular than ever as meeting places for men of letters and women of the streets, lawyers of the courts and artists of the stage. Should she go in? It had been two years. He was married—and had a son, according to the sign. She merely wanted to wish him well.

No, that wasn't true; she ached to see his face, hear his voice, just once more. It *wasn't* right. It was all wrong— and dangerous—but didn't she deserve this much? After all, she'd had a part in his success, though he might not realize it.

Heart pounding, she picked up her skirts and started for the door. Chocolate scented the immaculate interior. She opened her cape to the warmth. A young girl served hot chocolate from a pewter pitcher. Though Judith had never met her, she knew Evan's sister at once. She had the Dugdale green eyes. Judith found her very pretty and sweet looking. There were four tables with stools about them, all occupied by smiling men, many of whom wore beaver hats. The few female customers were accompanied by husbands or fathers. One of these dames, clearly from the country, wore a gown with a neckruff, while her husband wore full breeches, both out of style for at least a decade. They studied their steaming mugs of rich, frothy chocolate with suspicion. The man took a sip, and his eyebrows lifted in surprise. His dame, encouraged, tasted her own. Judith smiled at the sound she made, the predictable *mmm* of pleasure. Judith had made the same sound the first time she'd tasted the luscious brew.

She even remembered the things Evan had told her that day, trying to make her feel at ease in Mr. Netter's shop, things about the New World, the sacrifice of chocolate-colored dogs, a king called Montezuma. Was it really only two years ago, those few short months with music in them, and love? It seemed an age.

A counter spanned the back of the room, above which hung gleaming copper pans and pewter pitchers polished to look like silver. Behind the counter stood Evan himself, smiling at a customer as he poured hot chocolate into the man's cup. The passage of time had been kind to him; he looked more handsome than ever.

Judith knew the man being served, young Mr. Samuel Pepys. Sir Davenant had introduced him to her once. Would he remember? Would he give her away? Her heart thundered. He looked her way, and his brows contracted, as if thinking he should know her, but she wasn't wearing her makeup or stage wigs.

His notice caused Evan's wonderful green eyes to turn, and seeing her, his great grin of happiness faltered. Her own excitement fell suddenly dead. She'd made a mistake to come in. The love between them, the shared happiness was all gone. Destroyed. It could never be recaptured.

He came from behind the counter, wiping his hands on his apron. She couldn't move as he approached. The love they'd shared might be gone, but the lonely love she felt for him remained as strong as ever.

"Mrs. Hawthorne."

The name gave her a start, but of course he thought she'd married Matthew. She curtsied. "Mr. Dugdale. I saw the sign, and wondered if it could be you."

He lifted his chin. "As you see, it is."

"And you have a son." She looked away from him, unable to meet that fixed green stare. "It seems things have worked out wonderfully. I'm very glad for you."

He nodded as a small boy came toddling through the side door which led to the upstairs apartments, where no doubt Evan and his wife lived. "Da-da." He ran right to Evan and clamped his pudgy arms around one of his father's long legs.

Evan, smiling with a tenderness Judith remembered only too well, stooped to lift him. A boy with untidy dark hair and large green eyes. "Johnny, where's Nurse?"

The child pointed to a middle-aged woman puffing after him. "That baby," the woman panted, "gets away from me." She took the boy from Evan. "We're going out for our walk." As she moved for the door, Judith studied the child's face for a brief moment. Yes, Evan was in those features, and also Nancy Netter.

With the opening of the door, a little of noisy London entered the shop, then nurse and boy were out on the brick lane. Evan remained where he was, and Judith felt a new sense of loneliness—when she thought she'd already experienced every possible kind and degree of that emotion. But she was an actress. She could put forth whatever sentiment was needed. "He's a handsome boy."

"Thank you again."

"I have—" She'd almost told him!

The chill coming off him grew so apparent his customers began to glance at them. Judith grew self-conscious. "I wish you luck in your enterprise, Mr. Dugdale."

He nodded, no sign of friendliness in his narrowed gaze.

Back on the street, she pulled her cape close again, took a deep breath, and blinked hard against the weak, tired, self-pitying tears her eyes wanted to shed. He'd had the same effect on her as always; every sense and emotion felt sharpened to an almost painful intensity so that an unnatural brilliance glared from everything she saw. She walked away with purpose, running the gauntlet of London's carts, coaches, and carriages. She sidestepped the mud-choked gutters and ducked the low-hanging signs. Church bells struck the hour. She was late. There were over a hundred churches inside the walls of London, and once their bells had echoed in her deepest emotions. But not today. Suddenly she hated the sound of those time-keeping chimes calling her to a profession she'd grown to loathe. Her life without Evan now seemed almost too much to bear. Why had she gone into his shop? Now the years were unbound again, and the memories let loose to roam.

Evan turned back to his duties. This was his opening day, supposedly the day his dreams came true. Judith's abrupt appearance only pointed up the truth that it wasn't. Damn her soft brown eyes! What did she mean coming in here? In fact, what was she doing in London at all, especially dressed like that? The good Mr. Matthew Hawthorne lived in Newington-Green and was a strict Puritan. He'd hardly care to know that his wife came to town looking not Puritan "plain," but very colorful indeed. Evan's last sight of her out the door was of bright green skirts, the hems caught up high in the back to show a red-and-white striped petticoat. And the broad-brimmed straw bongrace on her head seemed hardly likely for a modest Puritan matron.

She'd always loved color. But Puritans weren't allowed such debaucheries as red striped petticoats. And their wives were never dressed as Judith was today. Be damned! What did it mean? Had Hawthorne proved an antimonarchist and had his inheritance confiscated by the crown? That still didn't explain Judith's dashing gown.

Evan turned to his sister. "Katherine, you're going to have to watch things by yourself for a while. Master Pepys at the counter needs his cup refilled once more before he leaves for the theater. Will you get it? I have to go out."

"Go out? Evan!"

"You'll do fine." He already had his apron off and was at the door, shrugging into his coat. "I won't be long."

On the street, the bells struck six o'clock. He hardly noticed the racket most of the time, yet it seemed part of the urgency he felt now to find Judith among the vast concourse of common people going home from work and aristocrats out for the evening. There seemed to be more of the latter than the former, masked ladies in coaches and men on horseback with sword hilts flashing, their mounts prancing and snorting, lifting their hoofs daintily. How the nobles liked their evenings at the theater. During Cromwell's day the good men of God couldn't wait to darken the city's stages, and when the monarchy was restored, the loyal men of the crown couldn't wait to light them again.

Evan had no idea in which direction Judith had headed. He turned left, striding up the brick-paved lane on his long sailor's legs. He caught sight of that red-striped petticoat as she stopped at an intersection for a snail-paced funeral procession. Not everyone showed so much respect for the

dead; several people bullied right through. It was a late
hour for a funeral, but these days anything could happen in
London, day or night. As the black coach, its horses decked
in black plumes, passed on, Evan got close enough to follow
Judith without being seen himself. Not that she looked back.

Her route took him a long way from his shop. Katherine
would be frantic. This was stupid; he should go back. As
he thought that, Judith arrived where she was going. In a
narrow lane of overhanging houses, she unlocked a door
and disappeared inside.

He stopped and looked about him. This wasn't the sort
of prosperous area he expected Matthew Hawthorne's wife
to live in. In fact, it was on the edge of the theater district.
Most of the people on the street were flamboyant stage-
types, easily identifiable by the drama of their dress: a man
in flame yellow, a woman in a costume so garish it made
Judith's look modest. What was she doing living among
such people, actors and gamblers and demimondaines? It
was too much of a mystery, one he told himself he didn't
care to solve. He was long done with all her caprices!

Yet he couldn't turn away. Instead, he went right to the
door and, aware that he was about to make a greater fool
of himself than he had two years ago, he knocked. She
answered the door herself, and her face showed her shock
to see him.

"Is your husband here?"

"My—? Oh. No." She seemed distracted.

"Where is he then? Did you desert him, too?"

"I don't know what business it is of yours, but I live here
alone—almost alone. I have a—" She bit back the finish.
A lover? he thought. Was that what she meant?

All he heard was that there was no husband, a fact that
gave him permission to shoulder his way out of the cold
and incessant clamor of the street into the narrow foyer. "Did
Hawthorne oust you when he found you were no virgin?"

She closed the door but didn't move away from it. He
wanted to go further inside, to see how she lived, but he
couldn't tear his eyes away from her face, from the lovely

skin that curved over fragile, arched cheekbones. "What's going on? Did you marry Hawthorne or not?"

She seemed to brace herself. "Not."

Although he'd half expected that answer, it hit him hard.

"I'm an actress. Sir Davenant helped me get on stage."

"Ah, Davenant. Old enough to be your father, but useful, I can see that."

She visibly checked her anger. "He's been a good friend to me. I work in his company. We do his plays, and adaptations of Shakespeare, Johnson, Fletcher—"

"The Duke of York's Players, isn't it?" He kept from insulting her further, though the desire was strong. His heart held a full nest of little wriggling, prickling spites. "Why, Judith? If you simply wanted to become an actress why that tale about marrying Hawthorne?" When she didn't answer, he said, "It doesn't matter, does it? Now at least I can stop regretting—" Too much. Far too much. He hadn't meant to knock at her door, let alone reveal so much of himself. She obviously didn't care what he felt, how he'd despaired. The air in the little foyer grew too charged to breathe. He had to get out. His shoulder bumped her again as he reached for the door.

But once outside, he still couldn't leave. In this dark little lane, night had fallen with a boom. Not married. An actress. Or was this just another batch of lies? Had he ever known her at all?

Oh, yes, he'd known her in the most intimate ways. And loved her, loved her slightness and fragile beauty, her gentleness and generosity and radiant grace, her determination and brashness and youth, her honesty. There was more here than he could understand, and he must understand it, he must. He thought of the several letters he still had in her flowing script. He'd long ago memorized them. The first began:

> *My Dearest Evan,*
>   *I know I should not be so bold as to address you so, but this is how I feel, and as you have already discovered, I do not know how to be coy. I am writing*

to confess my love for you. Yes, by God's blessing, it is true! And how it makes my heart sing to see it written in ink! I hope you are not burdened with the admission, that you are pleased. I have reason to believe you might be pleased, that you might even feel some affection for me.

How I wish I could see your handsome face, beloved, and say these things aloud to you. But I'm afraid I could not confess something else, which does not make me so happy, nor will it you, I fear. I am not free to love you this way. I have been betrothed since I was two years old to Matthew Hawthorne, in Newington-Green. My father says it's time for us to wed, and today I leave to visit Hawthorne House and discuss the arrangements.

It breaks my heart to tell you this. But do not lose faith in me just yet, for I have this hour placed my hand over my heart and vowed that it will stop pulsing if I ever marry where I do not love. Somehow, my dearest, I will get free of this obligation.

Forgive me for not telling you the truth yesterday, but I could not bear the thought that you might call me brazen and unfaithful. I suppose I am unfaithful to Matthew Hawthorne, but I shall never be so to Evan Dugdale.

Yet you have the right to be angry with me, and to withdraw that fondness you showed me beside the Thames. If so then you must not meet me when I return next week. I shall slip away—somehow!—and be at the gates of London Bridge at noon on your day off. If you are not there, that will be my answer. Oh, please be there, beloved.

There were others just as passionate. Why had he kept them? Why was he standing across the street from her house now? If she was an actress, she would be leaving again very soon. He felt a pounding in his chest like footsteps running away, but he knew he was going to wait and follow her again.

Judith stared at the closed door. She had an intense urge to run after him, to tell him. If only she could make him understand how truly she loved him, how impossible she'd found it to stifle that love. But it was best he didn't know, best he hated her. He had a wife and family. He was out of her reach.

A child came into the foyer from the drawing room beyond, a two-year-old girl who said, "Mama," and held up her hands to Judith. "Mama, story!"

"Sweetheart, Mama doesn't have time. Walters!" she called, ignoring the writhing of her guilty conscience. She had so little time to spend with Marguerite. She'd exchanged a life of two church services every Sunday for two performances six days a week. At least the theater wasn't as bare and cold as a Puritan church. "Walters? Where are you? I'm so late! Come take Marguerite!"

Minutes later, makeup case in hand, she left the house again, nearly running to get to the theater. To impede her were ballad-singers and beggars, satin-suited young fops and gentlewomen in black eye-masks, sober merchants and ragged urchins, and the occasional liveried footman making way for a sedan-chair containing a countess. The absurd web of narrow streets, the jumble of buildings had evolved over the centuries and made a sheerly random pattern. "Please don't get snarled," she muttered to the traffic as she fought her way through it. Everything could come to a complete stop—as it had come to a stop the day she'd met Evan.

She must keep her mind on her role, and put away the stunning fact that she'd seen him today, twice.

Would the king be there tonight? Charles II had fully recovered from his fifteen years of banishment, of trailing from one country to another, undesired anywhere because his presence embarrassed those bargaining with his father's murderers. Seeing him in the audience never lost its thrill.

At last, she entered the theater's backdoor—and at once heard the name she'd taken under Sir Davenant's advice. "Mrs. Wetstone! You're late!"

"I know, Mr. Kern!" she shouted back at the stage manager.

"Your cue is barely five minutes away! Get dressed, madam!"

Though the play had begun, the audience continued to babble noisily. Shouldering her way through the players, someone else said to her, "Dorea, you're so late!"

"That's now been etched in stone on the memory of God." She'd felt it best to hide behind a stage name so that people from her past would never recognize Judith Browne. "Carol, Eve—you don't go on for ages. Come help me."

Thank heavens her dressing room was empty. Since the advent of professional actresses, a favorite element of theater-going was for young noblemen to visit backstage. Many women forged "relationships" with male members of the audience, but Judith had a strict no-one-allowed policy. The two ingenues, Carol and Eve, entered the room behind her and set to helping her out of her gown and into her costume, wig, and makeup. "What are we doing tonight?" she asked distractedly.

"The Witch of Edmonton."

She mentally reviewed her lines as the women chattered about a duel two men had fought this morning over an actress from the Lincoln's Inn theater.

Mr. Randall had signaled the actors on stage to draw out their parts to give her time to make her cue. She stood breathless in the wings still patting her clothing when, hearing the line she needed, she stepped on stage. A spattering of applause greeted her, despite the fact she wore a wig of long, colorless hair and the haggish shift of a witch. "Dorea! Mrs. Wetstone!" She made a curtsy before beginning her lines.

Her first time on stage, she'd been as nervous as she was thrilled. Now it seemed more a miserable lunacy. She could be reinspired, though, if the king were in the audience. Was he tonight? She managed a sliding glance into the balconies where ladies of quality sat in the divided boxes, dazzlingly jeweled, with their husbands or devotees. Most weren't paying a bit of attention to her or the play. Essentially, they came to observe and be observed, to gossip and flirt. The play itself was a minor consideration.

There—dark, powerful, yes—Charles II. She remembered those deep set eyes with their look of private amusement, and that strong brow and vigorous beard from the day she'd seen him ride back into London. She'd arranged to meet Evan that day, and was taut with excitement and happiness that had nothing to do with King Charles.

No matter how hard she tried, it seemed her mind would ricochet back to Evan.

Evan sat on a bench in the pit. He'd never been a playgoer. He felt uneasy and strange in this world. The theater felt hot and stuffy after the cold outside, and smelled of sweat and perfumes. The audience was typically boorish. Despite the play in progress, half a dozen girls with baskets ranged around the apron-shaped stage bawling out their wares. "Oranges! Sweetmeats!" They charged outrageous prices. Evan felt disgust for the whole noisy, bad-smelling conglomeration. As he thought this, a lady in front of him spit backward on the shoes of the man next to him. The stranger jumped up, emitting a spectacular fireworks of cursing.

And the play went on. Evan heard a murmur that the king was in the balconies above, with his brother James, the Duke of York. On a less glorious level, Mr. Pepys come in with his wife.

Evan tried to concentrate on the play. The male actors on stage at the moment seemed to be overdoing their roles. He expected Judith to have a small part. This play was said to feature Mrs. Dorea Wetstone, a name even he had heard. As she came out now, dressed as a witch in a long, colorless wig and the petulant face of an elderly hag, as the audience shouted, "Dorea! Dorea!" he recognized her.

He recognized the love of his life, remembered her in his

arms, in his bed, her beautiful long hair scattered over his pillows. Judith. An actress. A harlot, too? Most of them were. He couldn't bear it. He looked for the door; he had to get out of there.

The story of Judith and Evan had started two years before, on the same windy day London had learned of King Charles II's impending return. Judith and her maid, Walters, were returning by hackney to her father's house from a social gathering. The coach was repeatedly jostled, and Walters said, "Dear, there's such a crowd out!"

Judith sat hunched in her seat, brooding about her ejection from Mrs. Rouie's sewing circle, in which the pious ladies of the church talked each Monday about the previous day's sermon while they sewed quilts for the poor. Mr. Rouie, a deacon, was always present in the next room, in case the ladies needed a male mind to explain any point too difficult for them to untangle alone. Judith had recently turned seventeen, and had been admitted to the circle only a few weeks ago. At first she'd kept prudently quiet, heeding the uplifting tone of her companions' comments—and more or less sitting still when she wanted to move about. But today impatience had overcome caution and she had disastrously spoken her mind.

Their Puritan reverend had yesterday droned on about death in the midst of life, evidently a barbed concept for Judith's companions. She finally said, impatiently, "He was simply talking about joy and resignation, how life is half full of sorrow and half full of joy, and how one forever sharpens the pangs of the other." It seemed so transparent that it bored her as much it had in the unheated, unadorned church yesterday.

If only she'd left off there, but no, she'd swiftly progressed from definition to debate. "The trouble I have with resignation is accepting that everything that happens comes directly from God. Does He really have that much interest in our daily affairs?"

Thus she'd run afoul of Mr. Rouie. Eyes bright and hard,

he suddenly appeared and asked her to leave. "Your comments are intolerable in the sight of the Lord, and unfitting for your gender. I've watched you grow up, madam, and I must say I think you have the personality of a traveling circus."

He'd expelled her from further meetings, and assured her that her father would hear of her trespasses. Judith didn't think of arguing with him. The word of a church elder was law. But it rankled her that no one, particularly no *woman*, was allowed to question anything that came from the pulpit. There were other things she doubted about the Calvinism in which she'd grown up. For instance, what was so wrong with reading Mr. Shakespeare's sonnets? It might let a little light into those closed-tight minds. She didn't understand, either, why they had closed all the theaters the year before her birth. Personally, she longed to see a real, live drama.

As her coach was jostled again, she admitted that she'd meant to sound brazen today. She'd found the sewing circle so boring that she'd been trying to stir up something interesting. She hadn't expected her tongue to get her expelled, however, and was a little stunned by this sample of what it meant to step out from under the umbrella of the religion in which she'd been reared.

She sighed. If only she had a man's freedom, a man's right to get an education. As it was, she had to do it all herself. Not an easy task, and perhaps not even righteous in the sight of the Lord. She moved uncomfortably, afraid she might simply be a sinner, and that Mr. Rouie really was God's instrument to disclose her errors to her.

But sometimes she felt so stifled!

She sighed again. Her father would be angry. He was sternly religious.

The hackney jolted more violently. "Dear!" exclaimed Walters. Judith sat up at last, and looked out at the bracing May afternoon, unusually clear for London, which typically sat under a pall of smoke and fog. Walters was right; the streets were uncommonly crowded. The coach was trying to move up a lane of houses huddled darkly together like gossiping women, but it was hampered by a stream of people shouting and rejoicing. Whatever was going on seemed to be a happy thing—thank heavens. Normally a shouting crowd in London meant a new outburst of civil war. Today, however, everyone was laughing.

"Long live his Majesty, Charles II!" This came from very near the coach, and now the door of the vehicle swung open. Their driver said, "Ye'd just as soon get out, ladies. I can't go further with this crowd." His face smiled with this news, and Judith saw that he wanted to be rid of them, probably so he could join the celebration himself.

"What on earth!" Walters complained as Judith exited the coach and turned to help her down—and at the same time struggled to keep her sober bonnet on her head and out of the snatching fingers of the clean, wild wind. Unlike Walters, she wasn't at all unhappy to be so unexpectedly dumped from their conveyance. Anything to put off the leaden inevitability of her father's displeasure.

The crowd was tremendous. The coachman, holding his horse, had already joined the merriment. Tradesmen had left their businesses. The distant, sullen toll of a church bell provided a counterpoint to the excitement. "Hurrah for the Cavaliers! The Cavaliers are back!"

Rumors of a restoration of the monarchy had been floating around since early March. In fact, since Cromwell's death two years ago, the call for the king's return had intensified. The Protector's son, Richard—Old Tumbledown Dick— was a glacier, frozen in time, incapable of acting. He'd been thrown out, and the old animosities rose again until it seemed war would break out afresh. London was tired of war, tired of the interminable adversities of the past twenty years. The people believed that a restored monarchy would bring back peace, at least. They remembered with nostalgia the old, familiar ways. On a new tide of royalism, the crown had been offered to Prince Charles, with no conditions other than a general amnesty, and for religious toleration and payment of the army's arrears.

Judith, who knew nothing of the old monarchy, felt her

heart lighten nonetheless. She'd secretly hoped for this day, unlike most of her Puritan sisters and brethren. She hoped that an age of prosperity and happiness would begin with Charles II's return—and that her own life would finally commence. What she meant by "her own life" she hardly knew, but it had to be better than the one she was living. And better than the one planned for her by her betrothal to Matthew Hawthorne.

"How will we get home?" Walters fretted, pulling her gray mantle closer.

"We'll have to walk," Judith said in a cheery tone. "We're not far from the bridge. Maybe we'll find another coach there." Taking her nurse's arm, she threaded a way through the crowd. The whole day looked brighter, for surely her father would be too irate about this news of Charles to bother with her ousting from the sewing circle.

Walking, however, was easier said than done. A frenzy of adoration had swept through the people. "Long live the king!" "Praise be to God for his Royal Highness!" When Walters's bonnet was knocked from her head, Judith saw the old lady was near to tears. She didn't have the stamina or the bravura to dare this mob.

What to do? Judith spied a swinging sign that said NETTER'S COURTYARD CONFECTIONERY. "There, Walters; we'll go inside and wait this out."

❧ Chapter 2 ❧

"A chocolate shop?" Walters balked. "Your father would never approve."

He wouldn't, but Judith had for a long time wanted to taste this fascinating imported oddity that was all the vogue. "He wouldn't want us to get trampled." She started toward the confectionery.

"Dear," Walters caught her arm, "you mustn't drink the chocolate, though."

Judith laughed. "We must order if we go in. And there's little choice with this crowd so alarming."

Walters followed her. The shop stood back from the street, allowing the owner to put a table outside. He'd erected a low fence around this, hence, the "courtyard." The women proceeded inside. A delicious scent enveloped Judith immediately. She paused, however, daunted by the all-male presence. The only other lady was accompanied by her husband. Walters whispered, "We should go."

Evan Dugdale, apprentice to the owner of the shop, saw the two women come in—and saw that the younger had the most beautiful face he could ever dream of or imagine. He wondered how she happened to be standing there, what her voice was like, and a thousand other ridiculous thoughts. Then he remembered—he was in charge in Mr. Netter's absence. He hurried to greet them.

"Ladies, Evan Dugdale, at your service." He sketched a perfunctory bow. "Have you come to seek safety from the crowd?"

Judith made her curtsy before she really looked at him—and felt as if a fist were squeezing her lungs. He stood more than six feet tall, with a look of robust fitness and strength. His dark hair fell in the shoulder-length style of a Cavalier, and beneath his apron he wore a short doublet and wide knee-breeches. But his good looks were spectacular. His green eyes left Judith so dumbstruck she hardly noticed that he too had a look of admiration as he gazed down at her.

Walters entered this odd silence to explain, "Our coachman put us on the street, and we are afraid of the throng, sir, else we wouldn't have come in unaccompanied."

"I understand. Here, take this table, which is as safe as can be." Though he answered Walters, he went on looking at Judith, who felt his gaze like a touch that warmed. A brisk sense of excitement rose to the surface of her skin.

Walters allowed herself to be seated, with Judith beside her. Mr. Dugdale asked if he could get them each a cup of chocolate. "You may," Judith said, ignoring Walters's worried look.

He smiled at her, but again, all she noticed were those strangely compelling eyes. His whole being seemed focused in them—looking only at her. "And how about a slice of Dutch gingerbread?"

Walters swiftly said, "Just the chocolate, sir. We're expected home for dinner."

Mr. Dugdale gave Judith another smile, flirtatious enough to leave her in a haze as he got their drinks. While they waited, she let her eyes steal to this table and that, inspecting the other customers. Most looked decidedly colorful, marking them as Royalists. Their shirts had elegant lace cuffs, something no Puritan would think to wear.

"William Shakespeare was brilliant!"

Judith's ears pricked at the comment made by a man with a chin as heavy as the defenseworks of a castle. He wore a bright green suit with red trim and aimed a long pipe at his companions as he made his point.

"He was *clever*," argued another, "especially in the playfulness of his young works."

Judith didn't hear the rest of the debate, for Evan Dugdale reappeared with a tray of three mugs of chocolate. "May I sit with you?" he said. He'd removed his apron.

"Oh, please, sir," Walters said gratefully. "We look so out of place with no escort."

"My pleasure." He gave Judith a glance of private humor. She hid her thrill by pretending to give all her attention to her chocolate.

"Mmm." She inhaled the steam from the mug before her. "It smells heavenly!"

"The natives of the New World call it the food of the gods." He smiled and waited as she took her first taste.

"Ohhh."

Walters looked at her mug suspiciously. At last she lifted it, and also made an "oh!" of surprise.

Evan said to her, "You chose a bad day to take a hackney, Mrs. . . ."

"Walters, and this is my charge, Mrs. Judith Browne."

Judith was grateful she'd called her Mrs. Only young girls were called Miss. And professed harlots, but she wasn't supposed to know about them. She said, "I've never seen the streets so crowded without some threat of violence, Mr. Dugdale."

She loved the way his dark hair fell over his forehead. "Everyone in England is out to welcome His Majesty home."

Walters blinked with alarm. "He's coming today?"

"Not today, but by the end of the month."

The man with the heavy jaw and the pipe called out, "Hurrah for Charlie! For eighteen years it's been no cards, no dice, no plays, no drinking—and now, *no Cromwells*! Long live Charles and all his excesses!"

Walters's mouth pursed. At home, the king's return would be greeted quite differently. Robert Browne had served under Cromwell at Edge Hill in 'forty-two, and become part of the cavalry troop known as the Ironsides. And in all his dealings he still exercised the stern discipline that had achieved his idol's fame.

"Those gentlemen," Evan Dugdale said, noticing where Judith's gaze rested, "are playwrights. They have more reason to be pleased about His Majesty's coming home than you perhaps. The one who spoke is Sir Davenant."

Judith studied the middle-aged man more openly. The famous Sir Davenant! She knew his tragedy, *Albovine*, by heart. Before her birth he'd been poet laureate, and had actively supported the old king. When he'd tried to lead an expedition of escaping Royalists to the Americas, he was captured and sentenced to death. Luckily, after two years in the Tower, he was released. Since then, despite the ban on dramatic presentations, he'd produced illegal performances in private London homes.

She whispered to Mr. Dugdale, "Is it true that he's really Shakespeare's son?"

"Judith!" Walters scolded.

Evan laughed—and his laugh affected Judith as powerfully as her cup of chocolate. It gave her a silken, melting delight. Evan said, "He hints he is, but I don't think so. His father was an innkeeper in Oxford, as much as that disappoints him. From what I can tell, Shakespeare might have been his godfather, though."

Judith didn't dare comment again, with Walters already frowning at her. Evan tactfully turned the conversation back to their refreshment. "Did you know that chocolate is made from the beans of the cacao plant? They were first brought from Mexico to Europe by the Spaniards."

"Mexico." Judith was entranced.

His smile showed white teeth—and gave her an even stronger melting sensation. "That's right. And I should warn you, it's mildly stimulating."

"Dear!" Walters put her mug down. "We're not allowed intoxicating liquors, sir."

"It's not intoxicating. In fact, it's mostly milk. By stimulating I mean . . . inspiring."

Walters seemed unsure. But Judith took a deep swallow of her own potion. It tasted quintessentially creamy and luscious. "Inspiring in what way, Mr. Dugdale?"

"Inspiring enough to take ships all the way to the Ivory Coast, to Nigeria and Ghana, even to Brazil and Jamaica to purchase it."

The names excited Judith. Or was it the chocolate? Or was it Evan Dugdale? "Have you been to any of those places?" He had the tanned look of a traveler.

"I recently returned from Jamaica. I was with the forces that took the island from the Spanish. I came home to help my sister. I hope to open my own shop one day."

Judith stared at him, drowned in awe and admiration. "Tell us more, please."

"Well . . . the Aztecs called chocolate *xocoatle*, and proclaimed it was a gift from the white god of wisdom and knowledge."

She tried to imagine it in a way she had, by closing her eyes and "seeing." Predictably, a vision sprang up in her mind, brightly rendered if wholly inaccurate, of New World heathens standing in dense jungle sipping chocolate from English pewter mugs. When she opened her eyes again, she found Evan watching her, amused. "Please, go on," she begged him.

"They served it only to male members of the court, to chiefs and warriors. Women weren't allowed."

"But that's so silly!" She stopped herself; she'd already been chastised once today for her outlandish viewpoints.

"In some places, sacrifice victims were given chocolate to bless their journey."

"Dear, dear! I don't think we should listen to such tales, Judith."

Judith looked at Evan. "We're Puritans."

His grin went wide. "I'd guessed as much."

Of course. They looked Puritan through and through. And provincial and unsophisticated. He seemed so very urbane that she wished she were a gay Royalist lady, her life brimming with color and spirit and adventure. She knew no more about that world than she did about New World heathens, of course. Her imaginings were all based on the merest keyhole observations. But she had a habit of envisioning herself as all sorts of different people. Right now, she wished desperately to be someone that this dark-haired stranger would admire. She positively *coveted* a personal connection to him. What was it about him that made her feel fully and completely alive?

Walters, as well trained as a turn-spit dog, glanced out the small window by their table. "It's growing dark, dear."

Evan agreed. "Yes, and the excitement is quieting down. You should probably get home." He walked them to the door and stepped out into the courtyard with them. The wind had died away, and though the sky was still mostly blue, a high-pitched moon had appeared already, thin and transparent.

"Isn't it the loveliest May you can recall?" Judith murmured.

"Yes, it is." Evan was looking at her, not the gently ending day, as if he wanted to say that she was lovely, or that the day was lovelier for her being in it.

"We haven't paid you, Mr. Dugdale." Walters opened her purse.

"Allow me," he sketched another bow, "since the pleasure was all mine." As he straightened, Judith stared up at him, unable to tear herself away. And he stared back at her. She felt her bones and muscles turn watery, and cursed herself for this wordless stupor. Usually pert remarks came to her tongue all too easily. Why did she have nothing to say now, when she longed so to impress him?

"You really should go," he said softly. "Your family will worry."

That soft tone, so intimate! A dizzy, powerful longing swept through her. Impulsive words sprang to her lips: I don't care! I don't ever want to go home again. I want to *know* you! Oh, let me stay!

But Walters kept her silent, Walters with her troubled, cautioning frown at this immodest exchange of looks. Judith dropped him a curtsy. "Thank you for your kindness, sir. Perhaps we'll meet again one day."

He continued to watch her face. "I shall pray for it, madam."

Did he mean it? Did he truly? The world spun into a color-streaked tornado as Judith turned away. She knew that the chances of that prayer being answered were nearly impossible. They lived in different worlds, she and Evan Dugdale, and it was unlikely their paths would ever cross again.

People were still on the streets as Judith and Walters dashed to cross old London Bridge before the gates closed. Even there, however, a group of boys wearing makeshift red sashes in honor of the Cavaliers had built a fire to roast skewered hunks of meat in derision of "the Rump Parliament." Judith and Walters edged by them cautiously.

The evening settled swiftly. Judith's father would be waiting. She saw his stern, lean, reproving face in her vivid imagination: *Judith, you know it's dangerous for a young woman to be out so close to dark*—as if she needed to be told! Even with Walters beside her, she was half afraid. Yet beneath her worries ran another current of thought: Evan Dugdale, so tall and broad shouldered, his hair as dark as ink. There had been something free and enviably assured about him. She'd never realized such a man breathed, and now that she did, some timbre of her life seemed higher pitched, some desire seemed more ardent and irresistible and tangible.

She and Walters at last entered their own familiar neighborhood of timber-framed homes with large gardens behind, all exuding a comfortable aura of abundance and ease. The Browne home in Manchester Square was a fine tall residence, unornamented save for flat stone pilasters. Robert Browne, who owned a tallowchandlery, embodied all the values of the Puritan ethic. He'd been a frugal, hard-working man all his life, and God had seen fit to bless him for it.

He stood in the paneled hall, the big oak staircase behind

him. "Judith, where have you been? Walters, I'm shocked that you let your charge stay out so near to dark."

"I'm sorry, Master."

"Father!" Judith flung off her cloak. "The king is coming!"

"I heard." His lean face held all his indignation and bad temper. He was a man of fair complexion, like his daughter, though his hair was graying at the temples now.

"There were *swarms* of people out. Our driver simply put us down in the street and refused to go on. We set out to walk, but the crowd was so *crushing* we had to take safety in a shop."

Walters hung her own cloak by the door, along with her bonnet. Smoothing her white hair, she said, "It was dreadful, Master, all the shouting and singing."

"Dreadful indeed, and the least of it the shouting and singing." He gestured them into the dining room where dinner waited. "I thought we'd rid ourselves of the Stuarts, and now—Charles II! What will England do with such a king? We fought so hard. Surely we earned the right to decency. But God's will be done."

Though his anger scorched Judith's secret enthusiasm, at least he hadn't yet touched on her banishment from the sewing circle. As she took her seat at the table, however, a certain thin-lipped look told her that he'd heard. For an instant she felt the church grasping her around the neck and squeezing.

Her father's eyes bore into hers as he lifted his head from the blessing. He knew but wasn't going to mention it until after dinner. That was his way. He saved up her sins. She would have to try to choke her food down knowing that once the meal was over yet another scolding was coming. Though the meal was well cooked and served, she only toyed with her smothered rabbit, the poultry in a piquantly rich lemon sauce, the boiled leeks, the sweet cubes of jellied milk for dessert. She sometimes made the effort to converse at dinner, but tonight she, Robert, and Walters ate their meal without talk.

The dining room displayed the comfort of the rest of the

house. Its walls were paneled oak, dark and luxurious. The chimney piece was sculpted with fruit and flowers. The floor was bare, and all the furniture was of the heavy, florid style belonging to the early years of the century. Sage brocade, worn to mellowness, cushioned the chairs.

After the meal, Robert asked Judith into his study. With the door shut, the room seethed with the ticking of his collected clocks. She stood penitential as he began. "I received notice of your behavior today. What exactly did you say?"

She tried to repeat it word for word. "I know now it was a question I should have asked you privately, Father, so that you could straighten out my thinking." Standing there as she had as a three-year-old, a seven-year-old, a ten-year-old, it seemed she must be growing more and more stupid. Why did she have so many questions about their faith? What was wrong that she couldn't accept it as everyone else did?

Robert might not be talented at dinner conversation, but he had a fine bent for religious monologue. "It's pride that drags you into these sins of thought."

Pride, yes, though she didn't know what that meant exactly. She was no more conscious of having pride than she was of having a liver or a spleen.

"And my own pride of resolution," he went on. "I resolved to rear you without a mother, and in that I fear I sinned myself. It's not right for a man to live without a helpmate, especially if he has a daughter to be brought up." He closed his eyes and pinched the bridge of his nose, as if parenthood utterly wearied him. "I thank God that soon you'll have the guidance of a mother-in-law. If anyone can correct your character, it's Mrs. Hawthorne. And Matthew, of course."

Judith resisted the urge to squirm at the mention of her betrothal. Matthew was five years older than her, yet the few times she'd met him the difference had seemed fifty. The last time, two years ago, he'd told her stiffly, "I dislike frivolity, Judith. I am a sober country gentleman who needs a sober country wife." All because she'd taken off her shoes and stockings to wade in the fountain of his parents' sober country garden. She'd been fifteen, and the fountain surely invited play. But maybe not.

She stood through Robert's reprimands, then knelt through his long prayer asking God to forgive her. Then came the evening's scripture reading in the drawing room, with the household staff in attendance. Then another prayer. Judith had the feeling that in some way, despite his prosperity, her father had lost out in life, and that all this religion was an attempt to replace something important that he missed. When at last she was allowed to retire, she climbed the stairs heavily, loaded down by guilt.

Her chamber held a stool by the fire, a chair and small table with a mirror, and her linen-curtained four-poster bed. Long draperied windows provided a view of the square. Walters helped her undress, then retired to her own chamber across the hall. Judith did as ordered: She knelt on the floor beside her bed for yet another hour of prayer. "Dear God, please grant me the strength to stand against the corruption within me."

The floor beneath her knees was cold and hard. She'd never quite understood why the Lord required people to be so uncomfortable in His name—if He did require it.

There, she was doing it again, letting questions sneak in right between her words of repentance. She redoubled her effort on behalf of her soul. "I am evil, Lord, corrupt beyond measure, wicked, wicked!"

By the end of the hour, she felt contrite enough to creep to her wardrobe. She opened a bottom drawer that, as far as Walters knew, held only a few musty items of her mother's, kept for sentiment's sake. Beneath those, however, lay a cache of forbidden poetry books, pamphlets, and playscripts. Tonight, she would burn them. Crouched before her hearth, she opened Middleton's *No Wit Like a Woman*, intending to tear the cover off and cast the impious comedy page by page into the flames. Instead, God forgive her, she read the first line, and then the second, and soon she was captured.

She owned twelve playscripts, and loved them for their worlds of passion and intrigue, so different from the frugal peace of her own life. She'd read them over and over, each time with the same absorption. She hardly realized what she was doing as she began to whisper the words, using different inflections for each part, as she supposed actors would. She studied a pamphlet of woodcut prints of scenes from *The Royal Slave*, by Mr. Cartwright. They showed a stage with curtains behind the players, an audience laughing.

She sat by the dwindling fire until she grew too sleepy and chilled to read on. With a sinking feeling of disgust, she put the forbidden collection away again.

At her windows, she parted the draperies to look out at the night sky. She would never make it through all that maze of stars to heaven. She was bound for hell, no doubt about it. It frightened her, confused her. Why was *she* so different, so weak-willed? What did the other young women of her faith do to overcome their forbidden questions and strong feelings? Or did they not have them? Why her? Why, why?

The tables inside Netter's Confectionery smelled of linseed oil. The fire had gone out on the small hearth, and only three candles lit the shining tabletops, circles of tiny moths darting about each flicker. As Evan swept the flagstone floor, his mind wasn't on his broom. He kept recalling that soberly dressed little Puritan. Her chaperon had called her Judith. She'd left him with a powerful afterimage. What would it be like to sit across from her at every meal, to see her when he woke in the morning and at night before he slept, to talk and laugh and share his thoughts with her? Despite her fragile beauty and her Puritan upbringing, he'd seen a spirit of fire inside her. He sighed. One day he'd be in a position to court a respectable girl, but not for a long while. He had to get his own shop first, so he could support his fourteen-year-old sister and himself.

Since their parents had died, Katherine was living with an uncle neither of them liked. Gregor Dugdale made head molds for haberdashers and milliners and was a notorious tightwad. He made Katherine work like a common servant, both in his shop and his house. It wasn't right, a well-brought-up young girl, and his own flesh and blood. It was fine for Evan to put in twelve hour days, but not Katherine. He'd do anything to get her out of that, but for the time being they had to wait. Rents for decent quarters were beyond his means. His tiny attic room was hardly big enough for one, and located in a neighborhood of jerry-built slums peopled by vagrants, vicious and destitute, unfit for labor or unable to find any except whoring or other debauchery. A place unfit for a decent girl.

He'd come home from Jamaica as soon as he could, and was working harder than ever in his life. He didn't resent it. Finally he had a purpose. Katherine's plight had given him the spark he'd lacked to settle down.

He finished the sweeping, closed the front door, and threw the bolt. When he turned, Nancy, his master's twenty-five-year-old daughter, stood trying to look nonchalant by the cold hearth. She'd almost married once, a ferryman, but he'd drowned and she'd never found another to replace him. Until she'd met Evan.

"Everything's closed tight as a sailor's knot." He took off his apron and brushed his clothes. He only had two suits, and wasn't pleased to see a spot of chocolate on his breeches. He'd have to wash it out before he went to bed.

Moving about the room, he blew out the candles as Nancy watched. She was a perfectly nice woman, only a year older than him, with eyes that were blue and limpid. You didn't notice them, though, because dividing them was a nose like a Roman emperor's. She was infatuated with him, and he should ask her to marry him, despite the fact that he felt about as attracted to her as to his own sister. Every morning, coming to work, he told himself he would do just that. Her father would provide them with lodgings, solving his problem of getting a place where Katherine could live with him. But everyday when he arrived and saw Nancy he knew he wouldn't. He held his tongue and tolerated her devotion with good-natured patience.

He brought the last candle to her, so she could see herself back up to her father's apartments over the shop. "There's a little raisin pudding left," she said, taking the nightlight. "We should finish it off, you and I."

"No, thanks, Nancy, I'm not hungry."

What he craved were a few rounds of bezique, but he wouldn't have those, either. He'd sworn off drinking. And whoring. Everything except working to get his own shop.

Nancy nodded. The candlelight, coming up from beneath her face, didn't flatter that fierce nose. "You're off then, I guess."

He smiled, knowing how badly she wanted to say something *interesting* to him. It was too bad he saw through her so easily. It wasn't fair. "Yes, I'm off, Nancy."

"I'll light you to the back door."

❧ Chapter 3 ❦

As Nancy bolted the shop's back door behind Evan, he shook his head. It must be sad to love someone who couldn't love you back. Nancy deserved better.

He shook his head again. Since when had he become so wise? When he'd sailed away to Jamaica, he'd been a wild lad, greedy for any foolishness, evading responsibility on any level. Foolishness and women and sack, that's all he'd cared about in those days. But a man grows up, sometimes rather suddenly, and realizes he's in the middle of a story that might have a variety of endings, some not at all to his liking.

The dark streets were empty now, the earlier hubbub done. What would it be like with the king back? Not dull, that was certain.

A plump whore stopped him just outside the door leading to his attic room. "Need a bedmate, me love?"

He was tempted. Women were cheaper than bezique, and he hadn't had one in a long time. In that earlier era he'd drunk women, lapped at them, gulped them, his thirst for female flesh unquenchable. It had been fun, if reckless. As soon as he imagined Rosy's plump rouged face on his pillow, however, the face of Judith Browne rose up again. She'd be pure and fresh beneath her plain clothes, like strawberries in winter.

The whore rubbed her breasts against his arm, reminding

him of a young cat with her tail raised, hinder-parts turned seductively upward. "I'd give it to ye free, Evan."

Even in the dark, her brown hair seemed lusterless, hanging around her pale, underground face. Her best feature was her plummy mouth—and those plump warm breasts of course. "You're too generous, Rosy. You should never give it away free."

"Aye, ye're right there, but ye're such a handsome bit 'o man it'd be a treat to have ye do the old jostle and bob 'atween me legs."

He chuckled. "You're tempting me—but I'm too tired to do you much good."

She giggled. "It's not good I want ye to do, but all the mischief ye can think of!"

Evan chuckled as he climbed to his room—alone, tired. The stairway smelled sharply of fried onions. The shabby chamber under the eaves held a bed, a broken-down wardrobe, and a stand with a bowl and pitcher. Its one asset was a window with a view over the roofs to the river, the great Thames, in all its tumult and changing light.

As he pulled off his clothes, he remembered the stain on his breeches with a sigh. His long day's work wouldn't end until he'd dunked his pants in a bowl of cold water. But he'd have something worthwhile for all this one day. He'd be his own master, have his own chocolate shop, his sister safe under his own roof. Then he'd look for a wife, someone fragile and fresh, with glossy, fair hair and enormous, soft brown eyes.

The arrhythmic ticking of Robert Browne's clocks echoed in Judith's confused thoughts. Sitting in the parlor adjoining his study she pretended to read a heaven-and-hell tome, but the dogma simply didn't interest her. The predominant theme, that life lead irrevocably to hell except for benevolence of God, was reinforced by verses: *Youths who make their parents bleed/ Should live to have children who/ Revenge the deed.* But even the threat of fire and brimstone could not get Evan Dugdale out of her mind. It had been three days, and still the meeting remained in her mind every minute. The life she knew seemed more intolerably dull than ever since his voice, his expressive eyes, had given her a glimpse into another world, one she passionately longed to view again.

Her father was gone on business, and Walters, growing older, had stolen upstairs for a nap, leaving Judith alone with a temptation such as she'd never felt before. Biting her lip, she put her book aside and went into the hall and listened. Nothing. Walters was asleep. Should she? No, she shouldn't. But she would. Quickly she wrote a note and propped it on the drawing room mantel. Then she threw on her cloak and bonnet and hurried out, heading for London Bridge. The note said she'd gone for a stroll—a sinful lie and not one that would ease Walters much, but Judith *had* to see Evan Dugdale once more.

Of all the days not to find a coach! She crossed the ancient bridge on foot again. The day was brilliantly lit and crowded with people still exuberant at the restoration of the monarchy and the lifting of Puritan repression. A group of returning Royalists on horseback drew wild cheers. Boys trotted beside the riders to touch their boots, and women leaned out their windows, and men stopped to take off their hats. Even Judith gaped at their colorful clothing, her appetite sharpened by a lifetime of plain dressing.

Royalists and their families were inundating London. The minute Judith passed through the city gates she felt as if she'd entered the heart of a celebration. She didn't forget her purpose, however, and moved through the lively jumble of shops and houses, passed unseeing through an open market occupied by an itinerant band of performers, and at last came to Netter's Courtyard Confectionery.

Since the day was pleasant, the outdoor table was occupied. Heavy-jawed Sir Davenant sat there smoking his long-stemmed pipe. Judith stepped just inside the courtyard, then stopped as doubt came on her like a thunderclap. What was she doing here? She couldn't go inside unaccompanied, and it wasn't likely that Evan would see her and come out. He probably didn't even remember her!

"Madam, you seem stymied."

Had Sir Davenant spoken to her? He lounged on his stool, a man not willing to move in a hurry. "Allow me to introduce myself. I am—"

"Sir Davenant. I know your *Albovine* by heart."

His brows raised. "I would have said by your dress that plays are forbidden you."

She blushed. "They are. I'm afraid I'm not, well . . ."

"Not a very good Puritan?"

She nodded. "I'm a terrible sinner."

"I see." He didn't laugh. "Of course, there's the possibility you aren't a sinner at all, but only rightfully caught up by the age in which you live. What brings you to Netter's again, madam? I saw you with another lady a few days ago, didn't I?"

What could she say? Her heart beat up in panic. Go! her mind said. She turned her head—and saw the man who had haunted her every thought and dream. Evan, coming into the courtyard, wasn't wearing an apron, but a blue coat and a tall-crowned hat. When he saw her, he stopped dead and stared at her with a look that made her skin tingle. He swept off his hat with as much gallantry as for a queen. "Mrs. Browne."

She smiled with relief—he remembered her! She curtsied, but then didn't know what to say. In his eyes and the expression about his lips was a kind of lazy merriment. It embarrassed her and made her feel helpless and tongue-tied and awkward—and angry, too, for being such a giddy peagoose.

"Where is Mrs. Walters?" he asked.

Heat flooded her face. "I came alone. To see you."

Now *his* brows raised. "Whatever for?"

"I . . ." Miserable chagrin set in.

"Forgive me," he said, stepping closer. "That was tactless."

"No," she said, ready to flee, "it was a mistake for me to—"

He placed his hand on her arm, and a new thrill ran through her at his touch. She turned her head at the sound of someone coming out the door behind her, a woman of about twenty-five, with a really extraordinary nose. She placed a cup of steaming chocolate before Sir Davenant, but her eyes were on Evan.

"Hello, Nancy."

"Hello." She flushed wine red and went back inside.

He said quietly to Judith, "This is my day off. I only came to pick up my week's wages. If you'll wait, I'll see you home." He looked at Sir Davenant, who was openly watching their conversation. "Can Mrs. Browne sit with you until I can accompany her home?"

The man's knowing smile made her wish she could crawl under the table and hide. When Evan disappeared inside, the playwright said, "Here, have this chocolate, madam. Mrs. Netter will bring me another."

"Oh, I couldn't."

"Now, don't turn silly just when I want a sensible conversation with you."

She accepted the chocolate, tasted it, and the rich, sweet flavor filled her mouth.

"Do you mind if I smoke?"

"No, sir; I like the smell of tobacco."

"Ah yes, but I dare say it will give me little return in the long run. You say you know *Albovine*. What is your impression of it?"

"Oh, it's wonderful! I act it out to myself sometimes." She recited several lines. "I've always wanted to see it staged, but . . . I'm not allowed."

"No. In fact, I'm curious as to how a sweet-faced Puritan managed to read it."

"I bought it without anyone knowing. I have several plays, and some poetry."

He chuckled. "I like your mettle, Mrs. Browne. I suspect there is an extraordinary hunger for life beneath that somber little bonnet. The way you said those lines, you'd go far on the stage. I've been discussing with my friends my desire to use women in the female roles when his Majesty reopens the theaters. Interested?"

He was only teasing, but—an actress! Imagine! She drank more of her chocolate, and was relieved when Evan reappeared. Rising, she gave him the brightest smile she owned. She barely remembered to thank Sir Davenant, who said, "My pleasure entirely," his eyes twinkling. "Perhaps we'll meet again one day, madam."

Evan offered his arm to escort from the courtyard. "This was very foolish, Judith."

She noticed his use of her first name, and loved it.

"You're only going to get yourself into trouble."

"I know." Walters's scolding would scorch her. And if her father should find out . . . but she would have this hour, whatever discomfort it might cost later!

Back in the open market they were stopped by a crowd around a sweating man waiting to have a rotten tooth pulled. Judith's face pursed in sympathy as the dentist took up his pliers. The crowd gasped. Judith turned her head into Evan's arm.

He pulled her away. When they were safely beyond the patient's grunts and squeals, he said lazily, "Why did you want to see me?"

They were threading a way between a fire-eater and a stilt-walker. A chapman vaunted the virtues of a collection of ribald poems: ". . . to purchase but an hour's charm, Of wriggling in a maiden's arms. . . ."

Evan hadn't forgotten his question. "Why did you want to see me?"

What to say? Lying in bed these past three nights, she'd imagined this conversation and in it she'd been very gay and easy. Now she had a wretched sense of inadequacy. Whatever she said was bound to seem ridiculous.

"I just couldn't stop thinking about you." Her stomach churned. "I tried to drag my attention elsewhere, but I couldn't. You've been in my heart and my mind every waking moment, and if I didn't see you again I don't think I could have survived the frustration. So when I found myself alone this afternoon, I felt I must do something."

He smiled down at her. "You haven't much practice at being coy, have you?"

Now he thought badly of her because she'd shown all her eagerness. "I haven't much practice at anything."

They walked on through the crowd. "What you should have said was, 'Mr. Dugdale, I found our meeting intriguing, and I believe you did too.'"

"Was it?" she asked, looking up into his face

He laughed outright, and she felt herself blush. He said, "As long as you went to so much effort, we might as well get to know one another."

Hot faced, she nonetheless answered, "I'd like that."

He laughed again, then bent to say softly, "You really mustn't wear your heart so plainly on your sleeve, sweetheart."

Sweetheart!

The street was too hopelessly crowded. Evan turned her into a long narrow alley that opened out finally among stacks of wood and coal at the river's edge. Saint Paul's bells began to toll four o'clock. "You'll be missed at home, surely."

"Only by Walters. My father's out of town for the night. Walters will scold me, but she won't tell Father. She's as afraid of him as I am. He's very strict."

"As he should be with such a rash hoyden for a daughter. If my sister behaved—"

"You have a sister?"

"Katherine. She's fourteen—but wiser than you, I hope." He watched her ivory cheeks go red again.

"Would you like me better if I were wiser?" The Thames watery light filled her soft eyes.

Don't answer, Evan. But something drove him. "I like you exactly as you are."

"Do you?" A smile lit the face within the plain gray bonnet. She was so clearly delighted to be with him that it was simply too much temptation.

"I do, yes. I admire your sweet simplicity, your beauty— and especially your impulses. You are the most beautiful woman I've ever seen, and I haven't been able to stop thinking about you, either."

She looked up at him happily, trustingly. He wouldn't kiss her, though, he wouldn't. He changed the subject. "Look." He pointed to the river. "There's a ship like the one I sailed on to Jamaica."

She turned to see the caravel under the arches of the bridge. "What does Jamaica look like?"

He gathered his thoughts. "At first sight, just a tiny cloud-blue mist low on the horizon. Nearer, mountainous. And subject to earthquakes and hurricanes. The rain is disgusting in the spring and autumn. The soil is fertile, the jungle luxuriant, full of cedar and rosewood. I miss the fruit, the bananas. And the parrots. There now, is that enough about Jamaica?"

That lazy note in his voice affected her strangely. She wanted to break through that veneer, to experience the stormy power she sensed lying underneath, carefully leashed. She heaved a sigh. "What a fine thing it must be to see the great world."

"Yet the prettiest sight of all is right here in London."

Judith felt his eyes on her profile, but she didn't turn into the inviting softness of his voice. Maybe she could learn to be coy. He stood very close, and talked some more about Jamaica, speaking easily, as if he'd known her forever. He pretended, as she did, that it wasn't strange for him to stand so close. She watched the flowing river and gave all her attention to the flow of his words, the deep resonance of his voice.

But after a while he stopped talking, and she felt his hands around her waist, turning her, drawing her even closer. She felt the powerful muscles in his thighs against her own, and her head fell back, her mouth lifted to receive her first kiss.

She'd often imagined being kissed, but the reality exceeded every expectation. It was as though the world were bursting. The touch of his lips stunned her. All strength left her. Thank goodness he held her waist tightly or she would have slithered into a boneless pile at his feet.

He kissed her several different ways, all lightly, first plucking her lips with his own, then moving his head to try a different angle, then he touched her lips with the tip of his tongue, then nipped her lower lip between his teeth. She stood unmoving, captivated by the novelty, dazzled by the intimacy, amazed by the feelings that boiled up and thundered inside her. When he lifted his head, it felt too soon. In the intimate silence between them, her fingertips stole to her lips. "Oh."

"My thoughts exactly."

It seemed incredible to her that life could change so swiftly, so irreversibly, in one short minute. He still held her waist, still held her close, and she couldn't recall ever feeling quite so safe and wanted. There was more, however, as one of his hands slid to her bosom. "Oh," she said again.

Evan explored the soft, warm weight of her breast beneath the fabric of her gown, and felt the hard responsive pucker of her nipple as he thumbed it. He said, gruffly, "This is what I meant about getting yourself into trouble."

"I thought you meant at home."

"I meant with me." He loved the way she looked up at him. How far would she let him go? Madness! "You should stop me. I shouldn't be doing this." He stepped back— wrenched himself away. "I should see you straight home."

"Not yet, I have a while."

He'd never felt so flattered. Her affection was so honest and the temptation so great that he *had* to seize this bit of quicksilver. His arms pulled her into the full length of his body. And she, innocent that she was, tipped her head again to meet his kiss. And slid both arms about his neck. The restraint he'd shown before vanished, giving way to a passion that was primitive and ruthlessly selfish. Yet still she reciprocated eagerly. Spurred by his mouth and his hands, her desire seemed to climb apace with his.

Finally, he stepped back again, breathing hard, knowing he didn't dare carry this any further. He'd never been so tempted, however, for he knew he had only to open his arms and she would step back into them. "Judith," he said. "Home. Now."

She nodded, though clearly sorry it must be so.

As they crossed the bridge, Judith's silence had to do with the revelation his kisses had brought about in her. She must be one of those sinfully sensual creatures reviled from the pulpit. There was only one place for sensuality, the marriage bed. But she was betrothed to Matthew Hawthorne and it was Evan Dugdale she wanted to go to bed with! All her rebellion rose up in her. She would *not* marry Matthew! Somehow she would be Evan's wife.

Almost as swiftly rose the teachings of a lifetime that said she must be obedient, dutiful, virtuous. This desire for a man not even of her faith must come from the devil.

Evan's voice brought her back, and what he was saying showed he was thinking along the same lines. ". . . no way I can marry right away. My parents died in a fire, leaving my sister in a bad situation. I've promised to get her out of it, but I have to save all my wages so I can open my own shop and have her live with me."

Judith murmured something in answer. A fire. His sister. His own shop. Couldn't marry soon, couldn't marry soon.

"The soonest I can leave Netter's is in two years—and that's a long time."

"Yes, it is." By then she'd be wed to Matthew.

Her agreement silenced him. He accompanied her the rest of the way without comment. She stopped him at a safe distance from her house. "I live in the square there, in that house." She pointed. "I should go the rest of the way alone."

He made her another bow, sweeping off his hat then turning to go. When she called, "Evan!" he paused. But she couldn't say what she wanted to say, and couldn't think of anything else. Finally, he nodded as if he understood. His face looked grim. "Goodbye, Mrs. Browne. It was . . . refreshing."

As the late May sunset planed through Judith's bedroom windows, Walters scolded her soundly. Judith refused to say where she'd been. With the kiss of a man, something had happened to her. She'd taken a first step out of childhood, for suddenly she didn't care about Walters's opinion. Her old nurse seemed to grasp that a change had come about, and the next day she watched Judith with searching worry. She never let Judith out of her sight, even when they made their monthly trek to Greencoat Hospital, in the shadow of infamous Bridewell prison. The women of their church made clothing and blankets for the parentless children who lived on the charity of strangers there.

Robert Browne returned that day to occupy the head of the oak table at dinner. Judith toyed with her roast partridge and boiled salad. Robert, who didn't notice the troubled silence between her and Walters, said, "We've been invited to visit Newington-Green, Judith. It's time you and Matthew made your wedding plans."

She had for some time expected to hear this news, yet she couldn't bear it tonight. She looked down at her plate, wishing with all her heart it was a mug of full-bodied, sweet chocolate. She recalled what Evan had told her about the Aztecs, that their women had been forbidden the royal beverage. What secret power did they believe it would unleash in them? "Father, I don't want to marry Matthew."

Robert didn't exclaim, didn't reprimand. He merely stared at her. "What nonsense is this? Shyness, I suppose. If your mother were here . . ." He cleared his throat. "Walters, you must talk to her, about . . . you know."

"It's not shyness, Father."

"What then? Not a desire to remain, er, a maiden. You know that's undesirable." Their religion preached that continence was unnatural and dangerous. Judith had heard many a sermon that went: "There is no necessity for a man to be a debaucher or fornicator. Let him marry, for that is the cure which God hath appointed."

"I don't want to marry Matthew because I don't like him."

Still no reprimand, but the stare became a glare. "Matthew Hawthorne is an honest young man." Robert clucked his tongue. "A man of honor and fortune, and any young woman would be glad to marry him."

"Nonetheless, I would like to wait a few more years." Maybe by then Evan would be free to marry her instead.

Robert would have none of it. "Nonsense. You should have been wed a year ago. Mrs. Rouie and Mrs. Wigglesworth have both advised me so and I should have listened." He rose. "We'll pray for you to undertake your future sensibly, Judith. Meanwhile, we'll be leaving for Newington-Green in the morning. Make the preparations for your mistress, Walters."

"Yes, sir." The aging woman gave him that expressionless gaze rendered to authority—which suddenly angered Judith. She wanted to say, Speak back to him, Walters! Say what you think for once!

"And Judith," he went on, unaware of her mute rebellion, "you will behave toward Matthew with consideration and respect during our visit."

She had never felt such a desire to mutiny. It took all her will to remain silent.

✵ Chapter 4 ✵

On his way to work in the morning, Evan felt the change in London. The years of Puritan-imposed discipline seemed to be exploding in laughter. People were abroad even this early, as if they were too ravenous for life to waste it sleeping. These reviving appetites boded well for a man who wanted to open his own confectionery.

At Netter's, Nancy surprised him with a letter. "It was under the door." She pretended not to be concerned as he tore it open. The multitude of dashes communicated Judith's rapid, ever-changing thoughts.

My Dearest Evan,
   I know I should not be so bold as to address you so . . . as you have already discovered, I don't know how to be coy—

He scanned on quickly.

. . . confess . . . betrothed since I was two . . . Matthew Hawthorne . . . Newington-Green . . . Father believes it's time for us to wed, and this very day I leave . . . discuss the arrangements.
   . . . will get free . . . You have the right to be angry . . . then you must not meet me . . . one week . . . gates

of London Bridge at noon—If you are not there, that will be my answer. . . . be there, beloved.

He wanted to crumple it, throw it in the fire, but Nancy, under the guise of straightening the cupboard of pewter mugs, was watching. He put the letter in his shirt, and removed his coat and put on his apron.

The shop wasn't open for business yet. He arrived early once a week to help prepare the cacao beans. Mr. Netter was in the kitchen, beginning the process that turned the beans into chocolate.

"Hello, Evan." He was a man of an unfortunate appearance. His sandy hair was as coarse as hog's bristles, his ears uneven, his forehead splattered with worry-wrinkles, his nose as unceremoniously flat as his daughter's was imperiously Romanesque. He stoked the fire over which the imported beans would be roasted.

In Jamaica, Evan had studied the harvesting of cacao beans. The gathered fruit was cured in its pulpy state for up to nine days, during which a fermentation took place and the beans turned a chestnut color. After that, they were dried in the tropical sun, cleaned, and stoned. As Mr. Netter carefully tended a roasting batch, they gave out their predictably delicious scent. Evan went to the table to shell some cooling beans. These he put into a small mill for grinding. Fat from the milled beans made the batch a sticky paste, which, if left, would dry to a dull brown crumbly substance that tasted like smoke from a rubbish fire. But Nancy, busy even now with a sugar grater, would add sugar to the paste and fashion it into small cakes for storage.

The Netters didn't flavor their chocolate other than with sugar. That was something extra Evan intended to do in his own shop. Montezuma had flavored his with ground vanilla. The Spanish made complicated recipes that included peppers, seeds, flowers, cinnamon, and nuts.

When chocolate became the fashion in Oxford ten years ago, the Royalists there believed it to be love-arousing. The first shop had opened in London just three years ago, and

Londoners knew only the milk-and-sugar brew. Evan planned to add vanilla, prized as an aphrodisiac on the Continent. As his customers took to that, he'd perk up the drink further with a sprinkling of cinnamon, then rose petals and other flavorings. Soon the rich would clamor for his brews.

The process in Netter's kitchen took an hour, during which time Evan felt Judith's letter in his shirt like a burr. Nancy gossiped about a ball at The Hague to celebrate Charles Stuart's departure from the Netherlands. Evan's mind was on Judith. Betrothed. No doubt Matthew Hawthorne was some clipped, odorless, self-denying Puritan. Evan felt betrayed, deceived, desperate. Did he have time to stop her?

"Evan! Is your brain hung in a smokehouse?" Nancy's voice caromed through his ears. He thought she'd been saying something about the king dancing with his sister, the Princess of Orange. "Sorry," he muttered. Mr. Netter had left the kitchen to conceal his hair beneath a wig before he opened the shop. The young people were alone.

Betrothed. And Evan was a fool to care. "Nancy," he said, "I have to make a delivery in King Street this evening. Would you like to walk along with me?"

"Why, yes, all right." Hectic spots of joy broke out on her cheeks.

Newington-Green lay to the northeast of London. Hawthorne House was one of its grandest estates. The senior Mr. Hawthorne had made his fortune as a hose factor, a wholesaler of men's hosiery. His business necessitated traveling, but he'd given those duties to his son, which was why Judith had seen so little of her betrothed during these years when they should have been growing to know one another. Her earliest memory of Matthew was of a spindly boy of eleven, when she'd been six. He'd read to her from his favorite book, Foxe's *Actes and Monuments*. The illustrations, fraught with raging fires and saints in the agonizing throes of martyrdom and other miscellaneous Christians being stoned, flogged, and decapitated, had given her nightmares.

Now a man of twenty-two, Matthew remained gangly, and

still had the same cautious, proper look Judith remembered of
the boy. He did what was expected of him always. No one
could say he was good looking, though his plain clothes
were exquisitely made and his short black hair well brushed.
Judith thought he looked like nothing so much as a corpse,
purged and fitted out and ready to meet his maker.

His parents were walking corpses as well. His mother's
only flare was in her nostrils whenever she was alone with
Judith. She reverted to an inert meekness in her husband's
presence. He was a gray man, with drooping eyelids that
seemed to beg for coins to hold them shut.

Though Judith had been admonished to show her fiance
honor and affection, she refused to do either. She avoided
him when she could, addressed him coldly when she
couldn't, and stayed in the room she'd been given for hours
on end. With her eyes so newly opened to love, she saw the
life planned out for her as intolerable. She saw these
Hawthornes—and her own father—with new insight.

Or was it that new? More likely Evan had only crystallized
a restlessness and yearning that had been working inside
her for years.

Toward the middle of their stay, Mrs. Hawthorne, with a
touch of duty, planned a dinner party to introduce Judith
to Newington-Green. The afternoon before, Judith couldn't
dodge an invitation to walk with Matthew in the knot garden
behind the manor. It felt good to be out in the fresh air.
Strolling at Matthew's side, she wondered how one man
could have such an imposing presence while another could
seem so pretentious, so shallow.

"Within these walls we capered as children, and came to
understand each other," her betrothed said.

"Do you think we understand each other?" She recalled
the incident of the fountain, when he'd informed her she
needed more sobriety.

"We understand as much as we need at this point. We can
look forward to learning more when . . ." He cleared his
throat, and Judith's heart pounded up, for she suddenly knew
what was coming. Of course! The dinner party was to

announce the date for their marriage. It was time for Matthew to propose formally.

"Judith, dear." He turned to take her hands. She felt the urge to pull away, to step back as he sank to one knee on the graveled walk. "Will you be my wife?"

She knew what she had to say, yet everything in her cried out not to say it. "Matthew—oh, for heaven's sake, get up! Let's sit on that bench."

He frowned, but brushed at his bony knee and took a seat. He reclaimed her hands, however, and looked moonish. "What troubles you, dear?"

She gazed away from him. A blackbird sang its heart out on a nearby bush. "Matthew, we don't even know each other, and I'm not sure we're well suited. In fact, I can almost guarantee I would make you a very unhappy man in no time at all."

His smile was superior. "You needn't be shy; I shall be the kindest of husbands."

"It's not that. You don't know how impulsive I am, how irresponsible. I have faults you can't even imagine."

"After you retired last night, your father appraised us of your little follies. Don't be angry. I'd already noted how your mind darts from subject to subject. You have all the consistency and wisdom of a weathercock, my dear," he condescended. "And a way, as Mother says, of twirling into a room like a top. A little streak of vulgarity, I'm afraid."

Though Judith raged inside, she managed to keep it hidden.

"But I find all that perfectly charming—if a bit thoughtless at times. It shall be my pleasure, with the help of God's grace abounding, to aid you in conquering the small defects of character you've acquired through being motherless and left too much to your own whims. That's a husband's duty. In fact, I've already given some thought to our wedding trip, and I think it a good idea to combine it with a pilgrimage of the soul. We'll visit Calvin's grave in search of your salvation, dear. And if that fails, I've observed that even the most hoydenish female settles after the, uh, first child arrives."

Judith shuddered. "There's more you don't know," she said in a hurry. "For instance, I don't like the country. It's so *quiet* here! I love London. I would pine for it."

"Pish! London is far too full of reprobates for anyone to prefer it over the country. Why, it's a filthy warren, all those narrow alleys and evil-smelling ditches. And that oozing, dung-choked abomination of a river." He shook his head. "We shall visit your father from time to time, but you'll soon realize how much nicer it is here.

"Now, Judith, no more of these petty protests, which only point out to me that you lack a strong guiding hand. Give over to my authority and there you'll find deliverance."

He sounded so saintly she was tempted to ask if he could also raise the dead and stir up fire out of snow.

"If you're too shy to answer my question aloud then may I seal it with a kiss?"

She didn't turn her face away quite soon enough, and his puckered lips caught the left side of her mouth. She jumped up.

He rose too, smug and condescending. "Your modesty pleases me. I wouldn't like you to be brazen in the, er, physical sense. You are impulsive and unpredictable, but I shall pray for the strength to mold your mind into a cast more becoming."

Back in London, Judith did something more desperate than ever before. She slipped out of the house right under her father's nose. Walters had taken her day off to visit a cousin, allowing Judith to claim at eleven in the morning that she wasn't feeling well. "I'm sure it's just fatigue from our journey," she told Robert in his study. "I'll have a nap. Don't bother to wake me for lunch. I'll be right as rain by dinnertime, you'll see."

Gambling that he wouldn't look in on her—he never did—she let fifteen minutes pass in her chamber, then crept downstairs again. As she'd hoped, he was still working at his desk in the roomful of clocks, their contrary ticking making noise enough to cover her quiet escape out the front door.

She hurried, her legs trembling beneath her. She had her cloak hood over her head, yet if her father looked out his windows, conceivably he could recognize her gait.

Her luck held. She safely turned the corner and put a large, solid building between her and Manchester Square. Finding a hackney to take her across London Bridge, she fell back in the seat, shaking all over.

Fog hung heavily, thickened with smoke from the fires of the soap-boilers and lime-burners' works. She alighted at the gates of the city with her legs still shaking. She'd dressed in a lavender-gray frock, the most colorful of all her gowns. But Evan wasn't there to admire it. She was early, but several church bells tolled the noon hour and he still didn't appear. Another five minutes passed, which seemed like five years.

Somehow she'd simply assumed he would come, but what if he'd laughed at her ardent letter? What if he'd tossed it in the fire and forgotten all about her?

Someone tall passed by. "Evan!" she called. The man's head turned. Tall, but blunt-faced. Not him.

A gleeful, yelling group of street urchins parted to pass on either side of her, and one of the rascals flipped up her skirt hem. She slapped his hand. "Heathen!" As she looked up again, there he was, Evan, not running but walking fast, clearly looking worried that he'd missed her. Dear God, he was handsome! He had the longest, most exquisite legs she'd ever seen on a man. He didn't hail her, and as soon as their eyes met, he slowed his pace. The worried look changed to a stony expression. Her smile failed a little in the face of that.

When he got near, he removed his hat and made a bow. "Your servant, madam."

"You're angry."

He stood like something fixed and unmoving since the making of the world. "Did you find your fiancé in good health? When will the wedding be?"

Matthew had chosen a date after Christmas. She hadn't been able to stop him, but she cried now, "I'll never marry that prig!"

"Did you tell him so?"

"I told him I would make him miserable." Which wasn't the same thing, especially since it had done no good. But the answer thawed Evan's reserve. She threw herself into his arms.

The strength of his feelings surprised Evan. This had happened so quickly he still couldn't quite believe it. He'd told himself he wouldn't meet her, and almost too late he'd thrown on his coat and hat and hurried to the appointed place. Still, he'd managed to keep himself in check—until now. A dam broke, and he knew that all the time she'd been gone—even when he'd been with Nancy—love for Judith had grown in his heart of hearts like a mushroom in the dark. He wrapped his arms around her and held her hard. "Sweetheart!" All his feelings were in his voice. "What shall I do with you?"

"Love me! Kiss me! I've kept myself sane by thinking of your kisses!"

He looked about them. "This isn't the place. Come with me." He took her down a stairway, and on the brick jetty at the bottom, with the Thames lapping at their feet, he pressed her against a brick arch and kissed her thoroughly.

She was so willing! Innocent, but eager to learn everything. He found himself doing things he'd done with other women, things that were second nature to him, but when he shoved up her skirts and let his hands roam her legs, she murmured, "Evan!"

He stepped back, realizing that even the fog didn't hide them completely from the fishing smacks on the river. "I'm sorry."

"I'm not." Her face looked strange, sensually open yet strained. "I want to be yours, Evan." She threw herself at him again. "Make me yours, please, today!"

He held her off long enough to ask solemnly, "Are you sure, sweetheart?" He'd never foreseen them going so far. But then he'd never foreseen falling in love with an obstinate little Puritan innocent, either!

She looked at him gravely, as if she knew this moment was a turning point in her life. Yet she didn't veer from it. "I'm sure. I've never been so sure of anything."

He looked for the least sign of unspoken reservation. When he found none, he said, "I can't take you to my room. It's not fit for a lady. But I know of another place."

He took her hand—and was hard put not to pick her up and carry her when she had trouble keeping up with his long-legged stride through the streets crowded with vendors crying their wares, housewives making purchases on their doorsteps, porters carrying reeling loads and swearing thunderously at anyone who interrupted their progress. Evan put his arm around Judith as they passed two fops arguing with drawn swords.

At the Inn of the Royal Axe, a man with a sour expression greeted them. Evan said, "We need a room for the afternoon." The jaded innkeeper didn't bat an eye.

Judith didn't fail to note her beloved's experience at this sort of thing. In front of the innkeeper, he behaved as casually as if he were escorting his sister up the stairs. At the top, the innkeeper opened a door and stepped back silently for them to enter.

The room was enormous, and so was the bed it held. Two tall windows were curtained with stiff red brocade. The innkeeper crossed to light the fire, and Judith moved toward it, for she felt a nervous chill. Behind her, Evan said, "We missed our lunch."

"I'll bring something up, sir."

"Fine—but wait an hour."

As the man went out, Judith stared into the fire, suddenly wondering what she was doing here.

* * *

Evan approached her slowly, thinking almost the same thing: What was she doing here? But sometimes a man doesn't have world enough or time enough for scruples. He wanted this woman, no matter the cost. And the cost would be high. Just the price of this room would set him back weeks of savings. But he must make her his. He felt an urgency to do it, today, before any narrow, eccentric Puritan could take her away from him. That she was of a different faith, that she was a complete innocent and might not even realize what any of this meant, even his concern for his own sister's miserable situation could not stand up against his need to claim Judith Browne as his own.

He took her into his arms and tried to make a joke. "Montezuma drank an extra cup of chocolate before he visited his wives. I should have thought to bring some."

When she didn't smile, he realized she was too unworldly for such a quip. "Judith, you do know why I brought you here, don't you?"

"To make me yours," she said with such honesty he almost winced.

"Do you know what that means?"

"I'm inexperienced but not ignorant." Something changed in her eyes. "I know people would say it's wrong, but why was love given to us if not to join us body and soul? When I press myself against you like this, it feels so right!"

"We'll make it completely right when we can—but I must be honest, I don't know when that can be."

"Then for now . . ." She lifted her mouth for his kiss.

He wondered how this had happened? How had this girl been given to him?

Somehow in the next few minutes, between kisses—oh, such kisses!—Judith was divested of all her clothes except her shift. Even her hair was loosened and fell around her like a mantle. "Wait for me in the bed, sweetheart," Evan said in a throaty tone.

Bereft of his arms, shyness overtook her—and panic. She'd spoken boldly in his arms, but she knew herself to be naive and sheltered. She wanted to move toward the bed but felt too weak to do it. Was she going to disappoint him after all? She took a step—and felt herself glide like an ice skater. Somehow the skater didn't fall, she got to the canopied bed, then Evan's arms came around her from behind and steadied everything again. "Afraid of me?" he murmured.

"Just parts of you." She felt the specific object of her fear through her shift. She felt the heat of it, its rigidity, its size.

He chuckled as he pulled back the counterpane and together they slid between the cool linens that were surprisingly fragrant with lavender. She kept her eyes steadfastly on his face, for he'd stripped naked, and she had a panicky dread of seeing the frightening apparatus about to be used on her.

"Can I take your shift off, sweetheart? I want to feel all of you against me."

She couldn't answer. It was as though her lips were stitched together. He unlaced the garment and pulled it over her head, and once she was naked against him, she found the sensation delicious. He felt warm, muscled, hard, and a craving to wrap herself around him, to twine herself like a vine, swelled in her.

He seemed to revel in letting his hands roam at will—but he was still hesitant, as if he couldn't believe she knew what she was doing. "Are you truly sure, Judith?" He framed her face with his hands, and studied her eyes.

"I don't want to exist as a separate being from you for another hour." She was glad her voice sounded level. And she was rewarded by his kiss. And another, and another. The bed became a warm nest, a protected encampment, a small world.

Evan loved the soft pressure of her skin all up and down his body. He felt her yearning, her timid, inexperienced passion. He'd had many women, but love made all the difference. He slid his hand up her thighs. She flinched, then surrendered and opened to him. He stroked her lightly, moving his fingertips carefully among the petals of flesh, caressing her gently. She surprised him when her hand trailed down his belly and her fingers tentatively touched him, explored him with shy inquisitiveness, then boldly took him in hand. The delightful feeling almost destroyed his intention to go slowly with her. He kissed her in a frenzy of desire, his own caresses between her thighs growing surer and seeking entrance—and causing a quick protest.

"It's all right," he whispered. And though he felt she was half mad with both passion and terror, she relaxed. He went on tenderly, and when he felt her body clench, heard her amazed gasp—"Ah, ah!"—he felt on fire to plunge into her. While she was still stunned by her first-ever climax, he positioned himself. He looked down at her, at her eyes half closed, her lips moist with his kisses, her cheeks flushed with pleasure, and his passion blazed. He moved into her, slowly, soon encountering her maidenhead. "Judith, it may hurt a little this first time."

She moved in a way that told him better than words that she was ready. He thrust. She didn't cry out, but only made a small sound in her throat. Then he was free to take her completely. The rapture was too much. Though he wanted to make it last, he couldn't hold back a moan as all too soon he reached his crisis.

He rolled onto his side, bringing her with him. They lay quietly in each other's arms as he recovered his breath. He drew a deep, luxurious sigh, and for a long moment felt he couldn't move so much as a toe. His hand stroked her warm bottom. The feel of her satin-skin fascinated him. He could fondle her like this for the rest of his life and never tire of it.

"Do you still love me, Evan?"

He felt her vulnerability. "I love you to distraction."

How easily those words came out. And on the tip of his tongue were more. *I want to marry you and keep you with me forever.* But he was in no position to do that.

So what was he doing, endangering her like this? She'd given herself to him in the belief that he would take care of her if she should find herself in trouble—and he would! Yet, as long as she wasn't . . .

❧ Chapter 5 ❧

Evan dressed in his hose and shirt to take the tray from the innkeeper at the door. A look at the food warned him that the cost of this afternoon had just risen another week's worth of savings. He didn't mind. He brought the tray to the bed, and shed his clothes again before joining Judith for a naked picnic in their own private pleasure garden. She tried to wrap herself with the lavender-scented sheet, but he teased, "None of that."

She acquiesced with a charming blush. Sitting on her knees opposite him, she said, "You're very sinful, Evan Dugdale."

He grinned, taking a forkful of fried veal sweetbreads as with his eyes he took in her beautiful breasts, still ruddy from his handling. "Why ever do you say that?"

"It's wicked to look at someone naked."

"Nonsense. Why would God make you so fair if not for me to prize His work?"

"That sounds like irreverence and blasphemy."

"I assure you, I'm completely reverent." He dipped his finger in his wine and anointed the tips of her breasts, which immediately gathered into tight points. "And it will be my reverent pleasure to taste that as soon as we finish this meal."

She blushed, but, bold as ever, said, "It's very nice, isn't it?"

He chuckled. "It is. And you need to eat, madam, to

restore your strength, because in a while I'm going to show you a few more nice things."

"Well, then." She started on a joint of chicken with such eagerness that he laughed outright. He took a bite of liver with a sweet eggplant sauce as she reached for her own wine. He nearly choked as she leaned with a wine-coated fingertip to anoint his own flat nipples. She gave him an uncertain smile, as if to say, Is this all right? He put down his food and took hers from her. "I haven't finished, sir."

"You'll have to finish later, sweetheart." He put the tray on the floor.

"It'll go cold."

"That's unfortunate, but it can't be helped. Now lie back on your pillow and prepare to be loved again."

He took her more leisurely the second time, and enjoyed more thoroughly her look of incredulity at the discovery of what pleasure her body could give her. And he enjoyed even more thoroughly the pleasure her body gave him.

Afterwards, she lay perfectly still, eyes closed, one arm over her forehead. He knew how she felt, warm and sleepy, marvelously content, and glad that this had happened. She had a lazy smile on her lips. He bent his head to kiss her. "I'm sorry."

That startled her eyes open. "Are you?"

He grinned. "Not really, no."

"Then may I finish my dinner?"

He put the tray back on the bed and went to refresh the fire. Returning, he paused to admire the sight of her sitting on her knees, naked as a pale garden statue, her hair hanging like seaweed. He climbed on the bed behind her, and nuzzling her hair aside, kissed her neck. She leaned back, allowing him to cup her breasts possessively. Though part of him still brooded about taking unfair advantage of her, he couldn't help but bask in the warm, arousing knowledge that she belonged to him now. "No regrets?"

"Not one." She turned her head and pouted her lips in invitation.

"And what does that mean?"

"It means I want you to kiss me."

He raised his eyebrows, at the same time stroking her breasts delicately with both hands. "Let me see it again. Hmm, yes, now I get the connection."

Her expression faltered. "Evan, does my mind swing around like a weathercock?"

He laughed. "Not until you said that."

"Do I twirl into a room like a top? And have the personality of a traveling circus?"

"You're absolutely perfect."

She smiled again. "That's what I think, too."

He frowned as it occurred to him who must have criticized her spirited ways, and in a flash he imagined himself riding hell-bent to find Hawthorne and smash his face.

"Well?" she said.

That delightful pout of her lips recalled him. "Well what?" He resumed his attentions to her perfect breasts.

"Kiss me, you simpleton!"

He gave her a quick peck. "Like that?"

"Hardly!" she laughed—a beautiful scarlet-poppy laugh, one he'd never heard before. Had he brought that out of her?

He pretended to look perplexed. "You'll have to show me what it is you want."

She turned in his arms, endangering the again forgotten tray of food. She took his face between her small hands and for the first time kissed him. Though careful not to take control, he found her innocent technique the most provocative enticement he'd ever endured. His hand, however, couldn't resist slipping between her thighs—now with all the familiarity of traveling a path known well. He lightly touched the golden-curled little grotto into which he had poured his heart and soul twice already this day.

She pulled back from his mouth and, still holding his face between her hands, looked straight into his eyes as he opened and caressed her. He moved closer, moved his knees under her, positioned her astraddle his lap, and pressed upward into her.

"Yes," she murmured, as he held her steady for his sliding ingression. "Yes, Evan."

He gazed into her beautiful face. The marvelous expression it assumed enchanted him. She sighed as he penetrated her fully, and her head fell back. His hands lifted and lowered her hips as he piloted in and out of her with long slow thrusts. Her soft climactic cry came muffled against his shoulder as she fell against him. "I love you!"

I love *you*, he thought as his desire jetted into her for a third time.

Returning to Manchester Square, the wonderful thing that had happened to Judith filled her. She feared everyone could tell how greatly she'd changed in the last five hours. Creeping back into the house in the late afternoon, she discovered her father had gone out. Amazingly, she reached her room with her outing completely undetected.

She had fooled him that time, and fooled him the same way a week later when once more she dared take advantage of Walters's day off. But she couldn't use the ploy of not feeling well a third time without her father insisting she see an apothecary. For nine days no opportunity presented itself, and she worried that Evan would give up on her. She realized she'd have to try something riskier than ever, because she *must* see him, be with him, lay in his arms. She felt that nothing could ever attach him to her enough; she wanted to merge completely with him. Therefore, she arranged for him to spirit her away from King Charles's entrance into London.

A frown darkened Robert Browne's lean, dour face at her announcement that she intended to witness the king's return. Before he could forbid it, she said, "There's no sense trying to ignore the monarchy. Matthew didn't object in his letter yesterday."

"You wrote to him about it?"

She carefully didn't answer directly. "If he is to be my husband, I must look to him for guidance—isn't that what you said? And his letter was full of advice."

That was true. It had been nothing but a boring missive

full of his mother's advice about her trousseau, what linens and woolens she should buy. But pretending she'd consulted him about her intention worked wonders in softening Robert.

The twenty-ninth of May 1660 began wildly. Men playing flutes and banging tambourines wakened the household on Manchester Square long before its usual hour. Judith and Walters left at six o'clock. Even so, it was harder to get to the spot she'd arranged to be in than she'd imagined. Several times Walters said, "Here, this is a good enough place, surely."

Judith insisted they move on over the bridge. People packed every balcony and window. All the way to Whitehall, pennants whipped gallantly on even the most common rooftops. Shop signs were draped with May flowers, garlands looped from window to window, and great arches of hawthorn spanned every street. Few people were dressed as plainly as Judith and Walters. That pious old look was suddenly shunned. Judith had dressed with extraordinary care in her grayest gown, however, not daring to display even so much as a ribbon lest her father use it as a reason to keep her home.

They finally reached the place where she'd told Evan to look for her, before the Turk's Head ale house. She saw her beloved only moments later, big, handsomely virile, his hair as dark as night. No wonder she'd fallen in love the instant she'd seen him!

She and Walters had a time keeping their places. Unruly onlookers tried repeatedly to elbow them aside or step before them. Though the procession wasn't expected until after noon, already by eight o'clock not a foot of standing space could be found.

As Charles II finally rode into the heart of this jubilation, the overheated crowd shouted their throats raw. Judith saw the procession coming through the narrow lanes, the horses' hooves clopping the pavement rhythmically, trumpets and clarinets shrilling, drums rolling with the sound of thunder. The Royalists were dressed in scarlet and silver, black velvet and gold, silver and green. Cheers went up for the loyal

Cavaliers who had fought for the first Charles and who had felt the heavy heel of Cromwell on their necks for the past two decades. They were now handsomely dressed and mounted and ready to serve their king again.

Then came Charles II. His brown hair was cut straight, just above his shoulders—like Evan's, Judith thought. His eyes weren't glass green, however, but slate blue, and striking, even from a distance. As he passed, Judith saw Evan standing almost at her side, only half-hidden behind another big man so that Walters wouldn't see him. Judith secretly nodded to him, then said to Walters, "We can go now." As the old woman gratefully turned for home, Judith stepped back into the crowd.

Evan had his arm around her in an instant. "Hurry!" he urged her.

At the Inn of the Royal Axe—now renamed the King's Royal Inn—they spent a delicious afternoon. "Evan," Judith murmured, feeling the full length of his body all along hers after their desire's first satiation, "you make me better than I am."

The windows were open, and the stiff red brocade curtains leaned inward on the breeze. He said, "That's impossible; you can't be better than you already are." His lips offered a cooling touch to her mouth. "What could be better than these pretty lips, or this tiny mole, close enough that when I kiss you properly I kiss it, too? Several lifetimes wouldn't be enough to appreciate all your perfections."

"What a shame, since you have only one."

"But I intend to make good use of it." His mouth took the lips he'd lauded.

His lovemaking amazed Judith. His tastes were so various, his appetites so keen. She knew she wasn't near to being perfect, but he was. She could never get to the end of him, he was so many-sided, his interests were so rich.

As the late afternoon sun filtered through the open windows, they dreamed of when he would open his shop and they could live together in the apartments overhead. There would be room for his sister, whom Judith would love as her own sister. Though he never said so, she knew these afternoons were actually prolonging their wait. This room was an expense. She wished she could help, but what money her father allowed her must be strictly accounted for.

When he left her outside Manchester Square, she automatically folded away her newly discovered true self, the imaginative, light-hearted self that Evan said, "has a way of changing everything into a celebration." Crossing the square, she stiffened her spine in preparation for confronting her father. She was going to have to explain her disappearance from the market. She felt guilty about tricking Walters, knowing the elderly woman must have had a harrowing time looking for her.

As for Robert's worry, she felt no guilt at all. He deserved it for trying to force her into a marriage with someone so dead to life as Matthew Hawthorne.

She found him standing in the usual place, as motionless as the oak stairs gleaming darkly behind him. "Are you all right?" he asked in a restrained tone.

"I'm fine." She hung her bonnet and cloak away. "I know Walters must have been afraid for me but—"

"Afraid? I had to send her to bed!"

"Oh, I *am* sorry. I must go and—"

Robert seized her arm as she tried to pass him. "Where have you *been*?"

"I won't lie to you, Father. I went to see a play."

"What!" He seemed genuinely stunned.

"I've always wanted to see one, and I knew that once I'm married I'll never have the chance. So I went."

"A *play*? You frightened Walters to attend a sinful drama? And me—I was mad for thinking what happened. Every day bodies are fished from the Thames—and you were at a play!" He released her arm. "May God forgive you!"

"He must be very large minded by now. He's seen so many human foibles."

Robert Browne's hand moved before she realized he meant to slap her. The blow took her by surprise. It knocked her sideways and backwards. Her ankles hit the first stair and she stumbled, catching herself against the bannister. She straightened slowly.

"I won't have you speak of our Lord in that casual, careless way! How dare you disgrace my name like this! Behaving like a strumpet! For years you've caused me nothing but trouble, and—*by the Lord above*!—I'm fed up with it!"

Judith heard a creak, and turned to see Walters on the stairs, her hand over her mouth, her eyes awash with tears. But Robert wasn't finished. "You will go to your room and pray for forgiveness. You will not come down for dinner, nor will any food be brought to you. You will pray and fast for your sins until dinner tomorrow night."

Judith returned his glare, sorely tempted to refuse, to run back out the door and return to Evan. But he had his sister to worry about. All their futures were in his hands, and the only thing he asked of her was patience. She turned and climbed the stairs without arguing, though in her head she shouted, If you only knew what I really did this afternoon— and it was worth a few missed meals, a few hours on my knees! A single moment in my beloved's arms is worth that and more!

The summer passed in a splash of sunlight, and the autumn in a swirl of leaves, and now mid-November stood full of gray mist. Manchester Square lay hushed as a graveyard, conforming to Judith's mood as she stood at the windows in her room. Since the king's return, she'd seen Evan once in August, once in September, and once in October, all three meetings the result of careful plans made to slip away from the house in the dead of night. That necessity had come about because Walters had been "retired." Judith had a new maid.

She regretted deeply that her tricks had caused her father to appraise her old nurse's age and vigor against Judith's growing independence—or defiance, as he put it. Judith could hardly believe his coldheartedness in dismissing the loyal old woman. She hadn't realized how much she'd loved Walters, who had been both mother and servant for as long as she could remember. With Walters gone, Judith saw that all that lay between her and her father was a relationship based on duty—and fear.

More fear than ever now. She stared unseeing at the day's white, whirling skirts. After Walters's dismissal, Robert had consulted with Mrs. Rouie and Mrs. Wigglesworth to help him engage a new chaperon for Judith. The result was Mrs. Ann Suckling, as watchful a creature as Puritan values had ever produced. She'd moved into the house in June, and until the very end of July, Judith had been hard put to think how to slip away from her. Finally, during a shopping excursion, she pretended a faintness—conveniently in front of Netter's Confectionery. She pleaded to be allowed to sit in the shop's courtyard, which led to placing an order for two steaming mugs of chocolate.

Seeing her, Evan had let a smile break across his mouth. But quickly surmising the situation, he grew distant. The ploy afforded Judith the chance to pass him a note explaining how hard it was to meet him. Before she recovered from her "faintness," he slipped her an answer: *Come out after they're asleep. I'll be waiting with a coach.*

To go out alone after dark would never have occurred to her, but knowing he was waiting made the risk delectable. The most precarious part was getting back before anyone arose. And leaving Evan's arms. That became more problematical each time.

She'd heard nothing from him since their assignation in October—but they'd arranged to meet again tonight for a few hours in their secret nest. She could almost smell the fragrant lavender of the Royal Inn's sheets. What a sensualist she'd become! But tonight there would be no lovemaking. She planned to meet him, but only to talk.

A knock at her door interrupted her thoughts. Couldn't she have just a moment alone? She barely turned as Mrs. Suckling came in carrying the wedding gown Judith was supposed to wear next month. "It just came." She hung it on the wardrobe door. "Isn't it beautiful? Just look at the bodice, and this lace!"

The heavy satin gown was embroidered with seed pearls, and had deep cuffs of cream-colored lace. Its skirt draped up over a petticoat of luminous silver cloth. It *was* beautiful, more so than anything Judith had been allowed before. But she could hardly bear to look at it. "Put it inside the closet, please."

"Aren't you going to try it on?"

"I'd rather be fitted for my graveclothes."

Mrs. Suckling's eyes became as dangerous as gun barrels. "What nonsense! I shall tell your father."

"That's what you're paid to do. And again I'll tell him I don't want to marry Matthew Hawthorne." Her audacity surprised even her, but her relationship with her father had deteriorated to the point of glittering stares. She couldn't forgive him for going ahead with this wedding despite her protests. "We'll quarrel again, and I'll be told to pray the night away—and what difference will it make? The smoke will go up the chimney tomorrow just the same as today." She practiced no pretense with this woman. She only put up with her at all because Robert had threatened to send her to live under her future mother-in-law's vigilance these last weeks before the wedding.

She turned back to the foggy day. Mrs. Suckling did not go quietly. And the smoke of her outrage did not go up the chimney at all, but lingered in the room. Judith summoned up Evan's large, confident presence once more. She would meet him again in the folds of the night—and what would she tell him?

Six months had passed since she'd first met him. They'd become lovers almost immediately, and as far as she could reckon, she was five months pregnant.

Pregnant! The word felt like a bare blade at her throat.

At first she'd wondered if his lovemaking alone was somehow altering her body—a pardonable error considering the repressive climate of her upbringing. The truth was almost too great to accept, especially under such distracting conditions. She'd finally deduced, though, that her absent menses meant something significant, and deduction had become certainty as her belly rounded and her breasts enlarged and grew tender.

For the past few weeks, she'd lived in dread of discovery, though so far her skirts disguised her condition. Looking at the ghostly reflection of herself in the window glass, she knew she didn't look pregnant. Pregnancy made women plump and rosy and placid, but worry had made her thinner. She jumped at the smallest sound, and felt easily angered.

"What's going to happen to me?" she asked that ghost in the glass. *Think*, *Judith*. Less than six weeks remained until the wedding. Not that she would ever don that gown in the wardrobe, that frost-pale dress and veil meant to denote her purity and virginity. She wasn't so low as to marry one man while carrying another's child.

She left the window to lay on her bed and stare up at the canopy. If she told Evan tonight that she was carrying his child, he would marry her, but at the cost of everything he'd been working for. How could she do that to him?

Tears seeped from her eyes and slipped into her hair, and finally she turned her face into her pillows and cried—softly, so that Mrs. Suckling wouldn't hear. She must cry it out now because she didn't dare cry tonight. She hadn't needed to think at all, really, because her decision had already been made. Tonight she must play a role, like an actress in a play. She must do it well, even better than the times she'd lied to her father and Mrs. Suckling, for unlike them, Evan knew all her different expressions and what they meant, and he might easily guess the truth—something he absolutely must not do. Somehow she must walk that path of burning stones without flinching.

At eleven o'clock, a coach stopped outside Manchester Square, and Evan stepped out. Ten minutes passed as he waited in the fog, then twenty. He couldn't help feeling annoyed at Judith for taking so long. To pay for both the coach and the room at the inn he'd dipped into his savings yet again. His annoyance raked his conscience, however, because he knew what he was doing was wrong. He should never have seduced her, and shouldn't be encouraging her to steal out of her father's house to meet a penniless apprentice who couldn't do the honorable thing by her.

Honor. What did he know about honor? Not a thing.

But he knew about love. The moment he'd first seen her he'd embraced love like a religious convert. He loved Judith, wanted her—and honor might as well be living in Jamaica. His life ceased to exist except when he was with her. Every conversation seemed painfully boring. He had little interest in anything except to see her again.

He assuaged his conscience with the thought that this affair would have a comfortable outcome. In the meantime, if only she would hurry! He peered through the fog, willing her to appear, willing his emotions to settle.

His inner struggle troubled him the more tonight because he'd been to visit his sister. Katherine stood on the verge of young womanhood. She had very soft, dark hair and thoughtful eyes that contained a look of wariness beyond her years. But wariness wasn't wisdom, and what he'd observed today made him more desperate than ever to get her out of his uncle's household. Sour faced Gregor Dugdale had recently engaged an apprentice, a young rake if ever Evan had met one (and he met one regularly in his shaving mirror). The knave had his eyes on Katherine and was no more able to marry than Evan was. And yet who knew better than Evan just how easily an innocent girl could be lured and debauched?

The coachman, bearded like most of his trade to save his face from the weather, cursed softly. "Marry come up! Was ever a woman born who didn't keep the whole world waiting?"

Evan muttered, "You're getting paid to wait." He fisted his hands in his pockets.

All his irritation vanished as he heard Judith's light running footsteps, saw her cloaked figure, her face damp with the fog. The only thing he wanted in all the world was to sweep her into his arms. No cost was too great. "Sweetheart!" He kissed her briefly. "Get in the coach." He felt the familiar urgency to carry her away and never bring her back.

❧ Chapter 6 ❧

Inside the coach, Judith felt shaky over the scene ahead. Evan pulled her close, one hand immediately seeking her breasts as his mouth sought her lips. For a moment she submitted, but then she pushed free. "We must talk."

"We can talk at the inn."

"Don't," she brushed his hands away, "don't, Evan."

He straightened away from her. "What's wrong?"

The rattletrap hackney jarred over the cobbles. "I've been doing a lot of thinking and praying," she began as she'd planned. "I was reared with strong beliefs about right and wrong, and what we—*I've* been doing is wrong."

He didn't say anything. Why didn't he say anything? Was he waiting for her to finish so he would know how to react? Every fiber of her being wanted to shout the truth: I'm with child! He would take her back into his arms and say they must marry right away. It would be so easy to let him sacrifice his future for her.

"Evan, I've decided to marry Matthew Hawthorne after all."

She sensed the hackles rising along his spine, like a wolf's. "You don't love him!"

"It all comes down to what I want out of life. Matthew and I will make a quiet and pleasant union."

"What are you talking about? Do you mean a *prosperous* union? You want the manor house, the servants, the gowns, all the things I can't give you? No, I don't believe it. You're not that way."

"I'm afraid I am." Her voice sounded regretful but sincere. All those secret hours of acting out her forbidden plays had prepared her for this dreadful hour. "What can you offer me, Evan? A life of hard work and frugality? A few cramped rooms over some shabby little shop—if even that." She felt his body clench. "I'm sorry, Evan."

"You're sorry." His voice came out flat.

"I am, but—" She mustn't falter now. "But I've already talked to my father and put myself entirely under his command. He's written to the Hawthornes—"

"Then why did you meet me tonight!"

"I felt it only fair to tell you face to face, considering how fond I am of you."

"*Fond*? We've been *lovers*! What's your Puritan husband going to think when he fails to find a virgin on his wedding night?"

"You don't need to be crude."

A moment passed, then his head moved again in denial. "You're lying. You fell in love with me the minute we met."

"I'm still young and foolish—and you're a handsome man. You tempted me to a wicked arousal, and I hope God will one day forgive—"

He took her in his arms savagely. "You're lying! Tell me you don't want me this minute!" He covered her mouth with his own and his hand swept under her skirts.

His first kiss, beside the river, had been the spark that had lit this entire conflagration. She couldn't afford to let him set her afire again. She clenched her legs together, and sealed her lips. Her mind held fast its terrible decision.

Her coldness seemed to provide the final proof. He released her, and after another moment of fraught silence shouted to the coachman, "Stop!" Before the vehicle fully halted, he flung himself out, calling up to the coachman, "Take her back!"

"Aye, and didn't I guess it? All that waiting in the damp for a cheap and cobbling bit of hasty work. If you've stained my upholstery—"

Judith slid across to the door. The coachman went on muttering, but Evan didn't speak again, only strode away into the fog.

She slipped back into her father's house silently, and went to bed. But she didn't sleep. There were night-long, strangling, whimpering tears. She fell into an exhausted doze just before dawn, only to start up, sick and juddering, when Mrs. Suckling entered in her usual intrusive way. "You're late for breakfast, madam." She threw open the heavy green draperies, letting thin November sunshine stream into the room. "It's a lovely morning with a flurry of birds singing in the square."

Birds singing? Judith rubbed her swollen eyes. Inside her flared an incandescent pain: that last sight of Evan disappearing into the fog. And more heartache was to come this morning. And beyond this morning—no, she couldn't look any further ahead.

" 'Pride goeth before destruction, and a haughty spirit before a fall.' " It seemed to Judith her father must already know about her. Mrs. Suckling made agreeing sounds, approving of his theology. Finally the end came in sight: "Praise be to the Lord, amen."

"Amen," Judith echoed. As she rose from her knees, she said, "Father, I must speak to you alone."

Mrs. Suckling gave her a supercilious gaze, but took herself out of the drawing room. Robert headed for his study. "I have a busy day, Judith."

"It's important." She followed him and shut the door—shutting them in with the tick-ticking of his clocks.

"What is it then?"

For just an instant she reconsidered: She could tell him the truth. *I met a man. I love him. I'm having his child. With your support, we could wed.*

Robert shuffled briskly through the papers on his desk. She spied an invoice for beeswax. At three times the price of hard, yellow vegetable tallow, it made gleaming white candles that burned with a brighter flame. He would never admit to the increase in his business with the Royalists' return, no more than he would help Judith marry Evan.

He glanced up, brows raised impatiently. She tried to take a breath, but her chest wouldn't expand. Something outside her squeezed tighter and tighter. "I'm with child."

She saw just how long it took those three words to penetrate his inattention. She saw the fingers of his right hand jerk just the tiniest bit, saw his thin mouth drop open, his eyes change, his expression grow blank. She must go on while she had the chance. "That day last summer when I slipped away from Walters, when I told you I'd been to see a play, I didn't tell you everything."

I spent those hours with Evan. She pictured their room at the inn, the rumpled bed, the lavender-scented sheets pulled into alps here and there by their passion.

"On my way home, a man approached me. I couldn't find a coach—the streets were so crowded that day, and . . . he accosted me." She blinked rapidly. Tears in her throat were doing odd things to her voice. "He pulled me into an alley and . . ." She dropped her eyes, unable to look at him. "He disgraced me."

"Who—" She'd never known her father to be at a loss for words. His fleeting emotions would settle soon like a stone however into righteous anger. "Who—tell me who would dare! What agent of Satan! Tell me and I will indict him before God!"

"I have no idea who he was." She had her voice back under control. "A man, dirty, rough—poor, I guess. Just a bale of sticks loosely tied together. But strong." She surprised herself with these improvisations offered utterly without feeling.

A clock began to chime, then another, and another, until they were all knelling, all at odds with one another as Robert struggled to cope. "That was . . . May?"

"May twenty-ninth, the day the king—"

"Five months? Then when we visited Newington-Green . . .?"

She looked at her clasped hands. "That's why I was so reluctant. I knew it would be wrong to deceive Matthew. I didn't know then . . . I didn't realize . . . but now—"

"You're sure? What do you know of such things?"

She looked down. "I know."

His anger narrowed and gained force. He leaned over his desk and concentrated a glare at her. "If you'd been obedient, but no, your heart is such a foul chamber pot of disrespect and *whoredom*!"

Judith stepped back. She'd expected fury, but not this. "Father!"

"*Father?*" His eyes gave off an icy light. "You call me that *now*, when you've rejected my authority again and again, when you bring this dishonor to my house? How many times were you told that sensible women stay out of sight! This is *your* fault! And I wish to God I could let you suffer it alone! I would put you out this minute."

"Father, please!" She felt herself growing white and ill. A polished, starless black rimmed her vision.

"I warned you not to soil my name, but you would, you *would*! And now you bring this sexual sin into my home!"

He sat down, still glaring at her. His hands gripped the watersilk arms of his chair, but now his eyes moved away from her, as if he couldn't bear to look at her. At length he said, grim and decisive, "No one must know. The wedding will be canceled, of course. Poor Matthew, this will break his heart—but not even he can know why!" Behind and beneath and all around his words came the clocks' tick-tick-tocks. "I'll say you're ill. I'll dismiss Mrs. Suckling. She knows the Wigglesworths and the Rouies, and I can't have any gossip. I'll hire someone outside our circle to tend you. I'll say you've been taken ill, I've sent you away to recover."

"Where?"

He eyes careened back. "*Nowhere*! You're staying in your room! As much as I'd love to throw you out, I can't afford a scandal. My business, everything I've worked for . . . you'll retire to your room and not come out until you're delivered of this bastard!"

Judith hardly dared breathe.

"When it's over, we'll pretend you've recovered—but you'll remain an invalid. You won't go out except to church. God knows you need the instruction! But you'll never marry. What man would want such a Jezebel?"

"It'll be months, Father." She swallowed. "In my room?"

His expression paralyzed her. "That's right—and don't you *ever* come out! I don't want to see you bloated with your iniquity!" His eyes bored into her belly. "By God's passion—" He left the curse unfinished, looked away again, and lifted his hand in repudiation. "Get out of my sight!"

She backed toward the door, felt for the knob, turned it and fled. Fled from that room of too-insistent time-ticking and sin-counting, fled to her banishment, to an imprisonment in her own home. That her father was forceful enough and bigoted enough and self-righteous enough to enforce his plan she had no doubt.

The new regime of Charles II and his cosmopolitan court brought cheerful times to London, especially as winter and the yule season approached. Christmas evening found Evan Dugdale miserable, however. He stood in Manchester Square, staring across the snowy cobblestones at Robert Browne's house. Was Judith still there, or was she already married? The thought of some other man possessing her set fire to his sleep some nights, and woke him sweating. A month had passed since he'd seen her, and depending on how much wedding fuss the families made, she might not be lost to him yet, but he had no way of finding out, short of knocking on the door and asking.

His frustrated love was like something alive in his belly eating its way out. *Judith! Was it really just a lark to you?* He still couldn't believe that. He'd learned her thoughts and hopes, discovered the fascinating breadth of her imagination, and the more he'd known the more he'd loved her. She should be his! He'd made her his!

He'd come here tonight knowing that he had to make up his mind about whether or not to ask Nancy Netter to be his wife. Katherine had been caught kissing that rake of an apprentice, and she stood in dire danger of being both cast out by their uncle and corrupted by the rogue. Evan had no choice but to wed Nancy in order to save his sister. Yet, God help him, all his passion belonged to Judith.

In Judith's room, the fire in the hearth ran grasping, phantom fingers of light across the floor. Near the hearth stood an old hooded cradle. Judith had asked her new "maid," Mrs. Riley, to bring it down from the attic. It was the cradle her mother had been put in at her birth, and the one in which she'd put Judith.

This had been a curious walled-in Christmas, not that Robert ever let her celebrate the holiday. But in previous years she'd kept it vicariously by watching others. This year, however, she hadn't even been allowed to go to church. She remembered the days when she'd dreaded yet another two- or three-hour church sermon, but after living in this room for over a month even that would seem a treat.

The day passed, hour after long hour, until she'd promised herself she'd at least have a glimpse of the world. Left alone for the few minutes it took Mrs. Riley to fetch her dinner tray from the kitchen, she doused her candle and went to her windows. She pulled back the heavy draperies an inch, feeling sure no one would see her. She forgot those running lines of shine and shadow from the hearth behind her.

The draperies had been shut for five weeks, not even the least flash of daylight allowed in. Mrs. Riley's orders were to see that she stayed "altogether away from the windows," and Mrs. Riley did exactly as Robert told her. The neighbors had been told Judith had fallen ill and was away in the country for a cure of rest and clean air.

Closed in with her keeper for so long, Judith had naturally put together a picture of Mrs. Riley. It seemed the grave woman had run away from a husband who "drank like a fish." She didn't want to lose this employment, even if her duties were odd. Despite her watchfulness, Judith found her less loathsome than Mrs. Suckling, perhaps because she wasn't always on her knees, sanctimonious, feeling a duty to help her frailer sisters—whether they liked it or not. Or perhaps Judith liked her simply because she seemed kind, if in a guarded way. For instance, she saw that the cook provided plenty of egg-rich custards, declaring they were good for mothers-to-be. And though her smiles were rare, when one did appear it was like morning light on calm water.

Peeping out the forbidden windows, Judith saw the square had filled with snow since she'd last looked at it. Otherwise, there wasn't much to see. She felt rather disappointed. In the glass itself, her reflection looked drawn, pale. If she'd pulled the draperies back more, she would have seen her rounded belly. That she didn't do.

The child moved, a familiar sensation by now. Three months until her lying in. Mrs. Riley had been a midwife in her youth, and Judith was glad to have her. Then what? Her father wouldn't let her keep her baby. She supposed he meant to hire someone to raise it. She would visit the poor mite often, though.

The logs shifted on the hearth behind her and she jerked, wary of being caught.

No one there. Looking out the window again, her eyes narrowed. Was that a man across the square looking at the house? She closed the draperies more, until she could just see out with one eye. It couldn't be . . . but it was!

Evan grew cold. It was insane to torment himself like this. But wait—the faintest sliver of light sliced out of an upstairs window. Was that a woman's head? Judith? If so, she certainly wasn't making any sign to him. She still planned to marry Hawthorne then. He would go to Nancy tomorrow and begin to court her properly. She'd guessed that there had been someone else for a while, so it wouldn't be decent to ask for her hand right away. Poor woman, she had the right to believe he'd fallen in love with her. Meanwhile, there was no use standing here yearning after a reckless girl who had never been his and never would be.

Judith's heart knew him even if her eyes couldn't be sure. He still loved her! Oh, how she wanted to fling open the window and shout: Rescue us, beloved! Yet all the reasons she'd decided to lie to him last month were just as true now. He looked downcast, lovelorn, but he was a strong person. He would get over her.

As she hesitated, he started from the square. "Goodbye, my dearest love." Her breath fogged the window, and when it cleared, the square lay empty.

When Judith's labor began, no midwife's chair was brought for fear the neighbors would guess the truth. Near the fireplace in her chamber stood a table with a pewter washbowl, a length of brown cord, a knife, and a pile of white cloths. She couldn't see past the curtains at the foot of her bed or she would have asked why the baby cradle was gone. As it was, she pressed her fists against the headboard as she pushed yet again. Her face screwed into a grimace of pain.

"It's coming!" Mrs. Riley said. During this terrible, endless labor she'd repeatedly reminded Judith to muffle her cries, smother her groans, be quiet, quiet, quiet.

Hidden, secret, quiet. Judith had lived on tiptoe. But it was almost over now. Just one more push. "Ah . . . *ahh!*" She felt the child slip from her.

"A girl!" Mrs. Riley said. "Perfectly formed!"

"Let me . . . see her," Judith panted.

"I'll just wipe her down first, dear."

Judith closed her eyes to wait. Delivered. The word would never mean the same thing to her again. Delivered of pain. Delivered of effort. Delivered of fear.

Her eyes opened as Mrs. Riley placed the blanket-wrapped

bundle on her chest. The two women briefly smiled at each other in utter agreement: We did it. Then Judith looked into the face of her daughter. The baby's features were compressed, and out of her mouth came the tiniest cry ever heard. Yet, even crying, she was beautiful—and so miraculously alive! "Darling, my beautiful darling. Don't cry. The worst is over now." The little face smoothed as if she understood. And she opened her eyes.

Throughout her pregnancy, Judith had hoped the baby would have Evan's eyes. And so she did, beautiful green eyes, as clear as green glass.

Judith didn't have the least idea how to nurse a child, but when she opened her gown, the little mouth eagerly sought her breast. Judith felt a sensation, in her breast and in her belly—and in her heart. A bell of stillness settled around them, like a soundless light. She bent her head to touch that whitest, softest cheek with her lips. It was a promise, as kisses are.

"There." Mrs. Riley had been tending to things "down there," intimate things which Judith didn't care to think about. Soon she lay on her side in a fresh bed gown, content, the warmth of her child beside her. "Sleep, dear, you deserve it."

Judith heard her go out, no doubt to report to Robert that after nearly twenty-four hours the child had been born. Please God, Judith prayed, let him relent and come up and greet his grandchild. For once in his life, let him commit a sin of sentiment.

Knowing he wouldn't, she snuggled her child closer, and closed her own eyes, and slid into sleep as a swimmer slides into a dark river.

When she woke, she heard her baby, but walls muffled the sound. "Mrs. Riley?" She struggled up.

"Now, dear, lie back. Your little one is fine. She's in my room across the hall."

"I want her with me."

"You need your rest now, and so does she. It's best this way."

When the baby's cries stopped, Judith relaxed a little. Her draperies remained closed, but she sensed it was evening. She'd slept all day. She smelled dinner wafting up through the house. Mrs. Riley brought a tray of guinea fowl boiled with radishes. Judith tried to eat, but when she heard her baby cry again, she said, "She must be hungry, too. She can't rest if she's hungry."

"She's fine, dear."

The cry escalated to a squall. "She doesn't sound fine. Bring her to me, please."

The woman took Judith's tray, but didn't go to the door. With her back turned, she said, "You must have known you wouldn't be allowed to keep her."

"But she must be fed, and as long as she's still in the house, why can't I—"

"She'll be given a sugar teat until—"

"That's ridiculous!" Judith threw back her bedclothes.

"Dear, you can't get up!" Mrs. Riley put down the tray and hurried to press her back into bed.

"She needs me." *Baby, Baby, Mother is near, don't cry!*

"There, she's quieting. You see?" Indeed, the child's cries stopped again. "You haven't named her yet," Mrs. Riley offered as a distraction.

The child did need a name. Judith had toyed with ideas— Katherine, after Evan's sister, or Clara after her own mother, but neither seemed just right. "What's your given name, Mrs. Riley?"

"Why, Marguerite—but you don't want to name her for me. I'm a stranger."

Judith sighed. "At the moment, you're my best and only friend in the world. Marguerite is a lovely name—if you don't mind, that is."

"Oh!" Mrs. Riley turned and stood with her face in her hands, her shoulders shaking with silent sobs. Judith watched her in consternation. Did it offend her to have a bastard child named after her?

No, something else was wrong. Something awful. "You must tell me what it is."

The woman's bowed head shook from side to side. "He's going to abandon her."

"Father? You mean he's going to send her away. Where? Not far, I hope. I shall want to visit her often."

Mrs. Riley straightened. "I'm to take her to the workhouse in Malden."

Judith gaped soundlessly.

"He says they take in a great number of fatherless children there, and feed and clothe and teach them, and eventually put them out to a trade."

"A workhouse!" Like Greencoat Hospital, where Judith took gifts of clothing to the penniless, wretched children of criminals, vagrants, and beggars. "No." Her emptied body filled with wild terror. "When, Mrs. Riley, when does he plan to do this?"

The woman struggled to recover herself. She wiped at her eyes, straightened her hoop-skirted gown. "In the morning. I'm to leave early so no one will see me. He's hired a coach to take me to Malden, and I'm to knock at the workhouse door at eleven o'clock and leave the child with the woman who answers. He's already sent money. I'm not to say a word to anyone, or give any indication who the baby is, or in anyway connect her to this house."

Judith saw in this plan the thoroughness that lay at the root of Robert Browne's nature, his passion for imposing conformity on everything. "He won't make you go tonight?"

"Oh, no, it's too cold out; the poor thing would freeze. Even he isn't—"

"Isn't that cruel?" Judith lay back. He was, but he wouldn't deviate from his carefully made plan. He wouldn't think of doing anything impulsive, not him.

Why hadn't Judith foreseen this? It seemed obvious to

her now that he wouldn't let her visit her baby, whether in the city or the country. She'd busily made up her own outcome, out of her own longings, while he'd meant all along to forsake her child and save his almighty respectable name. And what about his plan for Judith? He *had* spoken of that: semiconfinement under the guise of invalidism, presumably for the rest of her days, a spectator standing apart from life—a living death, in fact.

And she'd accepted it, building a fantasy of being allowed to at least see her child, watch her grow, take her little presents, love her and live through her. She might have agreed to anything, sacrificed every possibility of joy if he'd only given her that one small concession. But not now. Now all her independence of spirit rose up. "It won't happen. I'll never be parted from her."

Mrs. Riley said nothing, and Judith saw she believed nothing could be done. But Judith would defeat her father.

How? Go to Evan? For a moment she allowed herself to imagine it: His expression when he saw her, stern, resentful, not noticing the blanket-wrapped child in her arms at first. Then, his face changing—the shock, the surprise as she lifted the blanket and said, "This is your daughter." And as he saw Marguerite's green-colored eyes, like green stained glass with the sun coming through it, looking up at his own green eyes, the sudden breaking pride on his face, his smile, his white teeth glistening in his weathered face, his eyes moving to look into Judith's with the adoration of last summer.

She should have told him from the beginning. She'd hurt him for no good reason. It would be a struggle for them, but they would manage. She'd never known poverty, and frankly she feared it, but she saw now that worse things could happen to people.

She lay in her bed planning. She would take Marguerite to him, and he would forgive her and marry her, and they would find happiness despite the fact that some of their dreams would never come true. Life worked that way. You didn't get some things, like a chocolate shop of your own, but you did get others, like Marguerite. And love.

She would do it. Though tired yet, and a little weakened by her long labor, she would manage it. She would creep secretly out of her father's house one last time.

✦ *Chapter 7* ✦

At nine o'clock, Robert's step passed Judith's door. Mrs. Riley had tucked Judith in with tender sympathy before taking herself off to bed. Judith heard her baby cry just a little, but then the child settled again. She must have taken enough nourishment from the sugar teat to fill her little belly.

At ten-thirty, Judith rose. The shakiness of her legs distressed her. She knelt before her banked fire to put her hair up. She heard her father's voice in her head, echoing like the voice of God: *Your heart is such a foul chamber pot of whoredom.* . . . She'd made mistakes, but she didn't deserve to be so condemned by the one person she should be able to count on for forgiveness.

Would Evan be able to forgive her? Did she really have any hope of reconciliation? She had to have faith. A person didn't get over such a love as they'd shared, not in a lifetime, and certainly not in a few short months.

She felt stronger as she dressed and packed a single change of clothes. She couldn't carry Marguerite and burden herself with more. She had no money, no jewels to take. She must go to Evan just as she'd gone to him in the first place, empty-handed and trusting.

She'd learned how to leave the house silently last summer, but first she must collect her child. She opened Mrs. Riley's door quietly. The woman had left a night candle burning. The bed curtains were drawn. The baby's cradle stood by the low-burning fire. Judith's heart went out to her daughter as she knelt beside her. Extra shawls lay on a stool nearby, and a satchel of other things for the journey Robert had planned for his granddaughter. An envelope lay there, too. Judith opened it. Money! And a sheet of paper written in her father's hand: *Upon reaching Maldon, you will* . . .

She scanned to the bottom. The instructions had been left unsigned by her stony-hearted father. She threw them in the fire and put the money in her pocket.

She lifted the baby—and heard a sound behind her. Turning her head quickly, she saw the bed curtains move. Had Mrs. Riley peeped out? Judith waited for the curtains to move again, for a voice, an outcry. But nothing came. She considered again the things left ready, the shawls, the money. Had Mrs. Riley guessed?

She swathed Marguerite in the shawls and stood with her. At the door, she turned once more to the curtained bed. "Thank you," she whispered. Whether she was heard or not, she would never know.

She felt peculiarly hollow as she crept down the cold stairway, supremely aware that she'd recently labored through hours of hard childbirth. With only one extra gown, enough money to last a few days, and her child in her arms, she left the grim respectability of her father's house.

The March night felt as if it had come in over ice. The streets were so dark that the few dubious human creatures abroad at that hour were no more than thickenings in the blackness. Judith knew she should be afraid, but one thought alone filled her mind: She must get Marguerite to Evan.

She had to stop to rest periodically. She leaned against the wall near the bridge and panted. How could a child so small weigh so much? Her arms quivered.

Now she remembered she couldn't cross the bridge. Stupid, Judith! The gates at the far side would be locked. What to do? The baby stirred in her arms, and began to cry weakly. Frantic and weepy herself, Judith turned toward the river bank. She trudged along until she saw a fire burning. She blessed Mrs. Riley for the money that would allow her to hire a waterman to take her across.

In the silver-edged darkness on the icy black river, Marguerite continued to fuss. Under her cloak, Judith opened her bodice and comforted her baby, and relieved her own painfully full breasts at the same time. As the boat's bottom scraped the London bank, the child slept, completely unaware of her mother's desperation and danger.

Judith didn't know where Evan lived. She planned to go to Netter's and, even if she had to wake the household, find out his address.

In the dark, the city seemed old and ugly. The darkness fused with the shadows of the houses leaning over the streets, blocking the faint moonlight. Judith stumbled on cobblestones, and couldn't see whether the sewage kennels ran down the middle or along the sides of the streets. She had to let her nose guide her, since her eyes could not.

Staggering, she arrived at Netter's Confectionery—and found the windows still alight. As she paused in the empty courtyard, someone came out the door. The vague column of a heavy man's body approached her, and she shrank back. "Madam, are you all right?"

Blinking like a night bird, she recognized Sir Davenant. "I'm fine." But her voice sounded breathless. She couldn't stand much longer, let alone continue to hold Marguerite. Weakness and exertion had made her clammy, so that now she shivered. "My baby." She thrust the weight at the playwright and dropped the weight of her valise. She put her hands for support on the low fence that separated the shop's courtyard from the street.

"Madam, what . . .?"

"It's me, Sir Davenant, Judith Browne."

He bent to peer at her face. "Mrs. Browne? But Evan . . . I'd heard you'd married."

"I didn't. I had Evan's baby. This morning."

"This morning!" The man looked at the bundle held so cautiously in his arms.

"Yes, she's but a few hours old." She laughed a little

wildly, knowing she sounded giddy. "I had to steal away with her. My father planned to abandon her to a workhouse, and I—" she put a shaky hand to her forehead "—I need to find Evan." For an instant she closed her eyes and had the sensation of a slow, golden slide, like late afternoon sunlight down silk curtains.

"Here now, don't swoon!" Surprise gave new energy to the substantial body beside her, which seemed after all capable of quick movement: He shifted the baby to one arm and put the other around her waist.

"I won't." She wasn't sure she could keep her word, however. "Is Evan inside?" She turned for the door again, though still lightheaded—and afraid. She peered at the lighted windows. "Is this a private party? Is he working tonight?"

"It's a wedding party. Dear lady, Evan married Nancy Netter today."

The words stiffened Judith's legs. She stood straighter, and took a step toward the windows. She saw, through the steamed glass, the bride's father, the happy guests, the joyous Nancy. And the smiling groom. Bottles of sack and mugs of chocolate. The remains of a cake left uncovered on its plate. Evan wore a suit of new clothes, and looked more handsome than ever. Nancy looked pretty, too. And so deeply in love with her new husband that her eyes hardly strayed from his face.

"I'm too late then," Judith whispered.

"I'm afraid so—unless you care to go inside anyway and see what comes of it. The choice is yours, of course."

She shook her head slowly.

"Then what *will* you do?"

"I don't know," she answered in a monotone of shock.

"It seems simple. You must go home, even if your father is angry."

"And let him give my baby away? Abandon her on the steps of a workhouse?"

"That does seem harsh, but what other choice do

you have? The means of maintenance open to a young woman—" He clucked his tongue sorrowfully.

Judith felt beyond tears, and far beyond pride. "Will you help me?"

"What can I do—besides offer you lodgings for the night, of course."

"Employ me. You said you wanted to use women for your female roles."

"As an actress? I couldn't possibly. Why, you're a lady, a *Puritan*."

"I'm the mother of a fatherless child. I can never return to my father's house. Sir Davenant, I'm desperate. As you said, there aren't many means open to me, but make no mistake, I will do what I must if you won't employ me."

"That's ridiculous. Go home, Mrs. Browne."

She forced her mind to the lines of one of her cache of plays. "Let me be—*a poor player, that struts and frets his hour upon the stage. . . .*"

The playwright scowled fiercely. Then chuckled. "Little minx. No doubt you'll be trouble, but I'll find something for you, if it's only to light the candles around the apron."

How appropriate, she thought, completely sapped of the courage that had alone brought her this far. After all, she was a tallowchandler's daughter.

Judith, now known as Doria Wetstone, came back to her surroundings with a start of awareness: the theater, her role, her cue—which she'd missed again. The actor who had spoken it gave her a high-browed look as she lurched into her lines.

Whatever Sir Davenant thought of her prudence that night two years ago, he'd provided her with a livelihood, and not as a snuff-boy, either. She'd started with small roles and proved to be competent. She'd initially enjoyed the work. Its newness and Marguerite's needs provided diversion from her feelings of loss concerning Evan. She'd felt less enjoyment as time passed, however, and now would give it up in a moment if . . .

"Ye damned bawd! Are ye going to act or sit on yer chamber pot?" The catcalls from the pit warned her that she'd missed another cue. She glanced toward the prompter to her left, whose mouth moved, trying to give her the lines. She couldn't hear him above the noise made by the spectators seated right up on the stage:

". . . pheasant was tough and full of shot . . ."

The prompter, sitting on a high stool with his books, stretched his neck over the high-hatted gallants' heads, but she still couldn't hear his voice. The entire scene threatened to fall into confusion.

There—she caught a few words and rushed into her dialogue.

Her fellow actor sauntered across the stage and drawled in her ear, "Sweetheart, we're doing Dekker, not Sheridan, remember?"

Sweetheart. Dekker? She'd said the wrong lines. What were the right ones? What was *wrong* with her? She didn't usually suffer from a weak memory. *Sweetheart.*

A footman in the upper gallery threw an apple core at her. At the same moment, a man rose from a bench in the pit. The stage candles lit his face briefly before he turned his back. Evan? He must have followed her here. And now he was leaving. He'd seen enough of her acting—and enough of the indignity of her life to think he had the whole picture of it. He could go home to his family now, and his new shop, and feel smug that he'd done so much better.

A frenzy of feeling welled in her, sparked by two years of repressed heartache and struggle. She looked out at the faces shouting at her, the hands making obscene gestures, the mouths laughing, swearing, jeering. She deserved better. She hadn't gotten pregnant alone. She deserved at least for Evan to respect her, to understand that she was doing the best she could with the circumstances life had dealt her.

She turned away from those jeering faces, their insults and abuses, and strode from the stage. "What are you doing?" Mr. Randall shouted as she passed through the backstage. She didn't answer, but continued right on outside the theater.

With no cloak, still dressed in her costume, she began to walk in the direction Evan would be going. Blind to the stares that followed her, she walked faster, faster. A well-dressed woman unwittingly stepped before her, and Judith knocked her down. "Sorry," Judith mumbled.

"Aw, ye bitch!" Well dressed, but no lady after all. A bold, overpainted whore.

Judith hurried on. She saw Evan's unmistakable head above the moving throng, and she called his name: "Evan Dugdale!" He seemed *almost* to hear, turned his head just slightly, as a lazy wolf might cock an ear to a distant sound. "Evan, stop!" He turned, saw her, and watched her approach with a frown. She came to a halt before him, heaving in the cold night air to catch her breath. "It isn't the way you think. Not at all."

His mouth quirked in contempt.

"Don't you dare look at me like that! It's enough that I put up with it every night. Those cocksure dandies think they can say anything to me, make any proposition, treat me as if I were merchandise for sale—but I won't have it from you—do you hear me?"

"Everyone can hear you, Mrs. Wetstone."

"And don't you call me that, either! You know who I am."

"Indeed I don't. You resemble someone I once knew, or thought I knew. She seemed innocent and loving, but she turned out to be a liar, and very willing to sell herself as merchandise to the highest bidder."

She drew her hand back before she even thought, and delivered a blow that hurt her palm at least as much as it did his cheek. As the imprint went white on his face, and then turned fiery red, his eyes blazed with distaste. She saw he'd never believe her, she might as well try to wreathe iron pokers into love-knots. But her tongue always had lived a life of its own. "I lied to you about Matthew because I loved you. It was a mistake, but I realized that too late—the very night of your wedding, in fact."

He stood as stiff as a grave marker. All about them curled

the voices of others, the noise of strangers. "What are you talking about?" He flung up a hand. "No, I don't want to know. I have to get back. And shouldn't you be on stage right now?"

"You will listen to me! You owe me at least that much. You owe your daughter."

His closed expression accepted that without changing.

"I came to Netter's the night you married." She'd already said that. It was coming out all muddled and he wasn't listening anyway—but she didn't care, she felt so angry. "Sir Davenant found me in the courtyard, and I persuaded him to help me. He gave me my start in the theater—because I couldn't go home. Father had arranged to give away my baby. Our baby." There. Did he understand now?

They had stopped before a bakery. The golden aura from its window fell across his coat. His mouth opened, as if to make some sneering comment, but nothing came out except the smoke of his breath in the chill air.

Her own voice shook. She felt a knob in her throat. "Her name is Marguerite."

Still nothing from him. She felt a great disappointment, and realized that she'd foolishly hoped for surprise, delight: Judith! Why didn't you tell me sooner? She turned and rubbed her arms, feeling the cold at last. What was she doing? She took in the street, the people. Her costume was attracting attention. She touched her wig of long, colorless hair, her made-up face. What a sight she must make. What a fool she looked, and not because she'd come out dressed as a witch.

A hand gripped her arm, stopped her. "What are you saying, Judith?"

"It doesn't matter." Her lips barely moved. "I have to go." She held her face in a blank mask by sheer will, praying that it wouldn't crack, that she wouldn't humiliate herself further by giving away the fact that she'd just broken her own heart—again.

"Don't turn away from me!"

She looked over her shoulder into Evan's face to find it twisted with anger.

"If what you say is true, I have a right to know it all—everything!"

"You don't want to know. Go home to your wife and son, your pretty sister, your lovely shop." Every reason for not telling him sprang up now like the Hydra's heads.

His grip on her arm grew painful. "I swear, if you don't tell me—"

"You couldn't marry me so I told you I'd decided to marry Matthew. And then I told my father I'd been spoiled by a stranger. I spent four months locked in my room. He told people I was ill, that I was in the country recovering. I went along because . . . I was a fool. But when the baby came, he tried to give her away as an orphan.

"So I brought her to you. I realized I should have told you the truth, that we would have managed. But you'd married that very day." She forced her mouth into a bitter smile. "I don't expect anything from you, Evan. I saw you leave the theater, and suddenly I couldn't bear for you to think so badly of me." She managed an acid laugh. "I remain full of vanity to the end, you see."

"Take me to her. I want to see this child. *Now.*"

Evan paid for a coach to take them to her lodgings. They sat unspeaking, and he tried to ignore her shivering. He didn't want to give her his coat—or anything else. When asked if he had a handkerchief, he handed it over reluctantly, and pursed his lips as she ruined it by wiping away her garish makeup. She pulled off the wig and her hair fell down in that golden mantle he'd loved so well. He tried not to love it now. What was he doing, giving in to this absurd story? Even if she had a child, it could be anyone's.

She claimed Sir Davenant had championed her. Now that he thought about it, he hadn't seen the playwright since his marriage to Nancy. He'd assumed some other confectionery, or one of the new coffee or tea shops, had drawn the man's trade away from Netter's.

In this way, throughout the ride, his mind flared with vague then bright then vague again reflections—but with no clear vision of the one thing necessary, that Judith was telling the truth. He'd fought so hard for everything he had, especially his peace of mind, that he could scarcely bear to part with it now. He would pay almost any price to keep it, for if it were lost, how could he go on?

Her lodgings, beyond the narrow foyer, were not elaborate, consisting of a small and rather shabby parlor that smelled unmistakably of old cat urine, and a bedchamber beyond, lit by a single oil lamp. By its smoking light, he saw a woman sitting with her back to him in a very old oak chair. She was bent over, speaking low. To a child? She turned, stood, her hand going to her mouth. "Oh, dear!"

Walters, more elderly than ever. And at the moment as gray faced as cold ashes.

A child peeped around her skirts. "Mama!" She wore a clean little nightdress as she raced to Judith, who picked her up with a strained smile. "Mama funny!" She laughed, examining her mother's outlandish costume.

"Mama has been playing dress-up again." Judith and Walters shared a glance of apprehension as Evan stood in the doorway.

The child looked sturdy. She took her features from her mother, rosy and angelic, with long honey-colored eyelashes against white cheeks. Judith's daughter, yes, but who had fathered her? Part of him wanted desperately to go on believing she'd tricked him once and was trying to trick him again. It would be easier that way, more comfortable by far. But then the little girl looked at him, her head held birdlike to one side. "Man."

Evan stood transfixed. So like her mother, with a mind keen and fresh and alert for anything new and interesting.

"Marguerite, you mustn't be rude. This is Mr.—"

"I'm your father." What else could he say? Her eyes, green, were the Dugdale eyes he'd inherited from his own father and passed on to this child Judith had borne in secret, as she'd borne her father's abuse and two years of friendless responsibility. The enormity of what had befallen her—because of him—was suddenly and terrifyingly real. He took a step further into the room, closer to this frightening shock, to within a glove's length of it. "I'm your father, sweetheart." He sounded calm, yet he stood there stupidly, his arms hanging. He must do something. So he bent and kissed the perfect little cheek.

He heard Judith's breath catch, saw her enormous soft brown eyes fill with tears.

"You have a brother," he went on to Marguerite. Because he must say something! "He's younger than you, and can't talk so well yet, but I think you'll like him. His name is Johnnie. Would you like to live with him and be his big sister?"

"Evan!" Judith gasped, "you can't take her from me!"

"No, I meant . . ." He couldn't seem to get it out while looking at her, so he looked back at Marguerite. "I meant that your mother should marry me. Don't you think so?"

"But Nancy," Judith whispered.

"Nancy didn't survive Johnnie's birth. The apothecary tried everything, bled her, cupped her, used emetics, purges. She died anyway. I've been a widower this past year."

Judith's knees gave way.

Walters sprang to take Marguerite as Evan caught Judith. As he held her in his arms once more, all his checked memories came flooding back. He hadn't allowed himself to believe his life lacked anything, but he'd yearned for this, this woman as beautiful as morning, as gentle as a fawn, as sustaining as new bread and butter, her slightness, her golden hair, her gentle splendor. For once he wished he were more religious, because he needed a little divine courage just now. Making do with what he had, he said, "Will you forgive me, sweetheart? Can you?"

Her eyelids fluttered. Marguerite, in Walters's arms, surveyed them in a judging and intelligent manner. "Mama, say 'Yes, thank you, sir.' "

Judith laughed weakly. Then, strengthening, said, "Yes,

thank you, my dearest, my beloved sir." She put her arms around him.

Walters, sniffing and smiling, mumbled, "Come child, let's leave them alone."

As the door closed, Evan said, "I had no idea. I should have guessed. But I was so wrapped up in what I wanted. How can you forgive me so easily?"

"I never blamed you, beloved."

"Judith, I missed you so much. You'll never know."

She stroked the nape of his neck just as she used to do. "I do know."

In the morning's bitter chill, Judith woke reborn and in love with life. Evan called early to take her and Marguerite to meet Johnnie and Katherine. She loved Katherine immediately, especially her rich, juicy laugh. Evan made a tender and personal father. Marguerite and Johnnie wouldn't be brought up in a ruthlessly disciplined atmosphere ruled by a father who perceived himself as a stand-in for God. Evan showed her the apartments over his shop, and a great surge of happiness enveloped her as she went from room to room. She would live the rest of her days here.

They were married quickly. They held a party to which only their closest friends were invited. Sir Davenant came, and unexpectedly brought the famous actor William Rowly. During the flurry to welcome these lofty guests and serve them Evan's delicious vanilla-flavored chocolate, the playwright told the bridegroom expansively, "I brought Rowly because you may as well have some of this theater business. The bitter coffee these actors drink can't compare to a good mug of chocolate. Rowly's appetite is especially in need of revision."

Hearing this, the actor rewarded the party with one of his finest theatrical gestures: He touched his heart and swayed like a man seeking to hide a grave hurt from an implacable enemy. But when he tasted Evan's recipe, he declaimed, *"The little sweet doth kill much bitterness."*

Later, he bowed over Judith's hand. "I've admired your work, Mrs. Wetstone."

"I'm Mrs. Dugdale now, and happy to say I'm giving up the stage."

"A prudent choice," said Sir Davenant, smiling fiercely. "Your memory failed you grievously during your last performance. Perhaps you'll play the dutiful spouse better."

She answered tartly, "The devoted but *independent* spouse, sir."

Katherine laughed, and Walters smiled, covering her mouth. "Oh, my!"

The party became less quiet, and Judith's happiness felt complete. As she stood surveying the landscape of her bliss, she felt Evan's arm slide around her, and felt his gaze on her cheek as one feels heat from a fire. She turned to him with a full heart.

"Shall we retire, Mrs. Dugdale?" His head dipped to touch his lips to hers, almost chastely, but causing a smoldering fire to blaze up in her. They had self-consciously avoided becoming intimate while making their wedding plans, but the night ahead would be one of erotic indulgence. Yes, she wanted to be alone with him.

As they started for the apartments where their marriage bed awaited, their friends' bawdy remarks followed them. Judith didn't mind, for she knew they made an enviable picture, so in love, cocooned in a happiness of the sort that makes others happy to see it and makes the world a better place.

SWEET DREAMS

Sandra Kitt

✥ Prologue ✥

$\mathcal{M}$acKenzie Philips looked at his watch and shook his head at the excited cacophony of children's voices as they shouted over each other to be heard. Above it all he could hear the patient admonishment of the shop owner, who'd been warned in advance of the lunchtime visit of his nieces and nephews.

"You have five minutes," MacKenzie said firmly. The two older of the five children crowded against the display case of candy, turned their attention to him.

"Five minutes! But I can't decide," wailed eleven-year-old Cara, her teakwood-hued features a study in youthful confusion. She pulled absently on a braid extension in her ponytail, gnawing the beaded end between her teeth.

"I know what *I* want," her twin Casey said giving his order to the woman behind the counter.

"Uncle Mac, can I get both of these?" asked Aimee.

MacKenzie arched a brow at his niece, amused that at nine she'd already learned that a sweet voice and disposition, a guileless expression, would likely get her anything she wanted. Just like her mother, he thought. He shook his head.

"No way. You know the rules. One box apiece."

He noticed that the two youngest, Joel and Christie, seven and five, respectively, had finished their shopping and were proudly holding the wrapped boxes against their chest.

"Okay, let's get a move on. You kids have to be back to

school and I have to get to work. I need to make some money so I can pay for all of this." He grinned and winked at the saleswoman behind the counter, who shook her head and smiled.

"You sure are good to these kids. They're very lucky. Don't you have any of your own?"

Mackenzie chuckled silently and arched a brow. "Not that I know of," he said flippantly.

The woman nodded. "Ohhh . . . not married, either?"

This time he grimaced and his jaw tightened. His brown face took on an expression wrought of bitter memories. "Been there. Done that."

"I hear you," the salesperson shook her head wryly.

"Thanks, Uncle Mac," Cara beamed, skipping to her uncle's side and hugging him as she balanced her purchase under an arm.

MacKenzie accepted a damp kiss from Christie. "You're welcome, baby," he said.

While waiting for Casey to have his candy bagged, the other children gathered around their uncle exclaiming over their purchases and getting into the inevitable debate about which of them had the nicest box. He half listened, amused by their simple logic and funny observations. MacKenzie had come to learn through his sister's children that kids inhabited a totally different world from adults. If they were loved and made to feel safe and encouraged, then their views of the world were innocent and magical. As MacKenzie diplomatically refused to be drawn into the discussion the door to the shop opened and a youngster entered. He noticed that the boy and his nephew, Joel, were known to each other, as the two children briefly waved in acknowledgement.

MacKenzie paid attention to the seriousness of the child and the way he quickly looked around the small shop as if he knew exactly what he was looking for. MacKenzie had experienced from his own brood of nieces and nephews that kids were rarely, if ever, just quiet. But also, there was more thoughtfulness and consideration to this small boy, making him seem much older than his apparent age of seven or eight. He approached the display of candy and, with his nose almost against the glass, he carefully considered each row of chocolate samples. He wore glasses, making his small, dark face look owlish. The frames sat perched on the end of his button nose, adding to the incongruous image of an old man inside the body of a little boy.

"I'm finished," Casey announced, drawing his uncle's attention from the newest customer in the store.

"All right. Everybody wait right here while I pay," MacKenzie said, as he withdrew his wallet from the front pocket of his jeans and approached the counter. "What's the damage?" he wryly asked the cashier, absently watching as she rang up five items on the machine.

"Do you have any Sweet Dreams?" the boy piped up.

The woman behind the counter chuckled heartily. "Sweetheart, I *always* have sweet dreams. How about you?" Then she laughed at her own pun.

MacKenzie's attention was again drawn to the little boy. Of course he wouldn't understand the adult innuendo and sly joke. But his serious expression suggested he was thinking about it.

"It's candy," the boy said. His voice was young but with a surprising confidence.

"What does it look like?" the proprietress asked. "It is a hard candy? Does it have a nut and caramel center? Is each piece of candy wrapped?"

The boy blinked, and his glasses slid down his nose. "It's chocolate," he said, as if that should explain everything.

The woman was shaking her head. "I'm sorry, sweetheart, I don't think I have what you want. Never heard of Sweet Dreams before. I have something called Chocolate Dreams, how 'bout that?"

The child shook his head firmly. "It's not the same thing."

"Why don't you look in the case, then? Maybe there's something else you want." She turned her gaze to MacKenzie, who stood listening with interest to the conversation. "That'll be eighteen seventy-five."

He absently handed her a twenty-dollar bill and watched

as the young boy carefully scanned the candy in the case once again. He looked around the store before turning his attention to the staked boxes on the counter with their pretty floral wrapping paper and bright red ribbons. He pointed.

"How much for those?"

The shop owner looked at the stack of boxed candy, and back to him."That's the most expensive box of candy I sell. I don't think you can afford that, baby. How much money you have to spend?"

MacKenzie accepted his change and turned to his waiting nieces and nephews. Behind him the little boy zipped open a pocket on his jacket and stuck his hand in. When he withdrew it he was clutching a few wrinkled dollar bills and a fistful of coins. The woman reached over the counter to accept the money but frowned as she counted, an indication to MacKenzie that the boy did not have enough. He felt someone patting the side of his thigh and he looked to find Aimee whispering. He leaned down closer.

"He goes to our school."

"Oh, yeah?"

She nodded. "He's in Joel's class. And you know what else? His daddy died."

MacKenzie raised his brows. "Is that right? When?" MacKenzie asked.

Aimee shrugged. "A long time ago. Maybe last year."

"What's his name?"

Aimee pointed indiscreetly. "Shane Corey."

"I think I have something that would be nice," the saleswoman said to the boy, reaching for a box of candy that was considerably smaller and less attractive than the one indicated by him. "How about this one?"

The child shook his head and pointed to the box on the counter. "I want that one."

MacKenzie turned to the waiting children. "Wait outside while I take care of something. Don't you move until I come out. Cara and Casey, you two are in charge, you hear?"

With a chorus of "Yes, Uncle Mac," the children trooped through the door as they were told.

MacKenzie returned to the counter. He took out his wallet again and passed another bill to the woman. "Let him have the box he wants. I'll pay the difference."

"But it's almost fifteen dollars, mister."

"That's okay," MacKenzie said.

"Fine," she nodded.

While she rang up the sales and put the box in a bag, MacKenzie leaned against the counter and turned to the small child. "So, are these Sweet Dreams for you, or do you have a girlfriend?" he teased.

The boy peered at him through his glasses as if the idea was gross. The lens magnified his eyes to the size of chocolate kisses. "I don't have a girlfriend. It's for my mother, for Valentine's Day. But I can't find the one she likes."

MacKenzie nodded and pursed his lips. He took the large package from the saleswoman and handed it to the boy. "You were a little short of money, so I gave the cashier the rest. Here. I hope your mother likes the candy."

The child stared at the box. "I'm not suppose to take money from strangers," he muttered earnestly.

MacKenzie nodded. "Smart thinking." From an inside pocket of his jacket he withdrew a leather case with business cards. He gave one to the boy. "I tell you what. Here's how you can reach me. It has my beeper number. When you save up your allowance, you can pay me back. My name is MacKenzie." He held out his large hand.

The youngster hesitated and finally accepted the card and the candy. He put out his small hand and shook MacKenzie's. "My name's Shane."

"Nice to meet you, Shane," he responded, amused by the way the boy's hand disappeared in his.

The two left the store and MacKenzie found himself surrounded by children. He looked at his watch again. "We're gonna be late. Let's go, let's go . . ." He clapped his hands, and the kids began to hustle in a loose ragged formation toward their school, four blocks away. With a slight, nonchalant gesture of his hand, MacKenzie indicated that Shane should join them, and the boy ran to keep up with his nieces and nephews. Only Christie hung back to hold onto his hand as he slowed his long strides to keep pace with her short legs.

MacKenzie listened quietly to the childish conversations which now included the new boy, Shane. Their young voices made him feel oddly peaceful, if a little reflective. For one thing he wondered if he and his sisters had been like this when they were young. Not so much mindless, saying anything that came into their heads, as innocent. Being around his sister's kids often made MacKenzie wonder what it might have been like to have some of his own. His friend Conrad razzed him all the time about hanging out with "midgets," and Gina told him often enough that he enjoyed all the good stuff about being with kids without any of the work or worry. Was he using his two sisters' children for what he might be missing?

MacKenzie found himself studying the boy Shane, remembering Aimee's information about the death of the child's father. Which made MacKenzie wonder about Shane's mother. He tried to conjure up the image of a grieving widow raising a child alone and mourning a dead husband. Did Shane have sisters and brothers? Had his mother already replaced his father with someone else? He grimaced. She probably had. But MacKenzie considered the self-assured way Shane had gone about looking over what the candy store had to offer, knowing exactly what he wanted to get his mother. He was curious about a woman who could instill such love and devotion, inspire such thoughtfulness in a child so young.

They reached the corner and in the distance the school bell was already peeling the start of the afternoon session. With the kids preceding him like so many little ducklings, MacKenzie walked them across the street back to the school grounds. He stood facing them and raised a hand to get their attention.

"Okay, listen up. Number one, put your candy away in

your schoolbags as soon as you get to your classrooms. Two, don't forget to hide it until Valentine's Day. And three—*don't* eat any." The kids giggled.

"I'm putting mine under my bed," Joel declared.

"That's dumb. Aunt Laura's gonna see it when she vacuums," Casey snickered.

"Never mind all that now. Go on. Be careful and watch out for Christie," MacKenzie ordered, watching the kids hurry toward the building. Only Shane hung back for a moment, looking up at him thoughtfully, his eyes bright behind his glasses, his small brown face so serious.

"How come you didn't get a Valentine for your mother?" he asked.

Mackenzie studied him. "My mom passed away many years ago."

Shane thought about that and nodded sagely. "That's okay. I don't have a father."

"I'm sorry to hear that."

He blinked at MacKenzie. "Do you have a girlfriend?"

MacKenzie cleared his throat, thrown off guard by such an up-front question from a pint sized kid. "Sometimes," he hedged. He flicked his hand toward the school. "You better hurry. Be cool."

"I will. Bye, Mr. MacKenzie." The boy waved awkwardly.

MacKenzie stared after the little boy for a moment before heading toward his parked Jeep for the drive back to his work site. He decided that Shane Corey's mother was a lucky woman: A dead husband notwithstanding, she had a great kid. He thought of all the traps and pitfalls awaiting young black boys like Shane or his own nephews in the world at large, and in some black communities in particular. MacKenzie considered his sister's children. All in all they were good kids. Perhaps Shane's mother would fare better than many single moms. Although the chances were slim and none.

"Too bad," MacKenzie murmured to himself. Shane Corey

was already showing signs of growing up to be a smart young man.

And he wondered who Shane Corey favored. His mother . . . or his father.

❧ Chapter 1 ❧

*J*ill Corey couldn't decide what made her angry the most. That her car was acting up and threatening total shutdown, or that her son had disobeyed one of her cardinal rules: Don't talk to strangers. The car she could get fixed when she had available funds again. But her son was a different matter. She couldn't ever replace him.

She parked the Corolla in the municipal lot and gingerly turned off the engine, hoping that if she treated the troubled car kindly it wouldn't leave her stranded in downtown Chicago later when she wanted to leave. When Jill climbed out of the car her destination was made easier to recognize by the horrible racket of heavy machinery and the naked framing of a new building going up. She stood still for a moment, feeling the jerky pounding of a jackhammer as if it were inside her head. The February frost and the dreariness of the overcast day also seemed to seep into her bones, while her stomach protested what little she'd eaten for breakfast and the strong industrial type smells from the new construction.

For a moment Jill considered letting the matter with her son drop. It was only a box of candy after all, and it was the thought that counted. At least for Shane. She had no idea what was on the mind of this MacKenzie Philips. Taking a deep, fortifying breath and swallowing the faint hint of bile waiting at the base of her throat, Jill decided that as a mother she had to find out.

She crossed the street from the municiple parking lot. She was ignored as brawny and grimy workmen went about their business of the new construction. The noise was deafening and blasted out in all directions. The Chicago pedestrians around her, however, seemed more impervious to the racket than she was. Jill felt the tingling of sweat begin to break out on her forehead and neck despite the fact that the temperature hovered in the midthirties range. There was an angry twist of pain in her stomach which also made her hesitate. No matter how important *she* thought her mission was Jill knew that Maggie, her neighbor and erstwhile surrogate mother, would be fit to be tied if she knew where Jill was just then.

Jill spotted a middle-aged black man in clean khakis and a hard hat who appeared to be a supervisor. She approached him as he gave instructions to a worker. He saw her coming and stood to block her path.

"Sorry, lady. You'll have to cross the street. There's work going on. . . ."

"I know. I want to speak to whoever's in charge. Is there a foreman or someone like that around?"

He looked her over, the expression on his dark brown face changing from dismissive to open consideration. "You can talk to me," he said smoothly. "Maybe I can help."

Jill straightened her spine and gave him what she hoped was a cold look. "This is a personal matter. I want to talk to whoever is responsible for all the men on this crew."

The man was taken aback by the tone of her voice. He looked her up and down with a certain kind of insolence that suggested he didn't like women talking to him in that way.

"You sure make big demands for someone so little," he shook his head.

"Can't you answer a straight question?" she asked reasonably, as if she was chastising an adolescent.

He raised his brows and pointed to one of three white and blue trailers that apparently housed the management offices for the construction site. "Over there," he shouted above the noise and, having been discouraged from initiating any other overtures, he turned back to his clipboard and papers.

There were puddles of water and mud between the start of the construction barricades and the trailers. There were patches of what remained of a heavy snow fall, a week and a half earlier just after Valentine's Day, that were now filthy little hills of melting ice. Jill pulled her collar up and held it closed at her throat against the cold. She could see and feel her own breath turning to vapor as it hit the air. Stepping as carefully as she could she approached the one trailer that seemed to be where most of the workers came and went. She knocked sharply and pulled the door open without waiting for a response.

There were four men inside the trailer when Jill entered. They were lounging about having coffee, laughing in deep masculine tones over some joke or shared confidence. It all came to an abrupt halt when she walked in. Three of the men stood up awkwardly, clearly speechless at her appearance in their midst. The fourth man, seated behind a metal desk with one foot propped on a haphazard stack of technical manuals, merely put his foot to the floor and slowly sat forward to stare at her, bracing his forearms on the desk.

Jill remembered to stand as tall as she could, to keep her chin up as she met the steady and silent gaze of all the men around her. They towered over her, like giants. Sure of their power. Masters of the universe. She was used to that kind of physical posturing. She'd learned not to let herself be intimidated in any way by other people because of their size. Attitudes and deep voices did *not* make someone a man, she thought sarcastically. Two of the men were black, including the one seated at the desk.

"I'd like to speak with whoever's in charge here," she said clearly, sweeping her gaze around the narrow room. The silence was suddenly broken by the rustling of the men's movements now, a quiet chuckle here, a shifting of feet there. One man with iron gray hair and mustache and blue eyes shook his head and headed for the door.

"That lets me out. I just work in the trenches," he said exiting, followed by the laughter of his comrades.

Another man, adjusting his hard hat atop blond hair pulled back into a short ponytail, pointed in the direction of the other two men. "I'll be up on three, Conrad. We're going to need to see you about those changes." Nodding to Jill he, too, left.

Jill stood waiting as the exodus went on. Only the two black men remained. She didn't know which one was supposed to be Conrad, but it didn't much matter. She faced them both squarely, ignoring the grin of pure amusement and flirtation on the one man's face. It was a handsome face, richly brown with strong, well-defined features. Judging from the thorough assessing look he gave her Jill could guess that he was fully aware of his masculine good looks. She gave credit where credit was due. But she was hardly interested.

The man pointed both of his index fingers to the side at the last man seated adjacent to him, like he was directing traffic. "He's the one you want. But I'd sure help you if I could," he said with a charming smile.

Jill bet he could change most female minds on just about anything. She turned her gaze to the last man. He was checking her out, but not in the same obvious way as his coworker. She was aware that he had fixed his attention on her from the moment she'd walked in. He was the only one who hadn't spoken yet, but he was openly studying her. She returned his attention and was glad for the winter parka she wore that covered most of her body, leaving little for his interest or imagination to strip away from her. Her first impression of him was one of bigness. The broad shoulders under a denim jacket, which was worn over a chambray blue work shirt. He was clean shaven, unlike the other men who had varying degrees of facial hair. He had large hands, wide and blunt and clean as they played with a book of matches.

"Can I help you?" he finally asked.

She didn't let herself be swayed or affected by the rich deep smoothness of his voice, by the serious tone of his inquiry. "Are you in charge?" Jill asked bluntly.

The corner of his mouth lifted. Caution and amusement filled his dark eyes. "That depends."

The first man chuckled.

Jill ignored him. She tried not to grimace, but she slowly shifted from one foot to another and held her position. "This concerns my son. . . ."

The other man got up abruptly from his chair. "Ooops. I'm outta here. I have to see a man about a horse," he grinned, grabbing a hard hat and his jacket. He tapped the remaining man on the shoulder with his fist. "Talk to you later, man," he said significantly.

Jill waited until he was gone, knowing that her appearance was probably going to be the topic of some future conversation. When the door closed again she was left alone with the last man who faced her. Her impression of him shifted sharply when he stood up. He was not as tall as she'd first imagined, seated behind the desk. Not quite six feet, although that hardly mattered since the top of her head didn't even reach his chin. But what did strike Jill was the firm, athletic proportions of his body. He was lean and narrow in the hips and waist. No beer belly or flabby middle. Through the jeans was evidence of muscled thighs and calves. The cuffs and open neck of his shirt revealed thick wrists and the strong column of his neck. His face, the color of a walnut, was oblong with a square chin. He had prominent cheekbones and hooded eyes.

He came around to the front of the desk and, keeping his darkly intense eyes on her face, pulled a chair forward, scraping it noisily across the pine-wood floor of the trailer. The sound grated on her nerves and made her wince.

"Would you like to sit down?" he asked and stood watching her.

Jill accepted, more grateful than she could admit to in that moment. "Thank you," she murmured, sitting stiffly.

He sat on the edge of the desk in front of her, crossing his arms over his chest as he regarded her closely. "If there's a problem maybe I can help. I'm the boss."

His voice had a striking deep tone. His words were clipped with authority. He certainly spoke like someone who made the decisions and took charge. Jill shrugged her purse from her shoulder and reached inside the contents.

A frown of curiosity drew his brows together. "I hope you're not carrying a gun," he murmured flippantly. "Whatever the problem is, we can work it out."

Jill withdrew a large box of candy, beautifully wrapped and unopened, and held it up. "One of your men gave my son money to buy this." He pursed his mouth, his frown deepening as he flexed his jaw muscles. He reached out and took the box from her. He placed one end of the box against his leg and rested his hands on the upward end. "I have something I want to say to him," Jill said, letting some of her annoyance show in her voice.

"Yeah, I can see that," he nodded.

"His name is MacKenzie Philips."

He considered her a moment longer and finally held out his hand to her. "I'm MacKenzie Philips."

Jill stared at him, ignoring the extended hand. She hadn't considered that Philips and the man in charge would be one and the same, or that *this* man would be both. She looked him over again thoroughly. Jill realized now that she had expected someone rough around the edges, bold but simple. The man before her swept that image right out the window. She stared at his offered hand knowing she'd come to seek vindication. She looked into his face and her perceptions shifted again as she saw before her, not someone with masculine arrogance and macho ego, but a man with maybe some sense of protocol and civility. He was not going to puff out his chest and become defensive or try to blow her off. He was going to listen. Jill wanted to be angry and indignant. She wanted to set him back on his heels, but it was hard when he seemed perfectly willing to deal with her openly.

Jill slowly put her hand in his and felt the firm strength,

but also a gentle consideration in the squeeze of his fingers. "I'm Jill Corey."

MacKenzie nodded. "Your son is Shane, right?"

Jill wouldn't let herself be persuaded by the calm in his voice. If anything his self-assurance and tone irritated her, as if he hadn't a clue why she'd bother to track him down. All of Jill's anger and fears for her son quickly came to life and she narrowed her gaze on MacKenzie Philip's face. She pulled her hand free.

"You had no right to give my son money."

MacKenzie seemed only mildly surprised by her reaction. He tapped the box with his finger tips, his eyes bright with a suspicious hint of amusement as he stared at her. "Didn't you like the candy?"

She glared at him. "That's not the point."

"Okay, first things first. I didn't give your son any money."

"Shane couldn't have paid for that on his own." She pointed to the box. "It's too expensive. I can't accept it. Beside, I've told him time and time again not to accept things from strange people."

Surprisingly, MacKenzie laughed. The sound held Jill's attention. She was fascinated with the way it seemed to spiral up from somewhere in the center of his chest and bark forth in a pleasant but hoarse sound. It didn't have that kind of black-male cackle that sometimes got on her nerves when it was filled with contempt and vanity. Male posturing.

"Some people might agree with you that I'm strange," he said.

"I didn't mean it that way," Jill said stiffly.

"I know what you meant," he said. "Look, it was no big deal. You should feel good that Shane was thoughtful enough to remember you on Valentine's Day." He placed his open palm in the middle of his chest. "No one gave *me* any Valentine's candy."

Jill momentarily averted her gaze. She was tempted to grin. MacKenzie Philips didn't seem like a chocolate kind of person, but she would guess that someone like him probably reaped other kinds of rewards whether or not there was an occasion to celebrate.

"The store didn't have what he wanted. Something called Sweet Dreams. . . ."

Jill touched her hand to her forehead, briefly closed her eyes and sighed. "I wish I'd never told him about that. . . ."

MacKenzie noticed her hand was ringless. "He didn't have enough money for what the store *did* have. I only made him a small loan. I told him so."

Jill stared at the box of candy in MacKenzie's hands. Now she felt almost foolish for having gotten herself all worked up over some imagined pervert who'd tried to compromise her child. Leaning forward in her chair she was aware of the male sturdiness of this man, of his confidence and self-control.

"I still won't take it. Shane should have known better."

He nodded. "Shane told me he'd been taught to be careful of strangers. But the candy wasn't from me," MacKenzie said quietly, reasonably. "It was from your son. His heart was definitely in the right place. If you're going to give it back, you'll have to give it to him."

The reminder of Shane's good intentions made Jill reconsider. That was the point, wasn't it? That her son had the foresight and generosity of spirit to think of her. Last year in school he'd made her a cover out of popsicle sticks for the tissue box in the bathroom. The year before it was a decoupage pin made from an image of flowers found in a magazine. This was the first time Shane had attempted to save his allowance to buy something for her. And she had turned it down.

Jill avoided meeting MacKenzie's gaze, which she knew was watching for her response and reading into her actions, second-guessing her doubts and confusion. And she was not unaware that, in his own way, he was trying to make the moment easier for her when he certainly didn't have to. But it still annoyed Jill that although she knew she had a righteous cause, *she* now felt on the defensive.

"Shane and I have a business arrangement," MacKenzie

broke into her quiet thoughts. "I lent him the extra money for the candy, but he owes me. I wasn't trying to insult you or overstep your authority. I was just trying to help him out."

Jill wanted to apologize, but then realized she had nothing to apologize for. She was, after all, concerned about the safety and welfare of her child. Her anger was not inappropriate . . . simply misplaced. Jill silently reached into her opened purse and took out her wallet.

"Here, then. Take this and—" she held out several bills.

MacKenzie shook his head firmly. "No. I can't take that from you."

Jill sucked her teeth. This was getting ridiculous. She couldn't keep the candy, and he wouldn't take the money. She was cold, her stomach was acting up and she needed to get back home. She dropped her hand back in her lap, feeling exhausted.

"What is it with you? Why are you being so difficult about this? I'm the one who has a right to be mad."

MacKenzie carefully placed the box of candy on his desk and stood tall. He placed his hands in the front pockets of his jeans and looked down at her. "There's another principle here. Yours is probably motherly ethics or something like that. Fine. Mine is a male thing."

"A what?" Jill asked, irritated and incredulous.

He shrugged smoothly. "Shane and I have a business deal, plain and simple. If you like I'll write out an IOU for him. . . ." he leaned over the desk and reached for paper and pen. Bending over he scribbled something and then handed the sheet to Jill. "Think about it. If you give his gift back, how do you think your son is going to feel? If you don't let him finish with me himself, you'll short change him on learning how to handle situations he's gotten himself into. Let him deal with this himself. It's between me and Shane."

Jill reluctantly accepted the IOU and read it. Sure enough he'd written out the balance owed him for the candy. She didn't want to admit that maybe MacKenzie Philips was right. She grimaced at the roiling in her stomach. "This is getting too complicated. . . ." she murmured, ready to give up.

MacKenzie didn't answer. Instead he turned away from her and headed to a table that had all the makings for coffee or tea. He filled a styrofoam cup with hot water and poured in an instant hot chocolate packet. He returned to her, stirring the mixture before handing it to Jill. Surprised, she accepted it and sipped carefully at the hot liquid. Instead of sitting on the desk again MacKenzie took the seat next to her. Having him suddenly so close made her feel peculiar, like she wasn't going to get enough air and couldn't breathe. Like he was stepping into her space and was going to ask something of her. She looked into his face. Jill tried to guess how old he was, tried to see beyond the physical man to what might be inside. But it had been years since she'd had any interest in a man other than Keith, and her skills of curiosity and easy conversation were skewered. She didn't so much relax as give in to the recognition that her encounter with MacKenzie Philips was a draw. And he was actually being rather nice to her.

"Are you really in charge?" she asked.

MacKenzie smiled. "I own the company," he supplied.

"Oh," she said, truly surprised.

He shrugged. "I know. Still hard to believe. A black-owned company with this kind of contract. I'm also doing some work out at O'Hare. Some of us still have to prove ourselves over and over again, but I've been at this awhile. I have a track record."

"So . . . did you start out as a construction worker?"

He grinned at her naivete. "So to speak. I was with the Army Corps of Engineers for three years. I worked construction while I got my degree in engineering when I left the service. How about you?"

Jill hadn't expected the question, and she found herself shutting down protectively. She didn't really have an answer. So much of her life had changed from what she'd perceived it would be. She didn't know if maybe she'd had too many expectations . . . or not enough. She was still trying to find her footing after one too many crisis in the past several years. Too many disappointments.

"I'm a resource room teacher. I mean, I was. Then I went back to school for an MLS." She hid her confusion by drinking more of the cocoa.

"Ummm," he nodded absently.

MacKenzie watched her, noting the smooth, fine texture of her skin. Her face was tan, and her eyes were a translucent brown, like root beer. Her hair was shoulder length, curled loosely at the ends and with a fringe of bangs across her forehead. He was struck with how young Shane Corey's mother seemed . . . and not so much waiflike as just small. There were some very faint freckles on her cheeks and she had fine, straight brows that only added to a look that wasn't the least sophisticated. Her mouth was the most noticeable feature. Beautifully shaped, full and curved . . . and very inviting. There was a dimple in her chin. To MacKenzie, Jill Corey seemed to be a contradiction in terms. She didn't look particularly strong but she'd stormed his office to confront him, like a tigress protecting her young. And ready to rip his heart out.

MacKenzie came back to that one statement from his niece almost two weeks ago as they'd left the candy store. About Shane's father being dead. Now it returned with a compelling need for verification. He rested his elbows on the arms of the old wooden chair and made a temple of his clasped hands. He watched her over the peak. "I think it's important that you and Shane's father are teaching him to be careful. There are folks out there who can't be trusted. I just don't happen to be one of them. I have nieces and nephews who'll vouch for me."

The mention of her husband had an immediate affect. Her whole expression and body language changed. She finished the rest of the cocoa and stared into the empty cup. Her mouth tightened and her nostrils flared slightly. Jill stood up abruptly.

"Shane's father died last year. I have to go." But she didn't move.

MacKenzie stood up too, noticing in her response not sorrow or remorse . . . but anger. He was sorry now that he'd baited Jill Corey, however he was alert to her phrasing that it was her son's father who had died . . . not her husband. Standing next to her MacKenzie was again aware of how little she seemed, which really belied a certain steely internal strength he suspected Jill Corey possessed. He took the empty cup from her and placed it on the desk.

"I'm sorry," he felt the need to say. But she wasn't listening. She had placed her hand on the desk for support and stood with her features slightly tight and drawn. He frowned at her. "How far did you have to drive to get here?"

"From Oak Park. It's not that far." Jill took a deep breath and let go of the desk. Her features cleared. She glanced at her watch. "Shane will be getting out of school soon. . . ."

MacKenzie didn't really want to know too much about Jill Corey, yet he wanted to ask her if she was okay. He sensed that she might resent any inquiry that was too personal. He'd already put his foot in his mouth once. The door opened and another worker stepped halfway in. The sudden rush of cold air into the room made Jill shiver.

"Hey, Mac . . . need to know if it's okay to let the guys from local three on in. The BX cable and bundles of six-foot conduit were dropped off yesterday. The electricians are ready to move."

MacKenzie nodded absently, still watching Jill Corey. "I want to talk to the foreman first. I'm on a schedule and I don't want any games or excuses for overtime." He grabbed a yellow hard hat from a peg on the trailer wall.

"I better go. . . ." Jill murmured.

"Look, give me a minute," MacKenzie said and held up his index finger. "Then I'll walk you to your car." He left quickly before she could say no.

Jill stared after him, suddenly fascinated with the way he looked in the hard hat. It was just a piece of equipment, a simple prop. But it transformed him. MacKenzie hadn't bothered with a heavier jacket. His vitality made her feel even colder, but it also made him seem larger than life, capable . . . very sure of himself. It made him seem not so much big and hard, as solid and dependable. That was the way she'd first seen Keith, Jill realized. He'd seemed invincible. But life had proven that he was not.

The trailer was suddenly very quiet and she was cocooned against all the noise and activity on the outside. Nonetheless curiosity of another kind drew Jill to the door. She opened it and stood on the top landing watching where this man, who was persuasive and personable, was going.

Not far. Just to an open yard from where everything could be seen and MacKenzie could hold an impromptu conference with several men. Jill wondered about a black man who had authority and could command so much respect, who got the job done. The question brought on an anger that took her by surprise, and made her chest feel tight with sudden unshed tears . . . and made her ache deep within her soul. She absently hugged herself across the top of her stomach and felt overwhelmed by the memories of Keith, of all that had gone wrong between them.

Jill stared at MacKenzie Philips as he talked to his men, holding their attention. He talked with his hands, standing with his denimed legs braced apart. The hard hat was tilted over his forehead, shadowing his eyes, but she could see the movement of his lips. Jill quickly squelched the turn of her imagination as he moved a few feet to a stationary materials hoist and patted a thick coil of cable. She turned away from the scene, experiencing, for some unaccountable reason, the betrayal and disappointment of her past . . . sheer wishful thinking about the future.

She returned to the hard wooden chair to sit and wait for the return of MacKenzie Philips. She knew she should leave; now would be a good time and he'd never notice. But she continued to sit. Jill was glad that he'd persuaded her to wait. She was glad for the few moments alone. Already she was feeling better. Now she had time to consider the man outside who—the thought came unbidden to Jill out of the blue—already seemed the kind of whom heroes are made.

* * *

MacKenzie chuckled at the comment from the local 3 foreman as the meeting broke up and he watched them walk
away. But his mind was really on Jill Corey. He glanced up
toward the windows of the trailer, imagining her standing
and watching what was going on in the yard. But there was
no one there. He had felt surprise upon first meeting her
and finding out who she was, considering he hadn't given
that box of candy a second thought. The word *cute* kept
coming to mind, but didn't seem descriptive enough given
her caution and self-protective behavior. Now he wanted to
return to the trailer and see if his first impressions had been
right. MacKenzie wasn't really sure why it mattered. She
wasn't his type. His interest in Jill Corey was certainly not
sexual. She looked a little helpless, too, like a while ago
when he thought she was going to pass out. She had a kid.
But MacKenzie knew he was taken with her, the same way
he'd been with her son. There were a lot of questions that
came to mind about her . . . and her dead husband.

In the trailer she was sitting quietly, waiting. He'd half
expected that she would have left. Her eyes were bright and
focused on him; she stood up and they stared at each other.
Their individual appraisal was different from when she'd
first come into the office. Her indignation had been replaced
by tentative respect and admiration. His curiosity had been
replaced by a reluctant concern.

"I really have to go now. I appreciate what you tried to
do for Shane about the candy. I'll make sure he holds up
his end of the deal and pays you back."

MacKenzie shrugged. "No problem."

He held the door as Jill Corey passed through. He momentarily went back inside to retrieve a coat, catching up to her
in the yard. He was careful not to touch her, not even to lend
assistance on the messy cluttered ground. But MacKenzie
watched her slow and careful progress until together, they
reached her car parked across the street in the public lot.
He noticed that the dark blue sedan was covered in winter
grime and a fine layer of dried salt. He watched as Jill

awkwardly settled into the driver's seat and fastened her safety belt. She tried to turn on the ignition but the engine struggled and whined before finally kicking over.

"That didn't sound so good," MacKenzie observed with a shake of his head. "You should have it checked out."

"It's just temperamental. You know how women are," Jill said lightly.

MacKenzie raised his brows at the bit of self-deprecating humor. He hadn't thought Jill Corey had it in her. He grinned in appreciation. As she began to back out of her space he knocked on her window with his bare knuckles.

Jill braked and frowned at him through the glass which was clouding over with condensation. He used his hand to indicate she should put the window down. When she had done so MacKenzie pulled the box of candy from the inside of his jacket and handed it to her through the opening. She took it, wondering if he'd misunderstood her visit to his office. Hadn't she made herself clear?

Whether she had or not didn't much matter to MacKenzie. He returned the candy to her now for a different reason. One of his own. He watched Jill Corey closely, looking for any signs of rejection. But he saw only silent surprise in her eyes.

"Happy Valentine's Day. Again," he said.

✻ *Chapter 2* ✻

*J*ill tilted her head to the side and stood momentarily posed with a package of Raisin Bran in one hand and a jar of apple sauce in the other. She listened for the sounds of the Saturday morning children's program playing with frenzied and over exaggerated drama on the TV in the den. Then she heard Shane's delighted laughter. The sound was reassuring, and she turned her attention back to unpacking the three brown bags of groceries from the market. She made a mental note to change the linens in the two bedrooms, to look for that missing polo shirt of Shane's she hadn't been able to find for a week, and to start the laundry. She had an appointment to get her hair done, but thought that instead she would probably cancel and treat her son to a movie and McDonald's afterward.

She resolutely stayed away from the numerous other things that had to get done, opting instead to stay calm, do what she could, and not worry about the rest. Somehow, God would provide. She began folding down the brown paper bags, putting them away with others she kept stored under the sink to be recycled as liners for the garbage pail.

Jill heard the neighbor's dog begin to bark, but she paid no mind. The dog was always barking at something. Anything that moved within its line of vision, including cars just driving through the street. Jill checked the clock and realized it was time for her vitamins. Standing in front of the sink she ran a glass of cold tap water. As she was taking the last of the tablets, the phone rang.

"Hello," Jill garbled, trying to swallow the pill in her mouth.

"What's wrong with you?" came back the gruff question.

Jill laughed, hearing the instant concern in her brother's voice. "Hey, Jeremy. Checking in on me?"

He grunted. "How's everything going? How's the big guy?"

"He's good. I can't interrupt him right now. He's only allowed to watch TV on Saturday morning and he's been waiting all week for his favorite program."

Jeremy chuckled. "That's all right. Leave him alone. The last time I talked to him he wanted to know when he could come down and spend time with Tony and Brian."

Jill grimaced as the dog in the Jenkins' yard behind hers grew more frenzied in its barking. "I know he doesn't get to see his cousins very often. Outside of school there aren't that many kids in the community that he plays with."

"We told you you could send him down here for the summer."

She shook her head. Then she'd be all alone. "He's still too young to travel by himself."

"Come with him. You could both use a break. I hope you're not trying to run him around all over Chicago to do things," her brother commented with a warning note.

Jill leaned against the edge of the sink and smiled. Once a big brother, always a big brother. "I'm okay. . . ." She stopped suddenly, blinking at the dark shadow that passed just under her kitchen window. "I . . . er . . . I've been resting like I'm supposed to. And Maggie's been watching me like a hawk. I can't cough without her running over here."

"Good. It still makes more sense for you and Shane to come on down here with me and Karen. . . ."

"No."

"At least until you decide what you want to do—"

"No."

"Mama can help with—"

"Jeremy," she interrupted patiently. *"No."*

Jeremy sighed deeply. "You sure are stubborn."

"I don't need a babysitter. I'm doing fine. I don't want to . . ." The shadow passed again in the opposite direction. Jill felt her chest constrict and the barking became urgent, finally bringing her full attention to what was going on outside her house.

"Jill? What's happening?"

"Let me call you back. I . . . I think there's someone walking around outside."

"What! Don't go outside. Call the po—"

Jill hung up. She stood on tip-toe but couldn't get close enough to look completely out the window. She turned and hurried to the one just outside the kitchen but couldn't see anything from there either. She then opened the hall closet and took our her heavy winter parka. While she struggled into the sleeves, she reached inside the depths of the space and moved things around until she found a length of wood. It was Shane's hockey stick.

Jill peeked into the den to make sure that her son's attention was still engaged by his cartoon heros before leaving him alone. She exited the house through the kitchen door. It led to the garage, where the hood of her car was up and someone was bent over the opening.

"What are you doing!" Jill called out, all caution giving way to the fear that some thief was trying to steal her engine. She hurried around the end of the car, weapon poised. She gasped and stared with her mouth open when MacKenzie Philips stood up, holding a plastic bottle of blue fluid.

"Nothing illegal," he said easily as he screwed back on the cap to the unit under her hood where he'd poured the liquid. He then stepped back and closed the hood of the car with a firm push. "I was just adding transmission fluid."

Jill recovered, lowered the stick, and stared at MacKenzie. He was wearing a beaked navy blue cap, a dark brown leather jacket, beige slacks, and heavy winter boots. She blinked at him, having trouble registering that he was actually there. "Why would you do that?" she asked blankly.

"Because you needed it," he said. "I noticed that day I walked you back to your car." Then he looked at her. He noticed the stick and gently took it out of her hand. He chuckled and shook his head. "I'm glad you ask questions first before you start swinging. You could do serious damage with this."

"That was the idea. What are you doing here?" Jill asked, a part of her mind wondering if she looked perfectly awful. She'd twisted her hair into a knot because she didn't know what else to do with it. She wore no makeup.

MacKenzie hesitated, weighing his response carefully. He put the plastic bottle on a shelf. Then stood with his hands in the pockets of his coat and lifted his shoulders. "I was just passing through the neighborhood."

Jill chuckled silently and shook her head skeptically. "That's lame."

MacKenzie grinned and scratched at his jaw. "You're right. Shane called me."

She frowned. "He did? When?"

"Yesterday. When he got home from school. He said you were in the kitchen finishing dinner. . . ."

"That little brat!" Jill said with mild exasperation.

Mackenzie gestured over his shoulder to the continuous barking from the neighboring yard. "Good watch dog."

"Everybody just ignores the barking."

"But you didn't."

Jill shook her head. "I saw someone outside my window."

She stood wondering what to do or say next. Should she invite him inside? Should she call Shane and let him know he had a guest? Should she punish her son for daring to do something so outrageous behind her back? "You don't live around here, do you?"

"No. My sisters do. I live just outside of Lincolnwood."

She hugged herself. "It's . . . nice over there."

"It's cold right here. You want to go inside?" he asked.

Jill looked carefully at MacKenzie. She didn't see anything sly or calculating in his dark eyes. She believed him when he said Shane had called him. Her son was capable of independent and mischievous behavior. If MacKenzie had a hidden agenda she didn't want to stand in her garage thinking about it. She *was* cold.

"Sure . . . come on in. I'll tell Shane you're here," Jill said, leading the way back into the house. Then she hoped that it wasn't too much of a mess.

But that was not what MacKenzie saw when he entered the house. The first thing was that it reminded him of either of his sister's homes. Gina was a fussier housekeeper than Laura, but the one thing they both had accomplished were homes that felt warm, comfortable, lived in. There were pictures on the walls, framed photographs, and plants. There were magazines on the table and books on shelves . . . and children's toys all over. There was also a lot more noise, but sometimes that was a welcomed antidote to being alone. MacKenzie could hear the TV in a distant room, and that was part of a scenario he was used to as well. It seemed a prerequisite for families. TVs that were always turned on. The only time he ever watched TV himself was on Sunday afternoons or Monday night for sports. And then, more often than not, he did so by himself.

Mackenzie stood silently in the middle of the foyer, unzipping his jacket as he looked around. Jill hung up her coat and then reached for his, waiting. But his attention was caught by the astounding realization that Jill Corey was pregnant. MacKenzie tried not to stare but for some reason it affected him much more than he had any right to allow. It seemed kind of odd on her. She was this tiny woman . . . who had this protrusion from her stomach. Gina and Laura had both gained a lot of weight with each of their children. But nothing about Jill seemed out of proportion . . . except the bump that was her developing baby. Maybe she wasn't eating enough, he thought. Or maybe it was still too early. But if so, and her husband was dead . . .

It reminded MacKenzie, once again, that he couldn't understand why he was really there. Things had gotten out of hand. How had he gone from giving a small child a few dollars to a pregnant woman in just three and a half weeks?

Shane Corey had actually phoned him several times since he'd first met him, but MacKenzie now made the decision not to tell his mother about all of the calls. As with the loan of the money, it was something just between him and the boy. He also knew he could have found a way to communicate with Shane far short of coming to his home. MacKenzie knew he could have advised Jill Corey in some other way about her car's need for fluid. He didn't have to see her again. But, here he was, finding excuses for doing just that. Wanting to see if all the impressions he'd first had about her still held up. They did.

"You're staring," Jill reminded him flatly.

"Sorry . . ." he murmured.

Jill said nothing in response, a little unsettled that he was paying so much attention to her physical state. When she'd gone to confront him about the candy she could have cared less that MacKenzie Philips knew she was pregnant. But his awareness now made her feel conspicuous. But she couldn't deal with what MacKenzie might be thinking. She had her own issues to handle. When she'd hung up the coats she silently walked to the den with him following closely behind.

MacKenzie didn't know what to say to her. Should he acknowledge that she was pregnant? Did he think she expected him to? But he was so disoriented by the fact that he made an obvious point of ignoring it, as if it didn't matter to him.

"Did you ever open that box of candy?" he asked. He noticed that she walked gracefully despite the odd shape of her body.

Jill made a lopsided grin. "Shane opened it. He said I was taking too long and the candy was going to spoil. I got one piece. He and my next door neighbor ate most of it. Shane," she said quietly, standing in the den door. "You have company."

Her announcement threw MacKenzie off for a moment, because it occurred to him that Jill hadn't considered for a moment that he might have come to see her. Why would she when he'd been prepared to use her son as a reason?

But it was slightly annoying that she'd relegated him to being just Shane's friend, as if he was one of her son's classmates coming over to play for the afternoon.

For a moment Shane's attention stayed riveted to the screen. Then he slowly turned his head. When he spotted MacKenzie he came to life.

"Mr. MacKenzie!" He jumped up from the floor, ignoring his program. He only spared his mother one guilty blinking look before standing shyly in front of the tall man, a smile on Shane's small face, his glasses sliding down his nose.

"Just call me Mac."

Shane politely looked to his mother for confirmation, and she nodded consent for him to address MacKenzie Philips by his first name.

"Why don't you sit down," she indicated an easy chair to MacKenzie and avoided using his first name herself. She moved an afghan she'd been in the middle of crocheting, putting it in a basket. While she restacked some of Shane's books Jill glanced at MacKenzie and found him watching her closely. "Do you want to stay for lunch? Nothing fancy. Soup and sandwiches."

MacKenzie thought of all the plans he had for the day. He was supposed to meet up with Conrad for raquetball at his health club. He was supposed to drop by Gina's and help her husband Calvin move some boxes out of their basement. But Gina at least had Calvin. "If you'll let me take you and Shane for dinner some night." He could see the doubts forming. She was going to say no. "Nothing fancy. Red Lobster."

Shane bent his head back and glanced up at his mother. "Please, Mommy?" he asked in that beguiling way that children have.

She grinned, and used a finger to push his glasses up his nose. "Shane loves Red Lobster."

"Then it's a deal."

"We'll see. But thanks anyway."

MacKenzie felt himself sinking deeper and deeper. He could stop any time and he knew it. But he swept the warning signals to the back of his mind opting, instead, to find out more about this very likable—and lovely—woman. It didn't seem to matter that her hair wasn't styled, she was dressed in black leggings and an oversized cable knit sweater, or that she was wearing a laughable pair of bedroom slippers that looked like Porky Pig. What MacKenzie did see was that Jill Corey was poised and didn't seem coy. And she wasn't the least pretentious. There was some underlying unhappiness but he guessed that was to be expected given that she'd lost her husband. The fact that she was going to have another baby . . . well, MacKenzie frowned, he'd have to think on that a while.

Jill left them alone and headed back to the kitchen, wondering why someone like MacKenzie Philips would want to waste his time with a widowed woman with one child and another on the way. Beyond the shock of finding him in her garage doctoring her car was the thought that there was no reason in the world why she'd have thought to see him again. But now that he was here, everything she'd learned or thought about MacKenzie Philips in his trailer office that day changed. There was now a sense of familiarity but it still made her uneasy.

Jill couldn't tell if she was pleased . . . or just surprised that he'd found his way to her and Shane. Nevertheless, she quickly located a comb and ran it through her hair, pulling loose the haphazard bun and sweeping the bangs more attractively to the side. She found a headband in the bathroom to hold it in place. She added some lipstick . . . and then wiped most of it away so it wouldn't look so freshly applied. And then she tried to scrub it all off. Feeling utterly foolish and guilty Jill made a dismissing gesture and went to prepare the lunch. . . .

After a few awkward moments of wondering what the hell he thought he was doing there, MacKenzie settled on the edge of the chair, his elbows on his knees, listening to the childish chatter of Shane Corey. But it wasn't idle talk. Shane had first called him because he had the rest of the money from the purchase of the Valentine's Day candy. At first MacKenzie was going to tell Shane to forget about it, then remembered Jill's mission to his office, and how he'd defended the arrangement made with her son, and his motives. The fact that the little boy remembered his obligations said a lot about Shane and the training he was getting from his mother. It was that realization, that despite whatever hardships Jill Corey might be going through right now, and he would guess they were plenty, she paid a lot of attention to her son. MacKenzie liked that. But the other calls from the boy had been something else again.

Shane had once called just to talk, to ask questions. Questions he might have asked his own father had he lived. Things like, are there any black Ninja Turtles, or how come he never knows when he falls to sleep.

"Hey, you're missing your program," Mackenzie said now, finding it more difficult to talk to either Shane or his mother in their home.

"That's okay," the boy shrugged and glanced up at his guest. "Did my mom yell at you?"

"You mean, about the candy? Sort of. How about you?"

Shane pouted a little, but the affect was softened by the raising of his brows over the top of his glasses. "I got punished."

MacKenzie was relieved. Jill Corey might want to get her son to mind her, but she obviously didn't feel that a spanking was required. He would have felt somewhat responsible for that. "So, you had to stay in your room? No TV for a week?"

Shane shook his head. "No. I couldn't have any cookies and milk before going to bed."

MacKenzie tried not to smile. He wondered if Shane Corey had any idea how lucky he was to have Jill for his mom. "Sorry about that. Maybe I shouldn't get milk and cookies either."

Shane widened his eyes in horror. "But you're bigger than she is. She can't make you."

MacKenzie winked. "I bet she could. So, where's that IOU?"

Shane ran to his room and then returned with the now

limp and smudged paper. He handed MacKenzie a handful of money. It was exactly the amount owed.

"Thanks. That takes care of our business," MacKenzie said absently, still feeling reprehensible for taking this child's allowance. He sat staring at the money in his hand, his mind flashing on an image of Jill Corey as she'd stood in the hallway waiting to take his coat and cap. Her dark eyes staring up at him with so much self-assurance and strength. And not an ounce of embarrassment.

His first look around her property showed that the house was a contemporary, good size raised ranch on about a quarter of an acre of property. Everything was neat and clean and the house was obviously in good condition and well maintained. But MacKenzie had noticed that there were things about taking care of the house that Jill had let go. Maybe because the work was too heavy or because of her condition, although he wouldn't put it past her to try. MacKenzie would bet that the gutters needed cleaning, and he wondered if the oil burner had been serviced that year. There were no weeds in the yard but nothing had been planted for spring, either. With a sudden frown he wondered if Jill Corey had enough money to support herself and Shane—and a new baby.

MacKenzie initialed the IOU and gave it back to Shane. "There. We're square."

Shane frowned at him. "Can I do this again?"

MacKenzie raised his brows. "What? Borrow money? You just got out of debt. You don't want to make this a habit, you know." Shane leaned against the side of MacKenzie's chair, almost against his knee. MacKenzie lifted his arm out of the way and placed it around the boy, but not really touching him. With Joel or Cara or Christie he would have given an automatic hug. But he didn't have the right to do that with Shane, although he found the instinct was certainly there. Instead, he just let his arm hang as Shane sidled closer against him. The gesture made MacKenzie feel protective, but in a different way than he was with his nieces and nephews.

"I know. But Mother's Day is coming. I gotta get her a present."

"That's not for a couple of months yet. What do you have in mind?"

"Sweet Dreams," Shane said without hesitation.

MacKenzie laughed lightly. "That again? How about some perfume? Or a little purse or wallet. How about . . ."

But Shane was shaking his head, reminding MacKenzie of that meeting in the store when the boy had his heart set on a certain kind of candy for his mother. He came by his stubbornness honestly, he thought wryly.

"That's her favorite. I like Squashers, and M & M Peanuts."

"Squashers?" MacKenzie asked blankly. Shane nodded, leaning more into MacKenzie's leg, his small fingers playing idly with his watch band. "So how come your mother likes this candy so much?"

Shane shrugged. "I don't know. It has to do with before I was even born. My daddy liked Squashers, too, but he didn't like Sweet Dreams."

MacKenzie didn't have a clue how to respond to that. And that information didn't exactly answer the question. He was not surprised that Shane would have been left with such a strong impression of his late father and remembered so much. But MacKenzie was surprised to find that he was a little bit envious of that adoration. Yeah, his nieces and nephews thought that he was pretty cool, and pounced on him whenever he visited. Yeah, it made him feel special. But they were not *his* kids. MacKenzie stared pensively at Shane Corey, wondering what the boy's father had looked like, what kind of man he was. What kind of husband . . .

"Lunch is ready," Jill called out from the kitchen.

"We'll talk about Mother's Day later," MacKenzie said, committing himself further.

His confusion was compounded when Shane took his hand to lead him into the kitchen, and to the lunch nicely laid out on the round oak table. When they sat down MacKenzie suddenly felt very uncomfortable, as if he was being watched. He looked around the table, at Jill as she poured a glass of juice for Shane. At Shane as he peeked between the slices of the bread to see what kind of sandwich he had. MacKenzie felt as if he'd become part of the family just by being there. He rested his elbows on the edge of the table and quietly considered what it would really be like to have his own family. A wife and children . . . a son. But it's not as if he thought about it a lot. Paula had done quite a number on him and he only had to remember that for any kind of daydream to fade. He stole a curious glance at Jill Corey. She was nothing like Paula. . . .

"MacKenzie, MacKenzie, strong and able, get your elbows off the table," Shane chanted with a wide grin. Then he giggled.

MacKenzie squirmed as he obeyed and shrugged at Jill.

She smiled in apology. "He was taught in Sunday school that it's not polite to put your elbows on the table. Seems old-fashioned, doesn't it?"

"I was taught that, too. Don't tell anyone I had to be reminded by a kid."

"That's my daddy's chair," Shane announced innocently and bit into his sandwich.

MacKenzie stopped with his soup spoon halfway to his mouth. He looked at Jill. "I'll move. . . ."

She shook her head. "You don't have to. It doesn't bother me. I think Shane was just making an observation."

Jill looked thoughtfully at MacKenzie, for the first time wondering about his family and where he was from. It hadn't even occurred to her until that instant to think if he was married with his own kids. The sudden idea made her uneasy because it brought on the memories of a personal history that was not so far in her past that it couldn't still sweep her into momentary anger and despair. She tried a quick comparison of MacKenzie and Keith. But her image of Keith was overshadowed by her strong feelings of his betrayal.

MacKenzie felt Jill's gaze on him and looked up to see the wide-eyed consideration in her eyes. Questioning. He realized, of course, that they didn't know anything about each other. But already they were way past being strangers. Already there were things about Jill Corey that seemed familiar. And yet, MacKenzie felt more uncertain around her than with any other woman he knew. Maybe because all the others had such definite expectations and sometimes hidden agendas. Lumping all men together with suspicion. Some had serious attitude problems. They waited and watched, checking him out for signs of shortcomings. Jill seemed willing to give him the benefit of the doubt. To take him as he was and not ask too many questions. She didn't try to aid in his downfall by planting imaginary land mines. If he failed in gaining her trust, it would be his own fault.

The lunchtime conversation centered around Shane's need for new sneakers, a necessary visit to the eye doctor, and his desire to sign up for karate classes. While he ate MacKenzie mostly listened to the talk between mother and son. Some of it wasn't about anything important but he liked listening to Jill talk. She paid close attention to what her son had to say, as if there was great significance to his thoughts and ideas. She was patient. The teacher and mother in her were apparent.

For Jill it seemed easier to give her attention to Shane rather than to MacKenzie Philips who she was acutely aware of. It had been a long time since any man had sat at the table with her and Shane who wasn't family or Maggie's husband, Ben. Slowly more and more characteristics about MacKenzie were imprinting themselves on her consciousness. He was left-handed. She noted the way he held his sandwich, the slow thoughtful manner in which he chewed. How he tilted his head as he listened to the conversation. The way his gaze caught hers several times and held before they both pulled their attention away. Not from embarrassment but as a reprieve from their mutual curiosity.

"I'm finished. Can I leave the table?" Shane finally asked. But it was MacKenzie who spoke first.

"Why don't we clean up first. And then I need you to help me outside with something."

Jill stopped in the process of stacking plates. "Doing what?" she frowned.

MacKenzie stood up and gathered the soup bowls. "I thought I'd take a look at your garage door."

She felt herself flushing under her skin. Keith had been promising to do that for nearly two years. "You don't have to do that. The door's been up so long it doesn't matter any more."

"It does matter," he countered quietly, watching Shane take the juice container to the refrigerator. "It's too easy to get into your house through the garage. It wouldn't take much to trip the lock on the door into the kitchen." He nodded in that direction.

"But I don't want you to. . . ."

"I can help, Mommy," Shane said. "I know how."

Jill smiled at the eager expression on her son's face. She refused to look at MacKenzie. She didn't want to see any condescension in his probing gaze.

But again, MacKenzie didn't wait for Jill to respond. He picked up the bowls and took them to the sink. "Put the bread away, Shane, and then go get your coat." Shane quickly obeyed. MacKenzie looked squarely at Jill over the boy's head. He remembered what brought about their first meeting. "Okay?" he asked now.

Jill took a damp sponge and began wiping off the table. "Okay," she reluctantly agreed.

After washing up the few dishes from lunch she glanced out the living room window where now she could see where MacKenzie had parked his car. He had his trunk lid up and was reaching inside to retrieve something. Tools, she thought. But when he stood straight Jill could see he was holding two hard hats. His yellow one and one that was blue, which he now handed to Shane. She couldn't hear her son's reaction, but she could see his face. It occurred to her then that she hadn't seen Shane this animated or this talkative with anyone since his father had died. She grew pensive, wondering if her son had been able to sense the tension and unhappiness, all the anger between his parents. If he had he never mentioned it or even referred to it. Of course she'd never encouraged Shane to talk about his memories or feelings, because she had trouble with some of them herself. And Jill realized she wasn't really sure how much Shane might or might not miss his father. Watching MacKenzie with her son, however, made her pay attention. There was a rightness about the way they seemed to get along.

MacKenzie sat the hard hat on Shane's head and he nearly disappeared beneath it. Jill could hear MacKenzie's rich laughter, and the view from her window made her smile. She watched as he adjusted the straps and netting inside the hat. It fit Shane much better, but was clearly too big. It made him look like a turtle.

Then they both disappeared from her line of vision and in another moment Jill could hear a heavy hammering of metal against metal, scraping and grinding and rattling. Yet the mere sound of activity made her feel a bit languid. Suddenly she started and touched her middle. The baby nestled inside her kicked and shifted and made her stomach tighten and move. Jill stood still as it finally settled down again, but not before reminding her she had no right to fantasies about another man.

In another fifteen minutes she heard the distinct sound of the garage door rolling smoothly up and down on its track. When the kitchen door opened again Shane rushed in holding his hat in place with both his hands. He stood next to her and looked up. The hard hat promptly slid forward and down his face. Jill laughed as she grabbed it and set it back in place.

"Mommy, Mac and I fixed the door. Look what he gave me. I have a hard hat just like his."

His eyes were bright and large behind his glasses. His smile was enough to break her heart. She'd been so busy thinking about her own circumstances that she'd almost missed how lonely Shane might be. Yet, she should have known. She had only to listen to her own yearning. She looked at MacKenzie over Shane's head. He stood, large and sturdy and grinning in her doorway, and she was beginning to feel comfortable seeing him there.

"Did you say thank you to Mr. Philips?"

"He said to call him Mac."

Jill looked sternly at her son and didn't say a word.

Shane sighed. "Thank you."

"My pleasure," MacKenzie nodded, taking off his coat again.

Jill watched as he hung his hard hat on the kitchen door knob. There was something so familiar about him doing so. Like he was making himself at home. She gnawed on the inside of her jaw. "I appreciate you fixing that door. But I could have done it," she said confidently.

MacKenzie's mouth quirked at a corner in a barely perceptible smile. "You're welcome, too," he murmured.

"Can I take my hat to school?" Shane asked her now.

"What for? Aren't you afraid you might lose it?"

"But I want to show it to everybody."

"Show and tell?" MacKenzie asked.

Jill hesitated. "We'll see. Go hang up your coat."

Forgetting that MacKenzie was his guest and his attention span shortening quickly, Shane returned to the TV in the den. MacKenzie felt useless standing with his hands in his pockets as he watched Jill pick up a laundry basket and head for the washer-dryer in a little alcove just before the door leading to the garage. He followed behind and took the basket from her. She resisted for a moment and then let go.

"Thank you," Jill murmured. He held it while she efficiently filled the machine. She hastily stuffed clothing into the top loader, hoping that MacKenzie hadn't noticed her underwear. Then she added all her detergents and cleaners. "I'm sure this wasn't how you planned to spend your day off from work," she observed, avoiding his gaze. She felt a wonder and disbelief that MacKenzie Philips was even there, let along that he—engineer, business man, and small loan administrator—would stay to help with her laundry.

"I could be at home doing what you're doing and not

enjoying it at all. Instead I had a pretty nice lunch, and I made some money."

She smiled and grimaced. "I can think of at least five ways I'd rather spend Saturday myself."

He hazard a quick glance at her and became alert. "Oh yeah? How?"

"I'd *love* to go to some of the Saturday lectures at the Harold Washington Library downtown. I'd spend hours in a bookstore browsing and then buy a bunch of books. I'd meet some girlfriends for lunch." Her eyes was bright and whimsical. "I'd take Shane to the Adler. He's never been there and is always talking about the machine that makes the stars come out."

MacKenzie listened thoughtfully, completely taken by the simplicity of Jill Corey's wishes. He went through the list of women he knew and couldn't think of one whose idea of a good time was spending hours in a bookstore. "That's only four," he commented.

The light went out of her eyes. She finished preparing the wash and starting the machine. Jill took the empty basket out of MacKenzie's hands and put it away. "It doesn't matter. None of it is going to happen for a while anyway."

Jill faced him again, about to return to the kitchen. But MacKenzie was blocking her way. He, in fact, took up the whole entrance. His size made her feel so vulnerable. The way he looked at her made her more aware of her pregnancy. She was tempted to pull down on the hem of her sweater, but there was no point. She couldn't hide her condition. She wished she could. It might be interesting to know, for example, if he regarded her as attractive and desirable, or just in need.

She looked up into MacKenzie's face and found his expression pensive, and more than that. There was a deep consideration in MacKenzie's dark eyes, as if he was trying to figure her out. There was also ambivalence and curiosity, and even withdrawal before the ambivalence appeared again. Jill shook her head.

"Look, you can leave if you want. I'm not exciting company these days. You didn't have to come. You don't have to stay."

"How did your husband die?" MacKenzie asked straight out.

The question caught her off guard. The light suddenly faded from her eyes and so did some of her simple pleasure in the day, in having MacKenzie Philips's unexpected company. In having someone else in the house to talk to besides a seven-year-old or Maggie from next door. Jill hesitated, thinking he might apologize for asking so personal a question. But he didn't. He really wanted an answer. She wondered, abstractedly, why it would matter to him. She wondered how much to tell.

"He was killed when a burning building collapsed last December. He was a fireman."

MacKenzie didn't move. Nor did he immediately express sympathy. His eyes seem to watch to see how *she* reacted to the information. Then his gaze swept down the rest of her body.

"And there's another baby on the way."

"You noticed," she murmured flippantly. Suddenly Jill *did* feel awkward and unattractive.

"Yeah . . . I noticed." MacKenzie nodded his head.

Finally, MacKenzie stepped aside and she moved past him back into the kitchen.

"Would you like something to drink?" Jill asked, for want of anything else to say. "I can make coffee. Or there's apple juice. . . ."

"Juice is fine," MacKenzie said, watching as she poured a glass for them both.

Jill sat at the table again. MacKenzie remained standing, leaning against the edge of the counter. She glanced down at her lap, smoothing a hand absently over the mound of her stomach, emphasizing the shape and size. MacKenzie was fascinated with how comfortable Jill seemed about her body. She didn't try to disguise her condition. She didn't play on it or exaggerate. She didn't feel sorry for herself, under the circumstances.

MacKenzie watched as he suddenly tried to conjure up the image of the baby curled and resting inside of her. He felt an unbelievable tightening in his gut; an unexpected wonder. But also, an erotic intensity quickened his breathing at the thought of Jill conceiving. Before she became pregnant, when she was free to make love. He had no picture or perception of her husband as a partner, but it didn't matter just then. MacKenzie was really only aware of her as a woman.

"When are you due?" he asked, following the movement of her slender hand.

"June ninth, according to the doctors. But they're never right. Shane was almost a month early."

"Is it a boy or girl?" he asked, surprised at the depth of his interested.

Jill shook her head. "I don't know. I didn't want to know."

"What do you want?"

Jill considered the question, knowing that MacKenzie would have no idea that it was not a simple question to answer. What she wanted was for everything to have gone differently. She lifted a shoulder absently. "It doesn't matter."

Her response only mildly surprised MacKenzie. His sister Gina had said when she was pregnant that she only wanted a healthy baby.

"The baby will be a way of always remembering your husband, won't it? He would have liked that, I bet," he offered, but felt uncomfortable in the platitude, as if he didn't really believe that himself. Still, there was little reaction from Jill beyond a kind of blank stare.

"Keith never knew about the baby," she murmured. "I found out two weeks after burying him that I was pregnant again."

"Then at least you should be happy about the new baby."

Jill nodded, staring at the floor. She didn't smile or brighten at the observation. "Yes . . . I suppose." Another thought occurred to Jill and she glanced up at MacKenzie. "What was the real reason you came here today?"

He shifted his weight from one foot to another. He'd

hoped that she wouldn't question his appearance too closely. He didn't have much to offer in the way of explanation that wasn't transparent. It would sound strange to say he was just curious.

"I guess I wanted to apologize for getting Shane into trouble, for putting him on the spot. I didn't think about how you would react to that little deal he and I made. You were right to be mad. There are too many things that could have happened. I'm sorry I didn't think about it more carefully." He hesitated. "But ... I'm not sorry that I got to meet you."

Jill hadn't expected quite that answer, but she was impressed with his honesty. And surprised by his confession. If there hadn't been what she now referred to as "the chocolate candy incident," she wouldn't be sitting in her kitchen sharing apple juice with MacKenzie Philips. It made her warm toward him, knowing that he understood her concerns. Jill didn't let herself read anything more into his comment. She smiled slightly.

"Thanks for seeing it from my point of view."

MacKenzie grinned and glanced down at his boots. "Thanks for not having me arrested," he commented dryly.

The thought had crossed her mind. Before she'd gone to see him herself.

There was a sudden beeping sound that broke into their conversation. Jill watched as MacKenzie lifted the bottom of his light pullover sweater to reveal a beeper attached to his belt. He glanced at the top LCD panel, and then pushed the off button. He looked at his watch. He'd been with Jill Corey nearly the entire day.

"You can use the phone if you have to," she said.

"No, I don't need to, but I think I better get going. There's still some things I have to get done . . . and I have plans for tonight."

A date, Jill thought immediately. She glanced at MacKenzie as he finished his juice and rinsed out his glass. He retrieved his coat, putting it on but holding the hard hat in the crook of his arm. He put the navy cap back on. Jill began to absently construct in her mind the kind of woman MacKenzie Philips would be interested in. Tall for sure, Jill thought with a private grimace. Someone sultry and sophisticated ... sexy. She watched him covertly, sensing the athletic frame outlined under his clothing, the muscles across his shoulders and upper arms, in his thighs. His good looks were entirely different from Keith's. MacKenzie's brown features were more masculine, defined ridges and planes; a firm, hard jaw. Keith had been more tan and he had been more boyish looking. Eternally youthful. MacKenzie would grow old with a lived-in, mature look, a face full of character and soul. Keith would always have had a pleasant softness.

MacKenzie stood ready to leave. "Thanks for inviting me in. I really enjoyed being here."

Jill smiled. "Thanks for being nice to Shane. You're good with him and he really likes you a lot."

"He's a great kid." He hesitated, and then finally spoke again. "I was wondering, if it's okay with you, I could pick him up and he could spend a Saturday or Sunday afternoon with my sister's kid at their house."

Jill frowned. "I don't know."

"My sister won't mind. She might not even notice another kid in the house." She smiled. "Anyway, I think Shane would have fun, and he'd probably be a good influence on my nieces and nephews. . . ."

His beeper went off again.

He had to leave, Jill reminded herself. "The phone's in the den. You can say good-bye to Shane while you're at it."

"Right." MacKenzie nodded and headed for the other room.

Jill waited until he was gone before she let the tension drain out of her body. Her stomach felt tight and heavy, and she placed her hands underneath her belly, as if trying to alleviate the weight. She stared down at her own stomach and let her body relax so that she could try and feel what was going on inside. But she wasn't as in tune to this baby as she had been with Shane. She had anticipated her first child as if her baby was going to be the greatest miracle in the universe. Shane was God's gift to her and Keith when they were still so in love with each other. But this baby was different. She couldn't feel anything. The fetus was developing and growing and moving around in that tight little space that was her womb, making itself very much at home. To Jill what made it so much worse was that she'd long ago stopped loving Keith Corey. And now she was carrying a baby that only reminded her of all that had gone wrong.

Jill heard MacKenzie's firm footsteps in the hall and came out of her reflections. She took a deep breath and turned to face him as he reentered the kitchen.

"I gotta go." He stood awkwardly, as if there was something else he wanted to say. "It was a nice afternoon. I enjoyed getting to know you and Shane better."

She looked skeptical. "You must be hard up for a good time if you thought this was fun."

MacKenzie slowly grinned at her, because a sudden realization just crossed his mind. It was like when he spent time with Gina or Laura and their families. It wasn't glamorous. Definitely no frills. Even messy and noisy. But it was comfortable. "It was different. There's fun . . . and then there's fun," he teased.

She shook her head at him. "Bye, MacKenzie."

But instead of leaving, MacKenzie slowly walked toward Jill until he was standing right in front of her. She was forced to tilt her head back so she could see into his face. The simple movement again made him conscious of her size, but she also seemed must stronger and larger in many other ways. "I just want to say something else. I know it's going to sound stupid, especially coming from someone like me but . . . things are going to work out, Jill. You and Shane are going to be okay."

"What do you mean, someone like you?" she asked, ignoring his other observations.

MacKenzie hedged. He had failed once. "I only mean, I

don't have kids. I'm not married. I don't really know what you're going through."

Jill regarded him closely, remembering the way he was with Shane. "I think the best thing that came out of my marriage was Shane. You don't know what you're missing," Jill reassured him.

MacKenzie zeroed in on the loving and peaceful expression on Jill's face . . . and he believed her.

"You're doin' okay," Maggie Winston sighed, as she put away her stethoscope and blood pressure machine. "You'd do even better if you stopped running around all over the town trying to keep Shane entertained and got more bed rest."

"Nag, nag, nag . . ." Jill mimicked, sounding like an old shrew. She looked fondly at her next-door neighbor as she stood up from the sofa and pulled down the sleeve of her sweater. "I'm doing almost everything you told me to. And my doctor said all we can do is wait and watch."

"And don't do anything dumb," Maggie added dryly. "I know how you feel about this baby, Jill, but since you've decided to bring it to term you could try to be happy about it."

Jill was silent for a moment, absently straightening her living room while Maggie sat frowning at her. Her brown face, round and smooth, was wreathed in an expression halfway between wanting to fuss and mother her, and being an impartial health-care provider just doing her job. Jill liked the balance.

Her own mother, who suffered from arthritis, was living with her brother Jeremy in Memphis. Maggie was a warm and friendly substitute.

"I'm trying. I got some new baby clothes. I've been talking to Shane about his new brother or sister. I thought he'd want a baby brother but he said he'd rather have a girl."

"Uh-huh," Maggie murmured. "What do *you* want?"

Jill adjusted a baby picture of Shane at eighteen months that sat on an end table. "That there are no complications."

Maggie sighed again and shook her head. "Child, any good doctor can do that for you. But the rest is up to you. You have to *want* this baby."

Jill turned and her facial expression was blank. "How about some coffee?"

Maggie sucked her teeth. "You can go ahead and change the subject if you want to, but you better think hard and long about separating how you felt about you husband from how you feel about your baby. They're not the same thing." When Jill didn't respond Maggie gave in. "Coffee would be fine."

Jill left for the kitchen and after a moment Maggie got up, gathered her equipment in a black leather tote, and followed her young neighbor. She dumped her things on the floor and sat at the oak table.

"Who was that man I saw around here last Saturday?" she asked smoothly.

Jill smiled to herself. She had wondered if anyone had noticed. But given the way the Jenkins' dog had carried on, MacKenzie Philips's arrival could hardly be missed. Certainly not with people peering out their windows.

"He's a friend of Shane's."

"Ha!" Maggie barked and settled into an amused laughter. "He's a bit tall, broad, good looking, and too old to be one of Shane's friends."

"But he is. It's a long story. . . ."

"I got time." Maggie shrugged.

"Shane was in some store back in February to buy me Valentine's candy and didn't have enough money. Mr. Philips lent him the rest. He was here on Saturday to collect."

"That's what he told you. What's his first name?"

"MacKenzie," Jill responded, feeling her stomach suddenly quiver at Maggie's sarcastic comment. She put out a mug and toasted a bagel with cream cheese for her friend as the coffeemaker perked and dripped. Jill was reminded suddenly of the hot cocoa that MacKenzie had so thoughtfully made for her in his office trailer. She didn't think she'd tell Maggie about that. Besides having to listen to a litany of complaints about caffeine not being good for her or the baby, Maggie would question her to death about MacKenzie. Certainly Jill realized that she hadn't learned much at all . . . but what she did know she wanted to keep to herself.

"I saw him out my window. He was walking around your property."

"He didn't stay very long. . . ."

"More than three hours—long enough to fix that garage door."

"Maggie," Jill began in exasperation.

"Just looking out for you, baby. Ben was gonna come over and check the man out, but I told him to mind his business. If you needed help you would have called or screamed for help."

"Thank you," Jill nodded and poured Maggie a cup of coffee.

"So, is this *friend* of Shane's coming over to play again anytime soon?"

Jill squirmed uncomfortably but couldn't help laughing. "You're too much. . . ."

"And how does he feel about his playmate's mother?"

"I know what you're thinking and you are way off base. You saw him for yourself. MacKenzie Philips's not going to be interested in me. I'm pregnant, I already have a child. Men don't want ready-made families." She sat slowly. "And there's nothing attractive about pregnant women."

"Well, now that you're so clear on what *he* wants, how about you? What do you think about him?"

Jill stared at Maggie. The question was quiet and clear, and very serious. And it wasn't as if the thought hadn't flittered in and out of her mind over the past six days. She had been thinking a lot about MacKenzie Philips, and going over and over in her mind that Saturday afternoon with him and their odd conversation. She had asked herself repeatedly why someone like MacKenzie wasn't married, why he didn't have children. Jill was pretty confident that he'd be good at both. And she'd had other thoughts. Loneliness often made for fertile and wild fantasies which her active fetus kept reminding her were impossible and inappropriate. It had been easy to talk to MacKenzie. Keith had never been great about listening to her problems. It made him impatient, because he had his own.

As to MacKenzie . . . he'd captured her son's attention and affection. But it couldn't happen to her. She wasn't going to let it. Not now when it was too late.

"He seemed a nice man," Jill calmly answered Maggie's question. "Do you want more coffee?"

✷ Chapter 3 ✷

"Take it easy," MacKenzie chuckled, taking a swift glance at Jill as she sat stiffly next to him. "My sister doesn't bite. She's looking forward to meeting you and she's glad you and Shane are coming over."

Jill sighed and gnawed on her lip. She debated telling MacKenzie that she wanted to go back home. That her back ached a little, and she'd had cramps all through the night. The other truth was that she was nervous about meeting MacKenzie's family. What had he told them about her? What were they expecting? Jill winced. Wrong word. How would they treat her? And, as Jill felt the apprehensive beating of her heart, she wondered when it had come to matter? But every time she remembered the pleading look in her son's eyes Jill knew she had no choice but to agree to the Saturday plans.

"I just feel . . . it's not a good idea. I should have stayed home and let Shane come by himself," she said quietly.

MacKenzie thought for a moment. He didn't want to say anything that would make Jill change her mind about her decision. He glanced in his rearview mirror at Shane in the back seat as the youngster sat reading through a comic book. Next to him was a stack of games and toys Shane had brought along to share with Joel and Aimee. And while he was glad to be able to bring Shane Corey together with his nieces and nephews because he felt the boy needed the company of other children, MacKenzie found that it mattered more that Jill had agreed to come along, too.

MacKenzie suspected that Jill had talked herself into believing that it wasn't right for her to be out and about because she was pregnant, as if it was some sort of social disease. Not with her husband dead. And not with another man. But MacKenzie knew that he had never really connected Jill or Shane or even the coming baby with her late husband. Somehow Keith Corey didn't seem real. There were no pictures of him in the house other than in Shane's room. And except for that very first time he'd come to their house, Jill and Shane didn't ever talk about him. MacKenzie also suspected that he was afraid to acknowledge that he felt a genuine contentment being around her.

"This is getting to be a habit," MacKenzie murmured wryly.

"What's getting to be a habit?" she frowned.

"Having to talk you into everything. You made me work overtime just to take you and Shane to Red Lobster last week. And the Field Museum before that."

Jill twisted her hands together and glanced out her window. She did have to be persuaded each time MacKenzie invited her and Shane out, and it bothered her. Because she *did* want to go and Shane was the safety factor between her and MacKenzie. Jill felt her stomach muscles tighten. It wasn't the baby this time but the knowledge that she liked spending time in MacKenzie's company. They'd fallen into a comfortable routine. Too comfortable.

"I didn't think you would remember saying you'd take us to Red Lobster. You didn't have to. It would have been okay if you'd changed you mind."

"Do you think I'm playing on you? Do you think I have this thing for pregnant women. . . ." She gasped softly and looked sharply at him. He kept his attention on his driving. "Do you think I'm hard up, or that I feel sorry for you?"

"Well, do you?" she asked, irritated.

"If you thought that was true then you'd tell me to get lost in a heartbeat. So what do you think it is?" MacKenzie asked seriously and waited, as if he needed to know himself exactly what was going on. As if it was hard to figure out what the fascination was. Why this woman?

"I'm safe," Jill said with self-deprecating humor. "I'm unavailable."

"You forget something."

"What?"

Now MacKenzie did look at her and, for a brief moment, let his attention roam over the soft curling of her hair, the light application of lip gloss and cheek rouge that emphasized rather than hid her freckles. Her expression made him want to touch the tip of his finger to the dimple in her chin. She looked so youthfully pretty. He wondered if Jill Corey realized just how appealing she was. When he'd picked her up she was wearing a calf-length denim skirt with boots and a long tunic sweater that was loose and fashionable. It gently disguised the rounding of her stomach. "I think Shane is a very lucky little guy."

Jill stared at him. What did that mean? That he liked her? That he thought she was a great mother? A friend? She didn't ask, but nevertheless felt a twist in her chest of disappointment. But after all, what had she expected MacKenzie to say? What would have been appropriate under the circumstances? And the boundaries of their odd relationship kept changing.

When she silently turned away MacKenzie realized that he didn't see Jill at all in the ways she'd described herself. He had only just recently come to know, when he'd taken her and Shane to Red Lobster, that it was less a physical thing about being with her. It was more what he *felt* when he was with Jill Corey. Comfortable. Safe. Himself. She didn't ask or expect anything of him. MacKenzie hoped, however, that it wasn't because she might still see him as just caring about her son.

"I think you're quite a woman."

Jill smiled to herself. She didn't know what that meant, either. But it made her feel good.

When MacKenzie drove his car onto his sister's property there were already three cars in the driveway. Jill's anxiety was short-circuited and in any case there was no time to feel self-conscious, because once she and Shane walked in the door Laura Sexton treated her like a long-standing friend of the family.

"Nice to meet you," Theodore Sexton said in greeting. "Did you see my toolbox?" he added in passing to his wife, as he headed toward the basement.

Laura Sexton stood with fists planted on her ample hips and glared impatiently at her husband. "I don't use your tools. Do I ask you where my blender is when I can't find it?" Then she looked more carefully at Jill as MacKenzie helped her off with her coat. "Umph! How come you look so cute? When I was pregnant I looked like a whale."

Jill felt herself flushing under her skin, but Laura's blunt observation immediately dispelled any concern that her pregnancy was going to be a source of curiosity and conjecture. It was duly noted as a fact and that was it. There was no point in wondering what anyone thought about her being in their midst, a stranger, a widow—and seven months pregnant. There was too much going on and too many people. Gina Temple was also there with her three children, the twins Cara and Casey, and five-year-old Christie. Her husband Ken, a CPA, was at his office with a full schedule of clients lined up for the afternoon whose income tax returns he was preparing.

The six children seemed like a hundred to Jill, running through the house and creating pandemonium. Two Siamese cats were slinking around her legs and rubbing their bodies against her. MacKenzie and his brother-in-law, a cheerful teddy bear of a man, were trying to figure out what was wrong with the VCR. Laura, calmly accepting the chaos, did enough talking for everyone. Jill found that the only thing she had to do was to relax. She sat for a while in the rocker that was in the living room, and her backache eased. No one fussed over her or tried to entertain her and that was the way she wanted it.

She offered to help with lunch and Laura accepted, putting her to work mixing a macaroni salad and arranging cold cuts on a platter. MacKenzie came through the kitchen at one point and, in passing, briefly rested his hand in the middle of her back. The gesture startled Jill because it was oddly personal . . . and absentminded, as if MacKenzie took her presence for granted but liked knowing she was there. And it reminded her of the back massage he'd given her. That had been after the outing to the Field Museum. And the hatching eggs . . .

MacKenzie had called to say he was taking Joel and Casey to the Field Museum and would Shane like to come along. Another bogus invitation, she had thought . . . until MacKenzie had asked her to come along, too. The trip had been slightly wild with three adolescent boys who had more energy than they knew what to do with. Mostly they'd rushed through the exhibit halls of the natural history museum until they came upon the exhibit of the hatching eggs. Several of them lay in a glass box under hot lamps.

"How come the eggs are in that box?" Shane had asked.

"It's an incubator. That's a special box to keep the eggs warm so they'll hatch," MacKenzie had answered, but with a sudden quiet thoughtfulness.

"You were in an incubator," Jill had said to her son as the three boys pressed against the case.

"How come?" he repeated.

Jill was aware that MacKenzie was staring at her. It felt strange to be talking about Shane's birth while he listened so carefully. "Because you started coming into the world too early."

"You were still cooking," MacKenzie joked and the other two boys laughed.

"No I wasn't," Shane shook his head doubtfully and scrinched up his face.

"MacKenzie was only teasing you."

The boys had quickly lost interest in waiting for the eggs to crack open, but MacKenzie had stayed with it, waiting with unexpected fascination until, a half hour later, the first egg began to open. He called the boys back to watch.

"Where's the mother chicken?" Joel had asked.

"Probably resting," Jill responded dryly, sure the boys wouldn't really understand why.

"What about the daddy chicken?" Shane asked.

"The rooster," MacKenzie murmured in correction, his gaze fastened on Jill's face.

They exchanged looks as it became obvious that Shane regarded the eggs and chicken like a family. But Jill couldn't think of a single fanciful thing to say, or any answer that would easily explain the relationship.

"I don't know, sweetie," she finally shook her head.

"Maybe they don't have a daddy just like me. . . ."

MacKenzie had dropped his nephews home first, and then driven Jill and Shane back to their house. The full day of walking crowded exhibit halls had tired Jill and her lower back had started to ache. Shane had fallen asleep in the car. When they reached the house and he was awakened he'd gone, without protest, straight to his room to get ready for bed. But he'd wanted MacKenzie to help him.

Jill had sat on the edge of a chair with her eyes closed, her hands trying to ease and rub out the tension in her back from the baby pressing against her spine. She hadn't heard MacKenzie come back into the room.

"Let me try," he'd said in a quiet voice.

Jill had thought for a moment to say no. The sudden idea of MacKenzie touching her started an incredible riot of images and possibilities in her mind. Just his asking seemed to shift her perception of him even further, from erstwhile friend to virile and physical male. From innocuous encounters to personal contact. Nevertheless Jill swiveled on the chair presenting her back to MacKenzie.

"Here," Jill said, using her hand to indicate the pressure points.

She didn't realize she'd been holding her breath until she felt MacKenzie's large hands touch her back. She'd been taught how to use her fists to relieve the position of the baby's head, but MacKenzie had stronger hands, and she could feel his fingers resting carefully along her sides, and he used his thumbs to create a counter pressure almost at the base of her spine.

"How's that?" he'd asked.

Jill merely nodded. She thought she'd heard a strain in MacKenzie's tone, and it seemed similar to the one she was suddenly feeling in her chest. Because Jill realized too late that his firm and steady massaging of her back was unbelievably stimulating . . . and probably inappropriate. But the damage had been done. Jill let him continue. And everything changed.

The pain did begin to let up in her lower back. But it was replaced by a kind of swirling sensation of need in the pit of her stomach. She was beginning to feel languid. She was starting to enjoy his hands too much. But then MacKenzie stopped and stood up abruptly, turning away from her.

"I hope that helps," he murmured in a gruff voice.

"Yes. Thanks." Jill had responded, wondering if MacKenzie could hear the utter surprise . . . and longing in her voice. . . .

Jill took a deep breath to push the memory of that afternoon and evening to the back of her mind. By no means forgotten—just out of the way. The voices of the blended family surrounding her came into full consciousness as she glanced over her shoulder to MacKenzie. He and his brother-in-law joked quietly in the background while lunch was prepared.

And then when lunch was just about over Christie, the baby of them all, came to stand in front of Jill. She smiled at the little girl.

"Can I touch your stomach?" Christie asked quietly.

Jill blinked at her. "Excuse me?" She was aware that the other adults had heard the request and were all now watching for her response. Jill could especially sense MacKenzie's gaze on her.

"Can I touch your stomach."

"Oh, Lord . . ." Theo groaned.

Gina chuckled.

Laura tried to call the little girl away. "Come over here and leave Jill alone. Don't you know that's a rude question?"

Jill realized everyone was waiting to see what she was going to do. "It's okay. I don't mind."

"Me first!" Shane declared.

Jill looked at her son as he usurped the other child's position in front of his mother. He had never before expressed an interest in the changes in her body other than to say he hoped he got a little sister. Now Shane reached out his hand, and then he hesitated as if he didn't know what to do with it.

"Go on," she encouraged softly.

Shane gently placed his hand right on top. She never paid much attention to the movements anymore, unless the baby was especially active and made her uncomfortable, but now Jill found that she watched Shane's face to see what his reaction was. He was focused for a moment and then started to giggle and scrunched up his shoulders.

"It tickles," he said, laughing.

"Can I do it?" Aimee asked, and her response was the same as Shane's. The other children seemed disinterested.

"I think they're embarrassed," Gina said as they stood around awkwardly, just watching.

"Well, I don't have to feel Jill's stomach to remember what it was like carrying all of you around," Laura said dryly, and Theo laughed.

Gina shook her head in reflection. "I liked being pregnant but by the seventh month I felt like I was carrying a two-ton truck."

"Mac here is the only one who doesn't know what we're talking about," Laura observed.

Gina chuckled. "He can take one of mine, if he wants. He'll find out soon enough that children can drive you to drink!"

"He's a good uncle to the kids, but it's not the same thing," Theo said, looking at his brother-in-law and slapping him playfully on the shoulder. "You need to have one of your own, man."

Everyone laughed again, but Jill turned her attention to MacKenzie, and was riveted by the intense consideration in his eyes. He just sat staring at her. She could see his jaw muscles flexing, and something in his look made Jill feel a little breathless, more aware of her body and its awkward shape. More sensitive to what he was thinking, to what he saw when he looked at her. She had resigned herself to having this baby and she would try to make the best of raising a child conceived in lies. But MacKenzie didn't know that and the way he was looking at her suggested that he saw her pregnancy as something special.

After lunch Gina offered to clean up and Theo left to make a run to a hardware store to replace his garden hose. The simple domesticity lulled Jill into a comfortable state of peace. In the last years that she and Keith had been together, he was frequently away on Saturdays, leaving her and Shane to entertain themselves. The excuse he gave was special training, or overtime. It wasn't until after his death that she connected many of the absent Saturdays to a distraction of another kind. She had felt so isolated and so foolish when she'd learned of Keith's deception.

She was sitting alone in the living room when MacKenzie came to squat next to the rocking chair. His hand on the arm of the chair set it into a gentle movement. Jill could feel the natural heat of his body. His bigness. For a dizzying moment she wondered what it would be like to have Mac-Kenzie hold her against him. She looked at the wide, beautifully shaped male lips and thought about him kissing her. She could detect the faint outline of where his beard would grow in if he never shaved. He would look just as handsome, just as masculine. Jill shifted her attention quickly to his large hands, shaken at the drift of her thoughts.

"How are you doing?" he asked.

Jill smiled. She liked that he asked. "Fine."

"You can see, it gets a little crazy around here. There's always something going on."

"I bet you counted on that, MacKenzie," she said astutely.

He grinned at her, but neither confirmed nor denied Jill's

observation. "I hope the kids didn't . . . you know . . . embarrass you."

"Their curiosity is good. They should understand and be comfortable with where babies *really* come from."

MacKenzie chuckled softly and his eyes were bright as he leaned toward her. "How you make them is the part I like."

When he realized what he'd said and how it sounded MacKenzie became absolutely still. He expected Jill be to offended, to smirk and remind him to watch his mouth and his wayward thoughts. He grimaced and squeezed his eyes closed briefly.

"Hey, I'm . . . sorry. I . . . that was way out of line," he shook his head.

Jill looked at his bent head, the chiseled angle of his nose and cheeks. She thought she'd never known a man like MacKenzie before, whose masculinity was so firmly in place, whose ego was so healthy that he wasn't afraid or ashamed to apologize. And who understood when he should. He didn't seem to have an automatic sense of male superiority.

She reached out and touched his chest briefly. "It's okay. I know about sex and making love and what the difference is," Jill found herself admitting and then she, too, became slightly flustered at what they were talking about.

She was amazed at how bold and honest she was being with him. MacKenzie's head snapped up and his gaze narrowed on her face. She wondered if he was thinking the same thing that she was. MacKenzie was watching her mouth. It made Jill feel peculiar inside . . . overheated.

"As . . . as long as we accept the responsibility. As long as we don't forget that making love sometimes means making a baby—and raising a child."

"You're right. I know a couple of guys who haven't done the right thing."

Jill was mesmerized by the drop in his tone, by the way his eyes seemed so filled with sharp speculation. She had a lot of questions of her own about MacKenzie, like why wasn't he spending time with the kind of woman who could give him what he wanted? When had they become more than friends but far less than lovers ... someone she felt she wanted to trust. When had she come to wish fervently that things might be different and that there was a chance for something else between them?

His jaw tensed again and Jill thought about what was going through his mind just then ... and could he read hers?

"Now you know you're practically one of the family when I share my candy with you," Laura said, entering the living room and setting a glass plate on the coffee table. It was carefully lined with an assortment of chocolate candies.

If Laura was aware of the emotions developing between her brother and Jill she didn't indicate it. MacKenzie stood up and away from Jill.

"Do you have anything like Sweet Dreams?" he asked.

Laura frowned. "Sweet Dreams ..."

"Don't listen to him. It probably doesn't even exist anymore."

"What is it?" Laura asked, sitting on the sofa and letting one of the cats settle in her lap. The other marched across the coffee table, sniffed at the candy and, apparently not finding anything of interest, jumped down and ambled away, its tail curling in the air.

"It's a candy. When I was pregnant with Shane I had such a craving for it. They're chocolates with a raspberry cream center. I found them one day while I was out shopping for baby things." Jill smiled in memory. "I think I single-handedly kept that store in business. I was back every week buying more."

"When I was pregnant with Joel I wanted potato chips!" Laura laughed. "I can tell you that at least twenty of the pounds I gained had nothing to do with the baby. With Aimee it was blueberries and cream. Now I can't stand the sight of either of them."

"Shane tried to find Sweet Dreams to give Jill for Valentine's Day," MacKenzie informed his sister.

Jill raised her brows at MacKenzie. She'd never heard

the full story before. Now she understood why the box of candy had been so important to her son. "I remember that they were made in Waukegan. The candy store where I first got them is now a Gap."

"What do you crave with this baby?" Laura asked Jill.

Jill glanced down at her stomach. She thought about it for a moment and then looked at Laura. She shook her head. "Nothing."

"Yeah, Gina was that way. She gained a lot of weight when she was pregnant. She had *twins*. But she was able to take it all off. I hate her," Laura muttered and bent forward to sample a candy from the dish.

"Mommy . . . can I stay over with Joel?"

Jill glanced up as Shane came into the living room. He was in his stocking feet, his jeans were slipping down around his hips, and his glasses were slightly askew. "No, I don't think so," she shook her head and straightened her son's glasses. "Anyway, we should be leaving soon."

"Oh, let him stay. He seems to be having so much fun."

"I can bring him back tomorrow," MacKenzie offered.

Jill glanced at MacKenzie, wondering if he'd had this in mind all along. Shane put his thin little arms around her neck and laid his head against her chest, leaning his body against her stomach. She hugged her son close to her.

"Please?" Shane whined. "I don't want to go home, yet."

"You're outnumbered so you might as well give in," Gina chuckled. She came into the living room and sat in an easy chair. "When the baby arrives you're going to wish you had a day all to yourself without your kids."

Jill patted Shane's back and gave him a kiss on the cheek. "All right. But I expect you to behave and do what you're told."

"And on that note, I think I'll take Jill home," MacKenzie said smoothly.

She gave him a grateful nod. He helped her up from the rocker and while MacKenzie went for their coats Jill let Shane lead her to the room he would share with Joel.

MacKenzie was digging in his sister's hall closet for Jill's coat when Laura came up behind him.

"I like her," she announced, as if it was required for her to make a judgement.

"I thought you would," MacKenzie said.

"Now, I want you to tell me exactly what's going on in your head."

"What do you mean?" he asked, facing her.

"You're almost thirty-six years old. You've made it clear you're not interested in getting married again, that you're happy being a confirmed bachelor and everyone's favorite uncle. Then suddenly you show up with a woman who's pretty and friendly and sweet, it's true, but with a seven-year-old child, another on the way, and barely widowed six months. What's wrong with this picture?" Laura asked dryly. "I introduce you to some of the most accomplished, beautiful black women my church has to offer, and you're hanging out with a woman you can't have."

"I bet you've been wanting to tell me that for a long time," MacKenzie said.

"Don't get me wrong, Mac. You know I'd like to see you married. But I just wonder if you know what you're doing with Jill Corey."

He began to lose patience. "You can see for yourself there's nothing going on between her and me. She's not in any condition or position to get involved."

Laura made an impatient face. "Fool. That's why you're so attracted to her. You don't have to do anything. You don't have to worry about competition, or demands or commitments. That doesn't mean she might not care about you, or you about her.

"I know Paula did you dirt, but you were both just kids and too young to marry anyway. At twenty-two you didn't know a thing. She hurt your pride more than anything else. But Jill Corey is a grown-up and she has responsibilities. She's not going to care if you take her out all the time and buy her anything she wants. She's not going to throw tantrums and carry on. She's the kind of woman who wants someone she can depend on. Who'll be a partner and a friend and a lover. Who won't cut and run when things get hard. Whose ego won't need other women. . . ."

MacKenzie's jaw tightened as he waited out his sister's lecture. "You figure all of that out in just four hours?"

"Of course not. It took a whole bunch of mistakes, and being married to a wonderful man for thirteen years to know the difference. You should be so lucky.".

"Let it go, Laura. I'm just trying to be nice to Jill and her son."

Laura cocked her head and smirked at her brother. "Who appointed you Prince Charming?"

MacKenzie was glad there was no chance for Laura to continue when he heard Jill coming down the hall. But suddenly when he saw her, there was a funny surge of tension as he looked at her. He couldn't identify what it was. A cross between being fearful and holding back, and believing in a possibility that as yet didn't even exist. MacKenzie helped Jill into her coat and felt an overwhelming desire to hold Jill, to gather her in his arms as if the gesture would somehow clarify his feelings. MacKenzie felt it so strongly that he glared at his sister, as if it was her fault that the thought had even occurred to him.

Their departure was equally as noisy and confusing as their arrival. Jill felt like she'd just left the center of a storm. By the time MacKenzie had settled her into the passenger side of his car, she let out a long sigh. But it held more than weariness. She paid no attention to the silence from MacKenzie, thinking that like herself he was a bit worn out from the afternoon. Jill found herself smiling privately about how easily she had been accepted by members of MacKenzie's family. It had a bittersweet irony to it. They were virtual strangers. And yet, Keith's family made little effort to include her in their family gatherings even though they lived just a few hours away.

"Thank you, MacKenzie," she whispered, her eyes closed.

MacKenzie frowned at Jill's softly uttered words. His mind was suddenly a mess of thoughts and considerations.

He heard his sister's words again in his head, and felt guilty—and on edge. There was no reason for Jill to thank him. He wished she wouldn't. It made him feel too awkward. Laura was almost three years younger than he was, but she'd always been the advice giver in the family. The one who settled the disputes and clarified the issues and who could almost always come back later to say, "I told you so."

"What are you thanking me for?"

Lots of things came to Jill's mind. "I had a good time. You have a nice family."

"Do you have family in Chicago?"

"My mother lives with my brother Jeremy's family in Memphis. Keith's family is in Indiana."

"And your husband is gone," MacKenzie observed thoughtfully, wondering how much Jill might actually miss him. "But you have the baby. That will keep his memory alive," he voiced automatically, but in a strangely flat tone.

Jill didn't respond right away. She'd spent the past five months keeping her secret feelings to herself. Only Maggie really understood her painful ambivalence about Keith . . . about having his baby.

"Maybe it was just as well Keith never knew. It wouldn't have made a difference between us, I don't think."

"What do you mean?"

"I mean . . . there were other women," she said in almost a whisper.

MacKenzie frowned. "For how long?"

"More than a year."

"Then . . ."

"How did I get pregnant?" Jill chuckled but without humor. "The usual way, MacKenzie. I was going to leave him. He promised to stop and I forgave him. I tried. We got back together and . . ." She sighed deeply. "The week he was killed there was a phone call from a woman. She said she was from his union office."

"When you called back to check it out there was no such person."

"Right."

"You must have been pretty angry."

"Angry," she repeated vaguely. She turned to stare at him. "I was going to have an abortion. I didn't want to have his child after that. I made the appointment. I went to counseling. I showed up at the clinic."

"Why did you change your mind?"

Jill remembered so clearly getting changed into the hospital gown and being taken to the procedure room. And then feeling the nausea in her stomach, the pain in her chest so acute she thought she was going to be sick. She'd heard the faint crying of an infant out in the waiting room, and she'd started to cry herself. The nurse had led her back to the examination room and tried to console her. Even thinking about it now, Jill felt her throat closing up.

"I thought about Shane. I remembered that the baby is going to be half me. And I can't blame this baby because Keith hurt me."

There was a long silence in the car but it wasn't uncomfortable, just thoughtful. MacKenzie had a lot of information to process about how Jill felt about her husband. About how she was still not free. He couldn't get beyond that . . . or what he would do if she were.

"What about you?"

He shifted in his car seat. "What about me?"

"What's your story? An eligible black male, gainfully employed and kind to little children and pregnant women. There must be something wrong with you. Are you an ax murderer? Are you gay?"

MacKenzie shrugged and couldn't help chuckling at the exaggeration. "I was married once. It didn't last a year." He hesitated. "She was fooling around too, but they got married. They're still together."

Jill didn't ask how he knew that. "I thought so," she murmured.

"What?"

"You behave like a man who's had a bad experience with a woman. A little quiet and careful. Midthirties and no mention of a wife . . . or children."

"You're very observant."

"I'm a teacher, remember? And I couldn't figure out why you were so interested in me and Shane." *I'm still not sure*, she said to herself.

"Are you referring to your earlier list of options?"

She took a deep breath. "Being nice to me doesn't require any work, MacKenzie. It doesn't require much feeling."

"I never said I didn't have any feelings," he ventured quietly.

She sat still staring out the windshield, keeping any sense of hope in proper perspective. "Since you've been married too, you understand what it's like when it all goes wrong. It's too bad, though, that you didn't have a baby together. Even if the marriage didn't work a baby makes a difference. Don't you want children of your own?"

He shrugged but his hand tightened on the steering wheel. "I don't think about it."

"I don't believe you. I hope you're not going to spend your whole life being hurt and trying to get over it. You're only punishing yourself, not . . . your ex-wife." Jill hesitated for a second. The words seemed strange coming from her mouth. She realized suddenly that she could be talking about herself. "She got what she wanted. What about you?"

Jill turned her head and looked at MacKenzie. In the dark she was still familiar with the set of his head, the way his eyes could be both pensive and observant at the same time. Knowing that he never acted without careful thought. There was no knee-jerk reaction in MacKenzie.

"You're okay—for a guy," she teased quietly. "You deserve to be happy."

MacKenzie repeated Jill's words back to himself, let them roll around in his head. He didn't want Jill to just like him. He certainly didn't want her to be grateful for any attention he gave to her and Shane. But he also felt frustrated because for the life of him he couldn't seem to find the words that described what was really going on in his heart.

In a quick and spontaneous gesture she reached across the space between them and took hold of his hand. They said nothing, but their fingers laced together. Jill suspected already that they weren't so much taking comfort from one another as offering it selflessly. The silence stretched between them. It wasn't uncomfortable. And yet . . . there was a distance that remained between them; figuratively and physically. She felt safe being sympathetic. MacKenzie wasn't interested anyway.

It felt strange to Jill to enter her dark house and know that for the first time in almost ten years, she was going to be there entirely alone. It made her feel a little sad, because in a moment MacKenzie would leave. Jill put her purse and keys on the kitchen table. MacKenzie turned on the light, and went to switch on another in the living room. When he returned Jill had shrugged out of her coat. She stood with her hands braced on her lower back, arched it, stretching and poking her stomach out into the air.

Mackenzie felt an odd longing as he watched. He was deeply moved by the unique capabilities and the incredible changes in Jill's body. He felt curiosity again and, unexpectedly, desire. He tried to imagine what it would have been like to make love to Jill before she got pregnant; how different it might be now, to feel her small body beneath him. To feel her flutter and undulate against him, and know that it was with pleasure. The very thought suddenly made MacKenzie's groin tighten and he had to briefly close his eyes and take a deep breath to vanquish the fantasy.

Suddenly, Jill gasped and her arms swung forward to grab the sides of her belly. She grimaced.

"Oooh . . ."

MacKenzie came instantly to her side. "What's wrong? What's going on?" He took her hand and gently forced her to sit in one of the oak chairs.

She was silent for a moment, her expression frowning and pensive as she seemed to be listening to her own body. Jill squeezed his hand in reassurance and shook her head. "It . . . it's okay. It's nothing."

"It wasn't nothing. You looked like you'd been kicked."

She let out a long breath. "That's exactly what happened. The baby kicked. It also has the hiccups."

"The hiccups?" he asked, incredulous. ·

Jill nodded, absently rubbing her hands over her stomach, as if trying to quiet her tenant down. She glanced at MacKenzie and the expression on his face made her giggle. He stood bent over her, a frowning look of confusion and apprehension on his face. She was mesmerized by the thought MacKenzie was so concerned about her well-being. The baby kicked vigorously again and this time Jill winced and moaned softly.

"What can I do? Do you take a pill or something? Should I call someone?"

She shook her head, continuing to rub her stomach. "This is normal." She recalled the look on MacKenzie's face earlier, while they were at Laura's house, and the children wanted to feel for themselves what was happening. Now she understood what that look was all about and what it conveyed. Now she understood why he wasn't bored with her condition and didn't treat her as just a pregnant woman. Jill was startled by the realization, even as she recognized how much she wished their relationship could be something other than what it was. But MacKenzie wasn't going to let it—and she couldn't.

Jill took hold of one of MacKenzie's hands. "Here. Put your hand here . . . you can feel it."

MacKenzie held back. When he looked into her face he saw all that he had been missing and all that he now wanted. He saw reflected in Jill Corey's eyes the magic of the moment. He shook his head. "Uh-uh. I don't think . . ."

Jill pulled on his hand again and placed it firmly on her stomach. MacKenzie's hand was so big that it seemed to span the whole mound, as if her stomach was a basketball. The image made her giggle again. But when she looked into his face, her humor faded. MacKenzie's eyes were hooded and his brows were drawn together. His jaw was tensing. And his mouth . . . his mouth was poised in concentration. His whole face was set in surprise, and wonder.

"Can you feel it?" she asked quietly, but he didn't answer.

And he didn't have to. Through the fabric of her tunic sweater Jill could feel the incredible heat from his hand, and it was starting to spread throughout her entire body.

Jill suddenly knew that he was experiencing more than just the movement of her baby. He was bent down over her. MacKenzie tilted his head so he could look into her face. He was so close that she could see the gentle flaring of his nostrils. The dark intensity in his eyes. Slowly . . . very slowly, he bent his knees and squatted before her. He never took his eyes from her face. He was totally blown away and the naked longing in his gaze made her heart constrict.

The baby hiccuped for nearly a minute and in complete silence Jill and MacKenzie experienced the moment together. He put his other hand on her stomach and Jill felt like she was surrounded by him. The baby shifted and when it kicked this time, MacKenzie looked incredulous.

"Oh, man," he whispered in complete awe. He blinked at Jill. "Does it . . . hurt?"

She smiled gently at MacKenzie, enjoying his reaction, acutely aware of the feel of his hands on her. Feeling as if her sweater was superfluous. "Sometimes. It takes you by surprise."

MacKenzie began to take liberties. To slowly move his hands as if searching for another place to feel the baby's movement. Jill hadn't expected the sudden rush of heat that came over her as his hands explored at will. Her heart began to race. MacKenzie touching her this way became a sensual experience, and it was extraordinarily intimate.

He was still staring right into her face. And his expression changed again. The stunned looked was replaced by one that was much more personal. And much more expectant. Jill caught her breath and her lips parted as she realized that she and MacKenzie had stumbled onto another level of their relationship that made them aware of each other in a whole new way. Or maybe it only made them silently admit what was already there. She waited for him to stand up, to break the contact and put them back where they belonged. But that clearly was not going to happen. Nor did she want it to. MacKenzie had something else in mind, and Jill found herself waiting breathlessly for whatever was going to happen between them now.

MacKenzie was afraid to move. He hoped that nothing Jill saw in his face gave him away, because the physical contact of the moment was also intensely erotic. Then he saw the way she was watching him. He realized that Jill was also feeling something quite different between them. He took his cue from her and saw that Jill wasn't going to object to the liberty he was going to take, beyond what she had allowed. MacKenzie slid his hands to the sides of her stomach, and then closed the distance until his arms were around Jill in a loose embrace. Her stomach pressed against his chest.

"Mac . . ." she whispered nervously, using the familiar nickname for the first time.

MacKenzie ignored the hesitancy because it was natural. She didn't want him to stop, she was just expressing awareness. He felt her hands rest on his forearms, and then move up to his shoulders. Slowly he bent forward and lightly pulled a kiss from her lips. He created just enough space to test Jill's response, to look into the depth of her eyes and see acceptance and anticipation, and a bit of fear. When her eyes closed MacKenzie kissed her again, this time slowly and thoroughly. He was a little scared that it was happening but didn't want to stop. He didn't want this to end quickly now that they had come this far. Jill didn't discourage him. Her mouth was poised and ready and soft and he let his lips capture hers with tantalizing seductiveness. The connection was perfect and Jill's response was immediate. It was not a demanding kiss, or even one filled with passion. Their tongues were teasing and exploratory and said more about their mutual need for affection and tenderness than it did a desire for consummation.

When MacKenzie slid one hand further up her back, Jill was encouraged to lean forward, fusing their mouths even more as she looped her arms around his neck, one hand cupped around his nape. Jill could feel MacKenzie's innate strength in the tensing of the muscles in his shoulders and upper arms. She could sense a power in him that was appealing because she knew MacKenzie's true strength was in his ability to not use it.

She could hear his breathing. He could hear hers . . . and they both felt the life within her pressed in between them. MacKenzie would have been happy to continue to hold Jill and to kiss her until they were both mindless, but he knew he had to stop. When he did, pulling his mouth away even as his lips continued to need her, he heard the little sound of protest deep in her throat. For a long moment they stayed that way with their eyes closed, with their warm breaths mixing and the tips of their noses touching.

"Oh, man . . ." MacKenzie whispered, his voice gravelly and shy.

"Yes . . . you said that," she whispered in kind. But she couldn't look MacKenzie in the face. She was afraid that all of her secrets and her dreams would be exposed, and MacKenzie would see right into her heart.

"I've never kissed a pregnant woman before," MacKenzie said, as if it he expected to burn in hell for doing it now. He gently kissed her cheek. "Jill," he whispered her name.

"I haven't been kissed since . . ." She stopped just short of saying her dead husband's name.

"Is this when you tell me to back it up, or that it was a mistake?"

Jill felt sort of dreamy and soft. She began to shake her head as she touched MacKenzie's mouth with her finger tips and watched a muscle clench reflexively in his jaw. "Was it a mistake?"

He shook his head slowly. "I don't know. I'm a little freaked out about this."

MacKenzie thought that maybe Jill was right. And Laura. He considered all those years he'd spent feeling cheated and disillusioned by marriage and women . . . and love. He didn't know what this was that was going on between him and Jill

Corey. She was the kind of woman who could make him change his mind about a lot of things.

But he wasn't ready, yet.

MacKenzie tighten his arms around Jill just enough to force their mouths together again. He took up right where they'd left off, exploring her mouth. Their tongues stroked together until he could feel the telltale signs of rising desire in his loins. The fact that he now felt like he wanted to make love to Jill scared MacKenzie. When he broke the kiss this time he stood up, releasing Jill, letting her arms slide away from him.

"There's no place to go from here," he said.

"Where do you want to go?" she asked softly.

The question made MacKenzie uncomfortable and he frowned. "I don't know. I mean . . . it's not right."

"Why not?"

He looked at Jill for a long moment and felt like his past was merging with the present, and it was confusing. He couldn't straighten out in his head which one affected him the most. "I was crazy to kiss you. You've got a kid to worry about. You're pregnant."

Jill stared at MacKenzie, hearing his conflict. "You knew that from the start. I'm not always going to be pregnant. I have to go on with my life." She looked down at her hands. "That means . . . maybe some day I'll . . ."

"You're brave," MacKenzie interrupted quietly, looking into her translucent eyes. He didn't see any rejection.

"So . . . are you saying you're not a brave man? Some woman does you wrong and that's it? You give up?"

MacKenzie rubbed the back of his neck and sighed. "I'm saying—I don't know."

Jill pursed her lips and nodded. When she glanced at him again she made no attempt to hide the sadness. "I hope you figure it out," she murmured. "But I have my own stuff to deal with, Mac. I'm trying to start all over again."

MacKenzie felt her withdrawal and stared at Jill. He

couldn't do anything about it. He had the feeling she could see right into him, that his own doubts and the past just hung out there. He laid his hand against Jill's cheek as she continued to silently stare at him. He wanted to kiss her again.

"I guess I just need time. I don't know what I want."

Jill watched him as she brushed a hand over the rise of her stomach. "Well, no matter what I want *this* is also my future."

There was so much that needed to be said between them and yet, nothing that could be said in that instant that wouldn't break the spell and plunge them into confusion. But the phone rang and destroyed their fragile emotions anyway. They both started at the interruption. When Jill made to stand up MacKenzie put a hand on her shoulder to force her back into her chair. He reached for the wall extension next to the refrigerator.

"It's probably Shane," she said.

"Hello?" MacKenzie answered but there was an open pause on the other end.

"Who the *hell* is this? Where's Jill?"

MacKenzie held the phone out to her and frowned. "A man. He's pretty ticked off."

"My brother . . ."

But Jill didn't bother to acknowledge Jeremy right away. There would be a lot of explaining to do, but not now. Instead, Jill stared up at MacKenzie wondering if the sudden awareness found in their gentle lovemaking was now going to tear them apart. She couldn't think what was ahead for them, either. Maybe it was time to end it here.

Jill could hear her brother's bellowing voice through the receiver in her hand, but she made him wait. *This* moment between her and MacKenzie was too important.

MacKenzie knew the next move was up to him. But all he could do was to lean over Jill and kiss her again. He felt encouraged that she raised her head and closed her eyes, and parted her lips for him. The soft clinging of their lips was sweet. It wasn't enough but it would have to do.

And Jill did the one thing that she thought was best for both of them. She left everything as it was, sort of suspended and unfinished, and let MacKenzie leave. Because she understood that he had to.

❊ Chapter 4 ❊

"*H*ey, my man," Conrad said enthusiastically. "Smokin' idea. Who's paying for this bash, you or the company?"

"I *am* the company," MacKenzie responded laconically.

Conrad chuckled and tapped his beer bottle against the side of MacKenzie's. He pulled out a chair from the too-small bistro table and straddled it. As he sipped from his beer MacKenzie looked across the crowded bar at the two dozen or so men who were celebrating the end of their phase of work on the downtown Chicago construction project. Another union would take over for the next step the following week and his team would move on to finish work at O'Hare. Hosting an after-work dinner seemed a small enough thing to do for men he'd worked with and supervised for nearly four months, and who'd cooperated in bringing in the job on time and within the budget.

"You got anything lined up after O'Hare?" Conrad asked.

MacKenzie shrugged. "There's a big job I can have in Skokie. I have to let the builder know soon. And there's something in the works up near Waukegan."

"Skokie is a better commute," Conrad responded.

"Waukegan will pay more money."

Conrad cackled. "So, when do we start?"

"After I get back from Philadelphia. The home office wants me to fly out and work out the details."

"Sounds good."

"Hey, thanks boss," two men half saluted MacKenzie as they approached his table. "We gotta get out of here. The wives gets suspicious about these male gatherings. . . ."

"I hear you." MacKenzie nodded, shaking the two men's hands as they headed to the exit. "Put your name in at the union office. I'll call you if I can use you again."

The men left and for a silent moment MacKenzie and Conrad sat watching the remaining workers as they sat talking and laughing among themselves.

"Only thing missing is women," Conrad observed with a slight leering grin. "What say you and I kick back later tonight? Go home and change. I'll call Diane and you can call Carol. We can get together. . . ."

Already MacKenzie was frowning at the idea and shaking his head. "Don't think so. I'm not up to it tonight."

"Or last night. Or last week. What's with you, man? You got something else going on the side I don't know about?" Conrad leaned closer, conspiratorially. "Hey, if she's really hot ask her if she has a friend."

MacKenzie smiled cynically and arched a brow. "What about Diane? You two have been together for a long time. Almost two years."

Conrad shrugged and drank from his beer. "Diane's okay. But she's starting to push for getting engaged and all that."

MacKenzie glanced at his friend thoughtfully. "What's wrong with that?"

"I'm too young," Conrad said sarcastically.

"You two would make a pretty good couple."

Conrad pulled on his ear lobe and narrowed his gaze across the room. "I don't know 'bout that. I mean, Diane's talking serious stuff, man. Marriage and the whole nine yards. I don't know if I'm ready. I'm like you, Mac. I'm not cut out for anything permanent. I like things just the way they are. You know what I'm saying. If it ain't broke . . ."

MacKenzie found Conrad's philosophy interesting since his friend already had one son from an earlier failed relationship and a slew of short-term affairs behind him that hadn't worked out, either. He slanted a questioning glance at Conrad, wondering if he ever gave thoughts to the future. He behaved as if the party would go on forever. And he'd never have to face himself alone someday.

MacKenzie pursed his lips and nodded absently at Conrad's observation. Not because he was necessarily in agreement, but because he had already come to see that moving from woman to woman wasn't quite the right solution. He liked Carol Warren. He'd been dating her for almost six months. She was very pretty and poised. She had a good sense of humor and was fun to be with. She didn't make demands and she was independent. She owned her own consulting business, her own apartment, and her own car. If any reasonable man was going to be interested in marriage Carol was a sure bet. Except, MacKenzie considered reflectively, after months of dating her he had no fantasies or expectation. He'd enjoyed Carol's company and their intimate relationship . . . but Carol was not the person he had on his mind all during the day, or dreamt about at night. Not in the last two and a half months anyway, and he hadn't seen her in just as long. MacKenzie realized that he hadn't even thought to.

In fact, the only woman to actually give him sleepless nights in quite a number of years happened to be someone who didn't stroke his ego, didn't appear to need him, and had never given him an ultimatum. Jill Corey *was* inaccessible, MacKenzie realized, not because of lack of interest on her part, but because of wounded pride on his. For a brief moment MacKenzie considered confiding in Conrad, putting it all out there to see what he thought. But just as quickly MacKenzie squelched the idea. Conrad would laugh himself sick.

"So, what are you going to do if you ever come face-to-face with someone you think you could be serious about?"

Conrad laughed. "Run like hell!" He held up two fingers to the bartender. "Another round here."

MacKenzie's frown and unease deepened. He put down his empty bottle and stood up. "Not for me. I've had enough."

"So, you want to get together later?"

MacKenzie shrugged into his jacket. He could call Carol, he thought. Or someone else. But it would just be killing time and he wasn't all that sure he'd enjoy himself. He shook his head. "I don't think so."

Conrad shook his head sadly. "I don't know about you, Mac. There used to be a time when we'd tear up the town together. You must be getting old or something."

MacKenzie grinned slowly. Maybe age had something to do with it. More likely he was just getting selective. And he needed a lot more than just a good time. "Must be," he said agreeably as he prepared to leave. "Say hi to Diane . . . or whomever."

"Happy Birthday!"

"Thank you, sweetie," Jill murmured, giving her son a tight hug and kissing him on the top of his head.

"Here, this is for you," Shane said cheerfully, handing his mother a colorful package.

"He wrapped it all by himself," Maggie said, leaning over her dining room table to place a slice of cake in front of her husband.

"And he made us promise not to tell you what it is," Ben Winston said with a wink.

Jill smiled at her neighbors and added her son's birthday gift to the other two already stacked next to her. She kept one arm around Shane as he leaned against her. "Shane is getting to be very good at keeping secrets," she said.

"It wasn't a secret, Mommy. Mac said it's a surprise," Shane explained guilessly with perfect distinction.

"Oh, he did, did he? And when did this talk between you two take place?" Jill asked smoothly, clearing a spot for Maggie to place her slice of the cake. She hoped that she appeared indifferent, even though her stomach fluttered at the very mention of MacKenzie's name. She hadn't heard from him in more than three weeks.

"Last week," Shane garbled, spooning ice cream into his mouth.

"Don't talk with your mouth full," Jill admonished automatically. "I don't think you should be calling MacKenzie Philips all the time. The man is busy."

"But he told me to," Shane defended himself lifting his shoulders as if to also say, *the devil made me do it*.

"Is your friend MacKenzie coming to your mother's party?" Ben asked.

"I wondered about that myself," Maggie said, watching Jill.

Jill waited silently for her son's answer.

Shane shook his head. He had chocolate ice cream and cake crumbs on his mouth. "He can't. He said he had a prayer—"

"Prior," all three adults corrected at the same time.

"Comm . . . comm . . ."

"Commitment," they all added.

"That means he had a date with some woman," Ben chuckled knowingly.

"You hush," Maggie warned her husband quickly.

Ben's chuckle turned quickly into a hoarse cough.

Jill meticulously used the edge of her fork to cut off a small piece of her birthday cake. She kept her face blank of any particular expression. The weight and shape of her growing baby suddenly felt so heavy and made Jill feel clumsy and awkward. She forked some of the cake into her mouth . . . and it was absolutely tasteless.

"Mommy, you have to open your presents," Shane peered into his mother's face.

"Yeah, that's a good idea," Maggie nodded, looking at her watch. "I have to leave for the hospital soon and I'm not going 'til I see everything!"

"This is embarrassing," Jill murmured, shifting in her chair.

Maggie moved the birthday cake from the center of the table to the sideboard. Everything else was swept to the side and Jill's birthday gifts piled in front of her.

"Hey, it's bad enough we have to add one more number every year to how old we are. You might as well enjoy it and get something out of it," Maggie said dryly. "Besides,

I'm going to expect something great from you when it's my turn in September."

"I'll help," Shane said obligingly, handing his mother one of the boxes. "Open this one first."

"That's from me and Ben," Maggie said, her usual calm and good sense giving way to a shy anxiousness that the gift would be well received.

"Thank you, but—"

"We shouldn't have," Ben finished. "Yeah, we knew you were going to say that."

"This party would have been plenty. Maggie made a great dinner, the cake is beautiful. You've done enough for me already."

"It was such a small thing," Maggie said quietly, reaching out to pat Jill's hand. "It's been a rough year for you. I'm just glad there was enough money so you didn't have to work through these last months before the baby is born."

"Hurry up, Mommy," Shane whined, cutting into the sentimental moment.

Jill torn off the paper and opened the box to find an album of sorts nettled in tissue paper. It was a keepsake book meant for the new baby, covered in a white eyelet lace.

"How pretty," Jill smiled at Ben and Maggie.

"We know as soon as you see that baby you're going to want to start filling up every page," Maggie said wisely.

"Thank you, Maggie. Ben. I'll put it to good use. . . ."

"Now this one." Shane handed his mother another box.

"Who is this one from?" Jill asked, starting to peel off the wrapping.

"It came in the mail a few days ago," Ben said. "Addressed to you in care of us."

Jill hesitated over the unwrapping. Her mind grew fanciful and immediately she wandered about the possibility that MacKenzie had tried to communicate by sending her something. She wondered if Maggie and Ben were in cahoots . . . which she wouldn't put past either one of them. And then she was afraid to open the gift.

"I—I can't even think who would be sending me a birthday gift," Jill said uneasily as the paper disappeared. She could feel her hands shake with anticipation.

Inside the box was another box . . . and a videotape. Jill frowned at the contents and then glanced at Maggie and Ben but they seemed just as curious as she was. Inside the smaller box was a pair of pearl stud earrings.

"Real nice," Maggie nodded.

"It's just earrings," Shane said, clearly disappointed that it wasn't something more interesting.

Jill read the card that was in the bottom of the box. "It's from Nana, Jeremy, and Aunt Karen."

"What's the tape?" Ben asked.

Jill read the side label. "Homemade video of various things the family has been up to in Memphis."

Jill was looking forward to seeing new images of the rest of her family, so far away from her and Shane. But she found herself also experiencing a confusing blend of joy at the lovely present, and guilt that she'd hoped it was from MacKenzie.

"The last one," Shane said.

Jill grinned at her son and gently shook the package. "I know what's in here," she said.

Shane giggled and shook his head. "No, you don't."

"It's a new car," Jill said, causing everyone to laugh.

"Lord knows you can use one," Maggie murmured.

"It's on the list," Jill chuckled.

When the final box was opened, she sat staring at it for a silent moment. The thing that stood out immediately was the beautifully scripted package name: SWEET DREAMS. She blinked at it as Shane began to laugh, covering his mouth as if he knew another great secret. He did. It was bubble bath. Jill smiled in surprise.

"Look at this. I thought it was a box of candy." Jill looked brightly at her son. "Thank you, Shane. But where did you find this?"

Shane shrugged. "At the store."

Maggie and Ben laughed at the youngster's flawless logic.

"The drugstore at the corner sells that kind of thing," Ben said.

Another thought occurred to Jill and she frowned, narrowing her gaze on Shane. "And just where did you get the money?"

"My allowance."

"You mean . . . you didn't borrow from anyone?"

Shane shook his head. "Uh-huh. Mac told me not to. He said you wouldn't like it. He said I shouldn't buy stuff I couldn't pay for all by myself."

"Hmmm," Maggie uttered thoughtfully. "Who *is* this guy?"

"He's my friend," Shane announced proudly. "But Mommy likes him, too."

Jill felt the blood suddenly rush up her neck. Maggie and Ben sat staring silently at her. She began to crumble all the torn wrapping paper into a great ball. "Well . . . I know you have to go," she murmured quietly to Maggie. "Thank you for the lovely surprise party and the gifts. Thank you, baby," Jill said to Shane, giving him another hug.

"Are you going to use the bubble bath tonight?" Shane asked.

"Maybe not tonight. Tomorrow."

"Can I use some, too?"

"Sure you can."

Once she and Shane had left for their own house, Jill felt her spirits plummet. She was so grateful for Maggie and Ben's efforts to make her birthday a special day. She was proud of Shane's thoughtfulness. But she couldn't help herself from thinking of MacKenzie. The single most vivid memory that came to mind was him kneeling in front of her in the kitchen that night . . . kissing her as if it mattered. Not lightly, not opportunistically, but because the moment was so right. And she'd loved it.

Jill hadn't realized how much she'd missed being kissed and held, and the gentle euphoria of stirring desire. She had no guilt for her total lack of thought for Keith. She was only aware of the surprise of finding that she had feelings for

MacKenzie Philips, that she felt passion and need well up so strongly within her.

She put away the extra cake in the refrigerator and put her gifts on the coffee table in the living room. She and Shane would watch the tape together tomorrow.

"Shane, I think you should get ready for bed, now. School tomorrow . . ."

Jill heard some sort of response from her son and suspected it was a grumbling of protest. She turned and saw the flashing red indicator on her phone. There was a message waiting. Jeremy, Karen, and her mother, Jill thought, pushing the playback button. She was awkwardly bending to pick up one of Shane's library books from the floor when the voice on the machine came back to her.

"Jill . . . it's MacKenzie. . . ."

In surprise she tried to straighten too quickly and a pain shot through her abdomen. Jill gasped and sat on the edge of the chair. The pain rapidly faded but her heart thudded and raced briefly hearing his voice.

"Happy Birthday. Shane called and told me about the party. No deals between him and me on your gift this time. I just told him about the bubble bath. I know it's not the real thing . . . but we're getting close. Bye. . . ."

The machine beeped to reset and the instrument went quiet.

We're getting close. . . .

Jill continued to sit, repeating that message over and over again to herself. Finally she got her son to bed and took care of the mail and some bills. She sat with a glass of milk and tried to watch a TV program but was too distracted to follow the show. She went to bed herself finally, unable to shake MacKenzie's words from her mind. Jill lay curled on her side, absently stroking her stomach thinking how timing and fate played funny games that could really mess up a dream. She hadn't known how much she really missed MacKenzie Philips until she heard his voice.

And Jill admitted what she'd been avoiding for the past several weeks since she'd last seen him. Since he'd kissed her and touched her. That she was a little in love with a man she wished she'd met ten years ago.

It's too soon. . . .

The words sprang automatically into Jill's head as she carefully lowered herself into a chair. She'd been on her way to the den when the sudden spasm hit her. She closed her eyes for a second as she pressed her hands gently to her stomach. After a while the intense sensation of a fist gripping her from the inside loosened. Jill took several deep breaths . . . and started counting.

Finally she tried to stand up.

"Oooh. Sweet Jesus," she moaned as the fist tightened and twisted again.

It *was* too soon. Nevertheless Jill went through the mental list of what she had to do. Shane would just be starting school now, and Maggie would be home soon from her shift. She wouldn't bother her brother, yet. And she recited the two phone numbers she'd memorized from the hospital.

Just in case.

"When did you say you'll be back?" Conrad asked as he and MacKenzie stepped from the ground jeep and were pointed in the direction of the terminal.

MacKenzie checked his watch and shifted his leather duffel bag from one hand to the other. "By Tuesday. Wednesday, at the latest. I figure that as long as I was east in Philly, I might as well go into New York. There's some bidding going on for a government contract and I want a chance to get in on the deal."

Both men cringed against the roaring sound of a plane just landing on the runway some two hundred yards behind them. The ensuing wind melded their jackets to their backs. They entered a doorway into the building and climbed the stairs from the restricted passageway that lead back to the main terminal at O'Hare International Airport. They flashed their contractor's pass at the alert security who nodded them on their way.

"Getting a contract through New York should be a snap, man. The O'Hare people and the Chicago officials seem happy with our work. I bet it's a sure thing."

MacKenzie's beeper went off. He ignored it as he and Conrad continued down the corridor, busy with travelers and airport personnel. "Nothing's a sure thing until the ink is dry on the contract."

Conrad chuckled. "You got time for some coffee before I get back to the crew?"

"Yeah, sure," MacKenzie said as they headed for the cafe.

When the beeper went off again he turned to Conrad, handing him the duffle. "Here, take this. Let me answer the call and I'll meet you at the table."

At the bank of telephones he had to wait for a little over five minutes for one to free up. In the meantime the beeper sounded yet again. But MacKenzie didn't recognize the call-back number he had to dial.

"Miriam Summers speaking."

"This is MacKenzie Philips. I got a beeper message from this number."

"Oh, yes, Mr. Philips. Just hold on, please."

MacKenzie began to frown. Who the hell was Miriam Summers?

"Hello?" a childish voice croaked over the phone.

MacKenzie became instantly alert and his frown deepened. "Shane? What's up, buddy?" Shane was crying and sniffling. A sudden fear started building quickly.

"Can . . . can you come . . . come here?" Shane asked in a watery plea that was accentuated by hiccups.

"Here? Where are you? What's wrong?"

"At the hospital. My mommy's sick. . . ." Shane wailed, his anguish spilling out now that he could talk to someone he knew.

MacKenzie gripped the receiver. He leaned into the minimum privacy of his stall. He tried to keep his imagination in check. He didn't know what to ask first. He had to be careful what he said so that the boy would stop crying and know that everything was going to be okay. But mostly

MacKenzie realized that his heart had constricted painfully in his chest hearing Shane's announcement.

MacKenzie licked his lips, trying to think. "Okay, it's going to be all right, you hear?"

"Yes," Shane obediently responded.

"I want you to do me a favor. After you get off the phone, see if you can get a pencil and a piece of paper."

"How come?"

"I have an important job for you to do. I need you to try and remember when your mother got sick, when you got to the hospital, and what you've been doing since you got there."

"Why do you want me to do that?" Shane asked. He'd stopped crying and only a sniffle or two could be heard over the phone.

"Because when your mommy gets home she's going to want you to tell her all the important things that went on. You're the record keeper. It's very important."

"Okay. Can you come here, too?" Shane asked.

"Yes, I'm on my way. Put the lady back on, Shane."

In a moment Miriam Summers was on the line. "I'm the hospital social worker. Shane is keeping me company until we get more word on his mother."

"Is she okay?" MacKenzie asked, not realizing how strained his voice sounded. Not hearing his own concern.

"I couldn't tell you her condition at the moment, I'm sorry. Shane is fine, just a little scared. We have a playroom and he and I are going over for a while until we get more news. But he was really insistent that I call you. Are you a relative?"

MacKenzie hesitated. What was he to Jill and Shane? Where was his place in their family and in their lives? He could have given a simpler answer, like friend, but he felt like more than that. He wanted more than that. When he finally answered he knew he was taking one of the greatest risks of his life.

"Yes."

MacKenzie had no time to explain to Conrad. He simply

left his duffel in his charge and said he'd call when he could make it back to the airport.

It was more than an hour later when MacKenzie walked into the hospital and was directed to obstetrics. He found the playroom and when he quietly called out Shane's name, the youngster scrambled up from the floor when he'd been occupied with wooden toy trucks and raced to MacKenzie. MacKenzie caught the boy and lifted him clear off the floor. Shane's spindly little arms and legs wrapped around him.

MacKenzie patted the boy's back, realizing how great it felt to have his trust and his affection.

"Hey . . . it's okay, buddy. I'm here."

"Hi, I'm Miriam. We spoke on the phone."

Holding Shane MacKenzie turned around to faced a middle-aged woman with her wide cheerful smile. The gaze from her blue eyes was kind and alert. She held out her hand and MacKenzie shook it.

"Jill—"

"Hanging in there. You can go see for yourself. Why don't you leave Shane with me?"

MacKenzie put Shane down, reassuring him again that everything was okay with his mother. Then he followed the directions to maternity, but Jill wasn't on the ward. He was led to another wing where three large rooms were outfitted with the proper hospital bed but otherwise looking like someone's private bedroom. The rooms were complete with curtains at the window, a stereo, pictures on the walls and chairs and end tables and shaded lamps. Only one of the rooms was in use. There were two women outside the room comparing their chart work when MacKenzie approached. They looked up quizzically at him. One of them, a woman with dark skin and an air of no nonsense and authority, came forward to greet him.

"Are you MacKenzie?" she asked.

"That's right," he nodded, not showing any surprise at her apparent knowledge of him. He glanced toward the open door, and although he could hear two voices he couldn't see inside the room.

"I'm Maggie, Jill's neighbor. I work in surgery."

"What is this?"

"It's what we call an alternative birth center where woman can have their babies. There's medication given if the mothers want it. There's a doctor, of course, and a midwife. It's for natural childbirth."

MacKenzie accepted the information. "How is she?" He asked the one question he most wanted answered, next to seeing Jill for himself . . . if she'd let him.

Maggie grinned. "She's in labor. She came in on her own two days ago with false contractions, and she had already started to dilate. Nothing happened in the next twelve hours so they sent her home. She had to come back in this morning. This time it's for real."

MacKenzie stood with his hands on his hips, absorbing the information. "But, she's a month early."

Maggie cackled. "Babies don't work on nobody's timetable but their own. Jill is having that child today!" She waved him into the room.

MacKenzie stood at the entrance. He wanted to go in but he was afraid. Not of seeing Jill but of what he was feeling about her. He stepped into the room and stopped in his tracks when he saw her on the bed. She was mostly in a sitting up position with pillows propped behind her back. Her legs were up, bent at the knees, her feet in the metal stirrups. There was a doctor sitting on a stool at the foot of the bed, monitoring the dilation.

MacKenzie felt like he'd entered into something highly personal. He felt awkward. But he couldn't take his eyes off Jill and the heavy beating of his heart told him he was so glad to see her.

Their gaze met and held. Jill blinked at him, not sure she was seeing right. And the sight of MacKenzie made her want to cry. She had been feeling so painfully alone.

"MacKenzie . . ." she said somewhat breathlessly.

He couldn't move. He half expected the doctor to order him out because he was spreading germs or something—or because he didn't belong there.

"Come on in," the doctor said easily. "She could use some company. We're almost there."

MacKenzie didn't know what to do. But then Jill moaned deeply and her face contorted as some sort of pain ripped at her. She squeezed her eyes closed and grunted. She was clenching the bed linens and breathing hard.

"That's it, that's it—push!" the doctor said. "Push. . . ."

When Jill let out a short cry MacKenzie came out of his momentary paralysis and reached the bed in two strides. He grabbed her hand and was stunned at the strength of her grip. "Come on, Jill. You can do this. You can do this." He coaxed her confidently, even though he was nervous that he would say something stupid and out of line. She was panting rhythmically but it ended in another grunt. It was like a stab to MacKenzie's heart to listen knowing there was nothing he could do.

The doctor continued his instructions in a calm clear voice. The midwife came in and another nurse. They brought with them a portable incubator. The sight of it worried MacKenzie but for the moment he only wanted Jill to know she wasn't alone.

The contraction let up and Jill sighed as she tried to rest in between. MacKenzie pulled her up into more of a sitting position. It created a little bit of space between her and the pillows. He tossed the pillows aside and positioned himself behind her so that Jill could lay back against his chest. Her body was limp and small and damp against him.

"Mac . . . you didn't . . . have to come here," she said.

MacKenzie continued to hold one of her hands. His other he boldly placed on her stomach, astounded that she had gotten bigger in just the few weeks since he'd last seen her.

"I'm making this my business," MacKenzie said although he wasn't totally sure what that meant yet. But he had no intentions of leaving Jill again. "How long has she been like this?" he called out to the doctor.

"Almost two hours. But she's doing great."

"She's in pain," MacKenzie said accusingly.

"I'm . . . okay . . . okay," Jill sighed.

MacKenzie rubbed her tummy. He didn't know if it helped or not, but he needed to touch her. He nestled her against his chest, taking her full weight. He kissed the side of her temple and bent his head to whisper in her ear. "I'm with you. I'm going to stay. Is that okay with you?"

Jill nodded her head. She couldn't begin to tell MacKenzie how happy she was to see him, to have him hold her again. The doctor said the baby should have been out a half hour ago, but Jill felt as if her body was refusing to release it. As long as she was carrying the baby her anger and disappointment with Keith could be hidden behind the aura of sacrifice. But the baby was about to be born. It was about to become a person who was going to need her, and she wasn't sure that she could get past all those stored feelings of hurt.

"MacKenzie . . . I don't know if I can do this . . . I . . ."

A contraction started to twist and gear up again within Jill. She clutched his hand and her nails dug into his skin.

"Okay, don't fight it, let go. Come on, Jill . . . this baby wants out of there." MacKenzie coached, the stiffness in her shoulder and the way she pushed back against him telling him she was struggling.

"Here we go," the doctor said to Jill. "Push!"

MacKenzie whispered to her and said low, caressing words. He rubbed his hand over the hard, tight knot of her belly as Jill panted in short breaths. He found himself imitating her to make her keep the rhythm and to keep going, not to let the pain overwhelm her and prevent her from doing her job. At the end she collapsed against MacKenzie.

The doctor bent his head around her covered legs and peered at the two of them together on the bed. He nodded. "You're good with her. Don't stop now. I don't want Jill doing this much longer. She's getting tired."

MacKenzie hugged her gently. "Awright. You can do this." He kissed the side of her face and it was damp and cool under his lips. He could feel her rapid pulse in the vein on her neck.

Jill took deep breaths. MacKenzie was here. He had begun

to replace her past with new hopes for the future. But she was about to have a baby who, she was afraid, was forever going to be a reminder of Keith. She tried to think of what the baby would look like but only got an image of Keith.

"The baby is crowning!" the doctor said triumphantly.

Jill took another deep breath and began to cry softly. "I'm scared,"

"Of what?" MacKenzie asked, rocking her. "Do you want something for the pain?"

She shook her head. "Mac . . . I'm scared I won't . . . love the baby. I'll always think of Keith and what he did."

"No, no that's not going to happen. You said yourself you can't blame it."

"My poor baby," she cried. "I don't know what to do. . . ."

"Listen . . . listen to me," he said urgently in her ear, afraid of the doctor's words. Afraid that he would do whatever he had to to bring the child forth. MacKenzie was certain that unless Jill could cooperate and not fight it, get beyond the memory of her husband's betrayal, the trauma would be too much for her fragile ambivalence. "This baby belongs to whoever is going to love it. You love this baby, Jill. It's *your* child. The last seven and a half months it's been constantly with you . . . part of you. . . ."

Under his hand the next wave came quickly. Jill's back arched.

"Oh . . . my God . . ." she moaned, almost inaudible.

"Jill," he said smoothly. "Close your eyes and listen to me. Just pretend that this baby . . . is yours and mine."

MacKenzie didn't care if the doctor was listening or not. If he'd had another choice he would have found Jill and married her years ago. Shane would be his and this new baby would be his. But fate ran by its own rules, and he knew that his meeting Jill Corey was simply meant to be, to set the record straight. And save their lives.

Jill panted as MacKenzie continued the low cadence in her ear. "Our baby, Jill. . . . Don't be scared."

The doctor kept issuing instructions. The nurses came to

hover next to him. MacKenzie didn't know how much longer it went on, but the doctor suddenly murmured.

"Okay, this is it."

Jill pushed and pushed and MacKenzie couldn't imagine the pain of what she was going through. But he felt the most incredible pride and admiration that she'd cried not because of the struggle of giving birth, but the confusion over love. Already under his hand he could feel her stomach changing. Jill's next moan turned into a short sharp wail and then was cut off with a long sigh. Her stomach seemed to collapse.

"It's out. . . ." the nurse announced.

"You have yourself a fine boy, Jill," the doctor said.

"Did you hear that?" MacKenzie asked her. She nodded her head against him.

"We need your help," the nurse directed to MacKenzie. "We have to take care of Jill now, so why don't you have a seat over here for a minute. . . ."

He eased himself from behind Jill, kissing her as he left her. The other nurse quickly replaced some of the pillows behind her back. When MacKenzie was seated the first nurse approached him and held out a blanket bundle. He stared at it and felt his hands grow clammy.

"Here, you hold him," she said, not waiting for consent but placing the small bundle in his arms.

MacKenzie was speechless. The blanket began to move. A tiny curled fist, wet with its birth fluid, escaped the blanket and waved in the air. The rest of the bundle squirmed slowly against his arm. The baby never cried but soft little breathing sounds could be heard. MacKenzie tentatively lifted aside a corner of the blanket and stared down into the ashencoated brown little face that was Jill's new son. He was small but perfectly developed. MacKenzie felt the tightening in his chest, the awe which made his breathing shallow.

"Mac?" Jill said his name in quiet exhaustion.

"Oh . . . man," MacKenzie whispered, stunned to find the baby's eyes open and seeming as though they were focused right at him.

"Is he okay?"

MacKenzie chuckled softly, shaking his head in wonder. "This little guy is perfect." And despite all of his reassurances to Jill, and his own expectations aside, he personally felt relief that the baby very clearly resembled its mother. In curiosity MacKenzie peeled back the blanket to look at the tiny person he held. Jill's baby.

MacKenzie looked at Jill and found her watching him anxiously, her eyes drowsy. He could only stare at her, not able to find the words to describe this moment. There had never been anything like it in his life. He'd just witnessed a miracle. And he finally understood what his sisters meant about having children. MacKenzie winked and smiled at Jill . . . because he realized now that he had a few sweet dreams of his own to fulfil.

❊ Chapter 5 ❊

*J*ill was annoyed when she heard the Jenkins' dog start to bark. Now that the weather had gotten warmer it was left out in the yard most of the day. She never used to mind the animal's tendencies to bark at anything that moved, but she knew that if the noise kept up it would awaken the baby. She got up from the desk in the den where she'd been writing thank-you notes and answering all the letters that had come in in the past three weeks since Patrick Corey had been born. She'd even gotten calls from MacKenzie's two sisters.

Moving down the hallway, Jill peeked into the baby's room but found that he was still asleep, his tiny little mouth opened into an O, his fist resting on the pillow. She walked silently to the crib and peered down at her baby. Reaching in Jill used the back of her finger to gently brush it across the baby's silken skin.

Jill stared at Patrick in wonder, remembering that awful premonition which had paralyzed her at his birth with the assumption that she couldn't love this baby. What was not to love? He was beautiful and sweet and each time she lifted him into her arms or looked at him Jill knew she loved her son just for himself.

She didn't know if she had MacKenzie to thank for that or if her maternal instincts would have kicked in on their own. But having Mac's support had certainly helped. And she had not forgotten for one moment how he had talked her through it. *Pretend the baby is ours. . . .*

The repeated words, the image and memory never failed to evoke the most poignant desire in Jill. The very idea that she and MacKenzie might have loved one another and created this child made her heart beat faster and her breath quicken. It stirred a longing inside that made Jill giddy and wishful. But it had not come up again once Patrick arrived, and there'd been no time to try and evoke it.

She remembered how she'd begun to feel lightheaded after the umbilical cord had been cut and the doctor felt she was losing more blood than she should. She had gone into contractions once again, waiting for the afterbirth to expel itself, and MacKenzie had shown confusion and deep concern that she should still be in pain. The new baby, so incredibly tiny in MacKenzie's strong arms, had been taken to be cleaned up and to have his umbilical cord treated. He'd been asked to leave the room for a while but hadn't until he could lean over her bed again, kissing her gently, and assuring her that Shane was fine and he himself would be around for a little while.

But there'd been no time for them to be alone at all. Shane had been brought to the wing and allowed to see his mother for a few minutes. Maggie had taken him to see his new brother, and he didn't seem disappointed that it wasn't a girl. And then MacKenzie himself had had to leave. He'd told her about his trip. He still had to catch a flight into Philadelphia. His business associates were not going to wait on the birth of a child, especially someone else's.

Jill smiled down at her new son, touching his cheek once again before leaving the room. The other thing that kept happening to her is that every time she handled the baby she thought not of Keith, but of MacKenzie. Shane was anxious to see him again, but no more so than herself. He wanted to show MacKenzie the homemade journal he'd been keeping—the one MacKenzie had gotten him started on at the hospital—but Jill just wanted to find out if the energy and emotion which had come to life between her and Mac was real or not. Was it enough to build a dream on? Her heart skipped beats when she even thought of them face to face again, and what they would say to one another.

The dog continued barking. Jill felt a peculiar sensation sweep through her, a cross between premonition and déjà vu. She heard a car door slam and walked quickly through the kitchen to the door leading to the garage. The garage door was rolled up and MacKenzie's car was parked behind hers. His trunk lid was up and he was lost somewhere behind it. Jill felt her excitement and her fear rise at the same time. But she stepped into the garage just as MacKenzie lifted a very large carton from his car.

"Hi. You're back," she said, feeling foolish and shy.

MacKenzie shut the trunk. He put the carton down and stood staring at her. Her stomach was gone, of course, and Jill stood before him having reclaimed her body, thin and shapely. And while she still appeared young because of her petite size, there was something about the look in her eyes and the smile on her mouth that suggested a sensual woman . . . *not* a girl. She hadn't gained any extra weight with Patrick. But more than the obvious, MacKenzie watched her eyes and felt relief at the smile which curved her wide mouth. She had on a short little denim skirt and a white blouse, and for the world didn't look like she was the mother of one young son and an infant.

"You look great," was all he could say, because he still didn't know if he had a right to say anything else.

"So do you," she said quietly.

And it was so sincere that MacKenzie felt all of his questions and doubts sort of evaporate. He just started walking toward her and Jill had her arms open even before he reached her. They came together and MacKenzie's open mouth descended on hers. He sighed and groaned when his lips touched hers and his tongue thrust forward. Her body was so slender against his, the only obstruction between them was clothing. She stood on tip-toe to return his embrace and their mouths rocked together in complete satisfaction and relief. As if to make sure that none of this was a mistake or a dream, MacKenzie used the open palm of one of his hands to explore Jill's now flat abdomen. Their relationship was something entirely different now, and he didn't want there to be any mistakes or misunderstanding about how he felt. He pressed Jill to him, not bothering to hide his desire or the evidence of it in his erection. It would all be taken care of eventually, because Jill was right. He had all the time in the world now.

They said no more as they went into the house. MacKenzie retrieved the large box and brought it along. In the kitchen they faced each other and just hugged silently, no sense of urgency or the past to destroy the moment.

"Where's Shane?"

"In school. He'll be home in a few hours."

"The baby?"

"Sleeping. Shane will be happy to know you were here."

"I can wait."

"He'll like that, MacKenzie."

He glanced down into Jill's face. "What about you?"

Jill lowered her gaze and leaned back against his arms. She pressed her hands against his hard chest, loving the masculine feel of him, remembering how he'd talked her through that last hour before Patrick's birth. "I'm not in the habit of running into strange men's arms. You're still the only one I've kissed since Keith." She looked at him through her lashes. "Or who I care about. . . ."

"Things are going to be different from now on between us," he said.

He said it so definitively that she hesitated. "How?"

MacKenzie sighed and looked off beyond Jill into space a moment. "I'm falling in love with you. I think Shane is a great kid." He looked at her again, his eyes intense and bright. "I wish Patrick was really mine. . . ."

Jill was stunned by his confession. She didn't have to say she felt the same. Yet, she shook her head, bemused. "MacKenzie, maybe it's not real. We've never really dated.

We've never talked about what we want or the future. We've never made love . . . or anything."

His arms tightened. "I've touched you. I've kissed you. I've had dreams about what it would be like. Not with just anyone, but with you. It'll happen sooner or later. But that's not all I want. This isn't going to be a hit-and-run for me, Jill."

"Shane and Patrick are part of me. We're a package deal."

He nodded. "I know."

"It's a lot of responsibility, MacKenzie."

"I'll also be getting a lot in return. I'll have a family. I guess Keith had his problems, but you know what? He had you and Shane and didn't know how lucky he was."

She smiled into his face. "I guess this means we'll be seeing a lot of you."

He nodded. "Until you get tired of me."

She shook her head, and reached to stroke his jaw. "I don't think so. . . ."

From a room down the hall came the distinct whining of an infant fussing awake from sleep. MacKenzie had his head cocked toward the sound and Jill tried to free herself to take care of the baby. MacKenzie held her in place for a second and looked into her eyes.

"Jill? Let me get him?"

She blinked at MacKenzie. He was serious, and that only endeared him to her more. He wasn't going to wait around for things to take a course. MacKenzie had earned a right from the moment he'd struck a deal with Shane until he became the first person to cradle her new son. He had always felt like part of the family.

Jill nodded. "All right."

He stepped away and headed toward the sounds of Patrick as the baby started to wail in earnest.

"What's in the box? Did you bring something for Shane?"

"Open it," MacKenzie called out as he entered Patrick's room. "It's for you. . . ."

Jill found a scissors to cut the tape holding the top together.

She lifted the lid and scooped out a handful of the styrofoam chips that served as packing material. Underneath were neatly stacked boxes and boxes of chocolate candy.

Sweet Dreams.

She gasped and lifted a box to examine carefully. It was exactly as she remembered. "I don't believe this. . . ."

Jill took one of the boxes and followed behind MacKenzie. When she got to the baby's room she found him slowly pacing the floor, with Patrick's little body held carefully against his chest. MacKenzie's hands were so big that the baby seemed to be supported completely by his palms. He turned to face her and the look they exchanged said more than either could possibly have put into words.

Jill's eyes teared up, thinking how lucky *she* was. "Oh, Mac. How did you find these? There's a whole carton of it."

"I made a trip up to Waukegan last week on business. I remember you said that candy you like so much was made there. The company is still producing it, just not distributing in Chicago." He briefly rested his chin against the baby's head enjoying the incredible softness, the sweet fresh smell. "I'm about a week late but, happy Mother's Day."

Her voice shook. "I would have been very happy with just one box. The fact that you went to all that trouble . . ."

MacKenzie approached her and stood holding the baby as he gazed into her face. "I plan on staying around the rest of my life, if we pull this off. I wasn't taking any chances on running out. It's the first time I've ever made someone's dreams come true," he said wryly.

"What about your dreams?"

MacKenzie shifted his attention to the infant who was drooling down the front of his shirt, his wobbly little head trying to look around. "I guess this is as good as it gets."

Jill put the box down and wrapped her arms around Mac-Kenzie's waist with Patrick gurgling between them. She thought of making love with MacKenzie, of their growing love joining them together so that the boys had a father. She began to mentally plan and was pretty sure there would be no problem convincing MacKenzie to expand the family in the future.

"You're wrong, MacKenzie," she whispered, hugging her newfound joy. "It can *always* get better."

THE SECRET
INGREDIENT

Raine Cantrell

✵ Chapter 1 ✵

"*You* are a hardheaded, hard-hearted, opinionated, bossy, stubborn, annoying man!" Toe tapping to the tune of the waves of anger rolling through her, Miss Halimeda Pruitt ticked each fault off on her fingers, then snapped them beneath the nose of the recipient of her latest human good deed, one Cade McAllister.

"And you, Miss Pruitt, are the most—" Guilt snapped Cade's teeth together with an audible click. He glared around the shadowed interior of the dilapidated barn. Blue eyes glittered as his hands clenched at his sides to prevent him from lifting the chin-high shrew off the soles of her high-button shoes and setting her down in the newly delivered wagonload of fresh hay. Strength of will allowed him to close the mental door on the scene that would follow.

"Two more useless critters," he muttered. "Don't expect me to feed them."

"I never asked you to. I never asked you to do one chore on my property. All you need to do is rest, heal your broken leg, and leave."

"As soon as I can, Miss Pruitt. As soon as I can."

Hallie watched his limping retreat with a great deal of sadness. His muttering should have blistered her ears, but strangely enough, did not. She had deliberately provoked

Cade. He had been trying unsuccessfully for the past week to make her see the error of her ways. Cade didn't understand why she took in animals that no one else wanted.

But then, why should Cade be different from so many other men that had found their way to the spare room when no one else would take care of them? Gamblers all, regardless of how they had been wounded, from miners out of the Never Summer range above her deep valley ranch to those like Cade McAllister who had been taken in by a pretty face and robbed of all his savings.

Like her mother and grandmother before her, Hallie opened her home to them, but unlike the two loving women Hallie would not repeat their mistakes. She never allowed her heart to be involved.

When loneliness swamped her, she wanted to have someone to love, someone who would accept her and love her in return.

The animals posed no risk, unlike Cade McAllister.

She winced as the back door to the kitchen slammed and turned back to settle in the newest addition to her family. By suppertime Cade would be in a mellow mood. She had left him one of her favorite chocolates. Only Doc Burnswait was aware of the small addition she made to the confections.

After all, a woman alone had to protect herself.

When this reminder did not stifle the flush of guilt, Hallie thought of all the extra rest Cade McAllister was receiving, and the more he rested, the quicker he would heal and be on his way.

The thought did not cheer her.

Cade McAllister, all six foot two of lean, hard muscle, slumped against the door frame of his room. He stared at the sweet evidence that Miss Halimeda Pruitt left in his room. It sat in a lacy paper cup propped on his pillow like some unblinking eye of judgment.

Three days ago, driven by unquenchable curiosity, Cade committed an unforgivable violation. No one knew about it, least of all the woman he had sinned against.

After boarding with Hallie for five weeks, he still wanted to ridicule her attempts to dose him with confections to stop his craving a drink of whiskey. He longed to sneer at her offerings found whenever his back was turned.

Pathetic, infernal, interfering woman.

In the next breath, he amended his thought. How could he be angry with the woman who had taken him in when no one else would? He wouldn't be if she just once listened to reason and that was the truth.

Doc Burnswait said his leg was almost healed. He had taken off the cast. Cade figured in a few weeks he would be ready to cut his losses and ride away from this isolated, broken-down excuse for a ranch.

He could last a few more weeks here.

Couldn't he?

Cade didn't search deeply for an answer.

Only his desperate straits made him agree with Doc's suggestion to stay here. But the good doctor's solution created a problem—spelled with a capital P.

Pruitt. One Miss Halimeda Pruitt who did not know the meaning of the word *quit*.

Cade, feeling the aching throb of his leg, limped into the room and with a resigned sigh, closed the door behind him. He yanked off the sweat dampened neckerchief from his neck and started to unbutton his chambray shirt. His gaze locked onto the linen pillowcase and its sweet offering.

"What have I done to deserve this?" he muttered.

Too late, he thought to warn himself not to think of the answer.

The image of the sauciest bit of southern drawling baggage ever to grace a poker table rose in his mind like a haunting nightmare. No man liked being reminded of how he had played the fool, but that was the role Cade had played.

He had delivered a herd of cattle to the Double Bar J ranch south of Denver, and when the other men rode back to Texas, Cade decided to stay on. Spring had come to the Colorado mountains and Cade went looking for land to buy. He had found a grassland valley, but the purchase would take all his savings. Eager to increase his stake, he risked only the bonus he had received for bringing the herd up north earlier than expected.

Miss Lurette Beauclare, a widow fallen on hard times, had cleaned him out of his money, lured him to her room where two of her cohorts had beaten him senseless, stole his savings, and broken his leg when they dumped him in a ravine and left him to die.

A broken wheel led to Doc Burnswait discovering him. Without a penny to his name, no one would take Cade in until his leg healed—no one but Doc and Miss Halimeda Pruitt. The woman had even paid Doc his fee, then settled the livery bill so Cade could have his horse.

Guilt for his transgression rolled over Cade like a high mountain storm. His conscience was pricked like forked lightning had hit it. He didn't have the good sense God gave a mule to appreciate his Christian benefactor.

Or maybe he did. Maybe keeping his distance from the woman was enough. If it wasn't, and his thoughts about the hay and Hallie rushed back before he could stop them, maybe the best thing he could do for her and his sanity was to believe that fully healed or not, he should leave her and the sorriest excuses for critters that had ever been set on this earth.

The woman dared accuse *him* of being stubborn. Her streak of stubborness was so wide, the whole of the Colorado River could flow through it. She refused to listen to reason about her animals. She refused his advice, or had until today, in a gentle, admonishing tone.

How could she not see that she was in danger of losing her land if she kept feeding those critters, which included a sow too old to breed—named of all things, Eternal—and the dried up cow called Divine; to Faith, Hope, and Charity, three graceless swayback nags fit for glue and little else.

The woman coddled them all. Grain and corn, hay and apples.

He shuddered thinking about Sweetcakes, the most obnoxious billy goat born to bedevil a man, and Forage, a sheep that couldn't find a blade of grass unless it was under her nose, and wouldn't drink unless the water was freshly pumped into the trough and perfectly still.

Pruitt's latest follies came in the form of the newly christened Steadfast, a burro who thought itself a dog, so doggedly did the animal follow Hallie around, and Patience the mule, who would try a saint's patience with its ornery ways.

Unwanted every one of them. Unwanted that is, by anyone but Hallie.

Desperate. That's what he had been. Desperate and insane to allow the woman to get under his skin.

He didn't want to put up with more of Hallie's persnickety ways. Especially now, that he knew . . .

"No." The whisper fell from his lips as denial and prayer. Cade avoided the trap before he fell into it again.

He stripped off his shirt and tossed it on the chair where his gunbelt lay. Miss Pruitt did not hold with a man wearing a gun. He raked back the shaggy length of his black hair, once more looking at the pillow. He never wanted to eat another of her chocolate bonbons again, as a substitute for belting down a man-sized, throat-burning, gut-clenching glass of whiskey.

She refused to buy him a bottle when she went into Denver, rare as the trip was. He couldn't fight with her about it; after all it was her money, but she didn't preach to him about the sins of indulging in the devil's drink or remind him of the straits he found himself in because he had been drunk that night.

Oh, no. Not Miss Halimeda Pruitt. She used a far more potent weapon on him. She widened those green eyes with an oh-how-disappointed-I-am-in-you look.

"Lord," he muttered, moving as quickly as his aching leg allowed to snatch the chocolate off the pillow, "when you test a man's fortitude, you really test his limits with a woman like Hallie."

Because he was desperate to stop thinking about a drink— and Cade told himself that was the only reason why—he plopped the sweet confection into his mouth.

This one was new; beneath the chocolate coat was a fondant center filled with nuts and a hint of cherries. The candy disappeared in two bites.

"This is what I'm reduced to? Blazing hell! I can't take anymore."

Good for whatever ails you. Hallie's words. Hallie's belief. He grudgingly admitted that eating her chocolates mellowed his mood. But by the Almighty, he knew what ailed him, and confections didn't come close to being as good.

What's more, he knew what ailed Miss Halimeda Pruitt. Bonbons lost out in a minute flat.

So did whiskey and every other vice known to man or woman.

Hallie didn't need her store-bought confections any more than he did.

Miss Hallie needed a man.

Cade closed his eyes as he rubbed the back of his neck. For the hundredth time he wished he'd never given in to the urge to enter her bedroom when she went to Denver to replenish supplies.

Three days ago. Three nights of tossing and turning with a restless need that refused to let go of him—and that blind-as-a-bat woman had no idea of the torment she caused.

"All right, I used the hind end of a horse for judgment." The admission didn't help. That burning curiosity for a clue to Hallie's character got the better of him and he had opened the door opposite his room.

He hadn't even had the decency to hesitate when he lifted the latch.

Then he'd stood in her doorway staring like a wet-behind-the-ears kid caught with his pants down, muttering imprecations like a miner coming out of the mountains after working his claim alone for a year.

The thought of his reaction, the sight burned into his memory brought forth a low, deep groan. How could he have known? Hallie had been a shy little mouse until he had been able to move around and help her with chores. Then he made the mistake of trying to talk some sense into the woman, thinking she would welcome his advice, and she showed him a passionate side. True, that passion took the form of temper to protect her useless animals, but he'd wanted to discover all the hidden depths of Halimeda Pruitt from that moment.

And once he had stood on the threshold of her room not even the instant promise of being visited with the Lord's wrath would have stopped him from going inside.

The window of his room was open to admit the cool spring breeze sweeping down from the Never Summer Range, named by the Arapaho Indians for the snows that never melted off the mountains. But all Cade could inhale was the faint scent of roses, the scent that had swirled around him when he entered Hallie's room.

He closed his eyes, once more seeing himself gaze slowly around the room lit by dimmed sunlight peeking between the red velvet drapes on the two windows. Plush carpet had cushioned his steps.

Her dressing table was crowded with bottles and jars. He was drawn there first. Hood's Sarsaparilla, the strongest most efficient and cheapest purifer of the blood. Globe pills for headaches. Perfumes of White Rose, Rose Geranium, Blue Lilies, Persian Lilac, and Colgate's Cashmere. Sachet powders to match every one. Miss Libby's Face Wash and Hand Cream. He had lifted the crystal stoppers, opened jars, and smelled every one of them.

Intoxicating scents meant to cloud a man's thinking. Scents to entice, and arouse and seduce. Cade was not immune.

From the dressing table he had wandered to the red brocade lady's slipper chair in the corner and picked up a handful of lacy underthings. Pale pink ribbons and tiny embroidered roses, cobwebbed lace and sheer cotton made up drawers and camisoles. The froth of feminine underpinnings were enough to enflame an eunuch.

Or a saint.

Cade was far from either one.

He remembered how his gaze had skimmed over the bed,

then returned to feast on the large four-poster covered with a red velvet spread. The headboard was nearly invisible due to the pile of pillows. Red satin trimmed with black lace, white silk, and tassels; touchable, inviting pillows.

His hands curled at his sides, but in her room he had grabbed hold of the bedpost, fighting the image of Hallie in that bed.

He was reliving every moment again, losing track of time now as he had that afternoon, just as he lost control of his breathing. When he roused himself, he found his hand grasping the silky fur coverlet folded at the foot of the bed.

Jealousy rose with a growl from inside him. Hallie was no trapper. With the love of animals too useless to another, the woman would never kill one for its fur.

A gift then, Cade thought. He didn't like the turn his mind took from that moment. Didn't like or understand the unreasoning jealousy that prevailed.

He couldn't deny the fur. It was real. As real as his belief that someone had given Hallie a gift of precious furs.

His teeth were bared as he fought off the image of Hallie lying against the fur . . . waiting. . . .

He recalled the devil's own whisper guiding him to her writing desk between the windows. He seemed to be acting outside of himself when he had lit the crystal lamp. The whisper nagged, cajoled, and enticed him, but Cade ignored it to lift the lamp and investigate what hid behind the large painted screen. The paintings themselves held his attention. Each panel portrayed a lady at her bath. Roman or Greek maids, he saw, in various states of nudity, yet curiously innocent.

He discovered Hallie used Jubel's tooth powder and french milled rose-scented soap. A full-length mirror stood next to the washstand. The wood frame had been polished to a satin finish and he had stared at his reflection.

His shadowed, unshaven face added to his rough appearance and the reflection seemed to whisper that he didn't belong there. He had turned away only to brush his hand against the silken nightgown tossed over the dressing screen.

Cade realized then that he didn't known Halimeda Pruitt at all.

He had returned to the desk, intending to blow out the lamp and leave. But there, light pooling like a devil's promise, was an open journal. The pages were filled with Hallie's neat handwriting.

Had he hesitated once before he had lifted the open journal?

Cade groaned softly, squeezing his eyes tight, wishing he could remember, wishing he'd never let temptation allow him to read what Hallie had written.

Perhaps some good conscience would have stopped him if his own name had not appeared in the first sentence. He could see it as if he were still holding the leather-bound journal in front of his eyes right now. A familiar sexual stirring came within him, the same that had begun that day, the same that never truly left him.

He had read what Hallie wrote. Her most private thoughts. Her secret, vivid dreams.

It was enough to make a man break out in a sweat even then, and it did the very same thing to him now as he thought about that passionate woman hidden in homespun.

With a start Cade opened his eyes. He rubbed his forehead, realizing that he was in his room. He had done some foolish things in twenty-nine years, but he never thought of himself as a stupid man.

Stupid, dumb-as-a-doornail kind of stupid. That is exactly what he had been. Not once had he guessed what a bubbling cauldron of feminine longings Hallie Pruitt was by looking at her.

Tender, merciful, compassionate, yes. He could easily attribute these wonderful traits to Hallie. Bedridden and totally dependent on her care, he had not one hint, not one inkling of what went on in her mind. At first he had thought her as sharp and tough as a cactus thorn. But that sweet, oh-so-shy smile—dammit—the woman fooled him.

Since that afternoon three days ago, he had kept an eagle's

eye on her, watching for the signs he had missed somehow. They weren't there.

She still wore her hair in its neatly coiled braid. Dark brown hair, shot with a glint of red fire in the sunlight, rich and thick as a mink's pelt. Those eyes of Hallie's, green as high mountain spring grass, slanted like a cat's, never once gave away the sensuality of her thoughts.

He had never seen her dressed in anything but long-sleeved bodices, starched collars, and white aprons over long, dark skirts with layers of petticoats thick as a man's thigh hiding every inch of skin.

Now that he had a good idea of what the clothing concealed, he was in torment. Hell. Trapped.

Desire tugged at him like a relentless south wind.

Whispering. Luring. Enticing him to discover all her secrets.

Hallie—lush as a tree-ripened peach waiting to be plucked.

Salvation. Redemption. The Lord would offer more blessings than a man knew what to do with is a man put Miss Hallie out of her misery and into his bed.

Cade groaned again. He'd been doing that a lot lately. It was a deep, painful sound. His teeth ground together. His hands clenched at his sides.

He was harder than a whetstone, hotter than a steam engine's boiler, and crazier than a locoed bedbug.

That's what thinking about Hallie and her damn journal did to him.

He would burn alive if he touched her.

An intolerable, impossible situation.

The ranch—if anyone in his right mind wanted to call it that—could be built into a thriving concern. Hard work and money was all it would take.

Miss Hallie would be grateful if a man kept the wolves from the door.

A man would have his work cut out for him trying to get near her. He'd be crazy to try.

Cade would be crazy to try.

But what else could he do when a woman wrote down her dreams about him? Dreams so vivid that the words steamed up off the page to set his mind on fire and consigned his body to hellish longings.

That pouty little mouth of Hallie's and that corset-cinched body might know half the words she had written, for there was an undeniable air of innocence about Hallie.

Unfortunately, Cade knew.

Damn, did he know.

An honorable man would clear out. He was honorable, wasn't he?

Some saddle tramp might take his place.

Cade prowled his room. One hand raked his hair, the other remained clenched at his side.

Could he in good conscience ride away and leave Hallie to the mercy of the next man she took in? While Hallie fed him her sweet confections, some lowlife tinhorn would be thinking of feeding the hunger that sweet, lush body aroused.

Some other man might hurt Hallie.

He had not seen anyone but Doc in the past five weeks. She had no one to look out for her. After what she had done for him, he couldn't ride off and leave her as vulnerable prey for whoever came along.

And you wouldn't hurt her?

Cade hushed the voice of conscience. He remembered the feel of Hallie's hands on his body when he'd been at her mercy and helpless as a babe in swaddling. The memory of her husky, soothing voice washed over him. Heat pooled until the seams of his pants were strained.

Then the sound of her voice was real, calling him to supper.

Cade glanced at the closed door. *She's gotten along just fine without you. The fur coverlet, remember?*

The money to keep this place and feed those animals had to come from somewhere. He mentally slammed the door to the most obvious answer. If she had a lover, where the hell was he? If she had a lover why was she dreaming about him?

But the knowledge that Hallie was going to pump him full of sweet confections, pat him on the head, and send him on his way settled like a cold lump of grits in his belly.

She had never once hinted that he would be invited into her bed. That pricked his pride.

Hallie called to him again.

A wicked grin slashed his lips. Hallie was a bundle of intriguing feminine contradictions he'd just have to untangle before he rode away.

And maybe, just maybe, he'd make the shy Miss Halimeda Pruitt a very happy woman in the doing.

✳ *Chapter 2* ✣

$\mathcal{I}$t was time for Cade McAllister to leave. The decision had hovered at the back of Hallie's mind for the past two days. She had never turned anyone out of her home before Doc's allotted time to heal, but Cade was going to be the first exception.

Every waking moment was filled with an intense awareness of his presence, every sleep-filled hour was consumed with dreams of him.

She had never dreamed about any of the others.

Hallie called Cade to supper once more, then retrieved the basket of steaming corn sticks from the stove's warming oven. Setting the basket between the two place settings on the round oak kitchen table, Hallie sighed. She was twenty-five years old, long past nurturing girlish dreams of having a family of her own. At least she had believed that until Cade McAllister entered her life.

The man had made her dream again, not just at night, but daydream when practical matters required her attention. And he made her feel restless. At first she refused to recognize the signs but the longer Cade stayed, the more apparent they had become. It was his eyes, of course, that started a liquid warmth running through her. That intense gaze that seemed to peel away all the protective layers to see the secrets she hid. He couldn't know about the dreams she foolishly wrote down in her journal, but whatever had wrought the change in Cade, she couldn't ignore it.

For the tenth or was it the hundredth time since she had first set eyes on Cade, Hallie wished he had been less handsome. Not that she set such a store by a person's looks, but Cade McAllister was handsome as sin, and Granny Rose had always warned that sin brought its own kind of trouble.

Cade had the devil's own good looks, thick black hair that begged a woman's hand to tame it, eyes as hard and blue as a winter's sky that glittered with male power. Slashing brows bridged a straight nose, lashes a woman would be dead not to envy did nothing to soften that tough, sharp-jawed face.

But when Cade smiled, when those perfectly formed masculine lips revealed the dimples in the corners of his mouth, he blinded a woman with the sensual promise he implied.

Thinking about that smile caused her toes to curl within her shoes. It sent a flush of heat across her cheeks. Eating a whole tin of Sparrow's Empress double-chocolate, fondant nut centers wasn't as good as watching Cade smile.

Hallie closed her eyes. She had done more than look at Cade. She had had plenty of opportunities to touch him.

A hitch in her breathing warned her. But it was too late. That lean, long-limbed body, naked and helpless as a babe, seared itself on her closed lids. Oh, my, yes, she had certainly touched him. Cade would be shocked out of his boots if he had an inkling that he played the starring role in her too vivid dreams.

Hallie came to with a start. There, it had happened again. With a quick shake of her head, she snapped herself out of her heated musings. Her breathing was erratic, and a curious trembling beset her from the inside out. She stared down at the large tureen filled with the cooling chicken and dumplings. This would never do.

The man had to go.

She called him again, then fetched the pitcher of lemonade to the table. A dish of corn relish followed.

Hallie attempted to shrug off her pensive mood. She knew

she had a strong practical streak. Why did it disappear when she thought about Cade?

"Forlorn, love-starved, old spinster," she muttered, welcoming the anger the reminder brought. "You are a practical woman." And thanks to Granny Rose's trust, she was an independent one.

Practical, independent women with plain looks did not appeal to men like Cade McAllister. Aside from his most wicked smile, she had to remember Doc's warning. If she allowed herself to lose her heart she would repeat her mother's mistake.

Temptation teased her with the thought of what it would be like to cast off the cloak of respectability that wrapped her so tightly at times that she couldn't breathe.

And do what? Seduce Cade McAllister? Throw yourself at him? Ask him to take pity and make a lonely woman's dreams come true?

There was no longer a choice. Cade had to go before she did something foolish.

Briskly then, Hallie finished to set the table with the supper she had made. Chicken and dumplings was Cade's favorite supper. Granny Rose had taught her that a man's pleasure began with his victuals. Good food set a man's mood toward indulgent to the woman who provided it. Granny Rose would know. She'd been the toast of the Mississippi paddlewheelers fifty years ago. The thought was a strange one to have considering that she had made up her mind to ask Cade to leave.

Hallie turned from the table and found herself staring out the window over the dry sink. Strong, dying rays of the sun warmed her hands where they gripped the wooden edge. She didn't see the lush grass sprinkled with the spill of wildflowers. She was deep in thought of the three years that had passed, and how much that during that time she had missed her outspoken grandmother who held to her belief against everyone's opinion that a woman had the right to decide how she lived her life.

While Granny had been alive, Hallie agreed with her. It

was becoming more difficult as the years slipped away and the consequences of Granny's and her mother's beliefs forced her to live alone.

Cade felt the springy give of the wooden floor as he entered the kitchen. Dusk already layered the room in shadows. He sniffed appreciatively at the delicious aroma of the herb scented chicken stew set on the table, but noted with a frown that Hallie didn't seem to hear him. She hadn't lit the coal oil fixture above the table or answered him when he softly called her name.

Unbidden words from her journal came into his mind: *It was the surprise of those unexpected kisses that I treasure the most. He delights in catching me unaware. From the first he had discovered that most sensitive flesh at the back of my neck. Whether the brush of his warm masculine lips or the lightest touch of his teasing fingertips touched upon that place, tremors dance up and down my spine.*

Before Cade knew what he was doing he had moved up behind her. The fresh scent of lemon rose from her hair as he leaned close. A streak of sunlight cut across his vision. Sunlight that touched her hair with fire and picked out a series of golden needlepoints from the tips of her eyelashes which formed a fan of shadows across one cheek. She looked lost and defenseless. He felt her body heat through the layers of cloth between them.

He touched his lips to the back of her hair. "Hallie?" Cade moved his fingers to the bare skin of her neck, his thumb brushing her earlobe. He sensed she was aware of him now, every bit aware as he was of her.

Hallie stilled as a warmth seeped through cloth, going beyond skin, beyond muscle, to the core of her. The brush of his breath across her neck brought forth a tremor. The touch of his lips made her knees go weak. Her breath was heavy and fast. Goosebumps raced up and down her spine.

"Hallie?" Cade's voice was thick with a rush of emotions too tangled to name. It was the first time he had touched her and the sweet scent of her, the pale smooth skin drew his lips again and again.

She lost herself in the daydream, giving in to the impulse to tilt her head to one side, allowing freedom to the warm whisper of his mouth. The caress was as light as butterfly wings against her skin. Dreamily she sighed, unconsciously leaning back against his body.

Cade shifted his weight and the floorboard creaked.

Hallie lifted her head with a jerk and slammed his nose.

"Ouch! Dammit, Hallie, that hurt!"

Snapped from her daydream, she turned on him like a spitting kitten. "What were you trying to do to me?"

Cade rubbed his nose. "Damn, but you've got a hard head."

Hallie looked up at his eyes. They glittered down at her, full of nonsense blue. A very dangerous blue. "Why? Why did you . . ." Helplessly, she waved her hand in the air.

"To wake you up, Hallie."

"I wasn't sleeping."

"Like hell you're not." He said it so low he was almost certain she didn't hear him.

But she had. Hallie flushed. She kept her eyes on a level with the shadowed length of his throat. She could see the beat of blood just below the smooth, clean-shaven flesh.

"You had no right—"

"Don't expect me to apologize. You were temptation itself standing there, Hallie," he added for good measure.

"No." She blinked several times, then shook her head. He was wrong. There was nothing tempting about her. Her gaze slid past his shoulder to the crock of wildflowers sitting in the center of the linen runner on the sideboard. She should say something, make it plain that he did indeed need to apologize for taking advantage of her, for crossing the line that only confirmed her decision to ask him to leave.

Hallie couldn't get a word out.

"Hallie?" Cade couldn't keep a note of alarm from his voice. She appeared to have withdrawn without moving.

He stepped in front of her, tempted to touch the flush on her cheek. She seemed fragile to him, something he had never noticed before about her. His hand was on her shoulder before he thought about it.

"I didn't hurt you, Hallie. There's no need to have a maidenly fit of the vapors or something."

"Kiss my buttons, Cade McAllister. I am not about to have a fit or faint or give way because you forgot yourself. Supper's cooling," she said, then slipped out from under his hand. Her skin still felt the heat of his touch.

"I'd like to do that too."

The teasing note made her face him. "Do what?"

"Kiss your buttons, Hallie, just like you asked."

Under the curve of his wicked smile that turned her knees to unset jelly, Hallie could only sputter.

"Yep," he added, hooking his thumbs on the corners of his pants pockets so that her gaze dragged down to the indecent fit of his pants. "I'd number them among the other things I'd like to kiss."

"Try Divine, McAllister. Her tongue is as broad and slippery as yours." She walked past him to the table.

"Wouldn't do, you know," he murmured close to her ear as he pulled out her chair. "I'd need one that was smaller and softer to duel with mine."

Cade took his place across the table from her. She dished up their plates and refused to look at him.

"Chicken and dumplings," he remarked. "Third time this week."

"It's your favorite. You said so enough times."

"You're a kind woman, Hallie, to indulge me so. If I told you some of my other favorite things, would you be as indulgent?"

"Did you eat your chocolate?"

"My chocolate? What has—"

"Did you?"

"Yeah, I ate it. And all the while I still wanted a belt of whiskey."

In her lap Hallie twisted her fingers in her apron.

Maybe she should have given him two. Guilty she glanced up at him, then just as quickly looked away. Her gaze lingered on his hands as he buttered a corn stick. Long, strong-looking hands. A cowboy's hands, calluses on the fingers, across the tops of his palms. A working man's hands. But another image imposed itself. A lover's hands, sure and gentle enough to stroke a woman . . . *Hallie! What are you thinking of? That way leads to restless tossing all night long. And he's leaving, remember?*

But another little voice countered, only if you ask him to.

It was impossible to ignore his masculine presence. Even when she wasn't near him, wasn't looking at him, she was intensely aware of Cade, as though every nerve in her body centered on him. With her skin still carrying the heat of his light kisses on her neck, the sensations were ten times more powerful.

Feeling him watch her, she had to look up. His gaze was fixed on her mouth. Hallie tried to swallow and found that she couldn't. Her breath was lost somewhere inside herself. She forced herself to take a shaky sip of lemonade, then stared down at her untouched plate.

Hallie sensed something different about Cade tonight. She couldn't name it what it was, and it went beyond the liberties he'd taken, beyond the sexual teasing. From herself she wouldn't hide the truth. That was exactly what it had been. But why?

When the answer came to her, Hallie sat up straight, her eyes round as saucers, her lips parted, her hands clamped around her knife and fork as if they were weapons to do battle. Cade McAllister was a healing, healthy male, definitely hot as a horn! She wasn't positive what the last entailed. It was one of those phrases Granny Rose had been fond of quoting after a long association with Victoria Woodhull, a believer in free love and the first woman to run for president. The woman had left the country almost ten years ago to live quietly in England and Hallie had been one of many left with the legacy of her scandalous and radical principles.

She was the only woman here. Cade had not meant anything personal by his charming kisses. The man simply needed a fast trip to Miss Ada Lane's. Hallie wasn't supposed to know about Miss Ada or her girls or what went on in the big house, but Miss Ada had been one of her grandmother's intimate friends. Another burden to bear. How could she keep Cade's respect and make the suggestion that he should visit there?

How could she when she didn't want him to? *Hallie, take yourself in hand. You do not want him to stay.*

While she sat toying with her food, working out her dilemma, Cade refilled his plate with seconds. Normally Hallie would have been pleased. Tonight she wasn't. How could he sit there and eat as if he hadn't caught her off guard, daydreaming? How could he tuck into food when he'd left her insides feeling as if he had dragged them across the ribs of the washboard? And he dared to smile at her. She should have slapped that wicked smile right off his face. She should be furious that he had taken such a liberty with her.

So why wasn't she lacing into that smug masculine form of devil's bait?

"Hallie, what's wrong? Hallie?" Cade leaned across the table and waved a hand in front of her face. She gave a jerk, then her gaze focused on him.

"That's better. I asked if I upset you, Hallie."

The lie hovered on the tip of her tongue. She looked into twinkling blue eyes. "Yes," she blurted. "Yes, you did upset me. You had no right to take advantage of me. A gentleman would have waited for a—"

"Whoa! Hang it up, Hallie. If I had waited for a sign from you I'd be bald and rocking time away on the front porch."

Very deliberately, Cade set his fork down, planted his elbows on the edge of the table and formed a bridge with his entwined fingers to rest his chin. His narrow-eyed gaze took in her bewildered expression.

"Ah, Hallie," he began in a gentle admonishing tone.

"I told you the truth. I saw you standing there in the last rays of sunlight and you were too much temptation to resist.

When you didn't pull away or try to stop me I thought you welcomed my attention. Was I wrong?"

Cade held a bone-deep certainty that Hallie had never lied to him. He felt like the run-down edge of his boot heel watching her struggle to answer the question he'd already discovered in her journal. Beneath his chin his fingers tightened in a death grip. He was anxious for her to say it, to have everything out in the open between them.

"I won't repeat their mistakes," she whispered, then lifted eyes bruised with pain to his.

"Hallie? I don't understand."

She shoved her chair back, her napkin falling unheeded to the floor as she fled the room.

Cade repeated her words to himself. He tried to make sense of them. Without thought he found himself reaching behind him on the sideboard for the ever present fancy tin of chocolates. He was munching on his third piece before he realized what he was doing.

"Hells bells! That woman is enough to drive a preacher to drink and a drunk sober."

Sitting there, brooding and struggling to understand whose mistakes Hallie wasn't going to repeat was a waste of time. Cade stood up and began clearing the table. He knew where he would find Hallie when he was done.

Finding her was the easy part. Getting her to talk to him might prove more challenge then he had realized.

❀ Chapter 3 ❀

*T*he night was cool. A faint breeze murmured through the spring leaves. In the distance Cade heard the gurgling rush of the creek, and all around him were the pungent smells of animals and earth.

In front of him, he saw Hallie with her arms folded over the corral fence. She appeared unaware of him as the breeze tossed a wisp of hair across her cheek and she brushed it away. Moonlight touched her features, both delicate and strong.

Cade crushed the shawl he held, alarmed by the strength of determination that rose within him to pursue her. He limped closer and draped the light wool over her hunched shoulders.

"Why did you run away from me, Hallie?"

"I've been wondering the very same thing," she replied softly.

"And have you found the answer?"

"What I did was childish. I'm a grown woman—"

"Won't get any argument from me, Hallie."

She wanted to deny the words, deny the strange little shiver that raced up her spine, deny that sharp awareness of Cade in the darkness. What he said was nothing dangerous, yet she knew that is where the danger lay.

He trailed one finger across the open weave of the shawl from her right shoulder to the left, then back again. Cade couldn't seem to control his need to touch her.

"I love this place. I never want to leave here. It probably would be more practical to find a place in Denver but I like being alone." She felt the light touch of his hand, brushing back and forth across her shoulders and in an effort to distract him and herself, she rushed on. "My grandmother set up a trust for me, so I would never have to worry about losing this land and—"

"Was she one of the people whose mistakes you weren't going to repeat?"

Denial sprang to her lips. Hallie swallowed it.

Cade smiled as his lips touched the back of her hair. Although she had not moved he sensed that she was very much aware of him. He inhaled deeply and passion surged through him, but he quickly tempered it, for Hallie was ready to bolt and he didn't want her to leave him again.

"You're prying, Cade McAllister."

"You always use my full name when you want to keep distance, Hallie. But how else can I find out all there is to know about you if I don't ask?"

"Why ever would you want to? You'll be leaving soon." The gentle ply of his hands shifting to rub up and down her upper arms caused a hitch in her breathing. "I think you had better stop."

"Stop what? Talking to you? Touching you? Hasn't anyone ever courted you, Hallie?" *Courted*? Where the devil did that come from? "Can't you understand that I like knowing things about you that no one else does?"

"You can't."

"But I want to. I'm going to." He grimaced when he heard the smugness in his voice, but he did like the thought of knowing Hallie's secrets. He had no way of knowing for sure, but he imagined that like his mother, most women guarded little secrets from prying men. Determination washed through him. He wanted to be the only man who knew Hallie's secrets.

"You didn't answer me, Hallie. Hasn't anyone courted you?"

"No. I never allowed it."

He couldn't deny the pleasure it gave him to hear this. Cade found he wanted more. He wanted her to reveal the mysterious feminine dreams that had him playing the role of lover. While he continued stroking her arms, Cade reminded himself that once more she wasn't running off. He allowed himself to imagine what it would be like to have Hallie whisper the words she had written in her journal, to know all the things that made Hallie uniquely her.

The question of why Hallie was so special floated through his mind. Somehow from the moment he had left his room to tasting her skin for the first time, Cade realized that his priorities had shifted. He still intended to make Hallie a happy woman, but that happiness included more than the physical mating of male and female.

"Won't you look at me, Hallie?" Cade suited action to words and gently turned her to face him.

"I don't think we should be doing this, Mr. McAllister."

"I disagree, Miss Pruitt."

Courting. Had he really said courting? Hallie still sifted that word through her mind. Her concentration on what Cade was doing was minuscule at best. She couldn't stop herself from reveling in the heat of his hard, lean body. His breath smelled of chocolate, his skin like the sage-laden breeze. Was it so terrible to steal a few minutes to fill the need his closeness brought? Earlier she had felt threatened by his kissing. Not now. Now, she thought of how long she had been alone.

And hungry for someone's touch.

"I brought you a confection," he murmured, taking the sweet wrapped in its paper cup from his shirt pocket. "Will you share it with me?"

Hallie looked from the sweet held before her lips up to his face. "Where . . . er . . ." He touched the tip of the candy to her lips. Hallie turned her face. "Where did you get that?"

"Get it? From the tin on the sideboard." Cade lifted his head, perplexed. Hallie never denied him taking any of her sweets. In fact, now that he thought about it, she always encouraged him to eat as many as he wanted after supper.

Maybe Hallie had forgotten her own dream of sharing sweets with a lover? Cade smiled. He'd just have to remind her of that very pleasant interlude.

"Come on, Hallie. Share this with me."

"I can't."

"You won't."

"You're right." How many had he had? Hallie peered up at his face. He wasn't slurring his words. If anything, his voice was as coaxing as a feather tick on a winter's night.

"Can't understand it," he whispered, leaning closer. "You've seen all there is to see of me, Hallie. How can you refuse to share a bit of sweet with me?"

Heat spiraled through her in a double attack. It rose from her curled toes to stop where it met the heat that flushed her cheeks, swelled her breasts and settled down low in her belly.

"Ah, Hallie, you've always told me it puts you in a mellow mood."

Hallie worried her lower lip with the edge of her teeth. "Do you have a temper? Of course you do," she answered herself thinking back to the earlier set to in the barn.

"Of course I do? Where the devil—"

"You're a man. You have a temper."

"Glad you've noticed what sex I am, Hallie, but what in tarnation has my being a man got to do with temper? And, while you're answering that, think of one for what temper has to do with sharing a stupid bit of sticky, melting chocolate."

Her attempt to slide beneath his arm was blocked. There was nothing for her to do but own up to what she'd been doing to him.

"Share the damn thing with me. I'm trying to please you."

The command, issued in a voice of stifled irritation, only bore witness to her being right. When she pointed this out to Cade, his answer was to bite off half the sweet and hold the balance to her lips.

"We're standing in the moonlight, Hallie. The breeze while cool is not cold. You are sharing a piece of chocolate with a man who wants to kiss the sweet sticky stuff off your mouth."

"This is court—" The rest of the word was lost in the bit of confection he gently, but insistently, inserted into her mouth.

"Chew. Swallow. Then kiss me." What was wrong with her? Didn't she remember her own dreams? Was he going to have to remind her of every step? This was not what he had been imagining. He thought she'd fall right in, with every seductive curve of her body cooperating.

"Cade?"

"Are you done? Can I kiss you now?" He wrapped his arms around her and pulled her close. "Hallie, this isn't the way I meant it to be. I wanted to—ah, hell, words aren't very good. I'll show you."

Bemused by his shifting moods, she stood still within his embrace. She wasn't quite sure why she was going to allow this; it felt strange, and awkward, and terribly comforting. The warmth of his arms around her dispelled fear.

His heart beat with the steadiness of the enameled iron Waterbury clock on the parlor mantle. His shirt was soft against her hands. The heat of his body chased the night's chill.

"Hallie, you feel perfect in my arms. Doesn't this feel right, feel good to you, too?" Cade cupped her head within his large hands. His fingers stole beneath her hair and his thumb soothingly rubbed the tense cord of the nape of her neck.

"We're both alone, Hallie. We both have been alone for a long time. But if you truly don't want me to kiss you, now's the time to say so." He touched her temple with his lips. "'Cause I don't think I'm going to want to stop with one kiss, Hallie." The last was mouthed against her hair.

She tilted her head back to look up at him. Cade held his breath, ready to steal a denial with every coaxing word he knew. Her eyes were luminous in the moonlight. He retained enough sense to know she was wary and summoned all his willpower not to kiss her senseless. As it was, he tasted the tremble of her lips with the barest of touches.

Hallie closed her eyes as his head blocked out the moonlight. His lips were warm, his kiss one of softness, of simple sharing. Lips sweet with smooth velvet chocolate.

Slow and shy, Hallie brought her hands down to his waist, needing something to hold on to. *Foolish, foolish, Hallie.* She ignored the warning. This was a lost moment in time, and Cade, warm and strong, only filled her need to be held.

The breeze died. His lips strayed from her mouth to her cheek, into her hair. She noted the sudden hush of the night, then only had the alluring awareness of Cade.

The tips of her breasts just grazed his chest; her skirt brushed his thighs, teasing her into remembering the sinful thrill of seeing his long, lean, naked body. Her hands had learned the textures of his flesh. She knew she had to temper her wayward thoughts. But truly, Cade was a beautifully formed man.

Then his lips pressed against hers again, this time not quite so gently. This time he was making her aware of the shape of his mouth, of the taste of him, of all the coaxing power of a man who knew how to kiss. He almost made her believe she could give in to the seductive power of him, could unashamedly make every secret dream come true.

She could feel her resolve faltering. Cade kept rubbing his lips over hers. Her heart was pounding. An ache welled up inside her. His lips were hungry. She tasted his loneliness. Knew the bitter bite of her own. When he was gone the nights would be endless. Her hands dipped into his back pockets, holding him tight. Hallie swallowed his soft groaning sound. With a wildness she didn't know she possessed, she kissed him back.

This was more of what Cade had envisioned. Hallie flaring to life like tinder under the match. Her trembling lips withheld nothing from him. His tongue drove deeper into her sweet, heated mouth. His hands slid in a rush down her spine, her sides, wanting to learn every curve. He felt the smooth glide of cotton beneath his hands when he wanted to touch skin.

Mine. Every male instinct made the claim, demanded that he establish possession. He forgot where they were. The only thing that mattered was Hallie feeling as he did, that this was special and rare. Her kisses were bringing forth hungers he couldn't begin to name.

Her fingers sank deeper into his pockets. Hard, insistent desire pounded in his mind. Leaning into her, he pinned her to the corral fence with the hard length of his body, his arousal rigid against her belly. His palm strayed to her ribs. He heard her sudden intake of breath, savored it and plunged them both into a kiss of sexual declaration that promised wild, lush fulfillment. His fingers stole higher, gently rounding on the firm, taut thrust of her breast.

Hallie stiffened, then jerked her head to the side. "This ... has ..." She wet her lips as heart pounding, Cade stilled her move to flee. "... Gone too ... far."

Cade didn't think it had gone far enough. He released his stolen bounty with reluctance and cupped the softer skin of her cheek, forcing her to look at him. "Hallie" it was all he could manage for the moment.

He stared down at her with heated blue eyes, vaguely noting that neither seemed to breathe normally for a lengthy interval. He hoped Hallie was registering the minute degrees of pleasure inundating the senses just as he was.

He was doomed to disappointment for verbal acknowledgement. Dropping his forehead to hers, he rubbed the tip of his nose against hers, fighting to find a smile. He could almost hear the wheels of recrimination turning in her mind.

Even as Cade sought and discarded demands that she recognize the mutual need between them, he knew they were not going to be met. It was uncanny how attuned he had become to Hallie's moods and state of mind. Striving for a lighter mood as desire still clamored in his blood, he lifted his head but refused to allow her to turn away.

"Blame the chocolate, Hallie. Eating one piece brings sweet sensations. Think of the rush to buy such bounty by every male—"

"Oh, my Lord, you know!"

Such anguish snapped him into alertness. "Know what? Hallie, that doesn't make any sense. Confections can't make anyone feel what we did. I was only teasing—" Hit with a wave of dizzyness, he broke off. The edges of his mind were suddenly fuzzed with a thick cloud. Cade found himself leaning flush against her, crushing her against the fence.

"Your kisses pack one hell of a wallop." He muzzled her cheek. "I swear, Hallie, my knees are getting weak." Molasses thick and slightly slurred, his voice reached his ears as if from far away. "What did . . . Hallie?"

She slid her arms around his waist and with a great deal of effort managed to reverse their positions.

"That's just as good, Hallie."

Moonlight revealed the teasing grin of a young boy, while the voice was all male satisfaction as he nestled her hips against his.

"Cade, stop." Then she repeated it more forcably. "We need to get you into the house."

"Into bed, Hallie?" he asked, rocking his hips against hers.

Heat streaked through her. She fought a mighty and quick battle to subdue it.

"Hallie?"

"Yes," she snapped, attempting to wedge her shoulder beneath his arm. "Into bed we go."

"Ah, Hallie, you're a woman to make a man's dreams come true." He planted a sloppy kiss on her nose, then tried for her mouth. "Mine. All mine, Hallie."

"I'm not yours. Come on, help me, Cade." She pulled free. His arm slammed back to grab hold of the pole fence. This was not working. "A nice, soft bed, Cade, isn't that what you want? Soft and warm," she coaxed.

"You're soft." His hand slid from her shoulder to the upper curve of her breast. "And damn warm."

Hallie prayed he'd never remember this. She left his hand in place, urging him away from the fence. The sudden stiffening of his body alarmed her. "Don't pass out, Cade. I'll never be able to carry you." But when she looked up at him, his head was flung back, his attitude one of listening.

Moonlight slid lovingly over his handsome features. She could have spent the next hour looking her fill, instead, she tried to free his grasp on the fence.

"Bloody blue blazes!"

"Cade?"

"Get into the house, Hallie. Now." He shook his head like a maddened steer about to charge. "Move, Hallie." Cade found it easy to give her the order but he was having trouble making his body obey the same.

Dread—which had nothing to do with Cade's finding out he ate laudanum-dosed candy—forced Hallie to turn around and see what had alarmed Cade. His repeated order for her to run into the house and lock the doors registered at the same time she spotted the silhouettes of two riders stopped on the rise above the house.

"A strange time of night to be riding," she murmured. Hallie couldn't help but think that as long as they remained still, they might not be seen.

"Ornery female. Move. They can't be paying a social call at this hour."

"Stubborn cuss. I can't leave you here alone."

"Then run and get my gun, Hallie."

She quickly judged the distance to the house as she continued to watch the two motionless strangers. She would not, could not, leave Cade alone in his condition.

"Hallie, please."

"No."

Cade fought off the fuzzy cloud that threatened to buckle his legs out from under him. He knew she wasn't going to leave him. He couldn't even spare a moment to wonder what was happening to him. He had to protect her.

He saw the two urge their horses down the rise, not at a run, but at a walk, as if they were very sure of not finding any resistance when they reached the house.

"Get in the barn, Hallie. Don't argue. Just move."

✱ Chapter 4 ✦

$\mathcal{H}$allie propped Cade against the inside wall of the barn next to the open doors. The pungent smells of the animals assaulted her senses. Divine sent out a questing moo, followed by Forage's bleats and then grunts from a most disgruntled Eternal. Straw rustled as the other animals awoke and moved restlessly in their stalls.

"Just what we need," Cade muttered. "A damn welcome band to tell them where we are. Can't you shut them up?"

"I doubt it. If your sleep was disturbed—"

"Then tell me that you stash a shotgun in the barn, Hallie."

"I've never had a reason to. Nothing like this has happened."

Cade groaned. It had been too much to hope for. "Get me some kind of a weapon. And hurry."

She worried her lower lip with the edge of her teeth. Cade could barely stand. With his legs spread wide, boots braced on the floor, and knees jutting out, he appeared ready to slide down the wall at any moment. She didn't think he was capable of wielding a weapon.

Ignoring the rising animal noises, Hallie peered around the edge of the door. Her attempt to locate their unexpected visitors came up empty. The play of moonlight and shadows offered no clue to where they were now.

She wished she had Cade's ability to dismiss what had happened minutes ago. But the truth was, she was still reeling from the potency of his kisses.

"Are you so sure they are a threat to us?" she whispered.

"In my bones sure. A weapon, Hallie. Now," he demanded, in a testy voice. Cade had a feeling he was losing the fight with the fuzzy cloud that threatened to take over his body. It was too much to ask him to deal with a doubting Hallie who would likely talk him to death before she moved.

Over the pungent smells in the barn, he inhaled her much sweeter fragrance as she leaned closer to him. He wanted to grab hold of her and kiss her senseless.

Hallie had something else in mind.

Wagging one finger beneath his nose until he closed his eyes to stop them from crossing he stifled another groan when she spoke.

"I can't give you a weapon, Cade. You can't fight two men. Violence begets violence. Let them rob whatever they want."

"Including you? Don't get huffy, Hallie. Get me something to protect you."

"What would you like?" she snapped, alarmed by his insistence that she would be hurt. "A post-hole digger? No, you couldn't handle that. Too heavy. A shovel? The hay fork or manure hook? There's a hoe, rake, and scythe. Or an axe. Of course, I can't swear that the blade's sharp since I've been buying a wagon load of firewood from—"

Cade grabbed her shoulders and gave her a little shake. "Hallie, I don't give a damn what you buy, or from who, just get me something long and useful."

The fact that he had to let her go to brace his hands against the wall to stop a fall took the sting from his heated voice. Hallie wasted no more time.

She ran down the center aisle of the barn, easily dodging the staggered line of roof support beams. The new mule Patience brayed, which made the horses snort. By the time she reached the back wall and snatched down the buggy whip, Eternal's squeals reached an all-time high as the pig vied with Divine, Forage, the horses and mule, billy goat and burro. Hallie felt her way past the implements hanging from the harness hooks on the wall. She grabbed hold of the hay fork with its three long steel tines. Hallie stopped to open each of the animal's stalls as she made her return trip to where Cade waited.

She was immediately stopped as surrounding velvet noses searched for the treats she usually brought to her animals. Sweetcakes butted her thigh, Eternal's snout lifted the back of her skirt and petticoats as she wedged a place for herself between Hallie's legs.

Forage bleated like a lost lamb, while Steadfast planted a sturdy body in Hallie's path. Over the noise of the animals she heard Cade's furious whisper for her to hurry.

Hallie managed to untangle herself from Eternal. She led the way to Cade, all her darlings faithfully following her.

"Get rid of them," he ordered.

Hallie thrust the hay fork into his hand. "They'll be the perfect distraction. If you're right about those riders."

"Stop doubting me and get over here where I can protect you." Cade didn't wait for her to obey him. He latched onto Hallie's hand and yanked her beside him. "Did you get something for yourself?"

"The buggy whip?" she asked in a hopeful voice.

Cade pushed a questing nose away from his shirt pocket. He was breaking out in a cold sweat and his knees nearly buckled. He opened his mouth to answer Hallie, then snapped it shut. Two men were talking outside the barn. The fact that they made no effort to lower their voices told Cade more than he wanted to know.

"I done tole you it was wasted time to search in the house. I done told you I seen them head this way. I done knowed I was right. They're in the barn."

"Emmet, put a bit between your teeth. I can tell for myself where they are. Someone had to let those animals loose. But hiding in the barn ain't gonna help them. You go inside and I'll wait out here."

"You wants I should flush them out, Jeb?"

"Yeah. Flush them out to me."

"You real sure it's just him and that old spinster gal?"

"You heard, same as me, what Miss Lurette found out.

And remember what else Miss Lurette said. This time he'd better be dead. You understand that, Emmet. Make sure he ain't gonna be able to tell anyone what we done to him. Now move."

The moment he realized who they were, guilt swamped Cade. There had been no way to prevent Hallie from hearing them. He was the sole reason her life was in danger.

The gentle pat on his arm told him that Hallie didn't quite grasp how much danger she was in. He wasn't about to enlighten her. He couldn't divide his attention between one hysterical female and two men bent on killing them.

Cade had a more immediate problem to figure out. He had to find a way to get through Hallie's ragtag flock. All the animals ignored his nudges to give him enough room to lift the hay fork so he could tackle the first man through the door.

Fringes of fuzziness still threatened him, but Cade's night vision had always been excellent. He spotted the extended hand holding the gun before the man's full body came into view inside the barn doors. In the few moments that the man hesitated, Cade felt an explosion of fury that lent him strength. Sharp pokes to the animals cleared a path for him. He was ready to confront the man.

A few more steps . . .

Cade turned his head to Hallie. His lips found her ear. "Not a word," he mouthed. He thought she nodded her agreement from the way her hair touched against his cheek. With a solid grip on the hay fork, Cade awaited the perfect moment and readied himself to charge.

Hallie screamed. The air crackled with the snap of the whip. Faith, the youngest horse, shrilled a challenge—the animal had never accepted being a gelding. Hope attempted to rear. Charity lashed out with her back hooves. Patience followed suit, braying to wake the dead. The pig and cow added their own loud distress cries to the din. Sweetcakes, seeing it was a stranger and male, charged. Emmet's gun went off.

Cade came away from the wall. He had no strength to swear at Hallie for disobeying him.

Something tripped him. Thrown off balance, Cade's planned tackle went awry. He bit his tongue to bury a cry as his knee on the healing leg was wrenched. The hay fork dropped from his hands. Cade lurched to the side and hit Emmet as he struggled to rise. The gun went off again.

Panic cries from the animals filled the barn.

Cade went after Emmet's gun with a single-minded purpose. Forage bleated in his ear. A hoof came down on his hand.

"Not me, you jackass. Get him!"

Emmet bucked. Cade rolled over with Emmet on top. He managed to land a glancing blow to Emmet's face. Now, if the billy goat was worth his feed, he'd butt the stuffing out of the son of a bitch who wouldn't let go of his gun.

Cade heard the snap of the whip again. It was too damn close for comfort. But one of the animals must have felt sorry for his struggles. One got hold of some part of Emmet's anatomy. The man shrieked with a spine-tingling, curl-your-hair, shake-in-your-boots level that overrode the animal's varying cries. Cade quickly took advantage of the man's pain to grab hold of the gun.

A whack with the butt silenced Emmet's cries. Cade shoved the limp body off his own. He was on the opposite side of the barn now. Somewhere outside was the man called Jeb, who had orders to kill him.

Cade had no idea of where Hallie was and he couldn't call out to her. If the Lord took pity on a beleaguered male, He would keep Hallie safe and out of the way.

He managed to stagger to his feet. Keeping his back to the wall—a position that offered him needed support as well as protection—Cade inched his way to the corner, then moved along the front wall.

Strangely enough, the animals all milled about inside the barn and their initial panicked cries were softening. It was still too much noise for Cade. He couldn't hear a sound from outside. And he needed to know where Jeb was. Jeb had a fully loaded gun. Cade stopped. He felt the warm metal barrel in his own hand, counted the groves of the cylinder, and noted the gun was hammerless. A Smith and Wesson model with only five shots. Two had already been fired.

"Emmet? Answer me!"

Cade couldn't risk peering around the door to see where Jeb was. He had a feeling the man stood somewhat back from the doors. He had three shots and had to make one count.

A groan and a hard thump forced his attention back to where he had left Emmet. A choked sound escaped his lips. Hallie leaned over the downed man with the hay fork pressed against his chest.

Cade made a vow to teach that woman the meaning of obedience if it killed him. First he'd settle his score.

"You ain't fooling me none, McAllister. You ain't getting out alive. Better give yourself up or the woman will die, too."

Cade's directive of what Jeb could do with his threats was buried under Hallie's begging pleas. It took seconds for Cade to realize that from the sound of her voice that Hallie was moving. He tried to find her, but she was hidden behind the shadowy shapes of the animals.

"Stay put!" Cade yelled.

"Like hell, McAllister," Jeb answered.

Cade fired into the yard. He was rewarded with a string of curses. If Jeb was stupid enough to think he had meant the order for him, Cade quickly figured what worked once, could work twice.

Hallie once more had another idea. She shooed the animals out the door.

"No, Hallie!" Cade watched for her, intending to grab her before she could get outside. Jeb continued cursing. He fired his gun, once, twice. Cade flung his head back against the wall. If those animals did to Jeb what they had done to him the first time, he could almost feel sorry for the man.

Jeb's cursing turned to yells. Cade limped out of the barn. "Call them off, Hallie."

"I don't think so. He was going to kill you."

"Call them off before they kill him." Cade no longer saw or heard Jeb. "Hallie, I want to see them pay for what they did to me, but that's a job for the law."

Without a word she brushed by him, calling to her darlings. Hallie managed to get the horses to back away. Jeb swayed back and forth on his hands and knees. Sweetcakes found his position too tempting. Before Hallie could stop the goat, his butt sent Jeb sprawling on the ground.

Cade heard Emmet moaning. "Better get some rope to tie them up. I'll bring them into town in the morning and file charges against them."

Once Hallie had the animals back in their stalls and helped Cade tie up the two, she marched into the house. Cade was slow to follow. Now that the danger was passed, he felt drained.

Hallie stood at the sink, working the pump. He hung back from entering and watched her for a few moments. She soaped a rag and proceeded to wash her hands.

"Some fool would think you were angry with him."

"And you are not a fool, are you, Mr. McAllister."

"That doesn't sound like a question, Hallie." Cade still wasn't sure it was safe to step inside. "I don't know why you'd be angry with me. I did what I could to protect you. Of course, you didn't give me all that much chance. You just had to stick your—"

"If you don't stop right this minute, Cade McAllister, I'll stuff this soapy rag in that brazen mouth of yours." Shaking in the aftermath, Hallie turned around and brandished the rag like a weapon.

"Now, Hallie. You just be nice to me. I'm a poor, weak man in need of your tender attention."

"Like my foot you are."

"What's wrong with your foot?" Cade limped toward her. "Did you get hurt? I should've—"

"Done less than you did," Hallie cut in. She tossed the

rag into the sink and wiped her hands on the linen cloth. "Did you realize that you could have been killed?"

"I was more worried about you." Cade leaned against the counter. "They'll likely tell that they saw us kissing."

"I don't care if the whole county knows that you kissed me, but since you're obviously concerned, I'll lie."

Cade was too stunned to reply.

Hallie glanced around the cleaned kitchen. "Thank you for doing the supper dishes." She skirted the table, then couldn't help herself. She stopped and looked at Cade, hurt beyond belief that he hadn't denied what she said about kissing her.

"Stop looking at me as if you don't know what I'm talking about, Cade. You should see your face. If it became any more stiff and disapproving, I'll use it to starch my linens."

"Hallie—" A fresh surge of blood sent his flesh to fight the constraints of his pants, testing the tailor's skill and causing him to set his teeth in a wry grimace.

"Well, you're not denying it. And another thing, I'm not ashamed of myself. I won't let you make me feel guilty because I kissed you back."

"Hallie, I'm not trying to make—"

"You are." She glared at him defiantly.

"I'm not, dammit! You said you kissed me back?"

Hands on hips, Hallie eyed his erratic stalking walk. "So what if I did." She moved out of the kitchen and into the parlor, making sure the sofa was between them.

Cade couldn't follow as quickly and unwilling to let him trip again, Hallie hurried to light the lamp on the table. She blew out the match and had managed to replace the glass globe when he started around the sofa.

He started after her, spun around, groaned, and then collapsed on the sofa as though all vital energy had been sapped. When he clutched his knee, Hallie was beside him in seconds.

"Now look what you've done. Let me see."

Cade had his arms around her and hauled her onto his lap before she could blink.

"You tricked me."

"Sometimes Hallie, a man's got to do what a man has to do." His grin was sinful, so wicked that the temperature climbed in the parlor until she could feel a tiny pool of dampness form between her breasts.

"That makes no sense." His dimples fascinated her.

"Don't get your drawers in a twist, Hallie. You don't understand it because you're a woman. Now, tell me again about kissing me back."

"Why?" She squirmed, tilting her head to the side to give him a disgruntled look.

"Just do it, Hallie. Think of it as part of my reward."

"All right. I kissed you back."

"And you liked it?"

"Well," she said, releasing a long suffering sort of sigh, "you can hardly expect me to admit that based on one kiss."

Cade moved one hand up to thread his fingers through her dark brown hair. She'd lost most of her hairpins in the barn. He cupped the back of her head comfortably in his palm and made her face him.

"Hallie, I agree with you," he stated in a serious tone. "We should definitely test your reaction again. That's the part," he noted in a voice of hushed intimacy, "that I'm most interested in. Kiss me, Hallie."

"It's only a test," she murmured against his lips. "A reward, too," she added, sliding her hands into his thick black hair as he sealed their lips together.

Cade tested reality again, and discovered, if anything, that it was much, much better than the first time. Hallie's most enthusiastic participation allowed a leisurely indulgence, ensuring they came to no hasty conclusion.

Unfortunately Cade was forced to end the delightful interlude, not because he had any desire to do so, or for sudden lack of cooperation on Hallie's part, but for the reason that the pain in his leg reached an unbearable level.

"Hallie," he whispered, dragging his lips from hers. "You need to get up. My leg's killing me." His arms fell from her and she jumped up.

"Oh, Cade, I'm sorry. I'm so very sorry this happened."

He was left sitting there with the feeling that Hallie wasn't talking about his leg hurting, or the attack by the two men. But how could a woman be sorry for kissing him when she did it so well he'd have trouble unbuttoning his pants?

If Halimeda Pruitt thought he was going to let her retreat behind that polite wall she hid behind, the lady had better think again.

❧ Chapter 5 ❧

$\mathscr{N}$ear noon, Cade set the pole brake of Hallie's buckboard in front of the sheriff's office. He ignored the immediate crowd that formed, pointing and whispering about his prisoners. He vaguely remembered what Sheriff Mallory looked like from the two times he had questioned him after the robbery. But Cade's pleasure in turning over Jeb and Emmet to the law was dimmed by thoughts of Hallie's withdrawn manner as she served him coffee and breakfast, then helped him ready the buckboard.

Hallie had argued about her keeping the robber's horses. She had insisted that Cade turn them over as well. Patience the mule had proved docile once in the traces. Cade thought the beast had had all the excitement it could stand the night before.

As Cade stepped into the office the sheriff broke off his conversation with his deputy. "Help you? Wait a minute. You the cowpoke that Doc found? Where the hell you been?"

"Doc got Miss Halimeda Pruitt to take me in." Cade's hands curled into fists when he spotted the deputy's smirk.

"Old Pruitt's granddaughter, huh? Now, there was a woman." Mallory had a far away look in his eyes. "She's an independent woman like her mama, too. Guess the apple don't fall far from the tree. Miss Pruitt practice free love like her mama?"

It was asked in a straightforward manner, unlike the snigger from the deputy. A cold, hard stare from Cade shut the younger man up. "Sheriff, you're mistaken. Miss Pruitt is a lady."

"Ain't arguing that. But her mama, now . . ." Mallory then proceeded to educate Cade about the Pruitt women's history.

Given no choice but to listen due to circumstance and his own need to know, Cade seethed everytime he looked up to see the deputy smirking.

"So," Cade said as the sheriff finished, "her mama had a string of lovers dancing to her tune—"

"Yep. That's what I said. Mind you, just until she got in the family way. From what my papa told me, it was the same with her mama before her."

"And how many men danced to Miss Hallie's tune?" Cade hating asking, but he had to know.

"Nary a one, far as I know."

"Damn right. And I'll give fair warning. If I hear one slur against Miss Halimeda Pruitt's good name, the man'll answer to me. Now, we have business. The men that robbed and left me for dead are tied up in the buckboard."

"Caught 'em, huh?"

"Last night. They attempted to kill me and Miss Pruitt."

"That so? You ain't the only one that fell for that fancy bit of goods and got taken. But you're the only one that lived, McAllister. And you're a rich man. Pete Kent, who owns the saloon, and Joe Lassit, who owns the hotel, places where she and her cohorts plied their filthy trade here, put up a four-thousand-dollar reward. Couldn't prove nothing against them. But you'll stay around for the trial?"

"I'll be here."

"Jeffers," Mallory said to his deputy, "make yourself useful beyond holding up the wall and lock those men up. I'll take McAllister over to the bank to collect his money."

Cade followed the elbow-wielding sheriff through the crowd, still reeling over the information he had about Hallie's family. Well, the female side. No one knew for sure who her grandfather or father were. Then, the good fortune of receiving a reward amounting to more money than he had lost took second place to his churning thoughts about Hallie. He'd bet his half of the reward money that Hallie had not followed her mama and grandmother's path. The story gave him insight to Hallie's character and her contrary behavior.

Cade signed the receipt, opened an account for the balance less three hundred dollars cash. He was taking no chances of getting waylaid on his return to Hallie's driving a buckboard pulled by a mule that knew two gaits—slow and slower.

Pete Kent insisted on standing drinks for Cade at his saloon. Joe Lassit joined them on the way. He offered Cade the best steak dinner and room his hotel had to offer. Scam artists were a honest businessman's plague.

The liquor came from Pete's private stock. It was so smooth and aged that Cade thought he'd died and gone to heaven with the first taste. He savored that drink, thinking of the weeks he'd been craving one, but strangely enough, found himself placing his hand over the glass when the barkeep attempted to pour him a second one.

"Gentlemen," Cade said, shaking first Pete's hand, then Joe's, "appreciate the drink, the offer, and the reward, but I've got some mighty important things to do."

Hallie paused on the graveled path that led to the white clapboard house to watch the sun, wrapped in layers of color begin its descent on the horizon.

Cade had not returned.

Trudging her way into the kitchen, she worked the pump until the basin in the dry sink was half full, then added hot water from the kettle to wash after evening chores.

She didn't understand why she cared where he was or what he was doing. Cade McAllister threatened her peace of mind, her way of life.

And what happened to asking him to leave?

Hallie had no answer.

Cade had forced her to acknowledge her own deep need for human touch. Nothing had felt as good as the moments when he had held her. The man had awakened something she had never felt, but only dreamed about. Something that frightened her with its power. She thought of the way he had watched her this morning, with an intimacy that made her feel connected with him in some profound way. Hallie refused to name it.

"I do not want this," she whispered, grabbing hold of the edge of the sink. "I don't want to spend another day mooning over Cade's McAllister's dimples, or his kisses, his teasing, his very presence filling a room. I never want to think of how chocolate tastes when shared by the melting heat of his lips. I," she declared in a louder voice, "do not want Cade McAllister in my life."

"What did I do now?" Cade asked. He stood in the doorway, new hat in hand, innocent as could be, as if he hadn't spent the entire four-hour ride back recalling details from Hallie's journal.

Hallie blushed like a bowl of pickled beets. How much had he heard? She issued a barrage of silent warnings as she faced him. Drying her hands on her apron, she spotted the new hat he held. She didn't question the purchase. He had a right to take whatever money Jeb and Emmet had after what they had stolen from him. Her gaze strayed with helpless fascination to the faded denim the dark brown felt hat rested against, denim that gloved his thighs and lean hips with a soft, loving fit.

She briefly closed her eyes, overcome by jealousy for the cloth. She wasn't even aware that her hands clenched her apron as she denied the need to touch him.

An uncontrollable urge sent her gaze climbing upward, from his beltbuckle to the first button on the front of his shirt, then on up blue fabric and horn buttons to the open point where the cozy kitchen fixture's light gilded a V of hair dusted male flesh.

No matter how hard Hallie tried to look away, her stare drifted to his smiling lips or the mischief twinkling in his blue eyes, or to the soft sheen of his still-too-long black hair. Cade stood about six feet from her. . . . What possessed her to count the feet that separated them!

"You came back."

Cade swiftly sorted and discarded every smart-aleck answer and simply nodded. He could have pointed out the obvious, that he had to return Patience and her buckboard. Or the not so obvious to Hallie, that he wouldn't go unless she ordered him to.

"You didn't cut your hair?"

"Is that an accusation?"

"No. Just remarking about it."

"That's good. I didn't cut it, Hallie, because I like the way your hands felt sliding through it." There, he'd shot the first opening round.

That quickly the intimacy was back, filling the kitchen, filling her heart. A gust of love swept over her. The mere silent admission rocked her back on her heels. Love? When had it happened? He'd been gone all day and she had missed him so much everything was unbearable. Not even her animals filled the lonely void he'd left behind.

But Cade had learned the truth about her. There was no way he couldn't have once he'd told where he'd been staying. With her emotions running riot, Hallie knew she had to end this before he said or did something to hurt her.

"Last night," she began.

"Hallie, last night, you were supposed to sit by my bedside, wipe my fevered brow, and tell me how brave I was."

"What? But you didn't have a fever."

Cade should have taken pity on the confusion in her eyes. But he was not going to let her retreat. "You're wrong. I've had one from the moment I woke and looked into a pair of green eyes. I'll admit," he said, tapping the hat against his leg, "that I didn't know what it was then, but Hallie, I sure do now."

She wanted to tell him he didn't need to use his hat to hide the evidence. He hadn't been quick enough. It was no more than she had expected after he'd heard about her family. But expected or not, a deep hurt spread through her that Cade had come back thinking she'd fall into the nearest bed with him.

But isn't that what you want, too? Hallie refused to answer the little nag. Her chin rose and her eyes held a militant gleam. "Well, Mr. McAllister, if that was what I should have done, you were supposed to tell me that your heart ached instead of complaining about your leg."

Her steady gaze warned him this wasn't going quite the way he envisioned. He had not expected Hallie to fling herself into his arms—it would have been nice, damn nice if she did, but he had thought she'd be . . . warmer.

"It does, you know."

"What does? Speak plainly, Mr. McAll—"

"Cade. You said it often enough. I can't go back to being Mr. McAllister, no matter how much you want that."

"What does?" she repeated, ignoring the rest. Panic took hold. He shuffled where he stood.

"My . . . my heart aches for you, Hallie." Cade knew there was no point in mentioning now how the rest of his body felt. But if he didn't offer relief soon, his britches were going to strangle him.

Hallie wanted to believe him. She wanted it so much that she was shaking. This wasn't a dream. This was Cade telling her his heart ached for her. Horsefeathers! Bold and brazen as could be, Hallie marched the six feet separating them. She leaned close and sniffed loudly.

"You have been drinking. Stuff and nonsense is bound to come from any man who indulges."

He barely refrained from shaking the sanctimonious stuffing out of her. He smiled. If she still cared about his drinking, there was hope. "Now, Hallie—"

"Don't you now Hallie me."

"I'll do it all I want." Cade waved the hat beneath her nose. "No other man has the right. And I only had one drink. Wait till I tell you what I'm gonna do. There was a—"

"Pack your belongings and leave at first light." She spun on her heels and marched back to the sink.

Cade shook his head. He'd lost something somewhere. "I never said that."

"Look, McAllister, let's have a little honesty. You

brought those men to the sheriff. I am sure that he told you he was one of my mother's lovers. I am sure that he filled your ears with stories about my mother and my grandmother. I am not like them. I do not want a string of lovers. I do not—"

"How about one, Hallie?"

"I do not want you or any other man cluttering up my life."

The silence in the kitchen was absolute. Not even the cool night breeze dared to enter the kitchen. Cade needed long minutes before he could speak with any calm. It disappeared when he met that militant gaze.

"You," he said, tossing his hat toward the table and advancing on her, "are one bossy, opinionated female. Yes, I did see the sheriff. Yes, he told me about your mama and grandmother. And yes, I'll admit, it played hell with my good intentions to know they taught you to believe in free love. But if you don't sit down and hear me out, I'll tickle you till you can't draw a breath, Halimeda Pruitt."

Hallie folded her arms protectively across her chest. She couldn't move as he reached behind him and dragged a chair away from the table. She couldn't even draw a much needed breath until he moved aside.

"Sit down, Hallie."

Despite her declaration that she didn't want him here, Hallie greedily wished to prolong his leaving. She sat down, prepared to listen to him.

Cade snagged a chair for himself, placed it at her side, straddled it, his arms resting across the chair's back, and sighed. "You can be difficult."

"I—"

"Difficult, but not impossible. I don't give a hoot about your mother or your grandmother. I don't care who your father was. I do care that you've been hurt by stupid gossip. There'll be no more of it."

"Now that they know you were here—"

"Hallie, I swear I'll tickle you with a feather if you don't stop interrupting me. Tickle you," he warned, "till you can't breathe."

It was a mark of her upset that Hallie didn't question how he knew that she was ticklish. She wrapped her legs around the chair's, clasping her hands within the folds of her apron and nodded.

"Good. We understand each other. I also spoke to Doc. He told me that the other wounded men who stayed here never caused you any grief. A warning to me, I suppose. But before I get to talking about me and you, I want to tell you about the reward. We're splitting four thousand dollars." Cade placed two fingers across her mouth and shook his head.

"No interruptions. I left most of the money in the bank till we had a chance to talk about what we'll do with it." He liked the way her eyes turned dark and wide. "Yeah, you heard me right. We'll decide together. The sheriff also sent telegrams warning neighboring towns to be on the lookout for Lurette Beauclare.

"Now that's out of the way." Cade removed his fingers from her mouth and feather-stroked her cheek. "I have some ideas of what we can do with the money, Hallie," he leaned close to whisper, "you do know that I desire you a great deal. But what happens between us from tonight on is entirely up to you.

"And lastly, for your edification, Miss Pruitt, I had one drink. I am not drunk. I know what I've said. What's more, I meant every word. You can tell me to go or to stay, Hallie."

Please tell me to stay, his gaze pleaded.

Please don't ask me to decide, her look begged.

Once more, silence filled the kitchen, but this time there was an added tension.

Cade saw the indecision in her expression. He rushed to forestall her answer. "I had saved money to buy a spread of my own. You've got good land going to waste. We've been in each other's pockets for a few weeks and didn't end up hating each other. That's right, isn't it, Hallie? You don't hate me?"

"I don't hate you, Cade."

"That's good. Real good." He teased the corner of her mouth till she smiled. He was making a mess of this. "I need to put up the buckboard." He stood up, replaced his chair and raked his hand through his hair. "I bought something for you. I'll bring it in first."

The pleating on her apron required her attention as he went outside then returned. Hallie, still sorting all he said, didn't look up as something thumped on the table.

She started when Cade put his hand on her shoulder. "I'll be awhile. Hallie, look kindly on what I bought. I tried like crazy to find you some undernourished stray in need of a good home, figuring you'd appreciate a gift like that more than any other. Couldn't find a one in need of rescue. Fella over at the livery said his bitch's due for pups in a week or so. I told him we'd want the runt of the litter."

"You shouldn't have. . . ." *Don't cry. Don't you dare cry.*

"Don't spoil this for me. I wanted to buy a whole lot more. 'Sides, Hallie," he whispered, leaning down to nuzzle her ear, "you didn't see what I brought for you."

⚜ *Chapter 6* ⚜

The door closed but Hallie didn't look up. What exactly had Cade proposed? No, not proposed, she amended, stated as fact. "We're splitting the reward," she murmured. "We'll talk. We'll decide together." Cade's words, spoken as if the two of them were a pair.

The notion, too close to secret dreams, was painful to think about. He couldn't have meant it.

But he'd dismissed her illegitmacy as though it meant nothing to him. He had said that he desired her.

Hallie touched her fingertips to her lips. Did she dare believe him? The reward money meant his freedom. He didn't have to come back, didn't have to share it with her.

Her gaze strayed to where a large oval wash basket squatted over half the table. Imagine the man telling her he went looking for a stray. But what had he bought?

The moment she stood peering down into the basket, Hallie started laughing. Cade McAllister had certainly used a good part of his reward to shop. She lifted out tins of Driessen's cocoa, others from Philadelphia's H.O. Wilbur Sons, bonbons from Hugber's. Milk chocolate produced in Switzerland by Daniel Peter, semisweet solid eating chocolate imported from England. Boxes filled with delicious candy from the New England Confectionary Company and the two layers on the bottom were her very favorites, Sparrow's Empress Chocolates. She picked up, then shakily set down Runkel's Breakfast Cocoa, hardly able to see through the tears blurring her eyes.

He must have bought out the supply of every mercantile. She had enough chocolate for a year or more. And if Cade left she would need every bit of it.

"Good for what ails you. Oh, Granny Rose, you were so wrong," she whispered. Sniffing and wiping her eyes, Hallie had to repeat it again. Cade should have been running in the opposite direction after what he'd learned, instead he'd showered her with sweets and left the decision of his staying or going up to her.

But what if she were wrong? What if he changed his mind? She had had a taste of the loneliness he'd leave behind. And it had been just one day.

Impossible man. He wasn't reacting as he should, as she swore to herself he would. How dare he leave her to stew alone? Cade wasn't going to get a wink of sleep until they had wrestled through all his references of togetherness.

Hallie turned up the lamps on the coal oil fixture to dispel the corner shadows. She sat down to wait and took one of the Empress chocolate tins to open.

She thought about her dreams which featured one Cade McAllister—last night's being the most heated by far since she now knew what his kisses made her feel.

This is practical, Hallie?

"Maybe not," she answered the little nag and reached for another piece of candy. "But he risked his life to save mine. I think I'm in love with the man." She munched her way through the tin of candy without really tasting it as she made a mental list of Cade's faults.

She dismissed his tendency to be bossy as something she could manage, not unaware the fault was hers as well. He liked her cooking, she enjoyed his appreciation of that and all the other things she had done for him. She wondered what Cade would think of her bedroom, inherited along with the house and land from her grandmother. Since the day Doc had pronounced her grandmother dead no man had entered that room.

Twice she interrupted her musings to open the kitchen door. The sound of Cade's cheerful whistling in the lantern lit barn had her grit her teeth. The man was impossible!

How could she make a decision if she didn't know how he felt about her? Could Cade ever love her?

Hallie returned to her place at the table. The candy tin was empty. She reached over and opened another one, one to help her find courage. She had to confess to Cade what she had been doing to him. She wanted to be honest, and in return, needed Cade's honesty about his feelings.

Courage, Hallie. You can do anything.

She froze, frightened and held her breath. That had not been a whisper from the little nag. Hallie felt the cool brush of moving air against her cheek. She released her breath slowly, and with it, her initial fear.

"Help me, Granny Rose. Help me make the right decision."

"Courage is all a man needs to confront a woman like Hallie about her feelings. Isn't that right?" Cade asked the ragtag flock as he tore open a sack and scooped out a pail full of grain. "I made a mess back in the kitchen, but I'll get it right. She won't refuse me, will she? I mean a woman like Hallie doesn't go around kissing men and dreaming about them, does she? Not unless she has strong feelings for him?"

Not one grunt, bray, moo, bleat, or neigh came in answer. Cade surveyed the animals with their heads all turned toward him as he began to walk along, scooping out a measure of grain for each animal.

"I didn't understand what she was up to," Cade offered by way of apology. "So don't be holding it against me. Nothing else makes sense, does it?" He leaned over Eternal's pen. "Tonight your silence, pig, is not appreciated. Did she name you while thinking of the everlasting love and devotion every man and woman looks for in a mate?" Eternal lifted his snout from the trough. Cade took her grunt for agreement, desperate to believe he was on the right track as he moved to Forage's stall.

"You're still a fussy, persnickety ewe." He tossed the grass he'd picked into the sheep's feed bucket. "But I guess, and correct me if I'm wrong, that you got your name 'cause Hallie wants someone who's a good provider. Not a fancy one, mind you, Forage, but one who's got skills to feed a family."

The little burro stood in the middle of its stall. "Ah, Steadfast, I belittled your name, didn't I?" Cade rested his arms on the stall's gate. "Beg pardon of you. What woman doesn't want a man who will stand firmly fixed beside her in all things? Especially when a woman like Hallie would dare the devil himself for someone she loves." Cade grabbed hold of the top rail, closing his eyes briefly as he thought of Hallie and the danger she had placed herself in last night.

Faith, housed next to the burro, stretched her neck until her nose touched Cade's shoulder. He looked at the warm brown eyes and picked up his pail. Cade moved the three feet needed to reach Faith's bucket and gave the horse two scoops of grain.

"Hey, girl," he whispered, scratching her velvet nose when she made no move toward the grain. "Your name's easy, isn't it? Complete belief and trust. That's Hallie. We wouldn't have her any other way, would we?"

Across the aisle, the other animals showed signs of restlessness and Cade crossed over to them. Hope had a muzzle grayed with age and teeth so worn that Cade mixed her grain with water from her pail.

"You're all about her dreams, ain't you, old girl? Won't get much argument from me about them. I'd like to be able to fulfill every one of Hallie's dreams. Think I can do that? Blazes, what am I asking you for. Hallie's the only one that can answer it. Too bad you and your cronies can't put a good . . . er . . . so to speak . . . word for me."

"Hey Charity," he said, once more moving down the row of stalls, "guess if Hallie didn't have a heart full of generosity toward those in need, neither you nor me would be standing here having this one-sided conversation."

Patience, in the next stall, kicked her empty feed pail.

"All right, you ornery . . . no, I ain't gonna call you that."
Cade bent down to grab the pail. "You get three scoops, but
only 'cause you didn't give me a hassle on the way home.
Home?" he repeated, the grain pail dropping unnoticed from
his hand. "A home needs a woman who's patient. A woman
who'd show forbearance under all kinds of provocation.
Don't take a dumb mule to show me that. Guess I learned
to be a little tolerant—" Patience brayed, loudly, right in
his face and Cade backed off. "All right, so I got a ways to
go. But I'm heading in the right direction, you ornery cuss.
Leastways I was until you had to disagree. Can't you take
the same path as the rest of them? Don't see them giving
me grief, do you?"

Patience's head stuck over the stall. Cade eyed the move
with suspicion for a few moments, then closed the distance
and scratched the mule's nose.

"Guess you ain't so bad after all." He looked over at
Divine, placidly chewing her cud, large brown eyes watching
him with aged wisdom. Cade found himself smiling as he
walked over and set the grain pail into her stall.

"Divine, you of all gave me the hardest time to figure out
your name. But the way I see it, you got named for a marriage
blessed by the Lord. I thought hard about this one. You can't
give milk, can't breed, but there's still affection to be had
from you, ain't there?" The cow rewarded Cade with a lick
to his hand from her thick, pink tongue.

"Figured something else out, too. I'm just as dumb and
useless as each of you. Loco, too, for thinking that Hallie's
gonna know any of this without me telling her."

Rubbing the back of his neck, Cade stared down at the
sawdust covered plank floor. "That honest soul of goodness
took me in just like she took in each one of you. Guess it's
a good thing none of you were named honesty. Or worthi-
ness. How can I convince Hallie I'm either one of those
things?"

"You don't need to, Cade."

He twisted around so fast that his bad leg buckled and
he had to grab hold of the support beam to hold him up.

"Hallie!"

"That's my name." She stood with the shadow of the open doorway and made no move to go inside. Her heart was so full at this moment, Hallie didn't think she could move.

"How much did you hear?" he asked in a choked up whisper.

"Does it matter?"

"Sure as hell does. If you heard it all, I won't have to repeat it. If you heard half, I'll have to repeat it all. To make sure you understand the reasoning."

The caress in his voice was so enticing that Hallie could almost taste the honey in it. Joy whispered through her as she saw through her tears the odd, gentle expression on his face. His eyes rested on her, inviting her closer, flames kindling in the blue depths. All she could do was drink in the sight of him, trying to absorb him slowly, like the too rich sweets she had indulged herself in. He was standing quite still, the lantern light playing a pattern over his features.

"I . . ." Hallie began.

"You . . ." Cade started to say.

"Go first," she said, leaning hard against the door frame.

"No. You." He saw what was different about Hallie, she'd removed her starched collar and apron, and somewhere between his leaving and her arrival, most of her hairpins were lost. Mink dark hair rippled down to the waist of her reddish brown gown.

"Hallie, were you worried that I was out here so long?"

"No. Why do you ask?"

"Your hair," he said, gesturing with one hand. "You'd only take it down to go to bed. Wouldn't you?" he asked innocently, with hidden laughter and tantalizing spice in his voice.

"I forgot to thank you for the gifts."

"Morning—"

"No. It couldn't. . . . this couldn't wait until morning, Cade." She took a step inside. "There are serious matters to be discussed."

"Here?" Lord, did he sound too eager? Hallie seemed to

glide over the barn floor and Cade retreated. There was the small matter of Hallie and the fragrant hay that he couldn't get out of his mind.

"I've made some decisions," she informed him. Hallie eyed his hesitant backward walk and found she liked being the one to stalk him.

"Now, Hallie, there's no need to rush. Take your time. Think things over. These are serious issues."

"Yes, I realized how serious. But I don't believe taking time is possible anymore." The firm conviction of her belief rang in her voice. She noted how intrigued Cade appeared.

Cade skirted one of the post beams. "It isn't? Be very sure, Hallie." Cade knew how close he was to the pile of hay by the fragrant smell. *Come on, Hallie, a little bit closer.*

"Accept my word on it." She offered him a mischievous smile. "I am a woman who will always honor her word once given." *A few more steps back, Cade McAllister, and then I'll have you where I want you.* She refused to allow herself to think of what steps to take once she had him there. This business of seduction required thought and planning. Hallie knew her heart to be so full of love she could barely stop herself from flinging her arms around him.

She advanced on him like some warrior maid, and Cade delighted in letting her believe he thought retreat was the better part of valor. He deliberately stumbled, landing spread-eagled in the middle of the hay pile.

"Be real gentle with me, Hallie," he warned, then almost spoiled it with a stifled chuckle. "Please. You must remember you're about to take advantage of a recovering invalid."

The intriguing idea stopped her advance. "I've never taken advantage of a man before."

Don't quit on me now, Hallie. Show me the woman in your dreams.

"Hallie?"

"Hush. I'm figuring out a plan of attack."

"Nothing too violent, I hope." He watched the frown appear on her brow and his gaze slid down her slender figure to where her hands pleated the sides of her skirt. "Don't let lack of experience stop you," he urged. "As you can see, I'm quite helpless."

She saw he looked as smug as a bear with his own honey-bee hive. Helpless, indeed. If Cade became any more helpless without touching her, she would melt the hinges of the doors to hell.

"I meant what I said before, Hallie. There's no rush. We could talk about this decision of yours." *And I'll crisp the hay beneath me to a cinder.* Cade very slowly locked his hand beneath his head to show he wasn't going to grab her. When she still hesitated to join him, he tried for a lighter mood.

"What do you think they"—Cade freed one hand to gesture at the animals avidly watching them—"think about this?"

"You have the advantage there. I never thought to ask. But they can't be happy to see you claim their hay. What would I do if they took exception and said no?"

"We'll take them to task first thing in the morning. Threaten them with roasting. With work. We can plot all sorts of devilish torture for them. Stuff Eternal with apples, for one."

His teasing—and the merry twinkle in his eyes said it was that—brought her smile, then soft, delightful laughter.

"Hallie," Cade said in a honey-smoked voice, "they can't possibly know what you need right now." His extended hand reached out to her. "I do. Come here, Hallie. Let's be good to each other."

There was promise in his voice, in his eyes, a promise that gentled fear. Eyes bright with loving joy, Hallie settled herself beside him.

"Cade, I have a confession to make, and I don't want you to move or say a word until I am finished."

"Sounds serious." He thought of his grievous transgression and the words that confession was good for the soul. But telling Hallie he had read her journal would only hurt her. He could atone for his sin a hundred times a day for the next hundred years. He wanted more than anything to make Hallie a happy woman.

"It is serious. You'll be furious with me when—" The rustle of hay accompanied her move to hold his hand. Rather foolish, she told herself, to hold the hand of the man for comfort. But the touch of his large, warm, calloused hand did lend comfort.

"I've not been an honest woman with you. I've been dosing your chocolate with laudanum every night. That is why I encouraged you to have as much candy as you wanted. And that is why—" She paused, closing her eyes, only to open them as the image of Cade trying to do battle while drugged rose in haunting memory.

"I know you blamed my kisses and the candy for what you were feeling last night. But it wasn't that at all. You ate too much of the—"

"Hallie—"

"No. No," she said, squeezing his hand tight. "You must let me finish."

"I can't." He brought their joined hands to his lips, kissing the back of hers as he rolled to his side. "Sweet honest, Hallie. I already knew that."

❧ *Chapter 7* ❧

"*Y*ou . . ." she too, turned to her side to look at him. "You knew?"

"I told you I stopped by to see Doc Burnswait. Truth to tell, Hallie, I really was worried that I'd suffered some head injury."

"You blamed it on my kisses and the chocolate," she said in a cross little voice.

"And those sweet sensations were from them alone." He leaned over to nuzzle her neck, freeing her hand as he stroked her flushed cheek. "Your mouth is scented with candy." For long moments their gazes were locked. "I've discovered that I love the taste of chocolate, Hallie. Share with me."

Not a question, and not a demand. Hallie felt the soft mating of their breath as a kiss began long before his lips found and opened gently over hers. She closed her eyes against the overwhelming wash of sensations as she struggled with her burning desire to press herself against him and feel all his hard, lean body.

The kiss changed by heated degrees. The hard drive of his questing tongue made her feel her control was stretched to the breaking point. Cade McAllister, she discovered, didn't play fair. He wasn't playing or teasing now at all. The man was definitely an outlaw. He stole her reason. He kidnapped her emotions and held them for ransom with his sensuous, beguiling charm. When his lips glided from her mouth to her cheek, then to the lobe of her ear, a half shocked, blissful moan escaped her lips.

Hesitantly, she placed her hands on his shoulders. Beneath his shirt, he was warm and solid. His hand rested on her waist. A vision flashed in her mind like a streak of lightning. Hallie studied his face as he leaned back. The dreams she had had of him rushed back in all their erotic glory. But Cade was no dream lover. He was a flesh-and-blood man. His skin, the dark silky hair, the intensity of his blue eyes, and the heat of his lips brought fever to her flesh.

Lustful thoughts: She should attempt to control them. If he had a hint of what she had been dreaming and thinking about him, she would expire from sheer mortification.

"What is it, Hallie? You've gone away from me."

"I discovered a terrible truth tonight. Loneliness is a high price to pay for independence."

Cade braced himself on his elbow, and with his left hand stroked the hair back from her forehead. "Is that why you came out here, Hallie? You don't want to be lonely?"

"The truth?"

"Always."

"I truly wanted to know what you meant by all those *we'll talk* and *we'll decide* remarks."

"What did you think I meant?"

"Gracious, Cade McAllister, a woman could build a great deal on words like those."

"You'd make me a happy man if you did. Hallie," he whispered, "I don't want to steal your independence. Your kisses, yes. Your gentleness and caring and your love. But I don't want you to change." He kissed away the tiny frown that formed and brushed her nose with his.

Then, in a very serious, softly hushed voice, he said, "I discovered a few truths myself. I'm awfully glad you've never taken advantage of a man before. I want to be the very first, the only one. I want you, Hallie."

Melting just like a candy, Hallie drew his head down. "You have me." Made bold by the desire that flared in his eyes, she scattered kisses over the dimples she adored, until need spilled between them with broken words and heated kisses. Growing bolder yet, she touched the flesh-and-blood lover that haunted her dreams.

She felt enveloped by softness, the cool night breeze that draped lightly over them and the rising scent of the crushed hay beneath her. Her hands moved across his back, feeling the smooth, hard, shifting pattern of his muscles as he deepened the kiss, covering her body with his.

Their lips parted to the uneven cadence of indrawn breaths. "Darling, Hallie, much as I've indulged myself with thoughts of making love to you here, I'm ill prepared."

Not having the least notion of what he was talking about, and refusing to appear innocent, she smiled. "Don't give it another thought."

Cade stroked one finger down the line of her nose. "One of us needs to. I don't want your bottom scratched by the hay."

There was no help for it now. "Why in the world—"

His rich, soft laughter cut her off and he bent to nuzzle her ear, whispering his reason. When he lifted his head, he asked with all the loving indulgence she created, "Now do you understand?"

The blush began at her toes and rose steadily, heatedly until flags of color tinted her cheeks. "Well, if you thought I'd say no, you're sadly mistaken."

He stood before her next breath, lifting her up beside him. "Then we agree? We'll lock the doors and you'll let me love you by candlelight?" Once again he took her hand within his and raised it to his lips.

"Since yours is the greater experience in these matters, I agree. But be warned, Cade McAllister," she said, placing a kiss on his chin, "I fully expect turnabout to be fair play."

Drawing her to his side as they walked from the barn, Cade remarked, "That, Hallie, is one of my fondest dreams."

When she opened the door to her bedroom and lead him inside, Hallie lost her shyness. She lit the lamps and kept them low only to turn and find herself swept into Cade's arms.

"I've something else to confess," she whispered. "I can't wait to fall asleep at night to dream about you."

"Oh, Hallie, love, I can do better than that. Much, much better, my love. But you've got to promise to make an honest man of me as soon as we can arrange it or I'll tell our grandchildren how you seduced me."

She smiled, then softly laughed as he rocked her in his arms, loving him more in this teasing mood that dispelled all her fear and doubts. But the laughter died when she looked up at him and saw the love she had longed for there in his eyes.

She pulled the tails of his shirt free from his pants. "Shall we have children?"

"A dozen at least." His breath caught as she touched his throat and began to unbutton his shirt. Not one to be idle, Cade worked free the buttons on her bodice from the waist upward.

Hallie slid his shirt off with the most loving caresses, Cade kissed each bit of her skin as it became free of cloth.

"You'll allow me to keep my animals," she murmured, finding his belt buckle easy to open, but the buttons hidden by the placket of cloth below it were a sheer test of a woman's ingenuity.

Goaded by the ease that Cade used to strip her of her skirt and petticoats, Hallie, accompanied by a great deal of Cade's groaning admonishments that she was killing him by slow degrees—at which point she stopped only to hear his testy demand that she continue or he would die—Hallie, with single-minded attention that drew his praise, completed her mission.

As he kicked his pants free, and worked on removing his boots, she stood back. "Ill-prepared indeed. You're a fraud, Cade McAllister. There's not a union suit in sight."

His grin was unrepentant. "I cheated."

Hallie thought of the perfume heating several intimate places and wisely did not pursue the matter of cheating.

Clad in chemise and drawers, Hallie moved to the other side of the bed to turn down the spread. Nervous chatter filled the tense silence. "You must be wondering about the bedroom. It all belonged to Granny Rose. No one has ever been in here. I mean—" She looked up to find Cade next to her.

"Hallie, I don't want your family's history. I don't want to hurt you or order you. I only want to love you."

And it was love in his eyes, in every strong line of his powerful and aroused body. Love that sent her fingers to tangle with his on ribbon ties. Love that watched and waited as she stood proud and pushed the long length of her hair back.

"You are the most beautiful woman, Hallie."

In his arms, with his lips on hers, she felt beautiful as they sank together onto the feather tick. Insatiable kisses where their tongues curled and flattened, tasted and tempted, the duel heated and delicious. The touches were soft caresses, bold, bringing a furnace blast of desire and Hallie reveled in every moment. She'd waited so long. She'd waited for him, for Cade, a dream lover come to life.

He sensed her need before she drew his hand to touch, his lips to taste and tease, and found, with the aid of his shaky plea, that his needs mirrored her own. He kissed her breasts, her nipples, with a tongue made warm and wet from their kiss. Her heart hammered in her chest as his fingers worked a wicked sorcery on her.

The room tilted and swirled, spun with bright color, filled with heated sighs. She whispered yes at some point, repeating it and his name until it was one word, then dissolved in a sigh. She tensed briefly, his broad hands on her bare hips, holding her up to him. His whispered praise blended with love words, sharpened by passion and she dug her fingertips into the small of his back and moaned.

Cade's mouth simultaneously invaded hers. The kisses fierce, almost love-violent as the rhythmic movement of his hips changed from the gentle play that began making Hallie his. His breath moved in hot, shivery waves across her flesh as he coaxed her to melt for him. She was achingly tight and tender. He stole her cry and swore it was the last he would steal.

Love bathed her in a gauzy mist. Drenched with rapture she held him still within her body and saw above her his face sinful with unrestrained passion. Love flooded her, without limit and timeless. Eternal. Everlasting.

"I love you."

To Hallie the words were a delicate feast, balm and sweet sensation, rich promise and reverent vow.

It was later, the lamps extinguished, and they lay facing each other unable to cease the need to touch, when Cade spoke.

"There is one matter we didn't finish discussing, Hallie. About your animals—"

"You won't go back on your word?"

"No, love, no. I want your word that I can have my whiskey."

"Will you want a lot of it?" Her fingers curled within the hair on his chest and she gently rubbed the hard nub of flesh hidden there.

"An . . . occasional glass, love, no more." Cade groaned as her lips replaced her touch.

"Do you know," Hallie said moments later as she sought bolder game, "that you groan a great deal?"

"Only around you, Hallie."

"Well, keep it that way." She pushed him back against the tick and rose above him. "I'm a possessive woman. I definitely want to marry you."

Cade's grin should have blistered her skin. His gaze found hers. "I'm not sure I can keep up with you, Hallie. You plumb wore me out."

"I did? I mean, I did."

"If you're gonna seduce me every chance you get, I'll be old before my time."

"We'll ration," she murmured with stifled laughter. "But until it's necessary, you won't mind if I take my turn to be on top?"

Cade stretched beneath her. "You're a bossy woman."

"You agreed to take turns." Her lips hovered above his as she settled herself along his length.

"One last promise?"

"Only if you hurry."

"You won't share your chocolates or your kisses with anyone else."

Her head jerked back. He sounded so serious. "Cade, not even our children?"

"Not even them. Those sweet sensations are mine. All mine. You see, I'm gonna make you a happy woman, Hallie."

She shifted and squirmed and settled herself upon him with a startled cry.

"Hallie be gentle with me. This needs to last for a lifetime of loving you."

KAT MARTIN

Award-winning author of *Creole Fires*

GYPSY LORD
_____ 92878-5 $6.50 U.S./$8.50 Can.

SWEET VENGEANCE
_____ 95095-0 $6.50 U.S./$8.50 Can.

BOLD ANGEL
_____ 95303-8 $5.99 U.S./$6.99 Can.

DEVIL'S PRIZE
_____ 95478-6 $5.99 U.S./$6.99 Can.

MIDNIGHT RIDER
_____ 95774-2 $5.99 U.S./$6.99 Can.

ANITA MILLS
ARNETTE LAMB
ROSANNE BITTNER

*Join three of your favorite storytellers
on a tender journey of the heart...*

Cherished Moments is an extraordinary collection of
breathtaking novellas woven around the theme of mother-
hood. Before you turn the last page you will have been swept
from the storm-tossed coast of a Scottish isle to the fury of
the American frontier, and you will have lived the lives and
loves of three indomitable women, as they experience their
most passionate moments.

THE NATIONAL BESTSELLER

CHERISHED
MOMENTS